HER FAULT

Maureen Gibbon has always lived in London, and has worked in a variety of jobs. HER FAULT is her first novel.

MAUREEN GIBBON

HER FAULT

Futura

A Futura Book

Copyright © Maureen Gibbon 1988

First published in Great Britain in 1988 by
Macmillan London Ltd

This edition published in 1989 by
Futura Publications, a Division of
Macdonald & Co (Publishers) Ltd
London & Sydney

ISBN 0 7088 4283 6

Reproduced, printed and bound in Great Britain by
BPCC Hazell Books Ltd
Member of BPCC Ltd
Aylesbury, Bucks, England

Futura Publications
A Division of
Macdonald & Co (Publishers) Ltd
Orbit House
1 New Fetter Lane
London EC4A 1AR
A member of Maxwell Macmillan Pergamon Publishing Corporation

With love to Philip Leevers

Laura

The first time I went to hospital was when I had tried to poison my mother: kill her, that is. I was nine, and I had imagined her gone for years, because for years, as long as I could remember, I had not seen the point of her. She was a very imposing woman, especially to small children – tall, bony, dark-haired, witchy I'd have thought, if she'd read us stories about witches; or about fairies or railway engines or anything. If she'd had anything to do with us except hiss that we were to get out of the way it would have been preferable, but we were seen and unheard. Sometimes I heard her talking to the furniture as she tended it, and then I wanted to be made of wood because that would mean I would be rubbed, stroked, picked up and put down. She would use me but also she would want me.

'It would be better, wouldn't it?' I said to my sister Barbara. 'It would be better than this, nicer than how we live now?' But she didn't always agree.

The house we lived in was exactly the same as all the others in our street – two rooms and a kitchen and a cloakroom downstairs and three bedrooms and a bathroom upstairs – but it was different because everything was spotless. Immaculate, she said, and meant untouched. All the dark dining-room furniture shone, six sweet peas drooped onto a lace mat on the occasional table, flat cushions sat upright on the beige three-piece, curtains were drawn when the sun shone to stop the carpet fading. When we went to school our bedroom was inspected for tidiness before we left except no one but us ever saw inside it. When we were little and the children next door called over the fence my mother said, 'You don't want to play with them.' I didn't. I couldn't see any point in sitting down quietly with more people than Barbara, because that was what playing was. We sat on the stairs and watched, we sat in the kitchen, we sat in the hall, but the stairs were best because then we could kick our heels.

We were neat little girls. We were narrow-faced and had hair in pigtails and wore straight skirts and jumpers and long socks; we were uncreased and tight-mouthed and when our photos were taken we narrowed our eyes.

Until I went to school and my teacher smiled and sat me on her lap and I watched other children shout and jump it never occurred to me that not everyone had to behave like us. Even then it took time before I realised that I didn't like the way we behaved. It was arid and pointless and unhappy because there was nothing in it for anyone. If my mother had glowed with achievement at her shining saucepans or preened at her polished floors, it would have been some repayment, but she never did. She flung herself from one thing to another, and, less use than the Hoover, we watched. 'Move,' she said. 'Get off, out.' We never argued, we shifted out of the way, we got quicker and quieter and bigger.

As we grew older, because it was a tidy occupation, we watched television, and because it kept us quiet we saw whatever we wanted. When I was nine, in *Midweek Mystery Murder and Detection*, I watched a man die because he ate a meat pie doctored with crushed glass. It was a revelation. Every day as she screamed at my dusty shoes, the way my father ate, Barbara's books left lying on the floor, I'd said to myself, 'When she's dead,' but I'd never been able to find a way, and now there it was, in black and white, someone doing it, providing me with a practical solution.

I stole a hammer from the woodwork room at school and a drinking glass from the dining hall and a newspaper from the dustbin. 'I've got a project,' I said at home. 'I've got to be there early.' I went into the lavatories and banged and ground, a scarlet-faced little girl hunched against the wooden door, sweating, pulverising fragments into powder. The smell of disinfectant made me want to cry. Of course a hammer wasn't the right tool, and I was in too much of a hurry, they were lumps not fine grains; but one Friday I waited in the kitchen while she made tea, I tried to camouflage my navy tunic against the gas stove and when she turned her back to reach for the biscuit tin I emptied all the specks and splinters into her tea-cup.

'Sit down,' she said. 'Get out of the way.' I shivered on my stool and watched her drink, her throat go up and down and mine stopped, it dried up so I couldn't swallow a mouthful.

'Get on,' she said. 'I'm not sitting here all day waiting for you to finish, I've got work to do.'

I heard myself scream, I flung myself off the stool and across onto her lap. 'Don't, don't,' I cried. 'Stop it, don't drink it. You've got

2

glass in your tea, you've got to go to hospital.' She stood up, so I was left holding onto her chair.

'Don't be stupid,' she said.

I grabbed hold of the cup. 'Look, look,' I pleaded and then she did, she took the cup away and she looked at me. She tipped the tea back through the strainer and all the little pieces glistened against the curve of the cup.

'Get your coat,' she said. I ran behind her to the bus stop, sobbing, plaits thumping, breathless, and even when we got on the bus she never looked round to see if I was there. I fell as I got off the bus behind her and when I stood up she had disappeared. For seconds I wondered if it could be magic, and then I saw her through the glass door, waving her arms at a nurse, then pushing her fist into her wide open mouth and her hat bobbed on her tight curls and I wanted to laugh and she looked out and saw me.

'I'm having an X-ray,' she said when I went in. 'You wait.'

I sat on a brown leatherette bench and watched the clock not moving and when she came back she'd only been gone ten minutes.

'Are you all right?' I said, and I started to cry again because I couldn't believe my luck if that was true.

'They'll take you away,' she said. 'Shut up.' She went over to the desk and banged on it and when a nurse came I hid my face in my hands because I was sure she was saying what I'd done. But instead she came back and sat next to me again.

'We've got to wait,' she said, 'wait and see. I could tell them what to look for. You could tell them. You know what we're waiting for.'

'Don't,' I said.

She moved closer along the seat. 'It's too late for that,' she said. 'You should have thought of that before.'

'I didn't mean it,' I said. 'It was on television. I didn't mean it.'

'Liar.' She made a fist of her hand again. 'Little liar. I don't know where I got you from. I don't know what I keep you for.'

Then the nurse at the desk called her and she went over. They both had their heads together and I did not dare look up. I waited for the hand to descend on my shoulder, the voice of authority to summon me away, and when I saw her shoes coming I thought they had chosen her to be the one to fetch me. I stood up to save her the trouble of pulling me.

'Come on,' she said. 'We're going.'

I stared at her. 'What did they say?' I asked. It did not occur to

3

me that we were going home, I was waiting to find out where I'd be locked up.

'It didn't work,' she said. 'Nothing to see. Nothing to show for it. Out,' and she jerked her head towards the door. 'Move. Out of this place. Out,' she said. 'You. We're finished.

'I could have you taken away,' she said as we stood at the bus stop. 'You remember that.'

We didn't speak on the bus and when we were both inside the house she shut herself in the kitchen and I went to watch television.

When Barbara came home I heard her go into the kitchen, but there wasn't any screaming or shouting. I just waited until she came into the living room. She sat down with her back to me and unfastened her satchel and took out a blue exercise book. I pulled myself up in the chair to look and saw she'd begun to measure up lines with her ruler.

'I did something awful,' I said, and I went and leant over her shoulder.

She drew two more lines. 'What?' she asked but I didn't answer, I watched what she was writing.

Friends	Enemies
Susan	Caroline
Clare	Wendy
Penny	Peggy
	Elizabeth
	Jeanette

'I thought you liked Elizabeth,' I said. She shut the book.

'What did you do?' she asked. 'You might as well tell. It won't exactly stay a secret.'

I put my face into the back of her chair. 'I put glass in her tea and we had to go to hospital in case I'd poisoned her.'

'I don't believe you,' she said. 'You're making it up. You're as barmy as she is. No one could do a thing like that.'

'I did,' I said, 'really,' and I told her: the X-ray, the waiting room, the nurse, the waiting. 'I couldn't make that up,' I said.

Barbara didn't speak, she wouldn't look at me, she held her head in her hands and rested her arms in her lap and stayed quite still, as though she was frightened her head would break off.

4

'How could you? You're an idiot, you're mad.' She sounded as if she was crying. Then she said, 'I hate you. Why should you decide what to do, what did you choose that for? You're stupid, you never think. You never think of anyone except you, you never look at what you do. Look at it,' she told me, and then she sat up straight. 'Look at what you'll make her like now.'

'It didn't hurt her,' I said quickly. I wanted her to say it didn't matter, it would soon be over and done with, forgotten if not forgiven. 'And she might not even talk about it. She didn't tell the nurse, and she hasn't sent for the police. It might be all right.'

'Don't be stupid.'

She turned her back on me and opened the exercise book again. She looked at the page for a moment and then wrote something and then turned to stare at me. Then she glanced out of the window and started tapping her teeth with her pencil, considering the page from a distance. 'Look,' she said, as if she'd made up her mind to offer me something.

I went over to her and I did, I looked where her finger was pointing, underlining the work so it really stood out. Under the Enemies column was my name.

'I mean it, too,' she said. 'Really. I hate you. I could kill you too.'

Every time I went to a hospital after that I expected the worst. Death didn't lay the ghost, recovery and birth didn't prove me wrong; every time I was waiting for retribution, for threats to be carried out and promises to come to pass. Hospitals were where my nightmares happened, they were where it wasn't possible to pretend, however much you tried.

'They won't keep you, they can't,' I said to my grandmother.

'She's just like you, beautiful,' I told Barbara when Anna was born.

'He's fantastic,' I said when she had Tim.

'I'll get found out here, I can't believe I'll get away with it,' I said when my daughter Cathy was born, even though all I was doing was smoking, but I wasn't far wrong either. Not about that time, but the next one, the occasion after that when I had to go to hospital, because then I got all I'd been expecting for the last fifteen years.

What happened the next time started because I'd taken Cathy

5

shopping and left her carry-cot outside the supermarket. I lived alone with Cathy so I had to take her wherever I went, and usually I was a bit extreme about that, I never left her alone anywhere, but that day the shop was full and there were two dogs tied up by the door, barking, and I couldn't face them waking her up. She wouldn't get any wetter standing still than being wheeled along, I thought, and I only had a few things to get. It was odd because I almost dawdled round the shelves, picking up tins of lychees I'd never dream of buying, and jumbo packs of chips it would take me weeks to get through, telling myself it was neurotic to feel I had to watch over her every minute of the day, babies didn't get kidnapped in Shepherds Bush.

When I got to the queue at the checkout there was only one till working because it was lunchtime, but there were windows all along the front of the shop so I could see over people's shoulders, and the carry-cot was definitely still there and I could see another pram, a big high-sided one parked behind it, and a boy, quite tall, who was swinging on the handle. That made me a bit nervous because I thought, Supposing he kicks the wheels of the carry-cot, it could just roll down the kerb to the road, and there were traffic lights because it was a crossroads. Then I thought that was stupid, someone would stop it, and then I saw it happen. It was quite unbelievable, I saw his face jumping up beside the handle of that big pram and then he must have kicked mine as he fell, because I couldn't see him any more and I actually saw the hood of the carry-cot begin to move. I suppose it's possible I didn't put the brake on hard enough, but the frame the carry-cot fitted into was flimsy, it didn't take much.

For a second I just stared, then I shouted something, 'Look,' or, 'Mind,' and started to push people, squeezing past their trolleys, and some people stepped aside and others tried to make a fuss or ask what was the matter. I got stuck and rammed a man's back and it must have taken a couple of minutes, I could feel I was sweating, and I tried to explain by pointing out of the window. At one instant I thought again, Someone'll stop it; it won't happen, and then I fell over a pile of wire baskets and I didn't think I could get up fast enough, my body didn't seem to hold together. I saw people looking at me, a line of faces with baskets and raincoats and umbrellas and no one lifted a finger. Then I found I was running but it was too slow, I didn't seem to be moving, I wanted to grab the rail the barking dogs were tied to and pull myself along on that, but then I was at the door, and I could see the carry-cot, rolling, and I could see the lorry. It wasn't even all I noticed, I saw the traffic lights change and Fyffes written on a banana on the side of the lorry and a woman with a push-chair waiting on the other side of the road, but I couldn't see which happened first. Even though it was in front of my eyes I couldn't believe it was going to happen, because except for the very worst nightmares it doesn't. Either as the carry-cot went down the kerb it tipped over, or as the lorry pulled up it hit it, but either way there was a noise, a little bang as well as the lorry's brakes, and then everything turned upside down, and everything fell out, my string bag with vegetables in it, all the covers, her teddy, and Cathy. I screamed then because I couldn't believe that no one had done anything, no one had stopped it.

I don't remember walking or running or seeing anyone, all I thought was, Cathy, until I was next to her, and then I did notice more people, because I suppose the noise and me rushing out of the supermarket brought them out of shops. Another thing I noticed, not immediately, but afterwards while I was waiting for the ambulance, was that the row of yellow and blue plastic cats on elastic that stretched across the front of the carry-cot was all right; not one of them was smashed, they must have completely missed the impact.

But as soon as I got to the carry-cot I saw Cathy hadn't. You hardly ever see small babies bleeding, except war casualties, which is why it's so shocking, they can't do anything and you can't bear it for them. Except I don't think I had the chance to do anything because straight away there was a crowd and someone said I shouldn't touch her, I should leave her until the ambulance arrived, so I just crouched next to her in the road. She was crying, which someone else said was a good sign, but there was blood coming from her nose and mouth. She didn't cry loudly and I could see blood soaking through the Babygro all down one leg where she must have landed, and her eyes were funny, not looking at me; it was as if I wasn't there and yet she was five months, she was perfectly sensible.

'People are very kind,' you say afterwards, because they ring for an ambulance. Someone picked up all the vegetables that had rolled out of my bag and someone else brought my handbag out of the supermarket and said I'd dropped it, I'd better make sure my purse was all right. All I did was look at Cathy and think that in a moment it would have to get better, turn out not to matter.

7

I stroked her head for a bit, and said her name and a woman came and crouched next to me, but quite quickly stood up, and then no one got very close. I asked how long the ambulance would be and it felt as if I was acting, there wasn't a natural way to behave. I couldn't think of anything except I wanted to pick her up and try to put her back inside me, make her whole. I saw people in a ring round me, all the cot sheets and blankets around me, the bleeding going on, the lorry driver smoking, I smelt that and I wanted one, and yet I was watching, I didn't altogether seem to be in that place.

'You'll want your husband,' someone said.

I said, 'No, there's just me,' but then I didn't care, I wanted him too and so I told them Graham's number at work, and then the ambulance came. It'd been very quick; I suppose from start to finish the whole thing couldn't have taken more than ten minutes, and look at what it's done.

I was pushed into a white coat and Cathy was on another trolley and then I shouted, all I was saying was her name, that's all, but I was trying to pull her off the trolley, trying to push the nurses out of the way so I could get to her. I was shouting she was mine, they weren't to touch her. I suppose they didn't have much alternative but two nurses took hold of me and not pushed, but guided me, hard, into a little room.

'Sit down,' one of them said and, 'Take it easy.' But I closed my eyes and screamed and then I felt something cold rubbing on my arm. 'That's it,' I heard, and then I was quite limp.

'Keep still now,' the nurse said. 'You've had an injection. It'll take a minute.' I couldn't have moved if I'd wanted to, and I didn't.

'We'll take a couple of blood tests,' she said, 'in case they need to do a transfusion, and if there's the possibility of operating, we'll want your consent.' I nodded all the time, there was nothing else to do, all I wanted was to stop it happening. I could feel my head lolling and my mouth was very dry, so I told her that and she said it wouldn't last.

'It's a temporary effect.' She patted my hand. 'Don't worry about it.'

'I don't care,' I said. 'It doesn't matter.'

A few times the door opened and I looked up, expecting some news but then I closed my eyes. I could feel all my body twitching, head, shoulders, but I still couldn't move, I wasn't able to make my arms and legs react. Then my heart started to jump and when it took

8

an extra beat I'd feel as if I was going to get up and then find I was sitting perfectly still.

I've got no idea how long that lasted but then I heard the nurse say, 'Here she is.' I stood up, shut my eyes and held out my arms. Then the nurse said, 'Here's your sister,' and I put my arms round my head, I covered it up because I'd thought she meant there was Cathy, that was what I was waiting for. I couldn't move after that, I stayed in a hunched up heap. I heard the nurses talking and then Barbara said things, prognosis, informed, strength of sedation, all the right sensible things, just the right tone of voice, and when she stopped and the door opened and closed I knew she and I had been left alone.

'Laura,' Barbara said, and I felt her stand in front of me even before she started to unwind my arms from my head. I let her but then I held onto the arms of the chair and I didn't look at her. I didn't say, 'Barbara,' and let myself be hugged; I kept my distance and of course that meant she kept hers.

'They're going to investigate quite soon,' she said. Her voice was obviously meant to sound calm, quieten me down. 'You'll have to sign the consent form. It's her leg they're worried about.'

I nodded as though that was all right by me.

'Overall,' Barbara said, 'they're quite hopeful.' She moved closer to my chair then, and rested her arm quite lightly next to mine, but not touching, and although I could feel myself shaking, every so often I thought I ought to open my eyes and ask who was looking after Anna and Tim for her, but when I tried I'd feel myself clench up inside, I couldn't ask any questions about this because that would make it definite it was happening.

I remember some of the things she said, about how good the hospital was, and that a friend of her friend Geraldine had been on the bus that had stopped for the ambulance and telephoned her.

'That was lucky,' I remember remarking, 'finding one working. A phone-box,' I explained, as if that was all I could think about.

Then we didn't say any more. We sat there a long time before the nurse came back but when I heard her and Barbara start to talk I couldn't listen, I didn't want to hear technical words and promises and not believe them. I put my hands over my eyes, I wanted to shut it all out, I hated them for not making it go away.

'Come on,' the nurse said. 'Sit up now, sit up straight, look at me.' She took hold of my hands to move them, and I let her, and when I looked again Barbara had gone.

'Where's Barbara gone?' I asked. 'What've you sent her away for, what have you got to tell me? What's happened, why has she gone, why can't I?'

I started to struggle to get up and the nurse started to say, 'Nowhere, nothing's happened,' but I wouldn't listen, I'd found I could move again and I was ready to fight.

'Sit down,' she said and I shouted, '*No*, let me go, let me out too.' I was struggling and she was panting, it was like a real fight.

Then the door opened and Graham came in. He didn't tell me to stop, he just came and put his arms round me and I couldn't begin to tell him, I just hung on and wept and he held me very tightly and rocked me to and fro.

'Laura, Laura, sweet,' he said, over and over, and then I heard the nurse saying to someone who'd come into the doorway, 'We've finally located him, thank God. He's with her now.' I realised who she was saying it too, except Graham didn't, he tried to keep holding me and I pushed him away.

'Don't,' he said, 'don't,' and then I did say it.

'Let go, you've got to let go. Barbara's here.'

What the nurse didn't realise, and there was no reason why she should, was that he was married to Barbara. She was my sister, but there was also him and me and Cathy.

He did let go of me, in fact he practically pushed me over. I looked at Barbara. She was holding onto the door, half as if she was ready to go out again and then she made a noise, a coughing. Graham turned round and walked over to her. She stood quite still and suddenly he started to talk, rather loud, very flatly, as though he was reciting a dull set of facts to pass the time.

'The police rang,' he said. 'I was at work and the police rang. They were very unspecific, I'd got no idea, they didn't give any useful information, it could have been anyone, Anna, Tim . . .' He half-turned to Barbara. 'I'd got no idea. They just said to contact the hospital immediately, but I came, I thought that would be better. I got a taxi and came straight here instead.'

'It was me,' I heard myself say. 'I told someone. I said to someone when it happened to get in touch with you. I wanted you, I wanted you to know.' He didn't answer.

'Did you hear what she said?' Barbara asked, and she sounded conversational too, at first. 'Did you hear? The nurse, I mean what the nurse said, not her, not Laura,' as if she could have spat that word.

I started to answer and then I realised that for that moment I'd forgotten what had happened, it was as if I was being told now for the first time. I started to shout that I wanted Cathy, I wanted to wash her, she couldn't die, it couldn't happen. The nurse tried to hold onto me.

'Be quiet,' she said. 'This isn't going to achieve anything, it isn't doing any good either. No doubt she won't die, but you can't go on like this,' and she pushed me very hard into a chair. She was panting again and it was obvious she was angry. 'The doctor'll be down from your baby soon to tell you what's going to happen, but you won't see anyone unless you behave.'

I took some deep breaths and almost choked because that made me remember breathing when she was being born.

'Now be quiet. You've got to stay calm,' she said and I managed not to cry.

'All right,' I answered. I looked back at Graham and he'd gone to stand by the window. Even though all it seemed to face was a brick wall he was looking out of it, his hands in his pockets. He had his back to me and Barbara and she was leaning against the door, her arms folded, looking exactly like our mother, bony, disapproving, face all screwed up, ankles crossed, slouching as if you'd knocked all the stuffing out of her and all she had left was anger at what you'd done.

'That's better,' the nurse said, and she couldn't possibly have looked at any of us to say that. 'I'll see if I can get you some tea. Then you won't have long to wait for the doctor.'

None of us spoke, none of us even cleared a throat until the nurse came back into the room with a tray and cups and a sugar bowl and six ginger biscuits. She put it on a table and arranged chairs round it. I swear she'd have spread a tablecloth if she could have found one; she was determined to make something nice for us. 'There,' she said.

Everyone stayed exactly where they were and no one spoke. Nothing happened at all until I pointed, I looked at the tray and then at Barbara and I started to laugh.

'Just like home, look, Barbara, just like fucking Audrey,' I said.

Barbara didn't even glance at them, she looked straight at me instead. 'Shut up,' she said. 'I mean it. I hate you. I mean it. I could kill you.'

Then it took ages, all of us in silence, and after a couple of attempts even the nurse didn't talk, we all just waited there.

Eventually a doctor came and I signed the form for Cathy to have a transfusion and stitches. He said they didn't think an operation would be necessary, or the right thing, he chopped about in what he said. Graham asked two questions about X-rays and greenstick fractures. The doctor said yes and no, and that if I was calm enough I could go and see her in half an hour. I answered I was fine now and while the doctor was there, so there couldn't be any fuss about it, I turned in the direction of Graham and Barbara.

'If Cathy's all right,' I heard myself say. I knew I still didn't believe it, at the back of my mind I was waiting to go and find her torn apart or swaddled up inside a plastic tent, dismembered, unrecognisable. 'If Cathy's all right, I'd rather be by myself. Honestly. I'll be OK now. There's no point in you waiting. If you can't see her. And I'll have to stay so I can see her later again. Stay with her.'

Barbara nodded. 'You're probably right.'

'Yes,' Graham said. 'That's probably best.'

Then it seemed to happen like clockwork, people moving, following one another, doing up coats and putting collars straight, as if nothing more than walking in and out of rooms was involved. It was as if I wasn't there, they didn't have to think about leaving me behind, they could just get on with the business of going. When they were all buttoned up the doctor went out of the room to tell the nurse to come back and sit with me; and when he came back we all pretended we'd said our goodbyes, so he didn't notice that none of us had moved an inch nearer one another.

'Nurse'll be along any minute,' he said but I didn't care, all I could hear was them walking down the corridor, different length steps squeaking on the lino tiles, receding, and knowing nothing would bring them back again.

When the nurse did come back she said 'Ready? Come along.' She jerked her hand. 'I thought this was what you were waiting for. I thought this was what all the fuss was about,' and she would have been off down the corridor without waiting to see if I was following. I caught her up and stayed with her all the way, abreast of her black hair round every corner.

'Where is she?' I asked. 'Is she conscious?' She didn't answer, but jangled her keys at other nurses as if I wasn't there, or I was the one who was unconscious.

We went miles, I thought I'd never find the way out again. Secretly that was what I had in mind, snatching Cathy up and running out of there with her. We stood outside a lift for a little while. When the doors opened a trolley was wheeled out, the figure on it hooked up to a cylinder and a tube. For one second I thought it was her, that they'd brought her like that to show me.

'She's out of theatre now,' the nurse said, when we got out of the lift. I followed her again. She knocked on a door labelled *Mr Winch* and I went in. I looked all round for Cathy but the only person was a man. He looked a bit like Graham, medium height, bearded, brown eyes.

He said, 'Laura Harris?' and I said, 'Where is she?' and he said 'You'll see her in just a minute. There's just a few details first.'

I shook my head. 'No,' I said, 'no details. I've got to see her, you've got to let me. I'll listen then, I'll talk to you then.'

He started to argue but then he shrugged and said to the nurse, 'Get her fixed up.'

We went out again, down the corridor, through double doors. She tied a gown and a hat and a mask on me and led me through another set of doors. The doctor was waiting.

'She's still under sedation,' he said, 'so she won't know you. But no fuss. It's just to show you she's still in one piece.'

To tell the truth I couldn't have told if she wasn't. She was in a bed with a thin plastic dome over it and a tube strapped to her nose. All I could see was her head like that and the rest of her under a sheet.

'She's on a drip,' he said, 'just until you can feed her again.'

I grabbed his arm, I could have kissed him, because that was the first moment I really believed she'd be all right.

'I'm not breastfeeding,' I said. 'I only did that for three months.'

'But you'll want to give her her bottle,' he said, as though I was being absent-minded about my duties.

'What did you do?' I asked, but I didn't listen properly, he said contusions and possible crushing of the femur and the need for exploratory investigations.

'You mean you'll have to operate again?' I said then, because surely that was what exploratory meant. He said no, they'd seen all they needed and could find nothing wrong.

'The X-ray wouldn't give a clear enough picture, that was why we had to do it,' he said. 'They told you that when you signed the consent form.'

'I must have forgotten.' I tried to smile, pretending I hadn't been hysterical.

13

'It's a difficult time,' he said.

'When will she wake up?' I asked. He said less than an hour. 'And can I hold her then?' and he said he'd see, she was badly bruised, she might be better left still for twenty-four hours.

'We'll see,' he repeated.

I looked at her for a long time, watched her eyelids move and pinched myself and suddenly I said, 'Mentally? Didn't she bang her head, what about that?'

He nodded and said they'd done a brain scan and that was fine, too.

'You mean she really is all right?'

'I can't say it enough times for you, can I?' he said, and started to move away, opening the door for me to follow him out.

'I can't believe it,' I said. 'It's been a nightmare. I can't believe it's all right.'

'Not all accidents are fatal,' he said. 'It'll take her a while to heal, it'll possibly delay her mobility by a month or two. But she's got off very lightly. No lasting damage.'

'No,' I said.

At first while she was in hospital no one came to see us. I spent each day sitting by her bed, feeding, listening to her cry, even, at the end, being bored rather than grateful. I thought about why it had happened with Graham. I also thought that Barbara must have just as good an idea. She knew what sort of a shocking thing, maybe, it probably wasn't the worst thing that could have happened. It was the same as Cathy, it was damaging, but there wasn't anything tragic about it. A near miss, I thought, almost but not quite a lucky escape, except in the end, in the long run, I thought we'd all be able to say we'd got off quite lightly.

That was what I thought, and that was how I saw it; I could look back on everything between Barbara and me and Barbara and Graham and think, 'Not too good, but not the end.' I couldn't do without Barbara, I thought, and she must feel the same.

Two years ago, when Barbara was expecting her second child and Jas had left me to go and live with someone else, Barbara and I saw an unusual amount of one another. It was unusual, because however close she and I had been made to be in childhood, growing up had altered that, marked out the differences. My growing up was a series of different jobs and boyfriends, and hers was a series of well-organised achievements – typing, waitressing and three-month lovers as opposed to a university degree, teacher training, marriage and motherhood. But however I felt about those discrepancies, after I found the note from Jas, and I'd cried for two days, she was the person I telephoned, she was the only one I thought could even try to make it better.

What had happened was that Jas had gone to live with his best friend Barry's wife, Louise; Barry's firm sent him to America for six weeks, and no sooner was he on the train for Gatwick than Louise invited Jas to stay. Without a backward glance towards Shepherds Bush, he went; I ought to have foreseen that. I ought to have been suspicious at the number of weekends we were invited to stay, because Birmingham isn't everyone's ideal weekend retreat, and Jas could be fussy about getting bored with suburban landscapes. I ought to have noticed the smiles and nods and praises in Louise's direction and put them down to more than friendliness, and have known that because Barry and Louise had a daughter that didn't mean they were bonded for life.

Most of all I ought to have known Jas. I should have foreseen that the combination of always wanting what someone else had, and being offered a love nest in a large detached house with fitted carpets and french windows, was more than his total selfishness could withstand. I ought to have learnt that shits like him don't alter; that trust and generosity and sharing my two-roomed flat hadn't made any difference. Instead I was wise after the event. I screamed at him on the phone, wrote letters and tore them up, drank half a bottle of gin. Then I rang Barbara and said, 'Something awful's happened, Jas has gone, he's gone to Birmingham to live with Louise. I can't bear it,' and let myself cry a lot. She didn't even try and tell me it wasn't such a bad thing, that part of it worked, she didn't say a word against him. 'Come and see me,' I said. Straight away she agreed, she'd come at lunchtime when I finished work, she said, and she did.

The first day all I did was weep, the second I asked her how it had happened.

'They were friends,' I said, 'he and Barry were at school together. What do they think'll happen to Nicole? What happens to Barry being her father? How's Jas going to feel about that, when he gets over being in love? Why couldn't he talk about it? Why just write me a note? If we could talk we might be able to make it work again.'

By the third day I was desperate for consolation, advice, but it didn't happen. She came every day, her and Anna, the push-chair, the Tube, shopping, visiting, cooking my lunch and talking, except never about what I wanted to hear.

'I still can't believe it's happened,' I'd answer, whatever she'd just told me about the journey or the new supermarket at the Broadway. 'Read it again, read his letter again,' and I'd repeat the words in my head.

. . . this won't be any surprise because we can't go on destroying one another, and the dishonesty of pretending there's anything more than a long-gone good time between us is nothing but destructive . . .

'How could he?' I'd ask. 'How can I bear it?'

She'd pause for a bit and then say, 'It is difficult. I suppose you just have to give it time.'

She'd look out of the window for a bit at the vegetable shop over the road, or go to the kitchen and make tea and pick dead leaves off the tradescantia. I'd walk round the bed and wooden chairs and little table that were all imprinted with him and wait for the pain in my chest to go away. She'd sit at that table with Anna, and Anna would say, 'What's unhappy, Mummy, what did Laura say?' and, 'Am I being quiet enough now?' and, 'Have I been good enough for sweeties yet?' I'd curl up in the armchair and Barbara'd talk to Anna about the puzzle she was doing and ask if she wanted to make a cut-out picture now. Maybe she thought that no matter how many times I put my head in my hands and said, 'I hate him, I want him back,' I'd recover if I didn't dwell on it, so she tried to distract me with her views on Graham's job, Anna's playgroup, a new car, next year's holiday. I tried to believe she understood, 'She means well,' I told myself, and yet simultaneously there was a contradiction. I'd asked her to come and comfort me but what she talked about made my life, let alone what'd just happened to it, negligible. I was the one in need and yet I might as well not have been there.

'Look at what's happened, help me, make it better.' I wanted to shake her, and the next minute felt guilty because after all she had come, and then I wanted to shout, 'Stop it, you're behaving just like Audrey, stop pretending it hasn't happened,' and I'd push the letter into her hands again. She'd smooth her fingers over the awful words and then look up to see if Anna had finished her picture or found her doll's clothes and shrug.

16

'It's happened,' she'd say. 'These things do. Clear up, lovey,' she'd say to Anna and I wondered if she really meant me, if all she saw, looking round that high yellow room, the painted boards, wooden furniture and my misery was that the bed needed making; if all she noticed in the tiny scarlet kitchen was that the plants needed watering; if the only reason she came was to show me, by example, what I could aim at instead.

'Sit down, talk to me, be with me,' I wanted to say every time she stood up to go. Yet all the time she was there I felt as if she couldn't wait to leave. She made me lunch but she wouldn't eat too, she said she'd had hers; she wandered round and fidgeted with books and records and looked away. I sat chewing and quite often felt like a prisoner with a warder, as if she only came to see I didn't damage myself. Sometimes, if I was quiet, she'd flick through all the old magazines I had and turn the radio or television on. She might as well not have been there except she was company, and after three weeks of it I was almost as angry with her as I was with Jas.

'You don't care either,' I said one afternoon, when all she'd said in half an hour was that she'd have to leave early, Geraldine and Paul were coming to supper. 'Do you? Not about me. All you care about is how things look, how it'll look at suppertime. What you want is to congratulate yourself on how well you've coped with me and a Cordon Bleu meal. That's really it.'

She put down her magazine and reached for her coat. 'It's not,' she said. 'That's not true. You're upset, you're getting things out of proportion.'

'You wouldn't ask me to supper,' I said. 'I might cry or get drunk and show you up, you don't want to risk anything going wrong, you just want it to look as though you've done the right thing.'

'If you want to come to supper,' and she started to put on her coat, 'I'll invite you. Except I thought you said you were fed up with listening to chat about playgroups and husbands. But if that's not the case any more, fine. We'll fix a date.'

'Don't be stupid,' and I stood up too. 'You know that's not what I mean. Me coming to supper won't mean that you'll start caring what happens to me. Basically all you care about is looking right. You'll invite me because it's the right thing to do, just the same as you come here because you want to show me you know how to do your duty. That's all you really care about.'

'I've got to go,' Barbara said. 'I've got to take Anna home. I'm sorry, I don't know what you're talking about. I don't traipse here every afternoon to prove anything to anyone. If you want me to stop, if it's useless, that's fine, if that's how you choose to see it. I'll stop wasting my time.'

'I don't choose,' I interrupted. I wasn't going to let her go off in a burst of offended suffering. 'You make it obvious. I don't invent it, I don't get any satisfaction out of seeing that the only way you can behave is like Audrey, that the things you care about are the same ones she did—'

'Me? Like Audrey?' She stared, and put her hand on Anna's head as though that'd block her ears to what I was saying. 'You must be out of your mind. Audrey was a depressive, a hermit, I come and visit you, I go out of the house and talk to people and the reason I'm going now is because I've got visitors. I invite people, I make them welcome and I get invited back. The reason people come to my house is that it's nothing like Audrey's and because I'm nothing like her.' She pushed Anna's arms into the coat on the back of her chair. 'Hurry up,' she said. 'We've got to go. We'll be late.'

'No,' I said. 'Underneath you're exactly the same. Order, presentation, that's all you both care about. But you think you've got away with it because you've learnt a social veneer. Audrey shut people out physically; you go through the social routines, but you still keep everyone a million miles away. You think people don't know you're as isolated as Audrey so you're safe, but that won't work, you'll do just as much harm. Look at her,' and I pointed to Anna, she was half-stuck in her coat, one arm in, one out, because Barbara wasn't guiding her every move so she got it right. Barbara was rigid, holding her hands tight together: she couldn't move for anger. 'Look at her and Graham, they're the ones I really pity, living with someone who doesn't know how to feel. It must be exactly the same to them as it was to me, like living with a frozen woman, living in an icehouse.'

'You're mad,' Barbara said, 'you're vile. The only thing you're right about is that I shouldn't have come. I ought to have known how you'd take it. Poor hard-done-by Laura, everything's always awful for Laura. You can't grow up, you can't see anything's changed from when you were five years old, you're determined to wallow in being the innocent victim. If you want to distort why I came, if you want to distort my life, fine, but don't expect me even to discuss it. It's rubbish and I'm not wasting time on it. I'm going,' and at first I watched her, but when she'd packed Anna's paper and

18

scissors away and opened the door neither of us looked at one another. When I heard her go downstairs and slam the outside door I realised that for the time being at least it was final. And when I'd thought that for rather too long I thought instead that I felt sorry for her. In a way, looking at our mother, you could have seen it coming, but then if you look at me you see the opposite, so it's not inevitable. Equally, I don't think it's accidental – saying I won't grow up means that, as far as Barbara's concerned, if those hideous years are over, they're done with. And by done with she means now that she's an adult she treats Audrey as normal, as if childhood can be put aside as irrelevant now we're all grown up. I don't agree with that.

'Remember when we were little?' I've said to Barbara and every time she changes the subject. But I remember it quite well, I think it's important; I believe it's made everything that's happened between all of us, I believe in ghosts and reverberations.

Barbara and I were born, lived and grew up in Henley-on-Thames, where our father Leslie kept a butcher's shop and Audrey, our mother, kept house. In Audrey's life there were three times – when she went to grammar school and was so proud of her uniform, when she was evacuated to a Garden of Eden on a farm and finally, more relevant to her children, when she and Leslie found the house we lived in – that she liked to tell a little story about.

'They're nice stories' she said, and she certainly meant that because they were the only events she could dredge up from the whole of her life, the only occasions she ever referred to, that gave her any belief at all in being happy.

'When we decided to get married,' she said, 'we wanted a nice place, outside London. We didn't want to bring you up in all that.' So she and Leslie went up and down the Thames for a couple of months and when they arrived at Henley it was regatta week and they alighted in a paradise of old-world charm and gracious living.

'It took my breath away,' she said. 'It was like a film.' She'd been so moved by the sights they stopped and watched. They, too, sat at a riverside pub and had a drink, watched women with parasols, men in boaters and white trousers, all so graceful, everything so perfect, and as they were about to leave she slipped on someone's mooring rope. Straight away two or three young chaps jumped up to ask if she was all right. They wanted to buy her brandy for shock, they brought a rug out for her, even helped her up half an hour later when she'd finished another Babycham – she refused the brandy – and that was it. She was like Cinderella finally making it to the prince, she'd found a land that promised every one of her dreams; it wouldn't have mattered what house they'd seen, Henley and the house would have become one, the house would have been transformed into a palace fit for a princess.

I never understood that when I was a child; I found it impossible to believe that right from the beginning, from the first moment she looked at next door's sagging washing line and filthy dustbins and heard Mrs next door shout at her kids to come in for their dinner, she hadn't realised that the Promised Land would never lie in Medley Drive. I didn't believe she took it seriously.

'My home's something special. We're not like the rest of them,' she said, and she was right; the house was silent, gleaming like a morgue.

'Tombstone rooms,' I said when I was older. I still thought she was pretending, I could never get it into my head that she wasn't, that she wouldn't see reason. 'Why can't she see?' I used to ask Barbara ten times a day about some contradiction or another.

'Because she can't,' Barbara would answer, 'and don't try and make her. Leave it. Don't push it,' she'd warn me, and I never took any notice.

The most obvious contradiction about Audrey was that she had two children when what she wanted was an empty house, and the first thing I remember was that when Barbara went to school and there was only me left with her, that made it worse. Barbara not being there wasn't a relief to her, it was an incitement; it made it worse having me left behind, and so she shut me away. Not just mentally, not talking to me, but physically. I was too old for a playpen but she made a cage instead, a barricade out of the furniture to keep me in one place. She made it in the sitting room but she didn't use armchairs, something I could curl up in and be comfortable; she used all six wooden dining chairs, two lines of three, and at one end there was the sideboard and at the other end she put an old sheet, tied to the backs of the chairs.

'In,' she'd say, after Barbara went off with the woman next door – almost before Barbara was down the path she'd be darting round the room, pushing chairs up against one another, running upstairs to get the sheet. She was quite pink sometimes with hurrying, or excitement, anticipating shutting me away. 'In there, no arguments,' and I'd go.

'Here,' she'd say and give me a pile of comics and a box of bricks and a doll and a golliwog, 'that'll keep you quiet.' And it did, there was no point in doing anything else. She made a noise moving furniture and there were other noises, machines, the Hoover, the washing machine; sometimes, if both were on at once, I could shout because no one could hear me above them. Until I went to school all I knew in that house was a desert; all day, everything that happened until Barbara came back was nothing.

'Be good, be quiet, get off,' were probably the first words I learnt. 'Don't touch.'

Looking out of the window, looking at her back, looking at the door until it would open and Barbara would come in. I knew every square inch of my skin, every leaf of the tree in the front garden, I looked so hard. I learnt to tie bows, I learnt to plait my fingers, I could touch my nose with my tongue, they were amusements. Sometimes, if anyone came to the front door, she'd call, 'All right?' and I'd say, 'Yes,' back, and hear her chatting to the coalman or the electricity man, not to be friendly or ask them in, but to prove her manners were in order. After they'd gone she'd slam the front door, stand in the doorway and ask me what that was about, how she was supposed to get on with constant interruptions.

'You'd better be good, now,' she'd say. 'I haven't got time to waste on anything else,' and I'd hear her crashing all over the house until Barbara came home.

She'd always let me out by then, she'd got time to sit down for a cup of tea after seven hours of housework. We'd all sit together at the kitchen table.

'What've you been up to?' she'd say to Barbara. 'I hope one of you's been a good girl today.'

'She probably thinks you like it,' Barbara said to me when I cried because she had to go to school. 'It's like playing houses, she's got her house to look after so she makes you one to play in. That's all. It's all right.'

'You'd better get back in,' Barbara said sometimes when we'd had our drink and biscuit and gone back in the sitting room. 'Go on, quick, before she comes.'

'Why?' I'd ask. Barbara would just nod furiously, she looked like Audrey when she did that, her hair bobbed up and down in time with her chin and her mouth folded.

'Just do it,' she said, and when I was back between the rungs again she'd say 'That's better, that's a good girl.' She sounded like

21

Audrey, too, sharp and singsong at the same time. 'Don't move,' she'd say. 'I'll go and tell her. Stay where you are, though, you keep still or she'll smack you.' That would be the last I'd see of her until teatime. I'd hear her, I'd hear her talking in the kitchen, and even Audrey answering and I'd look at the sheet and wonder if I dared crawl under. When Barbara did come back in again she'd pretend not to notice I'd been crying.

'All on your ownio?' she'd say. 'At least you didn't get smacked.' I wouldn't answer and she'd toss her head. It would be dusk, it would be time to draw the curtains and put the lights on and I'd want to take away all the last half-hour, I'd want to change it to other days when Barbara and I sat next to one another on the settee and watched television. 'Be like that then,' she'd say, and go towards the door again. 'The cat who sat by herself,' and she'd make a miaowing noise. 'Good Pussy, stay inside,' she'd say and I'd start to cry.

'Let me out, it's getting dark, I want to be with you.' She'd shake her head and laugh.

'Cats can't talk,' she said. 'Shut up, bad Pussy, stop pretending. We'll keep you shut up all night if you can't be good.'

'Pussy's feed,' she said sometimes, and offered me a piece of bread through the chair. I'd reach for it and she'd smack my hand. 'Naughty Pussy, no claws. No tea for Pussy if you scratch.' She'd put the bread back on the plate and sit and look at it, not me, frowning, as if I wasn't there. 'Is Pussy going to be good?' she'd ask after a minute, and I'd nod.

'Miaow,' I'd mutter. It hurt, my throat was sore from not crying.

'What did Pussy say?' I'd repeat it and she'd pick the bread up, yellow and white, so small it was hardly worth having. I'd put my face to her hand and feed, chew it up and then lift my head.

'Miaow, more,' I'd say, and she'd feed me another piece, two slices cut into strips from the plate Audrey had given her.

'All gone,' Barbara would say, 'good Pussy. We'll let you out, then. She likes it. She wants to stay in there,' she told Audrey, whenever she stood in the doorway. 'Don't you?' and Audrey would nod. 'It's a nice game.'

But whenever I was ill I still said, 'Don't go away,' to Barbara, because being left in our bedroom with furniture that seemed to touch the ceiling frightened the life out of me. The only other room in the house I was used to was the living room. Although it was big, most of the furniture sat round the edge of it, and I'd got used to sitting on the floor with the chair-legs. But our bedroom was like a stranger's house; anything could be in the wardrobe or under the bed.

I waited for something with hair, jelly-like, spongy, to crawl over to the bed and crawl over me, smothering.

'She won't let me,' Barbara used to say. 'She says I might catch it.' But that wasn't the reason.

'I'm frightened,' I told her, 'I hate it by myself.'

'What of?' she asked, but I wouldn't say. I shook my head and turned over.

'I'll say I'm tired,' she promised. 'I'll come up early.' I would wait for the noise Leslie made when he came in, the sound of tea-cups, washing up, the news. I would wait and wait until the Archers' music because then it was time for her to go to bed.

'What frightened you?' she would ask, sitting on my bed. She'd bounce a little bit and even if I'd been sick I wouldn't mind, it was like rocking. 'Monsters?' she'd suggest. 'What did they look like?'

'Wet. Slobbery. Just frightening,' I answered. 'Like her,' I said eventually, 'like she looks. Big and bony except made of soft stuff.'

'Except she's more like a witch,' Barbara said. 'She's frightening, like witches are. They beat you and shut up and won't feed you and keep you away from your real mother.'

'She isn't one, though,' I'd say quickly, because the description was too accurate and that would be more than I could bear. 'And anyway, you can't ask a witch, it's too dangerous.'

'No,' Barbara would say. 'You certainly can't do that. What you have to do is be very, very careful. You have to be very careful she doesn't know what you think.'

'We'd better hide,' she'd say, 'that'll make us safe.' She'd take off her shoes and creep to the door and open it and listen, and there would be no noise. I'd move to one side of the bed and lift the covers and she'd whisper, 'Ready?' We'd lie side to side, face to face in the dark, with all the weight of the covers on top of us, and she'd whisper again, 'We're all right now.'

'Why don't we run away?' I asked when I'd learnt to read. The monsters I read about made me stop believing they lived in our bedroom, but that didn't make real life any better. 'That'd show her she can't go on like this.'

'Leave it,' Barbara said. 'All you have to do is pretend,' but it didn't always work. It failed when Audrey pulled my hair, vicious

23

with elastic bands, used a cold flannel to slap the back of my legs and stood over every unfinished meal until I gagged.

'You,' she said and it became the word I hated most.

The second most contradictory thing about Audrey was that she was married to Leslie, that she lived every day of her life with someone she couldn't stand. Looking back, I could have a small amount of sympathy with her over that, because Leslie was boring and ugly, all you had to do was look at their wedding photos to see how he'd changed from young, slight and dark to fat, middle-aged and balding, but then you looked again and saw that so had she, she wasn't the coy plump girl with sausage curls any more. She was scrawny and sharp and shouted instead of talked; she ought to be able to make allowances.

'You again?' she'd say when he came near her. 'What is it this time? Get off, get out of it, get out of the place.' So he did, and she hated that too.

I suppose it was gradual, but by the time I remember he was hardly there. Every day when he'd shut the shop and every weekend, Saturday afternoon and all day Sunday, he'd be off at the golf club, not to play but to drink with other shopkeepers and bank staff at the bar. It wasn't that he came back blind drunk, or brought other people home with him, he didn't break the rules like that; it was just the fact that he'd found a way of escape that drove her to a frenzy. Except not every time. You were never quite sure whether to nod when she said, 'The pig's out at the trough again. When do I get out?'

Because sometimes if you did, some evenings when you looked up from the television or your homework to agree, she'd turn and shout, 'What do you know about it?' Her eyes would pop with fury. 'What are you talking about it for?' she'd screech, and then she'd act as if he didn't exist, as if he was never coming home.

A couple of times, though, she tried something different, maybe she even wanted it to work, she acted as if he'd return transformed. 'Your father'll be interested in that homework, dear, keep it to show him.' Or, 'Put your blue blouse on, try to look nice for him when he comes back.' And then as soon as he walked in the door it'd be over before it even started. 'Back so soon?' she'd say. 'They've had enough of you too, have they? I realise,' she said, 'I realise, if you don't, how kind they are at that club. Putting up with someone like you. I hope you said thank you. Really charitable. Gentlemen, I suppose. Do thank them from me. Look at the trouble they save me.' And she'd throw up her hands as if she was praying. 'I can't be grateful enough.

'Tramp, tramp, tramp,' she would chant, over and over, she'd walk in and out of rooms, up and downstairs and none of us would move, we'd all sit absolutely still. 'Tramp, tramp, tramp. What you do and what you look like.' She sang it like a ditty, as though it was funny, a catchy little number.

'Don't tell,' Barbara said when he brought us back bars of chocolate, slid them under our bedroom door as he crept along to their room; we heard him half-stumble and then we saw the silver paper glitter on the red carpet.

'Don't be stupid.' We sat up in bed chewing fast, in case Audrey had the least suspicion. 'He's nice,' I'd say. I wasn't that sure how I knew, when we hardly ever saw him, or that giving us chocolate made up for that. 'I bet he doesn't like it, either. He might want to run away, too.'

'He could if he wanted,' Barbara said. 'She wouldn't stop him.'

'It must be because of us, then. He stays because he wants to make sure we're all right.' Barbara gave me the same look Audrey did when I said something foolish. 'We could ask him,' I said. 'We could tell him we'd go with him, tell him we'd be easy to look after.' I felt like a visionary, I could quite clearly imagine Barbara and me keeping house, Leslie returning flushed and cheerful from the golf club. 'We've made tea,' I'd say, and he'd kiss us and say it was delicious.

'Go where?' Barbara asked. 'The butcher's shop?' and I stopped because I couldn't picture Leslie buying furniture and curtains and cookers and beds for the new house we'd live in. But as I thought of that I had another idea, I was so inspired I stuttered trying to say it.

'She could go,' I said. 'We could stay here without her. We could get rid of her.'

Barbara folded up her chocolate paper, over and over, smaller and smaller. 'Don't say that again,' she said, 'don't be so awful. Where would she go?'

'If we had a different mother,' I said presently, 'pretend, just pretend if we started all over again, what would you make her like?' She'd think and we'd decide like Ann's, or Mary's, or even Mrs next door. 'But we'd keep him,' I said.

'Shake him,' Barbara said on Sunday afternoons when he stayed at home and started to snore after lunch. 'Go on, you do it, stop him, she'll go mad.'

'All right,' he'd say when I'd whispered a bit, jiggled his shoulder, and he'd struggle upright in his armchair. 'Get your things on,' he'd say then. 'We'll pop out for a stroll.'

'Coming?' he'd ask Audrey. She'd turn her back and put her hands into the sink, even if it was empty.

'Out with you?' she'd snort. 'Where to? The knacker's yard?'

'How's tricks?' he'd ask, as we walked either side of him. 'Everything all right.'

'You don't want to take too much notice,' he'd say. 'Her bark's worse than her bite,' and he'd make exactly those noises and I'd laugh and Barbara would cover her mouth. 'What d'you fancy?' he'd ask us. 'Trip round the boating pool, listen to the band?'

'Can we have an ice-cream?' I'd ask and he would not answer, 'What was wrong with your dinner, then, can't you see how much they are, want, want, want, that's all I hear from you,' he'd say:

'Vanilla, strawberry? Chocolate?' and then give us a ten-shilling note. 'Here, treat yourselves.'

I'd hug his arm because it was like a schoolday, for hours we wouldn't be told off.

'Just pretend,' Barbara said to me for years. 'Don't tell her. Don't ask her,' she said 'just do it. Make an excuse, make something up.

'We've got to get things for the nature table,' she said, and we were allowed to go to the park. 'The teacher's taking us swimming. We've got to have money to take for netball posts in the playground.'

It worked.

'Don't look at me,' she said most of all, 'don't let her see. Pretend we don't tell one another anything. Be careful,' she said.

So did the woman next door when we came home from school and had to sit on the back doorstep, because Audrey was still washing the kitchen floor.

'Be careful,' and she'd laughed. 'She'll throw you out with the dirty water next.'

Until I was eight I was reasonable. Going to school and playing and shouting and laughing and being with people all day was like going to heaven. But I could still see you had to live through the rest of life, and I thought Barbara and I had found a way to do that. I also thought all the reasonableness ought to add up to something, that there ought to be some reward for it; and I thought it was time I said exactly what I had in mind.

'I want a friend to come,' I said to Barbara. 'I want someone to come and play.'

She stared at me. 'Here? Someone here?'

I nodded. 'Why not?' I wanted it to be like other girls' houses, I wanted someone to call for me, games, I wanted to make us like other families, cure her abnormality.

'Don't be stupid,' Barbara said. 'Make people ask you to their house. Tell them your mother's ill, tell them that's why they can't come. That's what I do,' she said and I shook my head.

'You haven't got proper friends, though. You just go if there's no one else to ask. I've got Mary, I want her to come here. Why don't you ask her?' I said. 'You tell her it'll be all right.'

'Tell her yourself,' Barbara snapped. Then she laughed. 'Try, go on, I dare you. You want it, you tell her. You say it won't make a mess, it won't hurt.'

'Don't be stupid,' I said back, but Barbara started to think about it.

'You could,' she suggested, 'not straight out, but you could make an excuse, say Mary wanted to borrow a book. Say she wanted to come here because her mother wasn't in. You could think of something.'

'You'd be better,' I told her.

'I haven't got a friend,' she said straight away, 'remember? I only go if there's no one else to ask. You're the one who's got Mary, you're the one who wants it. She wouldn't say no about a book,' she told me, 'or if she'd got locked out. It'd only be for a little while, and once she'd got used to that you could do it again. She won't be friends with you if she doesn't ever come here.' She sniggered. 'Look what's happened to me.'

And so the next time Mary said, 'Let's go back to your house,' I said all right and when Audrey opened the door I said very fast, 'This is Mary, she wants to borrow one of my pony books,' and Audrey shut the door in both our faces. 'She must've smelt something burning,' I said, and because it was raining I knocked again. After a long time it opened again and I could see Barbara sitting at the top of the stairs.

'I can't ask you in,' Audrey said. 'I've told Laura not to bring people back without warning. Time and again I've told her. She'll forget her head next,' she added, and I held on to it because with her it was quite wise to take any warning seriously. 'I've got to keep things straight,' she said, 'I don't want just anyone coming and messing things up,' as if she was expecting some mythical visitor who would immediately recognise that all her years of inhospitality had been a preparation for this supreme visitation. 'I haven't done all this for any Tom, Dick or Harry. It isn't as though Laura hasn't been warned.' She bared her teeth at Mary, it must have been meant to be a smile of apology, hostess to guest. 'She just needs a reminder. I'll have a word with her when you've gone,' she said and started to close the door. I stepped back with Mary and Audrey's arm shot out and grabbed mine. 'In,' she said and I was, and the door closed and I could just move enough to turn my head and see Mary through the glass, going down the path, and then look back up the stairs and see Barbara covering her mouth with her skirt, her face as red as the carpet, she was bursting, she'd even risk making a noise laughing to go on watching what happened to me.

'I don't care,' I said afterwards, 'it didn't hurt that much. I hate you,' I said to Barbara. 'You knew it wouldn't work. You wanted that to happen. I hate you.'

I started to say quite often to Barbara, 'You're as nasty as she is,' but I knew that wasn't true. I think what made me try to kill Audrey was that I thought that would happen, though, that if I didn't put a stop to her she would get Barbara on her side for ever, there wouldn't be anyone to trust any more.

'Do you think it's easy?' I asked Barbara, when we watched murder plays on television, stranglings, shootings, and because sometimes we were both frightened enough by what we saw on the screen to sit together Barbara bothered to say:

'It depends. If someone doesn't know you want to kill them they aren't on their guard. It can't be that hard, then. You might not even get found out,' she said. 'If no one knows what you're planning there's no reason to suspect you.'

'It needn't even look like murder,' I said, 'if there's not blood, it could look like an accident,' and all the weeks we watched I knew all I was waiting for was a method I could recognise, a poison I could get hold of. 'Wouldn't you taste it?' I asked after we'd watched a man expire from the ground glass his wife had put in a steak and kidney pie.

'You can't,' Barbara said and yawned, it hadn't been very exciting, arguments, shouting, we didn't need television for that, 'otherwise he'd have stopped eating it.'

For the next two weeks I tried to be nice to Audrey, I said the stove looked nice and clean, I went to bed when I was told, I scrubbed the table when I'd upset some milk. Until I saw her swallow the gritty tea I never had a moment's doubt, but at that instant I saw what would happen. It would hurt her, she would scream and writhe with pain, she would collapse on the kitchen floor and I'd have to get a doctor, she'd go to hospital and we'd hear she'd died, she'd be buried, shut in a box for her funeral, it wasn't just that she wouldn't be there, I'd have to watch what I'd done to her and always remember.

'Stop,' I'd cried and thrown myself on her. 'Don't drink it, it's got glass in it, stop, stop,' and she did. When she poured the tea through the strainer I thought she would take all that glass and push it down my throat, I saw myself in agony and dead and buried, and so when she pulled me out of the house and round to the hospital and left me and hissed and threatened, it wasn't as bad, it wasn't nearly as awful as what could have happened.

'I hate you,' Barbara said when I told her. 'Look what she'll be like now.' I honestly could not see what would be different. I was shouted at if I left my coat on the floor, I was hit and sent to bed if I answered back. I did not see what else there was she could do to me, and yet Audrey didn't look at it like that. She must have thought I liked the attention she gave, that I enjoyed remarks like, 'You'll laugh the other side of your ugly face', 'Get out, go and make someone else ill', 'Pig-face, you've got his big piggy-face'; that I would miss it if she stopped making them. She must have thought that if she never spoke to me again I'd be sorry, and that when she started to give all that spare attention, everything that was left over from ignoring me, to Barbara, I'd be really upset and ashamed of myself.

Not at first, it took a little while, but when I saw properly what was happening, I couldn't believe my luck. She didn't expect me to provide pleasure in her life ever again, so it wasn't worth asking anything of me, but with Barbara it was the reverse. Not exactly from that moment, but intensified from that time onwards, came the idea that Barbara was meant to be all Audrey had never attained, have all Audrey had ever wanted, and in return be the appreciative and loving daughter. She'd be the one to give her conscientious mother all the credit she deserved, she'd make all Audrey's sacrifices worthwhile, never complain, never argue.

'It's only what I deserve,' Audrey must have said to herself, and she would have believed it, expected it to come to pass, because she had no idea at all of human nature.

'Top of the class this time?' Audrey said whenever Barbara came home with a report, and she never was, and Audrey would go through every line the teachers wrote about her. '*Lacks organisation*.' She'd frown. 'What's that supposed to mean? Untidy? I'll have a word about that, you can show me what it looks like in future. Do that again,' she'd say; it could be pages she'd make Barbara rewrite. 'You'll be sorry if I tell you again.'

'Tell her you did it at school,' I said. 'Tell her you haven't got homework,' because every night she spent hours writing, she hardly ever went to anyone's house.

'I don't mind,' Barbara said. 'She's right in a way.'

'All work and no play,' Audrey said one Saturday morning. 'Get your coat on, I've found a piano teacher.' She even took Barbara herself; they went along the road side by side and Audrey sat at the far end of the church hall while Barbara and two other girls thumped away. Not long after that Audrey said, 'She does ballet, too, that piano woman, Wednesday evenings.' Barbara was bought tights and shoes and a leotard.

'I like it,' she said, and spent what spare time she had practising in our bedroom. I hated that because Audrey came up to watch.

'Sit down, you,' she'd tell me and 'Straight back,' to Barbara. 'You want your Grade Two, it's no good looking like a crippled cow, I'm not paying out to see you fail.'

Barbara took deep breaths and turned her head sideways to watch her arms move.

'Stick yourself in,' Audrey said. 'No one wants to see you poking out like that. Lift and pause, wait and bend,' she'd shout. 'That's what she tells you, isn't it? It's very gracious, ballet,' she said. 'I've always liked the look of it.'

'I hope you break your leg,' I said to Barbara. 'I hope you fall over. If you don't pass that exam she'll beat you black and blue.'

30

'I will,' Barbara said, 'I'll be a credit to her. So what am I supposed to do, what would you do?' she asked. 'All you can do is what she tells you.'

'You can't stand it; I can't either,' I said to Barbara. For weeks one summer we'd been kept indoors for answering back, giggling behind her back. 'We'll have to escape, we'll have to run away.'

But before I even planned it Audrey must have got fed up too, because she started to organise outings, trips out on Sunday afternoons, when she and Leslie walked arm in arm with one another – the only time I ever saw them touching – and Barbara and I had to wear our school blazers and clean white socks, and every single time we went to the river. We'd walk along the bank and then go into the gardens and as soon as we got to the rose-bushes she'd be burying her face in Peace and Crimson Glory, saying, 'Oh, smell them, mind the thorns on your dress, oh, we could go to Kew next week, there will be bushes of bouquets there.'

I thought she meant it, I thought she was open to suggestions for making it better.

'Don't,' Barbara said, 'don't. Please don't ask,' but I did, I still made my suggestions.

'We could take a boat out,' I'd say, 'a rowing boat.'

'Him? How?' Audrey would stand up very straight so she was taller than Leslie and point at him, not laugh at all.

'Or get a bus to Marlow. Or Windsor, see the castle.' I was full of ideas.

'Windsor? With him?' She'd turn her back. 'I wouldn't go there with him if you paid me,' and I'd remembered when it was too wet for him to play golf and she'd shouted at us to clear up all our mess, pencils, paper, we had on the dining table, and he'd offered to take us out from under her feet for the afternoon and she'd laughed as if he'd made a joke.

'You? I wouldn't let a rat out with you.' 'I could, though,' she'd mused a bit later. 'You being an animal, too. Pig.'

He'd said, 'What does that make you then, Lady Muck?' and laughed back at her as if it was an affectionate nickname.

'All right,' she said one week, when I'd gone on about what the other girls did at the weekends, 'we'll do something to show madam what's what. I'll think of something,' she said, and perhaps she might not have meant it as a threat; it might have been intended as a promise of what we could look forward to in seven days' time, but it didn't sound like it. 'I'll come up with something a bit different.'

'I don't want to go,' Barbara said. 'I'm frightened.'

'What of?' I asked, but we both knew.

'What'll happen.'

'It might be nice,' I said, 'it might. It might be different. We'll try and make it. We'll both try. Go on.'

'It can't last for ever,' Barbara said. 'It's only an afternoon, I suppose.'

It wasn't even that long, because first we went for our walk. It was almost time for us to go home and I could see Barbara looking at her watch, wondering if we'd been let off, if Audrey'd forgotten or hadn't thought of anything, when she said, 'We'll go to the Elizabethan tea-rooms, I thought that'd make a nice change.' We all said yes, although we knew exactly what it'd be like, dark beams, hard chairs, families with mothers in cotton frocks and cardigans while Audrey had her linen coat on, everybody chatting and all of us silent.

When we got there it was so crowded Barbara said, 'We could leave it,' and Audrey folded her lips and said, 'We'll wait.' All the time I prayed there would be an emergency and it would close early, they would just send us back where we'd come from.

When we sat down Audrey told us to put our napkins in our laps and then she poured drops of milk into our cups.

'Rationed, is it?' Leslie asked. 'Or is Lady Muck counting the cost already?'

Audrey took no notice. Instead she beckoned the waitress and pointed to the plate of fancy cakes in the middle of the table.

'Not those. Plain sponge, if you've got it,' she said and Leslie laughed across at her.

'Nothing's for nothing. You've got to pay, see? Even Lady Muck doesn't get it for free.' The waitress stared at all of us and then shrugged.

'Plain sponge,' Audrey repeated, and she nodded at each word, 'if you have such a thing.' Barbara was so red I thought she would explode. I watched the marzipan and whipped-cream fancies disappearing.

'Why not?' I asked and Audrey pointed at the waitress's back.

'Five shillings each for those things, they count them, they count how many you eat. It's not the plate of them you pay for, not in a place like this. I'm not being jewed in a cheap place like this. You wouldn't realise,' she said to Leslie, 'you'd hog the lot, given the chance. Stuff your snout in while the rest of us sat and watched.'

He didn't answer straight away but then he said, 'Very likely, very likely,' and tipped his chair back and looked round over his shoulder until the waitress put the plate of sponge, eight yellow slices, in front of Audrey.

She offered the plate to each of us in turn. It was difficult to swallow because everyone was watching us, but she didn't take any notice. She crooked her little finger above the handle of her cup and smiled as if the rest of us were not choking.

'Enjoying yourselves?' Leslie said and winked at me and then at Barbara. 'Having a good time, girls?' and he let out a great burst of laughter.

'There's no need, no real need to behave like an animal,' Audrey said. 'There's a farm round the corner, we could take you there, if you'd prefer. This place is for people. Silly of me,' she said after a moment and playfully slapped her hand, twice, three times. 'I forget you can't help yourself. Animal.'

She nodded to us to eat up and patted her mouth with her handkerchief and coughed a little when a man nearby lit a cigarette, as if she was quite normal.

When we'd finished our slices she leaned towards Leslie and said, 'Another cup, Rover?' This time he looked at her. Quite deliberately, still watching her face, he picked up his cup and tipped it, grouts and brown liquid into his saucer, and it was brim full, overflowing. He bent his head down to it and lapped.

'Satisfied?' he said, and stood up. He put his hand inside his jacket and took out a ten-shilling note and put it on the table. 'What the animal earned,' he said and walked away, out of the place.

Other people started talking more loudly and Audrey nodded to the waitress and handed the money over. 'Do keep the change,' she said and even smiled.

'We can't go on like this,' I said to Barbara when we got home. 'It makes you want to kill her. I wish I had, I wish I had done it. I still could.' Barbara didn't answer. 'I still could,' I repeated and punched the pillow I was holding on my lap, 'really.'

'Leave her alone,' Barbara said. 'She didn't mean it to be like that.'

'Didn't mean it!' I hit the pillow harder than ever, I couldn't believe my ears. 'She always wants it to be awful.' Barbara turned over to lie on her other side so I couldn't see her face.

'She was nice before,' she said and I could hardly hear.

'Nice? What could she be nice about? What happened?' I asked. 'What happened, did she discover you were dying? She wasn't even nice when you got put in the A stream, she didn't care when I was Aladdin in the play, she doesn't know how to be nice.'

'I've started,' Barbara said. 'She was nice about that.'

'Periods?' I asked after a minute, although I knew straight away and I was dumbfounded, it wasn't fair that she was older, that it had happened to her first and I'd got years to wait. 'Her, nice about periods?'

'She tried to tell me about them,' Barbara had said once when we'd giggled over packets of Tampax in Woolworth's. 'She tried to explain.' I'd thought I'd die laughing.

'Her? Talk about that? Blood?' Barbara had nodded.

'I said she didn't need to. I said we did it at school and you would, too. Don't worry.'

I'd blinked, I hadn't worried, the picture of Audrey trying to explain reproduction, menstruation, filled me with delight, it would be my revenge, she'd have to talk about something that you couldn't clear up because it kept coming back.

'What about doing It,' I said. 'Did she tell you about that?'

'Shut up.' Barbara had blushed. 'That's all your friends talk about.'

'We're eleven,' I'd said. Barbara had taken my arm and led me away from the counter.

'People are looking at us. Stop it.'

'She gave me things. Pads,' Barbara said and looked up from the bed. 'Those things we looked at, I asked her, but they're for when you've had babies. You can't use them yet. She said if it hurt she'd give me a Disprin. She said to wrap all the old pads up and gave me proper little bags to put them in and a great big bag for the dustbin. She didn't tell me off,' she said. I had to admit that was quite an advance. 'She isn't always nasty,' she said.

'Not to you,' I told her, and then I said, 'I don't care, anyway,' and I didn't, I got my homework out and it made no difference any more that Audrey would be awful to me, and I wasn't jealous, I didn't mind if Barbara had an easier time. What I minded was Barbara going on to her side, that was what it was all about, sharing something that I didn't know about. What I minded was the thought of them getting together and leaving me out. 'I wish I had killed her. I still could,' I said.

I suppose I could have spent the next few years going on hating her and learning how to deceive her over boyfriends and going out, like I deceived her over schoolfriends. I could have listened to records at other people's houses, like Barbara did, and got a Saturday job and bought my own clothes and shouted back when she hated them. I wasn't unprepared to do that, wait to grow up and leave, and if Mercy, Audrey's mother, hadn't come to live with us I might have tried, and that might have been better. I'd still have gone on hating and Barbara would have gone on placating and pretending the rows could be discounted, that the everyday was bearable, concentrated on Christmases, birthdays, truces. I suppose we could have forgotten that she called Leslie pig – 'Go and get the pig for his food,' she said – and that he needed a trough, a sty, not a bed in her house and he spat at her. Once he hit her, too, so her cheek was red and the spit glistened on it and even when it dried the cheek stayed red. She stared in the hall mirror at it and strutted from room to room all day, pushing her face at any of us who went near her. She butted us, shoved us up against doors and walls to remind us what had happened. That could all have gone on except Mercy came and that changed the way all of us behaved.

Mercy came because her house had been compulsorily purchased and Hammersmith Council were going to rehouse her in a new block. It was hideous, she said, cardboard bloody rubbish. She made daily scenes at the Town Hall, and after she'd reduced a young woman to tears the housing office got on to Audrey and suggested she stayed with us for six months until they'd found a more suitable location. There were letters and Audrey went up to London to see what she could do, but they obviously got the better of her – she'd got a spare room, it was her mother, the only temporary alternative would be an old people's home; she wouldn't want that for her mother, would she?

'Answer that door,' Audrey said to me the day Mercy arrived. 'Take her up.' I carried Mercy's cases and Audrey refilled the washing machine and shut the kitchen door.

Mercy winked at me. 'Put them bags down,' she said. 'We'll see to them later. We'll have a look at my snaps now,' and as well as packets of photos in her handbag she'd got two bars of Double Milk chocolate. 'Be prepared, that's what I say.' She unwrapped mine for me. 'Better than her bloody mushy peas, any day. You get stuck into this, give you fillings in your teeth.'

All afternoon I'd looked over her faded pictures of people I couldn't recognise.

'Who's that?' I said, even when I recognised a face from another scene. 'Where was it, when did it happen?' I didn't want it to end, I didn't want her saying, 'That's the lot, go on, pack 'em up, I've had enough now.' That first afternoon I wanted to stay with her, I thought it would just be like an everlasting continuation of the times she visited. Once a month Leslie used to fetch her from the station and Audrey would go out in the kitchen and call Barbara to help and Mercy'd sit in the armchair and I'd sit on her lap and tell her things that made us sound like any other girls who lived in our street.

'Barbara's in the netball team. We cut up worms in biology and they kept on moving. We made shortbread in cookery, I've saved it for you, it's in a box in the kitchen.' I cuddled into her.

'She's nice,' I'd say to Barbara when she'd gone.

'How can you?' Barbara would answer. 'She's awful. She's ugly.'

'Not very,' I'd say, 'she's just different from us.'

'You can say that again.' Barbara would laugh and I would too, then, because she was an odd sight, short, bulging, and always with thick clothes, brown stockings that her varicose veins showed through. She sat with her legs spread wide apart under a blue dress in the summer and a brown one in the winter. Nothing matched about her, nothing quite fitted, and she was always pulling and hitching things up. Her hair was cut very short and stuck out all round; she wore glasses with bent frames and underneath her face was powdered white, then rouged over the top.

'Give us a kiss,' she'd say and leave her lipstick on your cheek, but it was better than spittle. 'You come tomorrow,' she said to me when Audrey finally called that it was teatime.

And every afternoon after that, when I got home from school, I'd go up and sit on the edge of her bed, trying not to crease the pink nylon cover and she'd put her arm round me. Sometimes, quite often, I didn't want to go, sometimes I envied Barbara doing homework in our nice clean bedroom while I had to sit with the smell Mercy made all day – because you couldn't pretend about that, you just had to ignore its existence. It wasn't her fault, because that room was where she always spent all of her day and because that was all she was allowed to do, that was why I went.

She was allowed out, from tea to bed, downstairs with the rest of us, and the rest of the time she stayed in her room. The whole time Mercy lived with us Audrey found her quite unbearable and she didn't disguise it, and because being shut up reminded me of the cage I'd had, that was why I took Mercy's side. The only way I could see of making her think her life hadn't been in vain, she hadn't existed just to be put out of the way in a spare bedroom in my mother's house, with me taking her poached egg upstairs, was to listen, was to act as if I was glad she was there.

Sometimes when I took her food up she'd say, 'How's the loony? How's the she-wolf? Loony bitch,' she'd say. 'She-wolf. I'll get her,' and stab her fork onto the bed or thump her armchair. 'I'll shove the bleeding toast up her, treating me like this,' she said. I'd sit on my side of the bed, feeling it shake, and I'd do the same, I'd be holding myself with excitement.

'My life and times,' she'd say other days, 'you get an earful of this, this'll tell you. When I was your age, I knew what was what, I was nobody's bloody old fool then.' I'd glaze over with boredom because I didn't want to hear again about when she was a child in White City, in and out of everyone's house, everyone poor, everyone helping one another, helping to keep the boiler going on washdays, brushing the totters' horses, unloading the rags from the carts, even laying out at funerals. Births, marriages, deaths, she was in the thick of everything. Life was making things happen, goings-on in alleyways, giving the lads a run for their money, making sure you didn't get copped, and then it went straight into being grown up. When the Great War came she was fourteen and when it was ended she was eighteen and then she got married.

'Eighteen wasn't young,' she said. 'I knew what was what by then. I thought I knew where I'd do better. I'd had enough of that titchy house, three in a bed, all day Monday in the scullery with the boiler going. I didn't want any more to do with it. We was courting,' she said, 'me and Will,' and then nudged me. 'But all good things come to an end. Will got the job at Dawson's and the house came too. That's all there was to it.' It didn't matter what I asked then, how I tried to get her to talk about it, she wouldn't say any more, not if she'd wished she'd changed her mind or what being married was like.

37

'What happened then?' I'd say, but all she did was stare out of the window. She didn't want to talk about being happy or what she remembered best, even when I yearned over her wedding photos she wouldn't tell me who anyone was.

'They're all gone now,' she said. 'Shut up going on about it. Leave off, leave it alone,' and that was the only time she got cross with me. 'I had Audrey,' she said, 'that's what happened next. Then I was widowed. That's all there was to it,' but it wasn't, she'd go on for hours about how Will was killed, burnt to death in a fire at Dawson's, how Dawson's tried to cheat her out of his pension, taking in washing to make ends meet, carrying baby Audrey with her at five o'clock in the morning to go scrubbing steps, hardship, counting pennies, doing without, worrying how they'd make out, and then suddenly Audrey was eleven and it was all right, there was all the money Audrey wanted, she'd never want again, and Mercy was livid. Instead of being pleased Audrey'd got a scholarship to grammar school and a grant from Dawson's to pay for everything, uniform, keep, for the next five years, Mercy was furious, she was ready to do murder.

'Dawson's fucking grant,' she said. ' "Fit her out," they said, "right uniform, right equipment," as if I wouldn't do it. As if I couldn't. They bought her,' she said. 'She took to money and that school and they took her away, they got her on their side. It was that that did it, their money, that school, her and them; after a year at that school she was nothing to do with me any more, she hadn't got two words left for me. They wiped it out, all the years I'd got by, they chucked that out as if I needn't've bothered, they'd see her all right now, I could hand her over to them. And she went; I didn't tell her, she went of her own accord, once they'd got their oar in she never had two words for me. Whenever I spoke to her she had her nose buried in a book, or else she'd be looking down it like I was dirt to her. "I'll kill you," I told her, "if you look at me like that. Bugger off, clever cuts, stick yourself somewhere else, I don't want you." Sneering,' she said, 'that's all she did, too. Pretending I was nothing. I could have killed her.'

I'd nodded. Whenever I saw them together in our kitchen I shuddered, thinking of them alone all those years together, opposites locked by blood, and I wouldn't have been surprised if there had been, except Audrey wouldn't have lifted a finger. I couldn't like the picture Mercy painted, screaming her head off, her whole fat body shaking with rage, hair standing on end, but when you saw my mother turn her back you could see how that prim little schoolgirl with her airs and graces had driven Mercy mad, cut out everything between them except anger.

'You ought to listen,' I said to Barbara. 'She's not awful, she's all right. You should hear what she says about Audrey, too. She can't stand her.'

'She should leave, then,' Barbara said. She didn't catch my eye and smile, she never glanced across the table at breakfast or teatime, she didn't look up when I went into our room and when she undressed she switched the light off. 'Haven't you got to talk to Mercy?' she said when I asked if she was going round the shops on Saturday. 'Hadn't you better see to her?' when I said we could go down the road after tea to see Anna or Mary.

'Leave her alone,' I said. 'She's got nowhere else to stay. Besides, why shouldn't Audrey have her? She had Audrey.'

'Is that how you'll feel?' Barbara smirked. 'Audrey had you.'

'Shut up,' I said. 'You don't know everything. It's me Mercy tells things to, you could do worse than listen.'

'Talking like Mercy won't make me,' and she turned another page of her exercise book. 'Actually, nothing would make me.'

'Go on, please,' I said another time. 'She was talking about when Audrey was evacuated, all that stuff she used to go on about, the Buckmans, going to stay in glorious Gloucestershire, you remember the awful way she talked about that place, her special voice when she said words like snowballs, bluebells, all that stuff about the lovely Buckman family and how they played games in the big house and huge garden. "It was my little bit of heaven," I imitated. "My own special bit to go back to one day."

'Go back to Mercy,' Barbara said. 'You don't want to talk to me, you just want to make fun.'

'You used to, too,' I said.

'Only because of you. If you don't have anything to do with Audrey, if Mercy's the only person you talk to, I don't have to any more.'

'I don't really want to listen to her every night,' I said one day when we came back from school together.

'Don't, then,' she shrugged.

'But she wants me to.'

'Then you'll have to make up your own mind.'

'Come on in,' Mercy said, 'you're late. I was waiting for someone to talk to.

'I was bloody glad to see the back of her,' she said. 'Evacuated, they called it, but I called it a blessing. I'd go and see her, mind, but a fat waste of time that was, all I heard was Mrs Buckman this, Mrs Buckman that, she didn't want a word of what I'd been through, nights in the shelter, glass everywhere, you could see people stuck all over with glass after a bad raid. And blown to pieces – it doesn't bear thinking about what you saw, but she didn't want to know. All I got was the cold shoulder, I'd spend all day going there, put up overnight, and all day coming back, I could have knocked her into next week the way she treated it like nothing. I could've knocked her into next week to get rid of that look on her face. She could be a real little witch, that girl, you forget that sometimes.'

Mercy had looked at me, thirteen years old, sitting on the edge of her bed, neat, uniformed, staring across as she rocked herself to and fro in her chair, pulling at the curtains when she got agitated, stroking her bulgy knees to calm herself down. Her bedroom was too small for us to be more than three feet apart and sometimes she'd lunge over from her chair and pull me off the bed to stand up against her, hug me really hard, fiercely, and then wipe her eyes. 'Time heals,' she would tell me then, and I'd look out of the window and think that was a good job, although it didn't seem to have done much so far.

'You don't learn, though,' she said. 'I still waited for her to come back. Once the war was over I thought she'd want to be back where she belonged.' I could see how she'd imagined a new life together for them, living happily in the two-up, two-down, Audrey getting a job, going out to dances, courting, getting married, that somehow she could join in with all that. 'And when she did,' and Mercy had covered up her face, 'it was horrible. We was like chalk and cheese, we couldn't stand one another. She got a job, that was one blessing, so she was out all day and then they sent her on courses and she'd be gone all week, but when she came back she was a walking misery. She never went out, never wanted any fun, books, shut up in her room, that was all she liked. "Go dancing," I told her, "I'll buy you a frock, enjoy yourself," but that was the last thing she wanted. She brought one young man back, and then another, two a year, and they were all skinny bookworms like her, mooning around, and then she found Leslie. She was lucky,' Mercy said and although I found it difficult I could see why she thought that. 'He'd saved, he was older, he wanted to get married. He'd spent the last couple of years in the Army, he couldn't see the point of hanging about. He'd even put up with all her airs and graces if he had to. She did the right thing for once,' Mercy said and sniggered. 'Even if it's gone wrong ever after.'

'Weren't they in love?' I asked.

Mercy laughed out loud. 'The only thing Audrey was in love with was the idea of leaving me. That's what Leslie meant, he was a meal ticket out of my house, he was a butcher to bring home the bacon. That's all he was.'

'It wasn't love,' I wanted to tell Barbara. 'We don't have to mind about them not loving one another,' but whenever I went up to our room the door was shut and there was a chair against it. 'Let me in,' I'd call and she would and straight away sit down at her desk again. She wouldn't ever look up from her history notebook or atlas, she'd go on writing notes as if her life depended on it.

'Go and watch television,' she said if I started to talk. 'I've got to get this done,' and I'd say, 'Fine, I was going to anyway.' After tea I'd help Mercy downstairs and we'd watch whatever was on, the adverts, the serials, the singers, and after a bit I didn't mind the way she tapped her feet to *Ready Steady Go*, and she stopped saying she didn't see how they got paid for caterwauling. We'd quite often laugh at the same things and then put our hands over our mouths, catch one another's eyes because we could hear Audrey starting to bang cupboard doors in the kitchen.

'Having a laugh doesn't make a mess,' Mercy would say, but under her breath, and sitting next to one another on the settee we were like naughty children, giggling, whispering, enjoying ourselves because we had to make a secret out of it. It reminded me of being very little.

Mercy lived with us for three years and told me her life story twenty times. She was the one I told when I was in the finals of the swimming gala at school and when I got suspended for smoking. She said, 'Tell your mother the teacher said so,' when I wanted a bra and, 'Don't you dare say a word,' when she sent me to the chemist for her medicines.

'You tell that Barbara,' she said, 'to get her nose out of books, it'd do her good to look round a bit. You have a good time,' she said when I told Audrey I was going to the school dance and I went to a disco in Windsor, and, 'You watch it,' she said the next week. 'Don't you go leading anyone on. Your sister,' she said, 'your father: I've had enough of them,' and I'd try not to listen, because that wasn't what I wanted, other people, all I wanted was someone to talk to, and she was the only one left.

'You ought to talk to her,' I still said to Barbara, but less and less often. I said everything to her less and less often because all she answered was, 'I've got exams, I can go to university if I get these exams.' I could see the point of that but it didn't bring us closer together.

At first when Mercy went to hospital I wasn't upset because I expected her to come out. I thought visiting her was so awful, that long walk down the ward, watching her old hopeful face as I tiptoed along between all the strange bodies, turning to wave goodbye and seeing how sad she looked, I couldn't think beyond that coming to an end.

'They're shifting me,' she said one day, 'putting me by myself.' When I asked why, I was quite unsuspecting, she clung onto me and cried and after that Audrey started to visit. I tried not to take notice of her dying so I suppose it was a shock, but as soon as it was over I put it out of my mind. I could no more bear to go over what she'd been like, pathetic, grabbing, pulling at me, and how still she'd been dead, than go into her empty bedroom. I didn't want to think or talk or have anything to do with that happening or that bit of the past, I wanted to skip it. It wasn't that I was particularly skilful, but I was very determined, and other things happened to make it easier.

The first was that as soon as I didn't have to spend time with Mercy after school I could join in with the girls who hung around outside the boys' school at four o'clock, and after a couple of weeks one of the sixth formers separated me off from Anne and Sonia and Lesley for long enough to ask me out. Going out, for all the time I knew him, consisted of cups of coffee and seeing how far either of us dared go sexually, but that was all we wanted from a relationship, so it was all right. He was called George, and though I told myself it was love, it was an obsession, and although that wasn't true he did make me feel excited about seeing him and not want to do my homework. We must have been important to one another because we got together again after he'd gone to university. Every so often he or I would break it off, though, because that was the only way to inject any drama into what happened – otherwise it was all handholding over coffee cups and, 'God, you're fantastic,' 'Don't make me stop,' 'Not there, I've told you not there,' and we'd go out with other people, but none of the boys I found were half as resourceful or good-looking as him, and those were the qualities that mattered.

The second thing was that, at the same time as Mercy died, Barbara went to university, and with only Leslie and her and me left in the house Audrey altered. At first it was just that she started watching television in the evenings, and then it was that she stopped telling me off.

'Out?' she'd say when I put my coat on, instead of, 'You don't think you're going somewhere?' and 'What time does this film finish, then?' instead of, 'You're to be back by ten'; it wasn't exactly that I could do as I liked but I could see George when I wanted and come home late and she didn't ask me about homework. Even when I failed exams she didn't threaten to throw me out or refuse to speak to me or scream or bully. She just got quieter, and I thought I hated that even more than all the silences and threats and bitterness because this proved they'd all been in vain. Barbara had got away, Mercy had disappeared, Leslie and I were acclimatised, Audrey less vigilant but no one had lived how they wanted. We all had to carry unhappiness around with us without there being any compensation. I felt worst about Mercy because when you were old you'd know things wouldn't have time to improve; I hadn't made enough difference to her. The only person, I decided, I could make a difference to was me, and the only way to do that was to do what I wanted.

I suppose at eighteen no one has very clear ideas except that they can be independent, and to that extent I didn't do too badly. Partly I was lucky in that because Audrey didn't want me around she only put up a token fight when I found a secretarial college on the other side of London, which meant I had to find somewhere else to live. I went back once a month for an afternoon, four hours every four weeks, that seemed to be an acceptable amount of time to spend with one another. When I went to see Barbara, she was always frantic about some essay, and whether I'd behave properly, and as she went out less than I did I didn't feel I'd missed out there either.

When I'd finished the course I got one job and then another; I wasn't very often without a boyfriend. I got quite good at dressing well, I nearly managed on what I earned, I made new friends at each job and lost them when I left. When Barbara came to London I'd meet her and Graham and I liked making him laugh about life in the typing pool. When he'd stopped smiling and Barbara had looked at her watch and started to fidget and he said, 'What are your plans, then?' I'd answer, 'Have another gin and then get a takeaway.'

I hardly ever thought, 'I'm twenty and I've got no idea what I want to do,' I was looking after myself, and if Barbara said, 'You'll have to alter one day,' I never imagined when or how. I just thought that as long as I didn't settle down with a pile of exercise books to correct every evening, like she did, I'd be quite happy.

I surprised myself as much as everyone else when I got the job in the old people's home. In fact all the time I was writing the letter of application I kept telling myself to turn to the next page of the Sits Vac. I was looking for employment as a courier not a skivvy. When I got an interview and found myself going to the library and taking out books on geriatric day care I pretended it was out of general interest, because of a television programme I'd stayed in to watch. When I got the job I said I wouldn't last more than a week.

'Why do you want this job?' the matron asked.

I'd said, 'I'd feel bad about old people if I didn't,' and a year later there were four of them, and Beryl who worked there, who I knew really well.

Mr Cathcart was seventy-nine, and lived for the letter he got from his daughter in Australia every month, and counted off the years of his life until she came on another visit; he'd been widowed for ten months, and still forgot, he'd still look round to show his wife when the post arrived with the precious pages, he still wanted someone to read it to.

Quite often Mrs Wells would, but that was because she read anything she could lay her hands on. She got through books more quickly than the library could send them, westerns, biographies, gardening, it didn't matter, and she recited a summary of the contents of each day's literature at the end of it, when the television was going full blast and the cocoa was growing chilly.

Mr and Mrs Thompson were one of the few married couples, and he was deaf and she'd been a teacher. Every morning when she got her paper she'd shake it at him and shout, 'Devils, look at what they're doing now.' He wouldn't lift his head from his jigsaw, and then she'd hobble down the corridor to the kitchen and shout at me instead, 'Ruining it, ruining the profession, senseless, senseless.'

I'd go over what happened with Beryl when we went out for a drink on Tuesday nights, when her fiancé did fire brigade advanced first aid, and then say, 'It's awful to talk about them like this, music hall turns.' She'd give me what she called an old-fashioned look.

'What do you think they say about us?' she'd ask, and swallow her lager and lime faster than I could keep up. 'I'm no better than I should be and if you're not careful you'll be left on the shelf. That's how they see you and me. They're still people, they're not saints because they're old.'

But apart from Tuesday evenings I didn't go out much for a whole year, and I was too busy to buy clothes, so I managed to save quite a bit, and I used it to pay the key money on a flat in Shepherds Bush. I pretended I didn't realise what was happening, that it was nothing like settling down, but when I'd moved in and painted the sitting room yellow and white and the kitchen red and bought rush matting and shelves, I realised it was just what I wanted, even if I wasn't sure why. I met Jas at a party six months later and when he moved in, too, I thought I'd finally got the life I'd always wanted. It'd be like this now, work, love, somewhere nice to live and then it'd become somewhere bigger to live, and children and still love. For six months it was like that, and for another six months I pretended. Because I couldn't visualise anything else, I didn't see any other logical outcome.

I'm not sure how I got through the six weeks after Jas did go, especially the three weeks after the row with Barbara, because mostly what I did was drink. I remember going to work but that's all, because every evening and Saturdays and Sundays I drank gin or vodka until I went to sleep, and if you're that drunk for that long you're unlucky if you retain much memory.

Also, the incentive to wake up was the sight of last night's glass and ashtray and the awful neglect of my flat, dusty plants, creased clothes, the smell, every part of it as abandoned as I was, so I became quite successful at unconsciousness. 'I'm trying not to think,' I told myself, and although I didn't succeed, at least sometimes I thought about something other than misery. I thought about trying to remember what I'd done with my purse the night before and feeling sick and aching all over instead of what Jas and I used to do on a Friday night or what he'd do if I got on a train to Birmingham and pleaded, said, 'This can't be right, if it makes me this unhappy it can't be the right thing for you to do.' Instead of missing Barbara or imagining apologies, instead of imagining the phone call to Louise where I persuaded her she didn't love him because he'd loved me so deeply, I used my brain power in the morning to wash and dress. In the evenings, if I drank fast, instead of remembering it wasn't long before I got past retribution and reconciliation and entered the downhill straight into resignation.

After a while I managed to say, 'Jas has left me,' to the people at work and, 'I don't want to talk about it,' nastily enough to stop Beryl trying. I spent a couple of Mondays and one Thursday in bed crying, but most days I felt a kind of relief that I had something to do for eight hours, that I was still alive enough to be distracted. I moved out of misery into hatred, and out of hatred and revenge into hope, and out of hope into hangovers. For three weeks that was it, weeping, swearing, blankness, putting things out of my mind, until one Friday I waited half an hour for a drink and it occurred to me that it must be about time that Barry was due back and that three weeks was a long time not to see Barbara. I knew that according to her rules, as I'd started the argument, I was the one who had to apologise but I couldn't begin to think of buying her a card or taking a plant round. If I thought anything it was that I'd try and engineer an accidental meeting, and then I decided I'd telephone her. I had a couple of drinks for courage, and then, accidentally, I wasn't thinking, a third, and by the fourth all the world was clear to me.

'Barbara,' I would say, 'I'm sorry. I'm telling you I'm sorry but not that it was wrong. You can change,' I'd gently offer. 'You don't have to stay like Audrey. Try and see,' I'd tell her and lean back, stretch out on the empty bed and look out of the window at the stars and see the infinity of comprehension. 'You don't have to pretend.'

But every time I picked up the phone to dial I found I'd put it down and put more gin in my glass because I couldn't do it. I couldn't think about hearing her injured voice, and picture her standing in her perfect home; I didn't want to talk to anyone, I couldn't speak clearly enough to say a word. I still sat by the phone, though, I did nearly every evening, and when it was time to go to bed, because the bottle was nearly empty, my elbow caught the receiver and simultaneously it started to ring. It took me a little while to understand what was happening, though, because the voice talking to me was drunk, too, so I thought it was some kind of echo, and then I said, 'Barry.'

He said, 'So you remember, there's one person who remembers. Louise won't, he won't, but you –'

I interrupted. 'What's happening, where are you, what's going on?' I asked because I wanted to make quite sure this was real, I wanted to be quite certain I wasn't inventing anything.

'I'm out,' he said. 'Locked fucking out.' Then I knew I wasn't imagining at all. 'She's changed the fucking lock,' he said. 'Let me in to tell me, announce what'd happened, and then booted me out, sent me packing. A hotel. A hotel,' he repeated. 'I had to find a place to stay in, somewhere for the night, and the next day I couldn't even get back in, I'd got to wait for them to answer or break the door down.'

'What did she say?' I asked immediately, because it might be that the end was in sight.

'What'd fucking happened,' he snapped. 'I told you. Her and fucking Jas, your fucking Jas. I had to go, she said, and when I went back the next day she watched me. "You can get your clothes," she said and then she watched me packing, she was in the doorway, twiddling her fringe the way she does, as if she was waiting to see if I'd take anything of his. All I'd take to him is a gun. Or a knife. Or a fucking bayonet, that's what I'd like, that's what I think about. That's what I've been doing, Laura,' and he half-laughed, 'since I got back, thinking of him with his insides out. Then this afternoon I rang them up, I'd got another idea. "I'd like to see Nicole," I told her, because I'd thought about her too, he's got her as well, but I was cleverer than that. "I've been away six weeks, I'd like a bit of time with her," I said. "She's still mine." I had this idea, see, that once I saw Nicole she'd want to stay with me. Louise said, "I'll come to the hotel foyer," anything so I wouldn't kick up a stink, but I didn't care by then, once I'd got hold of Nicole I'd have Louise too, she'd see sense after that, she'd boot him out and have us back –'

'But it didn't work,' I said.

'Too right, God, too right,' and he moaned. 'God,' he said. 'We went for a drive,' and then he stopped. He waited so long I thought he'd passed out and then he was suddenly very loud. 'I was so fucking stupid,' he said. 'Stupid. I should have told her to sit still, climbing all over me, all over the wheel. "Get off, Nicole," I should've said, but I thought, Let her, she's missed you, leave her –'

'Barry,' and I was loud too, 'what happened?' because I could see it and I could hear the impact and the ambulance and I wanted to know the worst very quickly. 'What happened this afternoon?'

He made another moaning sound. 'It's a write-off. Half the front stoved in, the offside, I ought to be grateful for that, a steering wheel through your chest isn't anybody's idea of a joke. We must've been doing sixty and I couldn't do a thing, straight across the central reservation, up over the hard shoulder, we must've been doing seventy when we hit the barrier –'

'What's happened, Barry?' I said very quietly. 'What's happened to Nicole?' Because that was what mattered, if Nicole was injured, if Louise had to be with her in hospital, devote hours to her daughter's recovery, that might alter Jas's devotion too.

'It was a miracle,' he said. 'Every day of my life I'll say that, it was a miracle. Compared to what could have happened it was nothing short. She bumped her head, that's what, she said it, we were sitting in that bloody great heap of tangled metal and Nicole's crying, "Banged head, banged head." There's cars stopping and no one daring to look and I get out one side and lift her out of the back and all either of us 's got to show for all that is one bump on the forehead. We just walked away. Laura?' he said after a minute.

'That is miraculous,' I managed. 'I don't give a fuck,' was what I wanted to say. 'She could have been killed,' I told him instead. 'So could you,' I added, and the noise he made at the other end was like laughing.

'I don't need you to tell me that,' he said. 'No one, not Laura or fucking Jas or Louise needs to tell me what could've been. I'm telling you.'

'I've listened,' I said. 'Yes.'

'I'm telling you another thing,' he said, 'and you can tell him. If, if that had happened, if more than a hair of her head had been damaged, it'd've been his fault. I wouldn't have stood that. It wasn't my idea to take her driving round the motorway, it'd be my idea to sit in my house all afternoon, and since he's stopped that, I'm holding him responsible. You tell him that, and you tell him what I'd've done to him. I'd've cut him up, I'd've—'

'I don't see him,' I said. 'I can't tell him anything.'

'You fuck off, too, then,' he said, 'if you weren't so useless he wouldn't have started on Louise.'

'Shut up, you fuck off, too,' I said. I put the phone down and poured the gin that was left into my glass, and then I took the phone off again because I imagined he would ring me all night. Then I started to cry, I was appalled at myself, really, that I'd reached a point where it mattered more that I got Jas back than that a child was injured, and I thought about it, I saw the car skidding and him trying to turn the wheel and the barrier coming to meet them, and that minute, that instant before Nicole started to cry, when he

48

didn't dare turn round and look, I looked at what he could have seen. Then I saw the look on his face when Louise told him to leave and I saw Jas in the bedroom waiting for her to come back. 'Bad? I'll make it better,' he'd whisper, his hands on her, his mouth, and when I saw him kiss her it didn't make me want to cry, it made me want to get out, find somewhere different to forget about everything that had happened. At that moment I knew I wanted something else to do, I couldn't think what or where, but I knew I had to escape, I was determined, and compared to how I'd been feeling it was like an instantaneous recovery.

By the morning I'd decided on two things, ringing Barbara and going on holiday, but I delayed the first while I arranged the second. Every time in the last weeks when someone at work had said, 'Why don't you have a night out?' I'd thought of Martine. It wasn't because I liked her, or saw her at regular intervals, but because she was the obvious person to have a night out with. Even when she'd worked night shift she'd managed to enjoy herself, and even though she was small and too plump she acted glamorously. I suppose I hoped some of that might rub off on me, I suppose I thought she'd give me the chance to be confident and amusing and make people interested again, and even if that magic didn't happen, at least I'd have made some effort. We could go for a drink, to the cinema, I encouraged myself. I didn't have to mention a holiday straight off, but I also knew that as Martine never saw anyone without an ulterior motive, she wouldn't be offended at anything I suggested.

'How's things with you? Jas still on?' was the first thing she said.

'No, he's gone. How's the job?' I said straight back. She couldn't ask that much because I'd taken great care she didn't meet him. 'How's the fantastic world of executive advertising?' I flattered her and she sighed.

'I'm out of it. The boss's wife found out. I'm in a boutique now.'

'How's that?' I asked after a minute.

I was astonished to hear her sniff, 'Not so good. I was a bit upset, to tell you the truth, losing Mike and the chance to get into PA at the same time – it was a bit of a blow. Still,' she said after a moment.

'Yes,' I said, 'can't be helped. Happens to all of us. Actually,' I said, 'I could do with cheering up, too. We'll meet for a drink, shall we?'

'Love to,' she said, straight away, and really sounded as if she meant it.

I told myself it was ridiculous to feel nervous about meeting her, and then when I arrived at the wine bar she was already sitting in a little red booth with a bottle waiting. The fact that she hadn't stood me up or even kept me waiting made me like her, and for ten minutes it went quite well, but after that we dried up. I didn't intend to bare my soul about Jas and all she said was, 'I'd say easy come, easy go, except Mike was gorgeous; I didn't blame his wife for fighting, I would, I just wish I'd got there first.'

I thought it was worse than embarrassing that we could exchange months of our lives in a quarter of an hour, that we had to make frantic efforts to talk about films, clothes, books I'd read, and every so often I'd see my anxious expression in one of the mirrors and think what a mistake I'd made. But then she ordered a second bottle and began to reminisce about where Mike had taken her, what she'd worn, hotels, restaurants, and she started to sigh a lot, 'God, men' and told me the women in the shop were young. She'd say, 'We ought to meet more often,' and 'Old friends are best.' 'You're someone to value,' she even said once and reached for my hand, and by the time we'd decided to leave I was rash enough to mention it.

'I was wondering about going away. Leaving it all behind for a couple of weeks, what do you think?' And of course she said, 'Wonderful.'

'It's not definite,' I said quickly, but she shook her head.

'Let's do it.' She clasped her hands together. 'I mean it, really I do. Ring me next week, no, I'll ring you, we'll talk about it. Promise. It's a wonderful idea,' and it was too late to change my mind.

After that I did ring Barbara and we had a short frosty little chat.

I said, 'Sorry,' three times and, 'Barry rang me. It was grim. Jas and Louise are pretty settled and he went a bit berserk and crashed the car with Nicole in it. I suppose I've got off quite lightly.'

'Is Nicole all right?' she asked. 'It sounds appalling.'

'I was thinking of going away,' I said after another pause.

She interrupted very quickly, 'Away where, who with, look, don't do anything hasty again—'

'I'm not,' I said. 'All I'd got in mind was a holiday.' She was quiet. 'With Martine,' I said. 'I know you don't like her, but it's me who's going. That evening you met her she was miserable, that's

50

why I asked her to supper, as soon as she left the Home she was much better.'

'Martine?' Barbara said, as if the fact that Martine had flirted with Graham meant she ought to have been deported. 'Her?'

'She's in a boutique now,' I said. 'She's getting me some clothes to take away, she gets a discount.'

'It's that settled, then? And you want to go?' Barbara asked.

'More or less,' I admitted. 'I've seen her for a drink and we've decided it's what we both want—'

'Only because you're both desperate. And she can't find anyone else. And using that as a basis to go away on isn't very sensible, that's all,' she said and I didn't answer.

'That's all right,' I said after a bit. 'I don't have your choice.'

After I had read all the brochures I got from travel agents I consulted Barbara very briefly and the library at length. Martine had said she didn't have the energy to worry that much, Corfu was hot and cheap, if that was what I was trying to find out. That was what we decided, and from then until we left, three months almost to the day after Jas did, I made a real social effort. I went out for drinks with Beryl and her boyfriend, and his friends, people I couldn't have found anything to say to in normal circumstances. I found it quite bearable to go bowling and to parties and giggle and shout; once I'd made the first step it seemed quite in order to behave abnormally. The one thing I couldn't stand was solitude.

'Life's looking up,' I told Martine on the phone, because once everything was settled I tried not to see too much of her. If I spent many evenings watching her flutter her eyelashes and stroke her cheekbones doubt would creep in about spending two weeks in her company. So we went to the cinema and I said I was working overtime for extra pay, a fourteen-hour day, I couldn't manage to go anywhere.

'I haven't had time to think,' I said to Barbara, when she rang before I went. 'I've been up to my eyes. I'm fine, though.' What I meant was, I've learnt not to, I've found out how to go blank.

The day we left I had to wait half an hour for Martine at Victoria to get the train to Gatwick. It was hot and when she arrived she looked like a very pretty ten-year-old.

'I had to get my hair cut,' she said and pulled the short black curls all over her head. 'I remembered that smashing bloke off Queensway so I dashed in and said, "Look, I'm going to Greece in an hour, please do something," and he did. It's going to be good.' She hugged herself and I knew from that minute how she was going to behave the rest of the time.

When we got into the carriage she kept bending forward to rummage in her bag and you could see down her shirt from three seats away. Eventually she got her passport out and offered it to me. 'I'm bound to lose it,' she said. 'It'll be much safer with you.' Then she started to read her book, *The Brothers Karamazov*, and I recognised the Lolita version of the intellectual nymphet, because she'd dressed for that part, too, jeans that were too tight, a blouse that looked as though it needed a school tie to keep it together. As she'd been known to wear plimsolls marked L and R I supposed I should be glad she wasn't cavorting with excitement. When she'd been at the Home, her fortnight, she'd jumped up and down in first-aid lectures, to get the doctor's attention, but then she'd decided she didn't like shift work and, even more important, that old people weren't sweet, and that no one who was really sexy could work just with women.

'Which way?' she said on the escalator. 'You'll have to be the one to deal with reality, it's like a Godard film, futurist, I'm lost, I can't keep my head straight.' But by the time we were on the plane she'd behaved enough like a grown-up for the man across the aisle to buy her two gins, and when she'd drunk them she fell asleep. I sipped my orange juice and read Olivia Manning for three hours. At the airport I waited for the cases and she cornered two guides, counting on her fingers as they taught her Greek numbers, and when we'd finally found our coach she bought a can of Coke for the driver. 'He's so sweet,' she said, and when she came back to our seat and looked round at all the people squeezed into the others, 'At least he's under eighty.'

I could tell her to pack it in or I could learn to ignore her, I reminded myself, so I looked out of the window. Although it was a bit dusty because the summer had been very dry, there were olive trees and it was hot and the sea was blue. I decided I could put up with quite a lot in those surroundings.

'Barbara heard of Kassioulla years ago when she was a student,' I said, 'when it was really small, a little northern inlet when the south was the only popular place.'

'Really?' she shrugged. 'It'll have changed from all that time ago. Quiet, unspoiled. Hope so, anyway.'

She was right, because as the coach went along the coast road there were hoardings, high-rise blocks, and when we came past the sign for Kassioulla there was a line of hotels and behind that a line of concrete chalets. We all sat in the coach with the engine running at the traffic lights and I could see that at the back of our hotel were big sheds like aircraft hangers with metal tables and chairs on the tarmac and signs that said BAR-B-Q, Spit-roasting TONITE and DISCO-DA-DISCO.

'There are bound to be some young people,' I said as we got out, 'there wouldn't be a disco otherwise.' It did look as though we'd arrived with a crowd of pensioners. She just tossed her head and made for the entrance.

The lobby was a couple of rickety tables and hard chairs. The floor hadn't been swept and as you went past the dining room the tablecloths looked grubby. We had to walk up to our rooms because the lift was out of order and the staircase was just like a hospital one, wide, marbled, with banisters for the elderly to hold onto. Each landing had a mirror and a glass of flowers. There must have been ten rooms on each floor, and when we got to ours, adjoining, level three, shared balcony, boiling, no sound-proofing, I thought mine was like a luxury cell. It was white, it had a bed, a cupboard, a sink, a shower, and it was built for solitude.

'We could go to the pool,' I called and sat on my bed. It was narrow and hard. 'There's the under-thirties club down the road. Perhaps they come here to swim. Or the beach. Or they'll come to the bar.' I was suddenly too depressed to move, and although I could hear her opening drawers she didn't answer, and then I felt even worse. I felt physically very cold and unhappy all through because I was in this strange place with Martine and I didn't want it, I didn't want to get brown or eat or drink or swim or smell the sweet warm scent that was everywhere. I wanted Jas and wanted to weep for hours and I lay down and curled up very tightly and didn't move. After half an hour I was stiff and bored enough to feel miserable instead of desperate and so I got up. I'll unpack, I thought, and shower and put something nice on for dinner and go downstairs, because that was what we were here for, and after another half-hour I was ready and knocked on Martine's door and straight away saw I looked like a pale clown in my black shirt and striped trousers.

She looked stunning, pink T-shirt, white skirt. She'd sat on the balcony and in the time I'd wept she'd got brown, and she smiled to herself.

'We'll go on the terrace,' she said. 'You can see it from the balcony, it's not bad.' We sat at an iron table by the wall and there was a vine growing over it, very dark and thick and the pool looked quite deep and the smell of chlorine had almost gone. We drank vodka and tonics with ice and mint and lemon and I felt better. Martine kept looking round, not saying what she thought of anyone, but earmarking people who were worth a second glance, and after the waiter came and we'd ordered another drink she leaned her elbows on the table and bent forward to me.

'The last thing I came for,' she said, 'was to get paired off on the first day, but there's a chap over there, don't look, who's out of this world.' She took a little sip, and then another, of her drink, and lit a cigarette.

'Really?' I said.

'Fantastic. And he's got a friend. At least, there's a man with him.'

'Thanks,' and I took one of her cigarettes. I'd been trying to stop the last month, but now it seemed something I ought to indulge in. 'I can choose for myself. If I want someone,' I said and she nodded, but not as though she was listening. I tipped my head back and looked at the sky. Usually when I did that sober I found it comforting, it put things into proportion, but before that could even begin Martine drained her glass and stood up and smoothed her skirt. She looked extraordinary in the twilight, her skin seemed to be glowing – even I wanted to touch her – and out of the corner of my eye I saw the man behind, to the left of me, get up.

In the dining room we all had to help ourselves and then find a place at one of the long tables. As soon as I'd got a plate I saw Martine and the man together, he was holding a bowl for her to take some fish. He was tall and dark-haired and graceful. His face was slightly lined and his hair curled over his ears but the main thing about him was the way he moved. I watched him all the time as he guided her over to a corner where there was just room for two people to sit. I told myself it didn't matter, it was only what I'd expected, and I forced myself to go and sit with a group I could hear speaking English. I thought that after half a bottle of retsina it wouldn't be too bad, and it wasn't, it was quite bearable. I decided I liked making conversation, it was interesting to talk to the man who

54

was obviously gay and waiting for his evening's excitement to start when the waiters came off duty. There were two young women who looked pleasant, no one was unfriendly. When I saw the man walking across the room to the bar and Martine got up and came running over to me, I knew she'd say, 'You didn't mind, did you, I just couldn't help myself,' and I wouldn't tell her off. 'Fantastic?' she leaned over my shoulder, she could almost have hugged me with excitement. 'He's called Dimitri, he's Greek, his brother owns this place, he's come over from England, he lives there, to sell some land. I think he's married,' she added, but I knew she wouldn't have cared if he'd been Bluebeard.

'So?' I said, and I didn't care any more either, because it was jolly and noisy and I was being invited to go on to the taverna. When I'd drunk a bit more I'd stop thinking about anything except dancing and lying in the sun tomorrow, and that it had been the right thing to go away. 'So what's diffcrent?' I said.

When we'd finished the meal I counted sixteen of us staggering down the road to the taverna, ten women and six men and I felt as if I was floating along on the pebbles, floating into the bouzouki music on the juke-box, immune to the wine that got poured and Martine leaning on the man's arm and whispering. After a little while they began to dance, very close and loving, and a couple more people joined in. I stopped wondering what would happen next, I stood up and said I was exhausted.

'Making tracks?' said one of the women I'd noticed earlier. She had a Birmingham accent that made me think of Jas again. They'd both been very cool and confident all evening, neat blondes in silky sundresses and suddenly they looked drained.

'Best thing,' the other said, and we all walked carefully out round the tables as people shouted good night, back out onto the road again. As we turned into the stretch up to the hotel I looked back and felt nearly nostalgic; it was bright and still noisy and it'd been a nice evening. It seemed a pity it was over, and I said so.

'Plenty more,' one of the women said, the taller one, but without a lot of enthusiasm. 'I'm Marie, she's Debbie. Been here before?' I said no.

'We had a week in Sorrento,' Marie said, and Debbie giggled. 'That's why we've still got a tan. Thought we'd get back into practice,' and she winked.

'Was it nice?' I asked and both of them considered, as if they never had before.

'There's more choice in Italy,' Marie said, 'with men. More English, here they're all sorts.'

'Who's complaining?' Debbie asked and giggled again.

They linked arms and Debbie offered me hers. 'Keep right on to the end of the road,' she said. 'Makes you long for a big red bus, doesn't it?' No matter how we tried to keep in step we stumbled around. It took us ages to get back.

When we got to the hotel lobby I looked at the three of us in the fluorescent light, creased, smudged make-up, nothing like the beautiful creatures we'd been under the stars, and I thought that this was what it would be like. Evenings out when you were transformed by wine and warmth, days recovering by the pool, struggling to feel well enough for a drink before lunch; the oily unread books, eating because it was paid for and broke up the day and when you got brown fat didn't show. Lots of solitaries coming together for ritual gatherings.

'Pleasant enough,' I said to myself as I hung my clothes over the back of a chair, put on a nightie, slid between the cool sheets. It was still hot. It would be sunny tomorrow, the sea and pool and vodka wouldn't go away, there were crickets chirping somewhere. It was pleasant, it would be nice enough.

If I hadn't dreamt every night I would probably still have believed that, although the first night was peaceful from that point of view, because the only things that disturbed me then were Martine and the man. As soon as they came in they gasped and yelped and crashed around and then started thrashing away, moaning, and every hour got up and started to run a shower. Although I didn't go and stand next to the wall to hear what they were saying, that was only because their voices carried through. It was all the usual stuff, the things Jas and I used to murmur and shout at one another, 'Love, love,' 'Please, yes, no,' and laughing, and quiet patches before the bedsprings started action again. I wondered if she was doing it deliberately, to let me know what hot stuff they both were, so I didn't make a sound, I listened as if it was all in a foreign language that didn't mean a thing to me.

About five it got light and they got quiet, so at seven I got up and ran the shower, and did the same at eight. That time I got under it, and opened my shutters loudly and let the cupboards bang and the door slam as I went down to breakfast. There was hardly anyone there, but there was coffee and rolls and a three-day-old *Daily*

Mirror. When I finished I went back up and pulled the shutters to and fro and rattled coat-hangers and kicked the door closed, enough to wake the dead and then I went down to the pool, which was at the back of the hotel. You could find your way by the smell, but it was a nice walk, too, bushes along the side of the hotel, thick green hibiscus leaves, and there was a lawn just before you got there, a bit brown, but with daisies on it, and the pool was practically empty.

I found a spot on one of the surrounds that was already warm and I got an umbrella to put on the sunny side, and spread my towel and beach-bag at a distance from one another so no one could get too near me. Then I lay down, and it was wonderful. I could forget all about what the night had been like, I could shut my eyes and pretend nothing mattered except that I could be relaxed enough to feel myself falling asleep.

I hadn't thought, let alone dreamt, about Mercy dying since I was sixteen and she had, but one of the reasons I went on working in the Home was because the idea of old people being lonely, dying alone, horrified me. It didn't hurt to listen or talk to them, and even incapable, incontinent, they weren't any more revolting than anyone else, just helpless. I suppose it had made an impression, but I'd never have said that it preoccupied, let alone obsessed me. It wasn't something I expected to haunt me because I'd put most of it out of my mind, and it had faded as all youthful experiences do – I'd seen other old women die since then, and of course it was sad, of course it was a reminder, but nothing more. Mercy didn't worry me because there was nothing I could do about her, there was nothing I could do about how she'd died, the only things I could do were to behave differently now, and keep out of Audrey's house, especially if I felt even the slightest bit unwell.

Mercy had come to live with us to die, but it wasn't until the last couple of months that she'd admitted it.

'It's my insides,' she'd said, 'they always play me up in strange places. A good dose'll clear me out. I'm not feeling too good, that's all.' So more and more often I'd have to go to the chemist's for Exlax and syrup of figs and liquid paraffin. I always went to the same one on the way home from school, and one week, instead of asking what I wanted, the assistant came out of the dispensary and took me to one side of the counter.

'You buy a lot of this stuff,' he said. 'Who's it for?'

'My grandmother,' I said. 'She asks me.'

'Why doesn't your mother buy them?' he asked. I couldn't think what he was getting at, I couldn't imagine anyone taking any of that stuff for pleasure, so I told him that my mother and grandmother didn't speak to one another. Then he frowned.

'I'm not prying,' he said, 'it's just not a good idea to rely on them, not in quantities like this. Has she got a doctor? Can't that be suggested to her?'

'By me?' I asked. When I got home I explained to Mercy why I was empty-handed. She wasn't angry, she didn't swear, she said she'd been thinking much the same, it felt like a lump nothing would shift.

'You give me a hand down there,' she said. 'You know where the surgery is,' and when I had she said, 'You needn't wait. I'll make my own way back.' But by the time I got home the doctor had rung and asked for her nightclothes to be taken to the hospital.

'Tests,' Audrey hissed. 'He wants tests done; they're keeping her in.' I've never seen her angrier. 'I'll never get rid of her now,' she said, over and over again, her teeth clenched. She shook with anger.

For days she polished and scoured and scrubbed the room Mercy had slept in, she would have fumigated it if she could, and her rubber gloves were worn thin at the tips. Every evening we left her to it: Leslie went to the golf club and Barbara did homework and I went to see the girls at the end of the road but in the afternoon, instead of going up to her room, I went to the hospital to see Mercy. A couple of afternoons Leslie was there when I arrived, and once a week Barbara came with me, but my mother didn't go until after the tests, after she'd seen the surgeon and been told Mercy wouldn't be coming back, coming out, at all. I know also that Mercy guessed because she never mentioned what she'd do when she was better. All she talked about, all I heard every hour I spent with her, was about other people's deaths, and until she died, every night when I went home, they were all I thought about.

I didn't dream about them then, they only took up waking hours, and then it altered, it changed over because the last few days she was alive I stopped thinking about her at all, I dreamt instead.

And from the moment I lay down beside that swimming pool, that afternoon, every afternoon I had a rest and every night when I went to bed, whether I was drunk, half-sober, calm, agitated, I dreamt about all of it all over again.

'It was wicked what happened,' Mercy said. 'No warning, no nothing.' It had been a nice day, sunny, warm for early April. She'd put Audrey down for a rest and gone to sit on the front steps of her house and started thinking about the summer, how Will'd have a week off and they'd go for a few days out, how it'd be nice to get away from sweeping up, cleaning windows, washing, cooking, it all took hours, all day if you'd let it. She said the cat came and sat on her lap and it was hot and heavy and she wondered how she'd manage if she had another baby – Will'd like one, a boy, of course, but she found one enough. She said that whenever she sat out in the afternoon she'd let her mind wander like that, and sometimes neighbours would stop on their way up to the shop to get their tea and have a word. 'Lady of leisure,' they called her, and she'd smile, cross her legs, and I could just about imagine her with curls like my mother's, her eyes screwed up against the sun, legs slim enough to cross, leaning against her front door, laughing back at everyone.

That afternoon, she said, the cat wouldn't settle. It kept kneading and sniffing and in the end she tipped it off her lap, and then she couldn't settle. And after a bit she thought maybe she'd left the iron on the stove, she kept thinking she got a whiff of a hot smell, so she went inside and had a look, and she hadn't, and when she went outside to sit down again she could still smell something. She shut her eyes, and when she opened them again, it couldn't have been more than five minutes, there were little black specks all over her arms, and her frock, and you could see them in the air, and no sooner had she seen them than she jumped up and at the same time a man came on his bike round the corner, shouting for her, Mrs Hart, Mrs Hart, and that was all he could say he was panting so much. He stood there, holding onto the handlebars, his cap stuck on the back of his head, swallowing, licking his lips, and he got out that it was the warehouse, Dawson's, where Will was. She didn't wait to hear any more, she could smell it now, everyone could, people were opening their windows and sniffing, and over towards White City you could see the sky was a different colour, brown, she just ran. She never thought of Audrey alone in the house, anything, she ran all the way past the laundry and across the allotments, down roads Will biked along to work every morning, and she could hear herself breathing. Every time she cut across a road people were out on their steps, arms folded round themselves, and when she got nearer there were other women running like her, dozens of them, and some of them had children they were pulling along. All you could hear was a roaring sound and sometimes a bell as another engine went past, but no one was speaking, it was just people panting and running feet. It was like a film, she said she thought afterwards, westerns with silent streets and two men waiting to shoot it out, except there weren't any men, it was all women. Before you got there, three streets away, it was appalling, it stank, it hurt you to breathe, people slowed down and walked and didn't look at one another. If it was like this here it didn't bear thinking about there. The ambulances sounded different in those days, they had a bell, not a siren, and you could hear them coming, too, by then, and it wasn't even that easy to see, the smoke was really thick. But the smell was the worst, rubber: it burns as fast as paper and it stinks.

The warehouses had concrete all round them for the lorries to drive up on and when you got to the end of Waverley Street you could always see them straight in front of you. There weren't any buildings around, there was that to be thankful for, the houses would have gone up like tinder. And that day it took your breath away, it was like an orange bomb, she said, and she hadn't seen any then, but that was all there was, an orange explosion. Even if you wanted to you couldn't get close, the heat suffocated you, you couldn't see or breathe except in patches. There were fire engines parked all round the concrete, not to keep people away, it turned out, but because they daren't go any closer, and ambulances, five or six of them were just standing there, the drivers, the attendants all out, watching, and that was all any of them could do. There were hundreds in the end, she said, half the neighbourhood, but for ten minutes or so there were just those women and firemen and ambulance men and no one said anything, except one fireman, that it'd have to burn itself out before they could get any closer, it was no good even trying to get the hoses on now, they couldn't risk any more lives, and then she said it came home to her. It wasn't that she'd thought Will was dead or alive, she'd lost all her thoughts because of not knowing what had happened, but it wasn't till then she realised properly that he was in there, and the others, they were in those flames, and she said as she realised so must the other women have done so, they'd all been too overwhelmed by the size of it till now, and there was this awful noise they started, all of them, a sort of wailing, screeching, and they started trying to push past the firemen, all bent over from the smoke and smell and they couldn't see what they were doing, and the firemen didn't like to manhandle them. One woman got past and she started running, well not running, because you couldn't, the heat was too much, but sort of sidestepping up the concrete, and she had her apron up over her face and her petticoat was hanging down under her dress and all the others behind the firemen started calling, louder. It was as if everyone was mesmerised looking at this woman, and then one of the ambulance men made a run at her and got hold of her arms and half-carried her back and that did it. The women all started screaming, shouting at the firemen to do something, they could see no one could get near, you couldn't do anything, but they were all being burnt alive in there.

After that, she said, it was just a question of time, standing what must have been an hour or more waiting, sobbing, but to yourself. And then the firemen went close enough for the hoses to be able to reach and when they did the women went behind, up as close as they could get, and more and more people came. It must have lit up the sky for miles. At one point she'd looked round and there was a ring of space all round them, her and the other women, all the people who were watching had left six feet, the length of a man laid out, between them and the women.

We were on our own, she said, and we were filthy, no wonder they kept their distance, we sounded mad and we were all black as soot. She said she didn't remember how long it went on, all afternoon, it could have been half the night, she said, you couldn't tell by the sky any more, we just stood and watched the flames, and thought about them inside and sometimes someone'd start screaming and then quieten down. People brought out jugs of tea from houses and they'd have a drink, and after a bit, perhaps it was the smell, perhaps it was water lapping round their feet, the crowd getting smaller, it seemed all over and done with and all she wanted was to be back indoors and forget it'd ever happened.

The next was the worst, she said.

When it was nearly properly out you could see better what'd happened. There was a skeleton of a lorry parked up alongside the entrance and something, a cigarette, a match, the petrol tank must've gone off, people said they'd heard a bang, and that'd done it. Not that far away from the lorry, quite a lot of them, were men's bodies, sprawled on the concrete, black all round them, black all over them, and they must've been inside, right at the back when it started, and tried to run through it, on fire, on fire themselves, and not got far enough. You could tell, she said, they'd been running away, and realised they couldn't go any further, they were shut in on the concrete, the fire moved faster than they did, they were engulfed in it. Imagine what they felt like, she said.

We couldn't identify them, she said, but we tried, and the firemen didn't try and stop us, but there wasn't anything to see, and if there had been we were past caring by then. We all walked from one to another of the heaps, really, that's all they were, and we looked at them and I don't know what they thought about, I didn't think about anything, you were past it. And then we went home. Not with one another, by ourselves, except people from our road had come to see and they took me back with them. I didn't care anyway, I kept waiting for it all to go away, I suppose all of us thought our one might be lucky, we might get home and find him waiting in the kitchen. I told someone to take Audrey away and I lay down and that was that.

She couldn't move, she said, for nearly a week, not wouldn't, but couldn't, and neighbours took it in turns to come and sit with her and she said all she thought of was a picture she had of Will falling, and before that screaming, covered in flames, his arms, his legs, his head, one great burning mass, and then falling, and it was the pain, she said, Will and that pain and I couldn't get rid of it. All of them, she said, all those men in agony, burnt alive. It didn't bear thinking about and you couldn't stop. She still got it, she said, and it got worse, the smell, looking at his eyes disappearing, his face cracking up and disappearing, seeing him scream. It was worst at nights. It was probably because it was a strange bed and all the medicines you got in hospital, and it was just like yesterday.

Some things aren't believable, she said, and yet they've happened.

After she'd told me once, the first time, she couldn't stop. Every afternoon I'd sit by her bed, my school panama on my lap. She'd sit up, hair on end, no make-up, no glasses, a rubbery lined old face and grab my hand and hold it tight. Then she'd go over it again, one part after another, running down the streets, all the women running, standing and watching, the woman who ran forward, the ring of them, how the water sounded when it started, the smoke, the bodies, Will on fire, Will's burning face and hair and body, it was always back to that, her picture of it, the nearest she could get to what he'd felt, and it horrified her.

I didn't tell anyone, either, because I couldn't see what they could do, except tell her to shut up or stop me visiting. And that wouldn't change anything, it had still happened and she'd still have told me, it couldn't be blotted out.

The last week she hardly mentioned it, she was quite different, so weak she hardly talked. Although my mother spent more time there, whenever she was just with me she'd hold both my hands and say there was nothing like it, it was as bad as Will, she could feel all his pain all over, not burning but stuck down.

'I'll never get out of it, it's all up, I'm not stupid,' she'd say. 'What's it for?' she used to ask and cling onto my wrists and start to shake all over. When she did die it must have been sooner than expected, because I was the only one by her bed.

She was quite quiet, as if she was asleep and then she opened her eyes and looked at me and I couldn't speak she was so frightened. She held onto me and swallowed and her head jerked and so did her legs, really hard under the covers, and she opened her mouth and I tried to bend and kiss her, put my cheek on hers and then she heaved herself up and tried to say – No – that was what it sounded like, and then she fell against me and I could hear the sound of nurses' shoes, running, and then she shuddered on me. The nurse laid her down and closed her eyes, and gradually her face looked more normal again, but I couldn't forget it. She'd been terrified and she'd died on me. It wasn't as awful as Will, I could see that, but it wouldn't go away, it wouldn't stop.

When I woke up that first time I wasn't sure which I'd dreamt last, her face or Will's, but it didn't make much difference as far as effect went. I was freezing, shaking, I couldn't remember where I was, I wanted Jas and I was crying. No one could see any of that because I put a towel round me and had sunglasses on, and after a bit the shaking stopped.

I looked at my watch and I'd been asleep about half an hour, it was only eleven, not even time for a drink. I sat still for a bit, then I had a swim. I sat down again with my book, but I couldn't read, I couldn't do anything. I looked round at the couples lying quietly, oiling one another's backs, the waiters leaning on the bar polishing glasses. Then I saw Martine, hanging on the arm of the Greek, his shirt over her bikini, and she waved and they both came and sat next to me.

'I'm exhausted,' she said and spread out her towel and lay down

63

and I thought I might say, 'I've just had the most appalling nightmare, I want to be comforted,' but instead I found myself thinking that I could telephone; I could ring Barbara and say I'd arrived, no more, like sending a postcard, and I would hear her talk for a minute. 'It's the heat; it's enervating,' I said but Martine smiled.

'Not the heat,' she yawned and let her hand rest, just brush through the hairs on Dimitri's brown thigh.

'I can't keep out of the water,' I lied, I didn't want to sit like an abandoned duck next to their pulsating flesh. 'It's wonderful exercise,' I said and stood up, but all the time I was swimming I couldn't stop watching them. Every time I turned my head I saw her tickling the palm of his hand and sometimes, when he whispered, she frowned like a puzzled little girl, as though it was vital she understood every syllable of his endearments, and then he'd laugh at her and I couldn't watch any more.

'Hungry?' she asked when I got out of the pool. We walked to the dining room together, but as soon as we were inside she and Dimitri walked over to a corner and sat on a window seat where there wasn't possibly room for anyone else. Instead of throwing my plate at them and running out of the room howling I turned round and chatted to the man behind me in the queue, and he said what food he and his wife liked. It didn't look too forced when I went to the same table as them. They came from Yorkshire so we talked about the lakes, and rain, and they said they couldn't have enough of this. When I went up to my room afterwards I didn't try and sleep, I just sat up in bed and read Olivia Manning for an hour and then sorted through my make-up and tried different clothes with one another until it was time to go to the pool again.

Marie and Debbie were there this time and we swam and lay in the sun and they said they'd looked all over for me in the morning, they'd been taking the hotel bus into Corfu Town, but I hadn't missed much because it had broken down. They'd waited two hours in the sun for the driver to change the wheel because the nuts had stuck, and by then all people wanted to do was come back here.

'Gives you the pip,' Marie said, and she sighed. 'Your friend fixed herself up double quick,' she said then, and stared at me crossly. Looking at her in daylight she was older than I'd first thought. 'Easy come, easy go. When she's gone there'll be plenty more where she came from.' I didn't answer.

'Not necessarily,' Debbie said. 'He looks really fond of her,' and Marie tossed her curls.

'Depends what he gets out of it.'

'I only came with her,' I said then. I tried to make it sound joking. 'I'm not in charge of her.'

'Sorry, I'm sure,' Marie said and turned her back for Debbie to oil it.

'I don't mind,' I said; it wasn't worth arguing or defending, it would be the same every afternoon, discussing the morning, waiting until it was time to go indoors, spending an hour showering and changing, going down to the bar, waiting for Marie and Debbie to sit next to me. 'You're probably right,' I added.

After supper that night we went to the night club instead of the taverna and I drank a lot and danced with a man called Ernest who was a widower and tall and thin, and Colin from Tottenham who said he was all out to score, and Brian who was shorter than me. Then Marie and Debbie and I came back to the hotel together and I knew we'd end up like this every night, too; and when Ernest said, 'Sweet dreams,' and Debbie whispered, 'It's probably all he can hope for,' we all laughed.

I could hear those words being repeated every night we were there. I thought I could see every minute of the rest of the time we were there and I didn't want it; all the rest of that night, every time I shut my eyes, I tried to open them. Every time I woke I expected to smell charred bodies, burnt tyres. When it was morning I looked round to try to find pieces of carbon floating in the air. I couldn't believe who I was or where I was, it was all at one remove. It's a hangover, I thought at first, because of the cotton-woolly distance everything had, and I was planning every movement, across the bedroom, into the shower, working out in advance because that was the only way I could function, yet my mouth wasn't dry and I didn't have a headache. I was surprised to find I'd got washed and dressed and gone downstairs, and while I was eating toast and drinking coffee I still expected to wake up and find I'd been dreaming, but when I'd finished I'd found that I'd folded my napkin and put the chair back and I was in the lobby, outside the phone-box, reading the dialling codes for all the foreign exchanges. I noted place names and then read the instructions, and I couldn't see why I hadn't done it before; it was easy, it'd take three minutes, it'd be a surprise, she'd probably be pleased I'd thought of her. All I had to do was find the change, wait for a couple of clicks and then the phone would be picked up and I'd say hello.

'It's me,' I said, 'Laura. I just wanted to see how you all were, and to say I've arrived safely. Hello?' I said because then there was silence.

'Laura?' he said, and I realised it was Graham. 'Laura? Fantastic,' and I heard him laugh. 'How is it?'

'Oh, fine, really, just what I expected. You know, sun, sea, just what the brochures tell you. Is Barbara there?' I said because I could imagine him standing in the kitchen, the sun shining in through the blind, stroking his beard, he'd talk forever.

'Not at the moment.' It sounded as if he was shouting, his voice was echoing. 'She wasn't well in the night. She's sleeping in.'

'What's the matter?' I yelled back.

'Nothing,' he said this time more normally. 'Just a tummy upset. Anna's here,' he offered.

'So she's not there,' I said again, although it was obvious that she was huddled under the duvet, she'd have it pulled up tight round her shoulders, she'd be buried in it. 'Give her my love,' I said, and at the same time he shouted, 'Shall I go and get her?' and I could imagine her voice. 'You had a dream about Mercy,' she'd say. 'You spent all that money and woke me up for that?'

'No,' I said, 'of course not, just say I called.'

'You must go,' he interrupted. 'This must be costing a fortune.'

'Wait for the pips,' I said, and then they went and he laughed. 'Lovely to hear from you, though. Take care, take care, Laura.'

'You, too,' I said, and then the line went dead, and even though I hadn't spoken to her I still felt better afterwards. I felt better all the rest of that day, more settled, more tolerant of Martine and Dimitri, more friendly towards Marie and Debbie. I chatted, I read, I even dozed without having a nightmare.

All that day I kept up being cheerful, and the next, and the next, on and on; for a week I showered and dressed, swam and ate, drank vodka and retsina and in the evening went to the DISCO-DA-DISCO or the BAR-B-Q without flinching. Every morning Marie or Debbie said, 'Come on, let's try and get into town,' and I refused. I needed routine, I had decided, because that made things more normal. I needed to know that I could lie by the pool and if I did close my eyes I'd be quite sure that when I opened them I'd see yellow flowers on a white wall, and that at eleven thirty I could have a drink and at twelve have another. I told myself I enjoyed the lunchtimes, smiling at the worn faces left over from the night before, and that it was good for me to read all afternoon, to lie still with the shutters closed and watch the sun change the shadows in the room.

I needed habit, familiar rituals to cling to. I didn't want to see anything outside that could give me any more ideas. Every evening we went to the disco again, the under-thirties, the taverna, night-clubs, and sometimes it was better or worse, more people got drunk, it was cheap, or the entertainment was appalling.

'You'd think they'd learn it in school,' Marie said, 'folk dancing. We used to.'

'They probably only do it for money,' Debbie told her. 'Bloody waste where we're concerned, though. What a dump,' although it wasn't a tatty place, it was quite nicely decorated in sludgy browns and reds. The tables were big enough for four people to sit at comfortably and the lights didn't flicker too much and the drinks didn't taste too awful; we were all just critical and disagreeable.

'You wonder if it's worth it sometimes,' Debbie said.

'It is for some,' Marie answered. 'We all know who's doing all right out of it.' We would look across at Martine and Dimitri, always entwined with one another. I watched them like that, staring, enraptured with one another, I looked at the flowers and sun and water, and people, and I didn't see any of them properly. All of it, especially the sky, the warmth and the sweetness appalled me, they were too beautiful to bear. I couldn't find any comfort and I knew there wasn't any pleasure in any of it because all day I dreaded the night, and all day I couldn't ever forget what I'd seen all night.

'You look miles away,' Martine said sometimes, if she saw me at breakfast.

'She is tired,' Dimitri suggested when I came back from a swim.

'You're a quiet one; deep,' Ernest told me as we danced, and I pretended to laugh. I tried to remember it to tell to Marie and Debbie.

'You ought to do a bit more, see a bit more of the place,' Marie and Debbie said.

'I'm tired,' I answered. 'I'm catching up on a year's rest. I don't want to move.' Every day I lied. 'I like doing nothing.' Every night I found it hadn't worked, I could keep as still and calm as I liked, I could pretend I was relaxed to my heart's content, but the dreams never stopped. 'Of course I'm enjoying myself,' I said and I had to force myself to smile. 'I just like a quiet life.'

'You look dead fed up,' Marie said one evening when I hadn't laughed at a joke for an hour. 'We'll leave you to amuse yourself, shall we?' and I almost cried because I knew what would happen next, misery was supposed to do that, mark you out as undesirable.

If I went on like this no one would be seen dead with me. 'No,' I said, 'no, I'm sorry, it's nothing to do with you.' She shrugged and jerked her head in Martine's direction.

'Fed up with her?' she asked, and she meant it kindly because she added, 'I know I would be. Having a good time's one thing, desertion's another. You come away with a person and all right, so they're not Superglue, but you expect a bit of loyalty. I know what I'd do,' and she drained her glass. 'I'd say, "How about us all having a day out? Come on, Dimitri," I'd say, "you're the one who knows the place, you show us what the real Corfu's like." You might as well get something out of it. She is.'

'Go on,' Debbie said, 'it'd be a laugh. We could all go. It'd be all right. Ask her now, ask before they get wrapped up in one another again, go on,' but I didn't stand up.

'All right,' I said, 'but not now. I'll do it in the morning.' Debbie shook her head. 'I will,' I said. 'I think it's a really good idea, but if I ask now they'll just put it off. If I do it then, they'll have to at least suggest somewhere. Really, it'll be better then.'

'Promise?' Marie squinted over her glass. 'Drink to it?' And we did, several times over, in the bar, in the taverna and back in Marie and Debbie's room. It was early morning before we went to bed, but that didn't help me sleep, it just meant fewer hours of fear to get through.

The next morning I waited until I heard the shower start for the second time and then I went downstairs. When Martine and Dimitri came into the dining room I was sitting at a table for six by myself and waving as they stood in line for their coffee and rolls. 'Come on over,' I called, so loudly they couldn't possibly refuse, but Dimitri didn't seem too displeased. As soon as he sat down he asked, 'Then what are your plans for today?' and I didn't even mind Martine rearranging their chairs closer together.

'We were talking about an outing,' I said. 'Marie and Debbie and me, that is. Somewhere that isn't a tourist tour.' I smiled at him. 'Got any ideas?' and although Martine put her hand on his shoulder I still went on. 'There's not much point in going up and down the coast in a bus to look at other beaches, we thought we'd like to do something more exciting.' To my astonishment Dimitri nodded, swallowed his mouthful of roll, put his plate in the middle of the table and moved Martine's hand so that he could stretch over to take some wrapped cubes of sugar.

'We are here. To the south.' He put a line of cubes along one side of the plate. 'The beaches are more sandy, to the north far rockier, more spectacular. Inland, there' – he drew a line down the middle of the plate – 'are the hills. Quite unspoilt, proper villages still with donkeys, snakes, little communities who farm and weave—' then he stopped. 'There are your friends,' he said and pointed to Marie and Debbie in the queue for breakfast. 'I will wait and we will tell them too,' and even though Martine pouted as they sat down he shook their hands and asked if they'd enjoyed their stay, what had they liked, where they'd been.

'Round and about,' Marie said, 'but one bit of coast's much the same as the rest. I fancied a trip into the interior.' Dimitri shook his head.

'Too far,' he said sternly. 'Transport would be impossible. We would have to go right back down to the south to get on a good road, and hire a car. No, there are other places nearer that would be nice for all of us to go to.'

Martine put her head down, like a cat resting, absolutely watchful, paws ready.

'Another day,' she said, half-closing her eyes, and I looked at Dimitri's hands, still playing with the sugar cubes, and thought they were nice, not hairy, quite long and slender. And beside the more obvious physical attributes, brown skin, black hair, he had a nice smile.

'Where do you mean then, Dimitri?' Marie asked and propped her chin on her hand. I saw Debbie brush her curls back, lick her lips and I thought this is disgusting, all of us performing, assessing him, wondering who he'd choose if Martine wasn't around.

'First we will take a bus,' he said, 'and then walk. Once there might have been donkeys to hire, but the villages I am thinking of discontinued that because it encouraged too many tourists. But I can show you the way. In the hills it's cooler, and very beautiful. We'll see some rugs, some stone ruins, have a drink and get the bus back in the afternoon. It will be good.'

'Today,' I said, 'now,' because suddenly I couldn't wait, I even put my hand on Dimitri's arm in excitement, 'go this morning, make today the day?' and he didn't answer straight away, but he didn't look at Martine, he looked at Marie and Debbie.

'Why not?' Marie said. 'It'd make a nice change from buying a bottle of Ambre Solaire.'

'We could get some different cards,' Debbie sounded eager at that. 'It'd be good.'

'We'll catch the bus,' he said, 'in half an hour. It will be good to show you something we make that isn't discos and barbecues.'

I was really pleased, I laughed. 'That's just what I hoped you'd say.'

After that Martine decided she wasn't hungry any more and so they got up from the table, but he nodded to each of us.

'Be ready,' he said, and we all drank our coffee quickly.

'Is that all right?' I said. 'Going today, I mean?' I didn't look at them because I didn't mean that, I wanted to be told how clever I'd been. 'You're not doing anything else?' Debbie giggled.

'I'll have a look in my diary,' Marie said in a pretend, executive drawl. 'I don't suppose it can't be cancelled, though. It's done you good,' she said as we waited for the lift. 'I told you it would. You look cheerier already.'

Because the bus was late we all stood outside the hotel for another half-hour waiting, hardly speaking, and I wondered if it hadn't been an awful mistake. I don't mean I had a presentiment, it was just Marie and Debbie asking one another had they got the lotion, what about water pills, perhaps a bit of fruit would be a good idea, and Martine and Dimitri leaning against the wall, not even touching one another, yawning and scuffing their feet in the gravel. I read my book and probably looked very calm and thought that if the bus didn't come in five minutes I'd say I felt sick and wasn't going.

When it came it was quite full, not of holidaymakers but men in suits and women with children, big ones, six or seven years old, on their laps and two extraordinarily pretty girls of fifteen or sixteen who kept looking at one another, and then at us, to and fro, giggles, glances, and even Martine looked used up beside them.

The journey lasted three-quarters of an hour and none of us spoke. We sat like lumps in the middle of all those Greeks talking and laughing with one another, not needing excursions for something to do, and looked out of the window, at the sea a long way below, and the stone and scrub and sky. The window was open and a hot wind came in that was almost unbearable. It was like being stifled, I thought, being suffocated by heat, and then suddenly we were the only people left and we were going through a cooler patch, through olive groves, and it became steep and the gears were grinding, nerve-rackingly, on every corner. Then we stopped again, outside a big dark building in a dusty square and Dimitri stood up.

'Come, hurry, then. This is it. Get out here,' he said and we did hurry and when we climbed down the whole place looked deserted. A little way away there were four flat-topped houses, but you could hardly distinguish them because the light was blinding, white hot, white stone, it was all shuddering with airlessness. We stood and watched the bus drive away, and it could have left us in another country.

'I'll see,' Dimitri said and walked away round the building calling, 'Stefanos,' and then Greek words, and then someone shouted back, and he disappeared altogether. I looked at three tiny children sitting by the roadside, some skinny chickens pecking in the shade, and at the flowers, all over the vines, all over the trees, yellow, blue and white, we were surrounded by blossom, silence and smell, nothing had altered because of us. For a long time no one spoke and then Dimitri came hurrying and beckoning and calling.

'Come, come, you can come now.'

We almost ran to follow him round the side of the building, and then stopped dead. There were two big wooden tables and benches that you saw out of the corner of your eye, but what you noticed was that we were right on the edge of a cliff. Where we stood the ground was green, grassy, and then only a yard away it ended, it dropped straight into layers of the flowers, and there were butterflies. Over everything, all the way down there were clouds of them, huge, transparent, like fluttering flowers, like reflections, and all the air was taken up with them, they made it seem as if there was no solid earth beneath, you could have fallen or floated on them, you had the sensation of both, and of very light air and very pure colour.

We all stared and after a little while sighed and then Dimitri touched Martine's elbow and we all went to sit on the benches, Martine and Dimitri next to one another, Marie and Debbie and I opposite. There were jugs and glasses ready for us.

'Lemon, orange?' Dimitri said and we all nodded.

'Where are we, Dimitri?' I asked. He shrugged as though it was nowhere special.

'A local place. Where we start our walk. From here we go up the hill to our left, a couple of miles, and there are two, three villages there. One of them is bound to have a taverna, we will get lunch and then we will walk down. The bus back is at four, now it is eleven, there is exactly the right amount of time. It is your day trip,' he said and smiled and drained his glass.

'I could just stay here all day.' Martine stretched and smiled at him. 'I could be quite happy in this place.' He stood up and put the glasses together on the tray.

'We'll get going,' he said. 'Off we go.' We waited while he took the tray back to the door of the house.

'Looks a fair step.' Marie pointed to the hill. 'Let's hope he knows the way,' and Debbie shushed her because he was waiting for us to follow him back to the road. That came to an end quite quickly and then we went along a grey lane that was shady and then onto a track.

'Who owned that house, then?' I asked, because it had seemed empty, as though a ghost had dispensed hospitality. Dimitri said friends of his family. 'It was beautiful,' I said. 'I really appreciated going there.'

'An old man lives there. He had six sons and all of them went away. He is waiting for one to come back. He keeps drinks ready for travellers.' He sighed. 'One day he will be lucky, maybe.'

'Let's hope so,' Marie said. 'It was a bit creepy, if you ask me.'

'It must be odd coming back here,' I said, 'and finding some things haven't changed at all when other places are unrecognisable. Tourists don't know anything about what it used to be like, you must wish sometimes they'd never come. Even though they make money, it's not for everyone; money's not always everything.'

'I left,' Dimitri said. 'I can't feel too bad about it.'

'But this is what you want to come back to,' I insisted and waved my arm over the scrub, desert, it almost seemed, we were in, 'isn't it?'

'Let's walk,' he said.

At first it wasn't too steep and quite shady, but after about ten minutes there weren't any big trees, just small thorny bushes, and the path got less and less visible. Dimitri had trousers on and I had a skirt that was quite long, but Martine and Marie and Debbie wore short dresses and it was obvious they were getting scratched, and that open sandals were unsuitable for walking through dirt and loose stones.

'Dimitri,' Martine called – I'd kept up with him but she was just behind and Marie and Debbie were yards behind her – 'is it like this all the way?'

'So, so,' he said. Martine made a face at his back.

'You should have told us to wear trousers,' I said. He turned round and I saw he was very red.

'That may be true,' he frowned, 'but I did not know. I did not

72

remember it like this. Soon we should come to open grass again.'
Then Martine caught up and the three of us stood to wait for Marie
and Debbie. 'Five minutes,' he said, 'only five more minutes and
then it will be grass again, soft, I am sorry.' They nodded because
they were too out of breath to argue.

It took another ten minutes before anything changed, and then it
was to big boulders, which made a relief from the gorse and pebbles,
but they also made it hotter. I heard Martine say that it was a stupid
time to walk, he should have made us bring hats, we were gasping,
and I looked back because I was in front of her, just behind Dimitri;
we were all strung out in a line, we looked like something out of a
film, explorers, refugees. He must have run through all this when he
was a child, I thought, and now he was out of breath and leading
four scratched Englishwomen on a stifling tour to a village none of
us would understand. He was taking us back to somewhere that
would mean nothing to any of us.

'It's like being in a lunar landscape,' I said. 'I remember when I
was really young, watching the first men on the moon, I thought it
was more frightening not to know what they'd find there than to
think about if they'd get back to earth.'

'One big step,' he said in a mock American accent. I laughed. 'It's
like wondering—' he said, but that was all, I couldn't hear the end
of his sentence because Marie screamed, and went on, high short
bursts, one after the other, and then Debbie screamed too.

'What's the matter?' I shouted. 'What is it?'

'Snakes,' Dimitri said, quite quietly, and then he turned round
and called back to them. 'Was it snakes you saw?' Martine and I
stood still, we wouldn't go back even ten yards to see what was the
matter because it meant walking back up again. 'Don't worry,'
Dimitri called, 'even if they bite they are not poisonous. They like
sunbathing on the rocks, like lizards, that's all. Grass, little ones,
they're not a problem, they run away, especially when you make a
noise.' He turned round and started to walk on.

'What about Marie?' I said, but he didn't answer, he just went on.
I watched his back, hunched, as he trudged a bit further and
Marie's and Debbie's faces as they panted up and Marie was pale
now and her cheeks were blotched with mascara because she'd been
crying. 'You poor thing,' I said and she made a noise in her throat.
'They're always a bit of a shock, we had them in Surrey, in the
garden. Once,' I invented, 'next door's cat tried to catch one. But
he's right, they don't hurt, they're not dangerous.' I repeated it

73

several times until she was breathing a bit more evenly, and then Debbie shook her head.

'It's not all right,' she said. 'It's ridiculous. It's completely pointless going all this way, look at us,' and I did, sweating, scratched, 'and look at this,' and she pointed round us, her hand shaking. 'There's nothing beautiful here, it's hot enough to burst, we ought to have brought a drink, we'll all be ill before the day's out if we go on like this.'

'There's some trees up there,' I said. She shrugged.

'So what? I've a good mind to say we'll all wait here till he comes back if he's going on like this.' Her voice sounded cracked. 'I've had about as much as I can take. You tell him, he's talking to you, he can get us somewhere for a drink, straight away, or that's the end of it.'

'Let's see,' I said because the trees weren't far and I could see the ground was levelling off, 'it may be all right now.'

The trees weren't thick but they gave enough shade to sit down in, but the best thing was a little spring and we all drank and washed our faces and put our feet in it. Dimitri said, over and over, when he saw Martine and Marie and Debbie hold up their scratched legs, that he felt terrible, he was so sorry, he had completely miscalculated.

'How far is it to this village now, then?' Marie asked. He said that truthfully it was minutes only.

'If you want,' he offered, 'you can wait. I will go and find out, or you can walk, you walk, too, and you will see it.'

'That's all right, then,' I said. Marie shuddered.

'I'm not waiting.' She shook her head vehemently. 'I've changed my mind. I'd rather be with people.'

'Don't worry,' I said and smiled at Dimitri. 'We're virtually there.'

We sat a little while longer, though, and it was beautiful, cool, green, sun filtering through leaves and reflecting on the water and I thought this was what we would all remember in future, the sound of water, the warm coolness, the smell of olives, shadows flitting around one another's faces under the trees.

'This was worth it all,' I said, not to him specially, but he was the only one who nodded.

Then we really did only walk a hundred yards, by the side of the stream, and then the trees opened up and we could see, absolutely clear in the sunlight, just a little way down the hill, about ten or twenty houses and a church with a tower, white buildings, and a few cats lying on top of a wall and I felt like cheering.

We walked down really fast, laughing with relief. 'This is all right,' I said, even Marie agreed, but when we got to the first houses we stopped. In front of us, in the middle of the square we faced was a wheel with a donkey tethered to it, walking round and round, and apart from that it was all silent, there was no one to be seen. All you could see, everywhere, were skins; on the ground, spread over walls, hanging from glassless windows. Some had fur on and others were raw, flayed, pieces the size of a cow, there was no one to be seen, all you could do was look and smell, and there was a smell not of leather, but fur, fleshiness, not rank but still there, heavy, dry, an outdoor giant butcher's.

'I thought you said rugs,' Martine said. 'I thought you meant woven.' She turned round and faced Dimitri, and tossed her curls like a cross schoolgirl who'd lost a hockey match. 'I want a drink,' she said. 'Isn't there anywhere for that, or have we got another five miles to walk?'

'I'll see,' Dimitri said. He walked to the wooden door of the nearest house, shut fast, and stepped round the skin on the ground outside. I walked very carefully backwards to lean against a wall and closed my eyes. When I opened them again the woman he was talking to had a cat sitting on her bent black shoulder, and when she pointed her hand shook. She put her hand on Dimitri's arm and pulled him to stand next to her and pointed again, stabbing her finger at a house the other side of the square. Dimitri nodded and bowed and thanked her and came back to us smiling.

'She'd feed us if she could but she's waiting for her husband to come back with the shopping. We're to go to her son, Spiros, the house with the half-door over there.'

'Isn't there a café, then?' Martine said. He didn't answer, just strode across the square, avoiding skins and all the cats there suddenly seemed to be, greys, tabbies, skinny, twining round in the shade of the trees.

'And look at that poor donkey,' Martine said, but Marie and Debbie and I followed Dimitri. He bent down and knocked at the low door and a man appeared immediately, he'd probably been watching out of one of the black, blind windows. He was taller than Dimitri and very brown and had a moustache and black hair and a white shirt and black trousers, so beautiful we all stared. Dimitri looked up at him, talking fast, pointing back beyond the village to the hill we'd walked up and the man fingered his moustache and nodded and Dimitri went on talking. Then the man said two words and ducked back inside the doorway.

'Water would do,' Martine said and leant against him, limp. 'Can't you just tell him that? I'm not hungry now, anyway.'

Dimitri looked past her, up at the trees in the square, at the low white houses, walls flaking, holes that were windows, doors that were like barricades, at all those skins.

'I remember now,' he said, not to anyone but between all of us, 'before when I came it was the opposite way. Where we will go down, I used to come up, so it was through another village. This one I don't know, but they will be hospitable. I mistook where to get off the bus, so it is the opposite from the way I went when I was a child. But that means the climb down to the bus will be pleasant, that will be grassy and quite easy.'

'You mean – ' Martine blinked at him with disbelief – 'this isn't where we're meant to be?'

'It will do,' he said. Debbie made a squealing noise, then laughed. 'It's just a cat,' she said, and it was, skeletal, furry, fastened against her brown leg like a bony growth. We all started to move, shuffle, as though to stop the same thing happening to us.

Then the man came out of the house again, spoke to Dimitri and Dimitri turned to us.

'If we would like to go through, into his garden, we can eat.'

One after the other, nodding and smiling at the man, we followed Dimitri into a central corridor with rooms leading off, except all the doors were closed, and out into – not a garden, but a piece of land covered in grass and bushes, with a wooden table and chairs. We all sat down and closed our eyes.

'What would you like to drink?' I heard Dimitri say and answered lemon, something long and cold, and then almost dozed off, quite peacefully, until I heard Martine saying wonderful and gosh, bread as well, and olives, and how she loved goat's cheese. We all sat up and pulled our chairs round the table and that was quite funny because they were all different heights and sizes and we felt quite close, unevenly reaching out for bread and warm tomatoes and cutting with blunt knives.

'This is smashing,' I said. 'The whole day's been quite –' I hesitated, 'extraordinary.' Dimitri caught my eye and I smiled at the way his head was bent over his bread, the way he flexed his hands as he sat back and chewed, uncertain, not quite at ease.

We ate without talking for a bit and then I got up and walked to the edge of the bushes. They were in a circle and below that it was scrubby grass and further down still was a road.

'Is that where we're going, Dimitri?' I asked. 'Is that where the bus drives?' He turned from the table to see where I was pointing. 'So where have we come?' I walked round the bushes again so I was by the corner of the house. 'Is this all a plateau, then? And we've come up one side and go down the other? How high is it?'

He shrugged and spat an olive stone into his hand. 'A couple of miles, up, not straight, though, or it would be like Mount Everest.'

'A couple of miles?' Martine sounded affronted. 'It must be more than that. When I've done hill-walking in the lakes, or when I was little and went to Wales I walked and walked then, ten miles when I was ten years old my mother says. It can't only be two miles.'

Dimitri shook his head. 'It feels more, in the heat, uphill, that's all.'

'The heat,' I nodded. 'It's amazing. You're surrounded, it's all you notice. It's why houses are built like this, why the vegetation is this sort and this colour, why the earth is brown and rocky and why olives grow. The heat governs everything, doesn't it?'

Dimitri started to speak but Martine yawned and put her head down on the table.

'I know what the heat does to me,' she said, and I saw her slip her leg round Dimitri's, and although he'd been listening, turned towards me, he put a hand in the centre of her back, ran a finger down and then up her bent spine.

'Siesta time,' she said, 'if no one minds,' and she got up very slowly and ambled over to the bushes. I'd noticed that close up the leaves weren't as glossy as English oleanders, but they were shady. Martine lay down, spread out her arms, yawned loudly. 'This is the life,' she said, quite loudly, and giggled.

'Will they mind?' I asked Dimitri. I suddenly felt very anxious we shouldn't abuse hospitality, shouldn't use their private garden like a public park.

'Well, I can't move,' Martine said and wriggled. 'I've got to have my forty winks.'

Debbie and Marie got up too and went and sat under another tree and Dimitri leaned back in his chair, and I thought how, despite eating together and the cats and skins we'd seen outside, we'd all be glad to get back to our separate rooms at the hotel. I sat down too, but facing away from everyone else, looking out over the plateau and wondered if I was glad I'd come away; with those dreams I couldn't be, and yet I felt changed. I was more recovered from Jas, but it was more than that. I wanted to see Barbara, I wanted to talk to her, I realised, get closer and show her the effect things – Mercy that is, and our mother – had. Jas leaving me and Mercy dying were all part of the same thing. If I'd been able to talk to Barbara, if she'd been able to listen, none of this might have happened; if Barbara had been able to let herself get close enough to comfort me when Jas left all this could have been avoided, this whole holiday could have been different, and that made me angry. But I could tell her, I thought. About the fire, about Mercy; and maybe if we swapped obsessions we'd both end up a bit more balanced. I stayed thinking and staring at the olive trees, roofs and then when I looked round I could see Marie had gone to sleep, maybe they all had. It was nearly three, we ought to leave soon. I put all the crockery and glasses together on the tray and Dimitri opened his eyes and watched me and mouthed, 'Thank you,' and then looked at his watch, held up five fingers and closed his eyes again. I picked up the tray and went to the corridor of the house. I could say thank you to the people, I thought, and ask for the toilet, they wouldn't mind that.

Afterwards I found it difficult to remember the exact order. I put the tray by the entrance and called, 'Hello', very softly. Because no one came and I thought I could hear someone round the side I started to walk there. By the bush just at the side of the house I saw, first of all, a skin laid out, not as big as the others and covered in a different sort of fur, bristling, grey, and I thought at first of a huge cat and then saw the head, blunt, big-nosed, and then again, immediately at the same time saw that of course it wasn't a skin it was a dog, a grey-black one, like a Dalmatian, but without spots. I stared at it for a bit and then I realised it wasn't asleep, it was looking at me too, and that it was making a noise, at first it had been very soft, like bees, low, bumbling, but it got louder, it was as if something was stuck in its throat. What I did next was stupid because even if there had been something stuck, a bone, a lump of meat, I couldn't have helped but I took a step towards it. I even held out a hand. Come on, boy, poor old thing, does it hurt? And it happened so fast I couldn't have described how it moved, whether its back or front legs got up first, how I even realised it was going for me until it was on me. It was quicker and heavier than anything and yet it didn't knock me down, it stood up to me, its front legs round me, like a performing animal I thought, in a circus, except it made

78

that noise, growling I realised, very soft, very deep and I was petrified. I could feel myself go cold all over, hairs I never knew I had standing up on end, behind my knees, the back of my neck, and I thought I mustn't, they smell fear, and opened my mouth and no noise came out and its legs got tighter and it leaned on me and I thought, I'm going to fall, and then it'll bite me. It was like a slow-motion film, I couldn't stay upright. It growled louder and I could see its teeth, and I thought, I wish I could faint, I can't bear this. Then I started trying to move, as if it wouldn't notice, and its legs tightened and then, the most awful thing, I could feel its penis, I could feel this thing getting bigger against my leg. I could feel its fur as well because it started kind of jigging against my leg and I imagined fleas jumping off the fur, and that made me shiver, I was goose-flesh all over and I could see inside its mouth, teeth, red, its eyes were red-flecked too and it was rubbing, it felt like bucking against me. I've never been so frightened, not even in the dreams. I had to keep my mouth shut because I knew if I started to scream I'd be hysterical. I suppose it couldn't have raped me, it would prob-ably have started to bite me, but I hardly thought of that. It stinks, I thought suddenly, it's got its stinking legs round me in this awful hot grass by this completely blank deserted building and all I can see is stone and bits of branches and I hate it, and it must have felt that because it barked and I knew then I couldn't bear it, and I opened my mouth too and then I screamed and at that exact moment there was another voice, cackling, high, and Dimitri saying, 'No, don't,' and I turned my head very slightly and saw the tiny woman in black holding a wooden bath and water glinting as she tipped it and then it hit us.

'Come here,' I heard Dimitri shout but I couldn't move, I just stood still, I was soaking, I couldn't breathe and it was still half on me. Then, straight away, the old woman started hitting it with a stick, screaming and I could feel the blows reverberating on me even though it wasn't holding that tightly any more. Then she shouted something at me, and I realised I had to move or it would realise I was paralysed and turn on me. She wouldn't be able to do anything then, so I somehow pulled away, flung myself away, I don't know how, and the old woman gave the dog a thump or two and then took my wrist and pulled me back to the side of the house and kind of propped me up against it.

Then she shouted at Dimitri, not for long, not even very loudly, but he bowed his head and shook it and tried to answer her but she went on shouting, shaking her hands. Then the man we'd first seen came round the corner, running, and he put his hand on the old woman's shoulder. She turned on him and just shrugged his hand off and hobbled back round the corner and inside the house. Dimitri and the man said a few words, and Dimitri said, as though I wasn't there, past me, 'You're all right, aren't you?' I said, 'Yes.' The man came and looked at me for a moment, soaking, still shaking, and I felt like a criminal, ashamed, as though it'd been my fault.

He said, very slowly, 'I am sorry.' I shook my head.

He spoke to Dimitri again and Dimitri said, 'He wants to tell you it's a guard dog.'

'Please tell him I'm sorry,' I said and Dimitri did and then I said, 'Can we go now?'

We walked back to the table again and the others oohed and aahed because I was dripping wet and Dimitri explained what had happened, but not properly.

'A dog jumped at her,' he said, 'and the old woman threw water to get it off.'

'Where were you?' Martine asked straight away. I said I was taking the tray back, I'd walked round the side of the house.

'And what were you doing?' she asked Dimitri.

'I heard the dog,' Dimitri said, and didn't look at either of us.

'Thank God,' I said, because I did; whatever reason he'd walked round there was irrelevant now, even if he'd wanted to find me, touch me, he'd have been hairy, smothering, I'd have felt almost as awful as I did now. 'It was appalling,' I said. 'It wanted to eat or rape me, I could even feel its thing up against me, it was—'

I could feel I was going to cry and took a deep breath instead, and looked out into the distance. All I could see was sky and trees shimmering because my eyes were full of tears. Marie put a hand on my shoulder and Debbie said, 'Dear, how awful, it must have been terrifying, I don't know how you stood it,' and then I heard the man's voice again and he was holding out his hand and so I stepped forward and took it. We all shuffled our feet for a moment, looking round at the table, the chairs, the crumbs on the flat grass where Martine and Marie and Debbie had lain down. Martine said, '*Epharisto*,' and we all repeated it and started down the hill, Dimitri leading.

We'd only gone a few yards before Marie stopped. 'Are you all right?' she said again. 'What happened?'

'I just took the tray back and went to look for a loo,' I said, and almost giggled. 'I thought it was asleep and then it jumped on me.'

'It could have killed you.' Marie shook her head.

'Or worse,' I said, and I did start laughing then.

'Dimitri,' Marie called. He and Martine were some way ahead, striding through the grass. He stopped really abruptly. 'Do they all keep dogs like that round here?' He shook his head as though he hadn't heard.

It only took about half an hour to walk downhill, it was really easy going. If none of that had happened and we hadn't had the space between us it would have been nice to admire the countryside and ask Dimitri about the other villages, because as we went down we could see little collections of roofs to the right and left of us. Who bought the skins? What did they grow apart from olives? What did they live on? I could imagine myself asking, all the polite questions that I pretended made me different, covered up for the fact that I was an intruder.

When we got back to the road the bus was there, half-empty, so we could spread ourselves out and sit on the shady side, but it was still sweltering. We stayed there in silence until it started up. After half an hour of stopping and starting I went and sat behind Dimitri and Martine.

'It wasn't my fault,' I said.

Dimitri went on looking out of the window. 'You were not meant to go out of the garden,' he said eventually. 'That was what he said to me. We had food, drink, the garden to sit in. There was no need to prowl around.'

'Prowl?' I was really affronted by that word. 'But I told you I was taking the tray back. I told you that then, you knew, and I said afterwards I was looking for a loo. I wasn't prowling, it was quite—' I stopped because my voice was shaking. I could have hit him for that, implying that was all, all day, I'd been up to.

He shrugged and Martine put a hand on his arm. 'Let's forget it,' she said and nodded at me to go away and leave him in peace.

'It wasn't my fault,' I said again. My voice went up and down. 'If it'd been Marie or Debbie you'd think it was stupid, if it'd been Martine you'd have been furious with the dog, but because it's me you're offended. And that's not fair. All I've been doing all day is trying to understand, that's all there was to it. It's got nothing to do with you, except you could be sorry. I didn't deserve it, I wasn't asking for anything; you ought to realise that. All I meant,' I waved at the signs we were just coming to, for DISCO-DA-DISCO and BAR-B-Q, 'was that I wanted you to realise I didn't think this is all there is to Corfu.'

'It makes money,' Dimitri said and went and stood by the door, waiting to get off the minute it stopped.

I stumbled when I got out, and again on the way into the hotel. As we were waiting for the lift I felt quite odd and Marie said she'd bring me smelling salts, and I think she did, but I lay down and fell asleep, straight away. When I woke it was still light. In fact it was light again because when I looked at my watch it said five o'clock and I realised it was morning, I'd slept for eleven hours. I'd missed a whole evening, I hadn't woken, and I had no memory of anything I'd dreamed about. I started to go through the previous day but I closed my eyes again and then I heard someone knock and it was Marie. It was nine o'clock, she said, how about a change of scene if I felt up to it?

'We talked about you all evening,' she said, 'and I looked in on you, but you were dead to the world.'

'I was,' I agreed. It seemed a fair description.

'If you're interested, Debbie and I thought we'd have a go at Corfu Town,' she said, 'get away from the great outdoors.' She laughed, embarrassed. 'It must've been dreadful.'

I shook my head. 'Over and done with. Corfu Town's a great idea,' I said. 'I can't wait to see some nice shops again.'

The last days of that fortnight were like the whole lot should have been, because I was a holiday person, I went back years to being good company. I heard about Ernest's wife, I asked Marie and Debbie about their jobs and ex-boyfriends, at mealtimes I sat with different English people every day. I even organised where we all went in the evenings. I also spent more time with Martine because I didn't feel ashamed of going to sit with her and Dimitri when they were at the pool or the bar. She'd come on holiday with me yet she'd treated me like an unfortunate appendage, ignored me, not taken any trouble to be quiet when they were making love. It was my turn to find out it was quite liberating to be insensitive and selfish. If I wanted conversation I demanded it, I didn't creep away and leave them whispering. I'd run up behind their chairs. 'Come and have a drink with the rest of us.' 'There's spaces over there, next to the lovebirds,' I said at mealtimes, and thought that it was survival, that was what I'd learnt in the last fortnight.

I told Martine about all the English girls in Corfu Town hanging onto waiters, how anyone could find a boyfriend, and laughed to Dimitri about the donkey rides, photographers, and the number of tourists complaining.

'Even the little children are miserable,' I said. 'The ones in Union Jack T-shirts whine, and the ones in culottes and espadrilles pinch one another. National dress is so easy to tell,' I said to Dimitri. 'You must be quite an expert too.'

He smiled at that and so I asked him where he'd been in England and when Martine was swimming he showed me photos of his children, two girls and a boy, rather plain and plump.

'Oh, it's nearly over, we're going soon,' I pretended to wail. I said that I didn't want to go, but I knew quite well that wasn't true. I was glad I'd come, I was glad I'd endured it all, but most of all I couldn't wait to tell Barbara what I'd learned from it. What happened in the last two weeks hadn't just been to do with me; I'd also felt for Mercy, seen what she'd experienced. At the same time I'd had a look at what I felt about her. She was selfish and she was terrifying, especially at the end, but I'd had to come to terms with that. And I had, I thought, and so should Barbara. It's influences and how you use them I thought, that was what you needed to examine, and I'd managed. I wanted to say, 'And so should you,' to Barbara, 'that's what you ought to try, it'd help, really'; that was the other part, that was the other important element in it.

On the last day, the morning when we had to get the bus, Martine was weeping all over the place. Even Dimitri didn't look too happy. Marie and Debbie had left by an early flight, so we'd said drunken farewells the night before, and when it was time to take our bags down Martine said she couldn't move.

'Fine,' I said. 'Stay. I'll leave you here and you can negotiate staying another week or whatever with the manager.' She sniffed and staggered and leaned against things all the way downstairs, walls, the lift, even the side of the bus, although that was baking hot. Dimitri was waiting to come to the airport with us. All the way there they were silent, holding hands, Martine's head on his shoulder, and when we arrived she was really crying in earnest. I left them alone, I wasn't going to provide an audience. For once I wasn't even sure she wanted one. When our flight was called and there weren't any delays, I marched over to where they were entwined on a sofa and I said I was boarding, she'd better get a move on if she wanted any duty-frees.

Once we were on it wasn't so bad. I said how pleased I was with my tan, how I had probably lost weight, and she pulled herself together enough to stop crying and look at least as presentable as me when the steward came round with drinks and lunch.

On the train from Gatwick she seemed to fall asleep, hand pillowed against her cheek, rubbing her eyes like a little girl when she woke up at Victoria, stumbling as she lifted her big heavy cases, and of course the man opposite offered to help and I went ahead to the barrier as if I didn't know her. When she caught me up we didn't bother telling one another what a great time it had been. We just said we'd give each other a ring, and I said I had to dash, I'd an awful feeling I might even be on late duty.

When I got back to Shepherds Bush it was grey and getting dark and my flat was cold. I rang Beryl and said, 'It's Tuesday, if you're not on duty we could go for a drink.' I came back not drunk but not too sober either, and hummed while I got undressed, and then I went to sleep and woke up the next morning dreamlessly.

'It's me, I'm back,' I said on the phone to Barbara. 'It was extraordinary. Not just the holiday itself but what happened to me—' and then I stopped. It'd taken me days getting around to ringing her and I couldn't for the life of me work out why.

'Come and tell us about it, come and have supper,' she'd say, and I'd know all was forgiven and forgotten.

'When? Let's make it soon, the weekend, then my tan won't have faded,' I'd answer, and then spend the next few days looking forward to it.

Normally I did look forward to going to Barbara's house, I quite appreciated civilised living at one remove, but all that week the prospect seemed to grate on me. I thought partly it was going back to work, the musty old smells, the gossip, feeling I didn't care if Mr Cathcart's daughter never wrote or Mrs Wells never again sang as she shut her library book, but it spread over more than that. In the mornings while I scraped my toast and looked at the cracks across the kitchen ceiling I thought of the sun shining through Barbara's conservatory, and when I wiped Mr Thompson's nose and shovelled away all the left-over cabbage at lunchtimes I thought of her dabbing Anna's little nostrils and rinsing the willow-pattern plates. Every day when I imagined going in through her front door, sitting at her wide oak table in her kitchen, instead of enjoying the prospect I wanted to point out faults to her.

'You haven't got any plants,' I'd remark, 'not even in the garden.' If we took our coffee upstairs to the sitting room, with its white walls and dried flowers, I'd say, 'This is a bit dated, isn't it?'

All along the hall and in Graham's study were old family photos, snaps of 1930s Liberals his parents had known, even Shaw and Dora Russell. I'd glance at those in passing and say, 'You shouldn't need to remember the dead like this. Especially when you never met them.' They'd been killed before Graham and Barbara even met.

'You're still living with them,' I'd tell her when I left my coat in their bedroom, which was dominated by his parents' big, dark furniture. The duvet and kimonos looked as if Barbara and Graham were playing at being grown-ups in an old married couple's room. The rooms I wouldn't comment on were Anna's and the bathroom. I couldn't find much fault with Beatrix Potter and Richard Scarry books and Galt toys and bunk beds, or thick towels and pine essence and Rousseau prints; everywhere else I'd remember supper parties. Other people ate and she watched, and then she sat on the edge of the sofa dispensing coffee and liqueurs, agonising over the creased cushions, silently lining standards and failures up against the wall.

Often people must have thought she was shy, listening rather than talking, but that was because they didn't realise she'd be storing it all up for use afterwards, cataloguing the evidence she got in exchange for hospitality. 'That went well,' she said when people left. Never, 'They had a nice time.'

'It was extraordinary,' I repeated on the phone, and I couldn't get any further.

'So what happened, then?' she asked after a minute, deadpan.

I gabbled, 'It was just an experience, it wasn't like anything else, it was split in two, reality and dreams, and reality was Marie and Debbie from Birmingham, and Martine getting off with the first Greek she met, and me being attacked by a mad dog, and the dreams were about Mercy and her dying—'

'Mercy?' Barbara said. 'Attacked? Badly? What happened?'

'That's not important,' I said. 'It was dreaming about Mercy that mattered, and how Mercy and Audrey connect with how we are—'

Barbara sighed. 'Don't,' she said, 'talk about reality instead. The Birmingham belles, Martine, the dog, why not stick to those?'

'It's what I was saying to you, when you came after Jas left, remember? How we've got to recognise what Audrey and Mercy did to us and how we've got to leave that behind—'

85

'When you apologised. And I told you I didn't see what we had to discuss about it. I still don't.'

'Because I've got free from Mercy,' I mumbled. 'Got free from what she was like, the effect she had—'

'Mercy,' Barbara said. 'I don't see the point of this. All right, Mercy was pretty vile. If you want to know what I thought' – and she could have believed it was the last thing either of us cared about – 'I thought she was pretty vile as Audrey's mother and equally unpleasant as a grandmother. All those visits when we were kids, all she wanted was to stir up trouble. She and Audrey didn't like one another, they couldn't get on, they couldn't adjust. That's all there was to it.'

'No,' I said. 'That's not true. Mercy needed to talk, Audrey shut Mercy away and Mercy wanted me to confide in, that's what I'm talking about. And she planted fears in me and now I've looked at the fears I dreamt those fears and found out how to survive. I did that on holiday. I stopped being frightened. It was an extraordinary experience,' I said. I wondered if she was still listening. 'Because it made everything that's happened clear to me, it confirmed things. I've had to look at her influence and what you've got to look at is Audrey's influence. I think we did a kind of swap in childhood,' I wanted to *will* her to remember, to join us together, 'I got Mercy and you got Audrey, and they were both overpowering and you have to try and shake off those influences or ruin your life.'

'Yes,' Barbara said. 'I have. As far as I'm concerned if you had nightmares about Mercy I'm sorry, but I can't do anything to alter that. If you feel dreams helped in some way, good, but I'm not involved in that either. I'm involved in the here and now – rather violently, actually,' she made a coughing noise, 'rather actively. Active participation is the best description I can think of for it.'

'I don't want to argue, Laura,' she said, when I didn't answer, 'and it's not a one-way process. You can't stand Audrey, you make that perfectly plain and I don't challenge that. It's me who has to go and visit them, I'm the one who tells them what you're doing, how you're keeping. I don't tell you what to do about that. I think you should allow me the same freedom. Listen,' she said; I had, I'd heard silence and all the words she'd stopped me saying.

'At least I look,' I wanted to tell her. 'At least I go beyond outward appearances. I lived her life through those dreams. Look, remember what she meant, what she showed us.' I was silent.

'I've got something to tell you,' and her voice was quieter. 'I wondered before you went, I suspected it, I suppose, really, I was sure, but I wanted to save it for a little bit. Laura?' she said to make sure I was listening.

'Yes,' I answered, 'what?' It should have been, 'No, go away, don't, it isn't fair, why, it was my turn to have you listen, you've done it on purpose, done it to stop me ever getting through to you.'

'I'm pregnant,' she said. 'I'm having another baby.'

I suppose I must have said the right things to her, how are you, when, wonderful. She told me she was sick rather a lot. 'But it doesn't matter,' she said straight away. 'Lots of women have that for months.' I could imagine how she would look, wan, triumphant, impervious. Last time she had been pale, and red blotches had grown and faded on her neck. 'Hospitals are stupid,' she said. 'I don't have much faith. I know my own body better, it's not as though I haven't done it before.'

She told me Anna was fine, she'd thought of repainting Graham's room to put the baby in. 'I think they ought to have separate places.'

I didn't answer, 'We never had,' and ask why. 'Work's a bit horrendous,' I said when she gave me space to interrupt. I heard myself and thought it sounded quite reasonable. I knew what I was talking about, too, I could converse about domesticity, pregnancy, Mrs Wells, rotas, as though that was all there was to everything, that was all that ever needed attending to or sorting out.

'So,' Barbara said when I'd had my turn, 'you'll have to come and show off your suntan. Come and have tea. Or supper,' she added and I wondered if it was an effort. 'When I feel like cooking again,' she added. 'Just come over, come any time, one afternoon, come one day this week, if you're free.'

Barbara

For quite a long time after Graham and I were married my chief fantasy was that I would be interviewed. For no predictable reason I would be selected by a newspaper or a radio programme; they would ask to pronounce upon my life, and I would describe it as pleasing. I rehearsed my words, I pored over a photograph to accompany the speech; the anxious eyes and untidy hair faded away. I was captivating with conviction, I shone with confidence. It was not to be boastful, I thought, it was not a question of pride, but confirmation, it was because otherwise I found it extraordinarily difficult to believe that I had come to this.

'It wasn't just that we fell in love,' I would confide. 'Everyone does that at university. It was the contrast. After years of uncertainty it was the joy of finding out that nothing went wrong. Weeks went by, and then months, and all those desperate unspoken worries about acceptability dispersed. They seemed to evaporate naturally, it was magic, not even as if Graham made them. Of course, Graham realised,' I would say easily, 'but he didn't specifically set out to alter me. He never questioned or dissected, that would have frozen me up, he treated me as if my uncertainties didn't matter. He asked what I thought, he wanted to know what I wanted, he wanted me around. It was as if it never occurred to him that self-doubt could be destructive. I could tell him I loved him. I wasn't afraid,' I would say.

'I could turn to him,' I would not say, I was far to shy. 'His brown head on the pillow next to me, his thin limbs wrapped round me, I could lean up above him and I would be besieged with tenderness. I would stroke, lick, kiss, I even bit, I yearned to bury myself, to consume enough of him to be swallowed into his flesh.'

'It was different,' was all I would say. 'Different from anything else in my life because I wasn't living in fear. All the awful times, living at home, testing friends, trying to live up to something, disappeared. And it shouldn't be like that, should it?' I would ask. 'It was a reversal,' and I would laugh. 'A reversal of perceptions.'

'Don't worry, you're not on trial,' he promised. 'Relax.' It changed me.

'You don't make judgements,' I said to him. He smiled. 'Open mindedness is so rare and so admirable.' He ducked his head with modesty. 'I love you,' I told him, and he agreed, and that it was rare, not only our state, but that I could believe I'd crossed the line into a world where life was there for the taking, where I could behave as if I knew what I was doing. It wasn't quite a constant state, though, I would admit. It had its ups and downs.

'He was older than me,' I would say. 'When he finished his degree he came to London. A year later I decided to do a teacher training course, too, and so I saw him every day again. We lived separately, in fact, but not for very long because after a year it seemed quite natural to get married.'

I never revealed that when all the other dreads had disappeared a new one formed, that he would leave me; that for six months I had tested him for signs, searched for boredom, constructed arguments, thrown tantrums, and although they had been fruitless I had not been convinced. It had taken the courage of desperation to plan to go abroad to work and I had been rewarded.

'Don't,' he had said when I started to pack. 'I'd thought of getting a special licence next week. Leave it till after that.'

'It was absolutely the right thing for us,' I'd say, and that I had not minded staying. Instead I had learnt to drive so that we could travel the world together in a Land-Rover, gone to Italian and Spanish classes to complement his French and Greek. 'It was one of the best times of my life,' I'd say. 'The other person,' I would remember, 'the other person I saw a lot of was my sister, but that wasn't quite as harmonious. Twice a year she came to see me at university and I never found how to deal with it. 'We're not alike,' I told everyone, and whatever she did – whatever excesses she attempted – I just said, 'It's only what I expected. It's something I've come to terms with.'

She'd tell me I didn't know how to enjoy myself – she'd shout across a room, brandishing a bottle like a microphone, and I wouldn't contradict her, I would rarely even turn round to acknowledge her. 'You never let go, you'd hate to be the life and soul, you're waiting for a miracle,' she said afterwards. 'You want someone to find your light under a bushel,' she'd taunt the next morning. 'People don't like caution,' and she'd try and grab me, pretend it was a joke, 'they like surprises. Relax,' she always said, too, before she left, 'it may never happen. You might even like it if it did.' She would wink then, as though she had a key to a secret, as though she was laughing because I would never be party to it.

'Togetherness,' she said when she met Graham and me in London, 'correcting exercise books together?' She'd lean across the pub table and whisper to him, 'Listen, listen to the story of the fumbler of the filing cabinets, that's the stuff jobs are made of, proper jobs, not snotty little boys. Come on,' she'd nudge, 'live dangerously. Come and have a curry. Forget that pile of essays on the bedside table, pretend tomorrow won't happen.' I would wish that she had a boyfriend who kept her tied to their bed, who never let her loose on the rest of the world.

'Have you seen Them?' she asked Graham at regular intervals – she'd grab his arm at the bus stop as though remembering a vital question – 'the dreaded Audrey and Leslie? I wouldn't let anyone near them.' She'd turn to me and laugh. 'He won't want anything to do with you afterwards, not once he's seen what he's letting himself in for.'

'I've seen,' Graham said. 'I don't mind. I quite like the prospect.'

When Graham and I married she said she wouldn't come, she would laugh too much, but afterwards she visited frequently, she brought wine, fashion magazines, different men, she preened and paraded and confided and entertained. She danced round me while I cooked, she said, 'Oh, leave it,' when Graham started to wash up. 'Run,' she'd say, 'run, there's just time before the off-licence shuts,' and when she left Graham chuckled and said, 'She doesn't change, whatever's happening she'll find something to celebrate.'

'Every time,' I agreed. 'Not a care in the world. Except her.'

'What is there to care about?' he asked. 'What's the point of worrying?' but after a year I did.

'How do you see the future? How should it work out?' I asked. 'The same? Same flat, same occupations? Same dissatisfactions, indecisions, don't they frustrate you? Don't you mind? I can't make out if you're tolerant,' I said, 'or indolent, or you believe in fairy stories, that one day your whole world will change effortlessly.'

'I don't want it to,' he said. 'I quite like the everyday as it is. I'm

91

not bothered with expectations. I don't believe in chasing perfection. I quite like the ordinary.'

'It's your parents,' I said, because he had told me enough of his childhood to see that their fervent Liberal politics had produced a chronic inability to decide. 'You can go too far, you know, following a good example.' If I was sour it was also because I was envious of that much-loved childhood, where opinions and discussion had been welcome. 'All they did when they listened was to turn every idea inside out, upside down, until it didn't matter whether you thought it or not. All they really did,' I taunted him 'was to teach you to change your mind, not make it up.'

I would look at us over our cramped breakfast table, his brown head bowed without a thought of anger, my fists clenched over the plates and cups that were all we owned, and rage that he had been deprived of selfishness, held back from any instinct to be independent, disagreeable.

'And you,' he would say, looking back at my screwed-up face, my bristling hair, 'have never learnt the other side.'

'I don't want it to end,' I said to myself, frequently, because I was also quite convinced that I had no desire to live alone or with anyone else; all my past had been riddled with swamps of uncertainty, what I most longed for was a present I could be sure of.

'I've just got to decide the best way for it to go on,' I reassured myself, and avoided noticing that I had no idea how. We never discussed what Graham made of the situation.

Sometimes I would be seized by a panic that there was no difference between him abandoning a long-held view on the detrimental effects of corporal punishment and deciding he no longer wanted to live with me.

'I've changed my mind,' I could hear him saying, without malice, and there would be no course but to agree to separate.

'There has to be more to it than this, more to give up. It has to be too hard,' I decided.

'This idea,' I said one day, 'of buying a VW to go round the world with the money your parents left. Are you that set? We talked about a house, too, and that's the thing that's beginning to seem more real to me.'

'I'm easy,' he answered after a while, 'if that's what you want.'

'I'd just like to look, really.' I backtracked. 'Probably I'll hate everything I see and then find a marvellous van. Work it out of my system. Not that we can't do both,' I added, 'in another year. We can easily save, we won't be spending money on rent. It might be more sensible this way round.'

'It's big,' he said when I took him to Dunster Road. 'Three bedrooms.'

'One could be your study,' and I led him all over it. 'It reminds me of your parents' house. Those old photos. Doesn't it you? We could hang them on the stairs. Or in your study. It'd be nice to have them to look at.'

He'd nodded. 'But then I suppose with any house one thinks of family. It's inevitable.'

A week before we moved I stopped taking the pill and six months later I became pregnant with Anna.

'We're delighted,' I told everyone I knew with absolute certainty, because by that time I was altered. Half a year in that house had achieved exactly what I intended. I no longer feared that there was a price to be paid, that one morning Graham would announce that he was leaving, that one night the house would fall down. I had no qualms about anything. It was correct that pregnancy made me feel sick, hungry, tired, energetic, erotic, sluggish; it was even right that I should relish the unpredictability. I did not ever imagine any sensation presaging catastrophe; it was the reverse, every day I was more confident, every day I thought that perfection was more nearly within my grasp.

'You think you've got it made,' Laura said to me between moving jobs and boyfriends, 'the wife and mother bit. Nice house, nice friends. But isn't it ever boring?'

'Not to me,' I said. 'I like knowing how good things are.' When Anna was born I recognised her immediately, I knew straight away that she provided me with a new means of achievement.

For another three years I persevered without doubts or nervousness. Certainly I took immense care – of Anna, Graham, the house. I encouraged Anna's progress, issued invitations to Graham's colleagues, carefully chose furnishings, food, and, among other mothers I met, Geraldine and Jessica for friends. I was cautious, I was punctilious even, but I was not fearful; I did not live in dread of loss, of making mistakes. 'Fine,' I said, whatever I was asked: I, Anna, Graham, his job, his new job, the house, were always fine. I behaved as if I had been born with a knowledge of how to make them so. I would not have said I was content, I would not have closed off the possibility of improvement, but I acknowledged that I had a good life; all I had to do was live up to it.

'What do you really want?' Laura would come and ask, as though I habitually practised both deceit and self-denial. 'What is it you're trying to get out of this?'

'I get exactly what I want,' I would answer. I'd laugh. 'Don't judge everything by your standards.'

'Come on, Barbara,' and she would grab my arm. 'Don't you want to say, "Sod off, Geraldine, stop pontificating", "Shut up, Jessica, stop moaning". Don't you ever want to explode all this homely myth—' and she'd whirl round and round the neat kitchen like a dervish weaving a spell to make the place disappear. 'Be free of all this?'

'No,' I answered and I would stroke a chairback for reassurance. 'We just have different perspectives. We make different choices. I don't see the problem about that.'

'Three years is an ideal gap,' I said to Graham when Anna had passed her second birthday. 'It's not fair to have an only child. Your parents would have had more if they hadn't been so old. She'd love it.'

Even though it took me nearly a year to conceive I was neither initially impatient nor eventually surprised. I now found it quite reasonable to receive what I wanted, to know what to expect, and I was confident that this pregnancy would be exactly like the first. Inevitably it would be less exciting, but the advantage would be that I would have advance information. I would be aware that at the end of the sixth month I would be exhausted and at the beginning of the seventh I would be energetic. I would not, however, be worried or very sick or doubt for one minute that anything untoward would happen.

After a month I discovered that I was mistaken, and for six weeks I was firm with myself, believing that the more normally I behaved the easier I would find it to forget nausea; I would not be overtaken by it; if I pushed it to the back of my mind my body would follow suit, I would adjust to the child I was carrying. But I did not. I was disabled, I was continuously aware of nothing but discomfort that nothing alleviated, nothing obliterated.

'I'm incapable,' I said to Graham, and tried to laugh, 'as incapable of cleaning up, cooking, looking after Anna as if I'd been paralysed.'

'It'll go,' he said, 'don't worry. That won't help. I'll look after things.' But I did not want to relinquish the everyday order, the reliable patterns and places. I needed the reassurance of that creativity.

'Rest,' he answered. 'That's what your body's telling you, anyway.'

'I hate it controlling me,' I said. He shrugged and said it was a matter of attitude.

'Try and relax,' he urged. 'You're the one who's trying to control things, not the sickness. It's just a physical reaction, it's not out to destroy you. Leave it, wait until it goes.'

'I just need something else to think about,' I said, 'anything would do,' and after two months, when Laura rang in tears because Jas had left, I thought I had found it.

Laura had lived with Jas for a year. I had met him half a dozen times and I had not liked him; I had thought the gap in their interests and cultures far too large to overcome. He had been scornful of Graham and me, and it had been plain that his relationship with Laura was unequal in affection.

'He exploits her,' I had said to Graham. 'He'll love her and leave her. And she could see that if she wanted to look.'

But when she rang and I told her I'd come that afternoon I had disregarded the fact that between two and four I was often incapable of moving. I would have to make an effort, get the better of it.

For a week I travelled to her flat every afternoon with Anna, proving I could still negotiate Tube trains, avocado pears, omelettes and conversation, and I listened. I had not tried to comfort her, I could not see the point of encouraging self-deception; instead I had tried to distract her. I had talked about Anna's playgroup, shopping, I had tried to provide topics for discussion, but she was obsessive.

'Help me,' she repeated. She sat rocking in her dressing-gown, agonising over his letter, threatening his life.

'You have to give it time,' I said. 'Of course it'll get better, of course you'll get over it.' I tried to sound appraising rather than impatient but every evening when I arrived home I was angry and feverish.

'It's a waste of time,' I would complain, 'and look at the effect it has on me.'

'Don't worry,' Graham always said. 'I'll see to things,' and I went up to bed and listened to him joking with Anna. I lay very still. I did not want to discuss or consider anything, it was unthinkable that this extremity of reaction was to continue, or that it was of any significance.

'Graham would say something,' I told my face in the bathroom mirror, 'or Geraldine. Or Jessica, they've been pregnant. It'll go, it's nothing.' But whatever I did, the visits, invitations, taking Anna to the playgroup or park, were only effective as temporary distractions. It waited, it lurked, all the time I was alone it never left me.

Sometimes I would allow myself five minutes, because for that long I was safe, to think of toasted cheese, of crusty soft bread spread with pâté and mayonnaise, of slices of tongue, thick and oval beside red beans on a white plate and I would fantasise with disgust, my mouth dry and my stomach aching, because I could see them, fantasy foods, with far more clarity than my embryo.

'I need to get up, I can't be still twenty-four hours a day,' I said to Graham. Every morning I hauled myself out of bed and, while Anna was out of the house, pushed the Hoover, cleaned the stove, polished mirrors, ironed clothes. If I moved slowly and did not bend over it was not too distressing; it expanded my world, it saved me from the state where everything, day, evening, night, was centred upon disquiet.

'Tell the doctor what you feel like,' Graham insisted. 'They must be able to suggest something.' On my first visit to the ante-natal clinic, after weighing and measuring and urinating, lying still, obliterating any image that might cause my stomach to turn while I was examined, I steeled myself.

'I am just a bit worried about the baby if I don't eat; being sick so much,' I said. The doctor asked me about vitamin pills.

'Your weight's fine.' He took my file off the table and looked at the one beneath. 'You don't realise how much you're putting away. Just because it's not roast beef and two veg. A little of what you fancy,' he said, 'as long as you're sensible.'

I started to explain but the image of wrinkled meat, gravy and Brussels sprouts was so intrusive I did not say that in order to be sure not to be sick that afternoon I had only drunk water for twenty-four hours. Swallowing was impossible.

'If it goes past next month,' he said, 'we'll do a few tests, find out what's causing the upset. See if we can find something to quieten it down.'

I had thought of Thalidomide, of needles and tubes and endless visits constantly to confirm that something was amiss.

'I'm sure I'll be fine,' I said, and he patted my file papers.

'The doctor said my weight was nothing to worry about,' I told Graham that evening.

'That's good.' He ate very fast when I was not at the table with him.

'Laura's awful, though,' I said. 'In comparison to her I'm a bundle of fun.'

'Maybe you ought to stop racing around,' he said. 'Cut out the errands of mercy to Shepherds Bush. She wouldn't want to exhaust you like this. Tell her,' he urged. 'She'll understand.'

'You weren't like this with Anna,' I could suddenly hear her saying, 'what's gone wrong?' and I said it was impossible.

'I'll be all right soon, there's no need yet to explain. She'll fuss, I couldn't stand that. I can't tell her now, not when she's just finished with Jas. She wanted a child, I'm sure. It's not fair to spring this on her so soon.'

'Did she?' He sounded surprised. 'I thought she liked being footloose and fancy-free. Surely,' he said, 'that's the essence of her, Laura, keeping moving from one thing to another, not wanting to be tied down?'

'That's one way of putting it,' I said. 'It's one definition of the way she lives. She's lonely. I can't abandon her.'

And after that first week I did not want to; she was not appreciative, she made it clear that I was not successful in consoling her, that all I provided was company, but it was not unrewarding; it did not only distance me from sickness, it put it into a different perspective.

'Good girl,' I would say to Anna and settle her with her jigsaw, her cut-outs. 'Just say if you want any help.' I would walk round Laura's big room, her little kitchen, while she ate the food I had brought. I would dead-head her plants, wipe her sink unit, read through her dusty book titles, and I would not repeat to myself the criticisms she had made of domesticity, I would not return to her arguments of freedom versus habit, but they were never far from my mind. It had not got her far, I thought, her independent yellow walls and scarlet shelves; they did not sit there and talk to her.

'I'm still glad it happened. Jas happened,' she said. 'It was still worth it.'

I did not answer. I turned on the radio or television, I found a magazine to read.

'You don't care, you don't try and help,' she accused. I would remain unprovoked, remind her that often it was her choice to ignore my conversation.

'You don't talk, that's not conversation,' she would answer. She would pace about, walk up and down, come and stand in front of me. 'You don't look at what's happening to anyone, you don't see what anything's really like. Listen to me,' she would command. 'Do something. Stop pretending it's all right.' Once, twice, I wanted to, I had difficulty refraining from shouting back, from hitting her, mocking back for every comparison she had made of our lives.

'I won't stay long. I can't stay late,' I started to say when I arrived, and it was not rejection, it was establishing the terms of the visit straight away so there could be no accusations when it came to an end.

'Don't bother,' she would answer, and all the time I was there she would not say a word, she would hunch away from me on the corner of her bed, she would nurse a grubby mug of cold coffee. 'You might as well not come,' she would rouse herself to say when I stood up, 'for all the good it's done. You try and pretend it hasn't happened, you try and gloss over all this, misery, grief, you don't really mind. You only come out of duty.'

'Do something,' she challenged me. 'Invite me to supper instead of Geraldine and Paul, risk me making a fuss, but you won't, all you care about is appearances. You're like her,' she said then, 'her, Audrey, that's who you remind me of. It's Anna I feel sorry for, Anna and Graham, they're the ones who suffer, living with you, like I did living with Audrey, frozen – 'and I told her to be quiet then, I said I would go; she preferred suffering, she had chosen that role from childhood. She had chosen from childhood never to alter, to pretend to victimisation in order to justify every disruption she inflicted upon others.

'You're lying,' I said, 'you always lie. About me, about how you're treated, you can't face the way things are. You want to destroy the world and put it back together for no good reason other than selfishness, you've got no justification for wallowing in feelings of being hard done by. Poor Laura,' I said, 'everything's always awful for poor Laura. You can't grow up, you can't leave anything behind, you don't want to change.'

I had been shaking as I finished dressing Anna; it had taken all the physical control I had to get downstairs, along the road, find a taxi. I had pinched myself, pulled folds in my wrists to stop myself crying. It was not worth it, I should have learnt that fifteen years ago, when our grandmother came, and Laura had made it quite plain to me that I was right to think there was nothing to be gained by caring.

'She doesn't want help,' I said. I said it aloud, to Anna, I suppose, on the seat beside me. 'She sets you the impossible and gloats when you fail. She loves criticising, she gives herself the right to reject and then blames anyone she can lay her hands on. She doesn't care. She never has.'

Sometimes, while I was growing up I used to wonder if I'd had two and a half years of quite different memories from Laura, if there was a remote chance that her birth completely changed our mother's character and that when I was very little she was a generous, hospitable, relaxed woman. But that was not the case. I watched, I listened, and over the years it was not difficult to realise that the circumstances, the conditions that motivated Audrey had existed from her birth. She never had any choice about the way she behaved. What had happened was not that she had ever treated me with more tolerance, but that surprisingly early in life I had appreciated her lack of alternatives.

Before Laura was born I have only two clear impressions. One is of being held up by Leslie, high, so that my face was on a level with his. I could see individual brown hairs on his eyebrows, and bristles where his moustache ended, and it was very precarious. He was supporting me, I was not in danger of falling, but it was a dangerous thing to do. It must have been exceptional, it stands out, it seems to be the most extravagant gesture of affection.

Apart from that it is most true to say that I remember Leslie as part of the furniture, on chairs, on the stairs, in bed, because that is also how I remember myself. I know exactly what it felt like to play in the saucepan cupboard, because I spent days sitting surrounded by pale wooden walls, the door propped open with a flat iron, piling up, balancing, fitting together aluminium pots and lids, watching my mother's feet and ankles and legs up to the bottom of her apron walk over the floor, or her face come level with mine, wide-eyed, flat, as she washed or swept or polished the floor near me. I would not be surprised when she did that, it was not part of a game, because I would have heard her fill a bowl of water or seen the brush and pan or polishing rag sweep over another part of the floor, we would look past one another, unremarking because it was a normal stance for us to take, one on hands and knees, cleaning, the other in a three-foot-square enclosure.

I think that the reason I did not complain was not because I was unaware of different ways of behaving but because very early on I saw what she was doing it for. It was what she needed. She must have conveyed satisfaction, even contentment, or I would have reflected her unhappiness or restlessness, and I was not a miserable child. It seemed a reasonable way to go on, a justifiable use of the days.

I might not even have been forewarned of Laura's birth; certainly I was not prepared with stories of a little sister or brother. One day my mother was not there and the woman next door was, and I sat at our kitchen table crying, because I could not recognise where I was. There were bags of vegetables, tins of food, open pints of milk, the neighbour's dog gulping from a bowl on the floor and her two small children, with shoes on, running cars over the cupboard tops. I was not frightened that my mother would not reappear but I could not understand what had happened. I was certain this was not meant to happen to her room and that this was why it was important for her to keep things otherwise.

Perhaps to comfort me, perhaps coincidentally, another day Leslie and I sat at the table and ate an entire box of chocolates my mother had been given and not wanted, and I arranged every wrapper to fit back into the box. I kept it under my bed to demonstrate how neatly I had joined them together, but I could never find time, the right moment to show her.

As soon as they came back from hospital Laura slept in my room. It was a room full of all the furniture she and I would ever need in our adult lives, two single beds and half a discarded bedroom suite of my parents: two wardrobes, a dressing table, a stool, an armchair, and then Laura's cot. I would wake up when she cried to be fed and watch the door open and my mother quietly move between all the large brown wooden shapes to pick her up. Sometimes I could hardly see Audrey because it was dark and she sat very still while she nursed. I would think she had disappeared into the armchair until she stood up and changed Laura's nappy and laid her down again.

When my mother went out of the room I would get out of bed and pull the stool over to the cot. I would stand on it and lean over the bars until I could climb in, absolutely noiselessly, and then I would smell her. I would sniff and, holding my breath, put out my tongue to taste her skin. It was salt and sweet and moved as I licked her forehead. I would stroke, then hold, then clutch her hand or fat knee or ankle and she was unresisting, fleshy, pleased. Later, when it was just getting light I would hear my mother go downstairs and I would get out of the cot and creep along the landing to the top of the stairs and watch her. She wore her brown dressing gown with an apron over it and her hair was in silver curlers across her forehead. She had a broom with a sheet tied over the bristles, and some sponges, and every morning she washed and swept the hall, kitchen, all the downstairs floors that weren't carpeted.

Sometimes I'd go back to bed because I was cold, and sometimes I'd watch to see her carry out every cushion, singly, on tiptoe, like a series of secret parcels from the sitting room to the back door, and bang each one and then take it back and fetch another. When I could count, three on the settee, two on each armchair, I was surprised it was only eight journeys to and fro, it seemed more like twenty. She never saw me, and I never called to her. She looked, as far as a three-year-old can judge, quite happy.

I think I have few memories before Laura was born because life was eventless, passionless, and it was only after her arrival that I learnt to be expectant or to experience physical pleasure. I looked forward to that round baby in the cot, and from when she was very little I said I wanted to look after her.

While my mother was busy I found it far more interesting to sit on the settee opposite Laura, make her laugh, even bounce up and down a little than sit alone, but I had to take care because from quite early on, from before Laura could crawl even, I would look up and see our mother watching.

'Keeping her quiet,' she would say, 'that's the way,' and she would nod and go back to the kitchen, not quite closing the door behind her.

As Laura got older we had a game to play where we smacked one another's hands; I would always be the one to stop, stop giggling. 'She'll come,' I'd say and sometimes it was a near thing, we would only be quiet seconds before her shadow was on the glass of the kitchen door. She would not have found anything wrong but before she was back at the sink or stove, too soon, Laura's hand would creep out again, illicit, conspiratorial.

'Let's go and look,' she would say. 'She's busy, she won't know. Let's do it again.' So when Audrey had taken all the curtains down to wash we would creep upstairs into our parents' bedroom. It was at the end of the landing, huge, white, with a white bedspread and net curtains and a wardrobe full of black clothes.

'Touch,' Laura would say, 'go on,' and put her fingers on the brushes and combs on the dressing table, the two cut-glass bowls, lift the lace mats on the bedside tables, switch on the lamps. 'Come on,' she would say finally and lie down on top of the bed. 'Come on, quick,' and she would wriggle, she would wrinkle the cover until I had to join her. We didn't speak, we hardly touched, we were both dying for the ritual to be over. Almost immediately we would get up.

'Be quiet,' I would say going downstairs, 'hush.' We would clutch hold of each other, clinging with the desperation of relief.

Before I went to school I had been in our house, our father's shop, the greengrocer's, the baker's and the newsagent's. I had spoken to Laura constantly, and our mother at regular intervals. Less frequently I talked to our father, Mrs Tillson who worked his bacon machine, the fat lady who sold papers and the baker's boy. I was quite unprepared, when I went into a classroom, for the number of people, and even less for the noise and movement they produced. I remember bewilderment and uncertainty, but not fear. It was strange, it was exhausting – running, shouting, laughing, hands and bodies everywhere, an unchecked carelessness of activity, I could not visualise it ever happening again, it used up so much energy, and yet every day it recurred. I watched, I was relieved when it was over, but I did not mind it once I was there. What I minded was leaving and going back home. I was not jealous of Laura staying there with my mother, but I was worried, all day it bothered me what Laura might do.

'Be good,' I used to say to her when I packed my satchel, and until I found how my mother dealt with her I dreaded what games she might have attempted, what accidents her presence would have provoked.

'Keep still today, don't make her cross,' I used to warn, as though she could help it, as though her very breath was not disruptive. When I came home and found her sitting still, chairs and table keeping her safely immobile, I was relieved beyond belief.

'She likes it. It's a lovely idea,' I told my mother. 'I'll play it, too. It means nothing happens,' I told Laura. 'It means you'll be all right,' and that each morning I could leave the house without terror, every evening I could return to it intact.

I did not like to think, now I had an alternative, of being shut in all day long, of what it made you feel like, but I could not alter the arrangement they had managed to come to because it was the only way we could all survive; it was the only way Audrey could accept the differences. I also realised that Audrey was different, she did not like the outside, she behaved differently in it.

After Laura went to school I started to recognise differences more easily; good and bad, times of day, bad weekends, bad holidays. Bad evenings began at six thirty when Laura and I had eaten the tea and biscuits Audrey laid out, when we got down from the table and she asked, 'What are you doing now?'

We would lean against the door to the dining room, or Laura would loll in an armchair, and I could see as Audrey drew in her breath that she was frightened. All day had been devoted to ordering and it could all be undone in seconds, not because we were destructive girls who would run amok but just by our presence. We were not neat and inanimate, we could not be fitted into four walls like a sideboard; we were active, allied with disruption.

'Go upstairs. Homework. Revision,' I learned to say, but sometimes Laura refused and I could not stay and watch that. Laura would move round the room, not touching necessarily, but hovering over rugs, the occasional table, the mirror, the tablecloth, the glass cabinet. Audrey would close the kitchen door on her, wash up our three cups and saucers, three plates, the table, the floor, beneath our chairs, the plastic covers of the seats and the washing-up bowl. When she could bear it no longer she would fling open the door again. Laura would be staring out of the window, not touching the net curtains, but the room would be changed. It would not be ruffled or rumpled but it would no longer be pristine.

'Get out,' I would hear Audrey say, and Laura would not disobey, she would come upstairs, and then, not looking at one another, we each sat on our beds, fiddling, twisting our fingers, school ties, satchel straps. We would hear the Hoover, the banging of cushions, her footsteps as she went to the broom cupboard in the hall. Sometimes she cleaned the stairs as well, it sounded like thunder, and then Laura would throw herself down on the bed and cover her ears.

'I didn't do anything,' she would shout into the pillow. I would not answer.

In the afternoon when I came home from school Audrey would be waiting. She would stand by the stove, kettle at the ready, longing for tea to be over and done with. All through the summer I was eleven I stayed late to practise for a swimming gala. She did not like that; it upset her timetable.

'Sorry,' I said every evening as soon as I went into the kitchen. 'I'll eat it really quickly.'

One Friday she was sitting at the table and it was bare; cups and saucers, teapot, biscuits, were nowhere to be seen.

'What's the matter?' I said. I darted looks all round me to see if the walls had cracked, up at the ceiling, because only imminent destruction precipitated such departures from routine. Audrey could not answer. Quite gingerly I went over and sat beside her because she was moving her hands and from where I stood I could not see why. I did not touch her, I just leaned towards her. It was a paper bag she was fumbling with, tearing apart, folding each piece over and over, tearing, refolding, and then I noticed all around her chair tiny brown pieces; centimetre by centimetre she had ripped dozens of them to shreds.

'What's happened?' I said and without considering I put my hands out to still hers. 'What's the matter?' At the same instant I took them back, it was like being burned; it was impossible to imagine that anything would want to be near, you could not survive it. It was as if she was contaminated with deadliness, as if proximity would infect, I would reek of this, too, if I stayed by her; it emanated from every part, her bent fingers, her shoulders, her crumpled scarlet face. I could not remain, I got up, I almost ran away over to the door.

'What's the matter?' I asked again. 'What's happened, what?' and then she answered. She did not look up at me, she took a very long time to open and close her mouth, make sounds, words, a sentence and then she pointed with her head to the living room.

'Ask her,' she said. 'Ask her, that one in there.'

I went in and sat down and took my exercise book and pencil out of my satchel. I put my ruler level to draw columns and then I looked up at Laura.

'Well? What's the matter?' She did not stay where she was to tell me, she came and leaned over my chair, she even brushed her face against mine and said, 'I did something awful. I put glass in her tea. She had to go to hospital. I tried to kill her.'

I was immobilised. I listened while she recited details; I kept my shoulders away from her and scored lines on the page so hard the paper was torn.

'Look what'll happen,' I said when she had finally stopped talking, when she had pretended that nothing would come of it, that there would be no repercussions. 'I hate you.' It was the first time, and it was justified.

'Look,' I said and I wrote her name, too, I put it in capitals at the bottom of the column. 'You're my enemy,' I said. 'That's where you belong. I hate you more than anyone else.'

Not that evening, but every other day of the week, Audrey gave us supper at six thirty. If Leslie was back we all had a meal and if Leslie had not come in, because he had stopped at the golf club for drinks, or golf, or a combination, we watched his food cool on a plate and then rest on a saucepan of hot water, another plate on top, and listened to the extractor fan whirring above the dry meat, the hard potatoes and soft cabbage while we silently ate. When Leslie was there he did not eat silently, or smoothly. He carved his potatoes, he bared his teeth at his knife, he shovelled huge speechless forkfuls. I used to sit opposite, watching, and thought his mouth was like a cavern that would demolish every morsel around him, that it was ravenous, insatiable.

We would sit one on each side of the table, Laura and I eating, Audrey watching, and in the pauses when Leslie raised his head to chew and swallow she would convey small neat packages, tasteless chop and carrot to her own mouth, stare him out as he bent over his plate again, noisy, cheeks bulging.

In his wedding photos Leslie was slight, mousy-haired, slick, but after Laura was born he did not stay like that. He had a very high colour because even when he was at home he drank a reasonable amount, and small eyes and a small fat body with short arms and legs. He stuffed himself to saturation and then he said, 'I'm ready to burst. I'm ready to go off pop.' I wondered what Audrey would do with his pieces, if she could reassemble him to look anything like the man she had chosen to marry.

Laura and I ate out of hunger because they were small meals and because we got nothing afterwards. After supper the kitchen was cleaned ready for breakfast and the door closed tight at eight o'clock. Sometimes, when Audrey had placed her knife and fork on the edge of her plate, she would say, 'What's the news, then?' and Laura would be willing to talk about school, rounders, quizzes.

'Really, dear,' and, 'Goodness,' and 'What a to-do,' Audrey would say, as if she was listening with interest. 'More?' she would ask Leslie, and deposit a congealed spoonful on his plate and stand and watch.

Five times a year, though, there were different meals. Christmas, June when Laura and Leslie were born and January when Audrey and I were. At two p.m. at Christmas and seven p.m. on the other days Audrey roasted a chicken and baked a cake and Laura and I would wear our best dresses. In December and January we pulled crackers and in June we had ice-cream and every time we talked about previous birthdays and the presents we had received. Half an hour after we sat down Laura and I would stand and offer to wash up and Audrey would agree we could help.

'That's that, then,' she'd say as we put the last plates away. 'Over and done with. Back to normal tomorrow.'

'Let's do something,' Laura would say as we grew older. 'Whatever she says. Let's go out. Let's ask someone round.' I agreed to provide reasons for our outings, I didn't mind that; Audrey, too, liked to have us out of the house, but her other prohibition did not seem unreasonable. I would look at the polished tiles, the runners arranged on armchairs, the tiny vase of flowers, at every flat opaque shining surface, every closed drawer and for all the time I was at school I never brought friends home.

I recognised that for all the time I spent in the classroom I could acclimatise myself to noise, ruthless fidgeting, talking, moving, but I could also see that it could be unbearable, I could see more easily how she felt. I had learnt how to manage, but Laura would not. She tested, she provoked, she tried to force alteration.

'There's a robin in the garden,' she would remark. 'We had Mrs Biggs for biology again, she's useless,' and go on talking as if every remark was answered by a mother who sat smiling at the kitchen table instead of one who stood mute with her back against the door.

106

When I went up to our bedroom to do my homework Laura switched on the television in the sitting room.

'Look at this, it's fantastic,' I'd hear her call, and her voice had an echo to it because no one ever answered. Until Leslie came home, no one ever did, and although he watched he never talked about it.

In the summertime it became worse, or I expected it to be so, because every Sunday we went for an outing.

'You're not the only one who wants a break,' Audrey said. 'Whatever you'd like to pretend. I,' and she rapped her thin chest, 'I'm the skivvy who doesn't even get two weeks' bed and breakfast away. You'd think an afternoon out wouldn't be too much to ask.'

I was terrified. I did not want to see her dressing up, wearing clothes we had not known she owned, high-heeled shoes and a smile, her arm latched into Leslie's. I did not want to hear her confess, laughing, that these excursions to houses and boats and flowers were to look at places she had once aspired to live in. I hated to see her sigh against Leslie's shoulder as she pointed to mansions with private moorings and murmur, 'We all had our dreams.' I did not see why she should become pitiable. It had seemed to me that although she chose a life that involved considerable difficulties for others it was still legitimate. I did not blame her for pursuing solitude and order, preferring them to uncertainty and disarray. In return I did not want to be presented with her actions as a pale emulation of unattainable pleasures. Nor did I want her to come home disaffected, yearning for an ideal that tidiness, cleanliness had not provided. All the time we paraded beside rose-bushes and public lawns I could not wait for it to be over, for her to be shut up safely again.

'Let's go home now,' I would say every week, long before it was time. 'Don't, please,' I would plead with Laura. 'Don't suggest anywhere else.' At every proposal she made – Windsor, Maidenhead – I held my breath, because it was appallingly obvious that Audrey also regarded them as dangerous.

'With him?' she'd say. 'I wouldn't trust him with a rat.' And she'd laugh at the feebleness of her excuse, she meant it was unthinkable to stray so far from the familiar, she meant she had no confidence in anything outside her own surroundings.

'I like the rose-garden,' I said. 'I don't want to go as far as Kew. I don't feel like walking. I'll get sick on a boat.' But Laura took no notice, it did none of us any good.

107

'We'll show madam,' Audrey said one week. 'We'll give Madam Laura a treat for her to boast about.'

We went to a tea-room, that was as much of an excursion as we dared, and it was as catastrophic as I expected, screaming, wailing at one another over a strange table of dried-up cakes, slopping saucers of tea, and what frightened me most of all was that I did not see how it was possible to grow up, away from this. If all that hatred and anger could surface over sandwiches and sponge cake I did not see how the rest of the world, jobs, people, travel, could ever be contemplated.

She was obviously right; for survival it was necessary to stay at home.

'She was really nice to me,' I said to Laura when I started menstruating. I had lied because that was easier than to explain.

'Come here.' She had grabbed me. 'You're bloody,' she had accused, 'go and see to it. Don't ask me, I can't do anything, I can't stop that muck.' I had known that this was the last chance, that I had been waiting for womanhood to provide her with the opportunity to reward me. 'Poor Barbara,' she could have said, she would not even have needed to touch me, 'you're one of us now.' 'Go and stop it,' she had said. 'Get those things off and cleaned.' I had known nothing would ever make any difference, that I had been quite mistaken in believing that she would ever take and comfort me under her wing.

'She can be nice if she tries,' I said. I did not need to, Laura would have been the first to sympathise with my distress, but I could not bear it, to lose the fantasy of all those years, to discover loss of past, present and future at the same moment, and watch Laura gloat over my disillusion.

'Stupid,' she'd say. 'I always told you she was wicked.' I could have argued about the occasions when she had meant well, the piano and ballet lessons she had forced upon me, the homework she applied herself to check. 'Only to spite me. She favours you. That doesn't mean she likes you,' Laura would have answered, and she would have been right.

By the time Laura was thirteen and I was fifteen I was ready to go; I was only waiting for a feasible plan for supporting both of us to present itself before I announced this to Laura. I was not unhappy, I thought, I had simply decided that it would not be any more unreasonable for us to leave than for my mother to continue to behave as she did. I acknowledged that her view of life was not untruthful, and that her means of pursuing it was not therefore cruel, but she refused to accept my understanding. In those circumstances all my presence indicated was opposition; it would be better to get out altogether, and there was even less reason for Laura to remain. I decided I would stay at school until Christmas, learn to type and then find a job in London. When I found somewhere there for us to live Laura could change schools. I worked out how much I could ask my parents to contribute towards our keep, because once we left they would not pay for our food, and ordered two local London newspapers from the agent near the school so that I could see the price of flats to rent. Twice, two Saturdays, I said I was invited to Anne's and caught the train to Victoria. I examined noticeboards for rooms to let, bought an *A to Z* and walked around Kennington and Vauxhall. They were shabby places but they were full of people who had no plans for my life and I felt excited. I could see forward, I could envisage Laura and me in those streets together, there were lots of girls like us, everyone was young, I could foresee a time when we would have nothing to worry about.

After Mercy came to stay, when she had lived with us long enough for me to realise that it was quite impossible for me to leave, I told myself that I was fortunate that had happened before it was too late for me to make up lost ground academically. Now I still had the chance to work for O levels, go on to A levels, even university. If it had been three months later I would have left it too late to revise and then I would have lost everything. After Mercy had lived with us for three months I did not expect anything at all from Laura, nor did my presence alleviate the way Audrey felt about Mercy, or even demonstrate my sympathy for her; the reason it was quite obviously impossible for me to go was that Audrey could not be left alone with her mother.

On the day Mercy arrived, Laura took her cases up and stayed with her. I crept to listen outside the door and I could hear the murmur of voices, no arguments, no reproaches, just talking. At teatime Laura took a tray up to Mercy and the next morning took her breakfast. At that early stage even Laura could not have intended betrayal, but that did not affect Audrey.

'She's got what she wants now,' she said, slamming dishes as I wiped up. 'She's in a position to take. That's all she's ever done, my mother, take, that's all she gets pleasure from,' and it became very clear that Audrey was right.

'I'll go up and give it to her,' Laura said every time Mercy's meal tray was ready. 'I don't mind. I don't mind seeing her.'

'Little lamb,' Audrey would say. 'She's got you where she wants you.'

'She's nice,' Laura said to me. 'Guess what she said about Audrey when she was young. You ought to hear her. She hasn't got a good word to say for her.'

She spent hours in Mercy's room. She watched television with Mercy, she giggled with her; I heard them while I sat upstairs revising, while they sat together on the sofa. They became a unit, Mercy and Laura, and they were quite deliberate about it, they knew quite well the way they affected us. From when Mercy first visited us, every other Sunday for tea, I knew why Audrey hated her. She would droop in one of the armchairs, spilling over the sides, her legs open, and hold out her arms and Laura would go to her. She would stroke Laura's knees or her cheeks and I would shiver. As soon as Audrey had made tea I would go out of the room.

'How can you?' I used to ask. She would just shrug.

'She's all right when you get used to her.'

'She's hateful,' I would say, and at times she was.

'It'd crack Aud's face to smile. She's a real scrubber, floor, tables, chairs, whatever she can lay her hands on. Nothing's too dirty for our Aud,' she would say when Audrey was out of the room. There was nothing to say back, nothing to do except avoid her smile. When she came to us she screeched, 'Aud,' and you could hear her wherever you were in the house, the incessant complaints about television, bus services, newspapers, industry, government. She swore viciously about the lot of them. It was hateful, all that hatred and destructiveness welling up all the time in her, and it was through my mother that she wanted to let it all out.

'Listen to this, Aud,' she'd yell. 'Get a load of this,' whether it was something she had just heard on the radio or some remembered event in her life. She would shout through closed doors; heard, unheard, it all came to the same thing.

After only a week my mother made her stay in her room for all her meals. Laura thought that was unkind and went and sat with her. 'You come,' she said, but I would have locked the door and starved her, poisoned her. I would have smothered her.

110

When she was downstairs she knocked, bumped, jarred, she did not walk through a room or sit in a chair without deliberate disruption. At teatime on Sundays, when we did all eat together, she cut her food, poured her tea with such ferocity that it seemed unbelievable she had not scarred her plate or hurled the pot.

'She's lonely,' Laura said. 'She wants someone to talk to. And she's interesting.' I did not answer. I wanted to tell my mother that I knew; that it must have been appalling to live with all that flailing, all those reversals of anger and love, hugs and screams; it must have been appalling to learn to survive in a world where the only reality was a vicious chaos. Order was the only form of protection available to you, I wanted to say. It was not harmful, it was courageous.

For the three years Mercy lived with us there was no way of making it better; silence, co-operation were best, but they were palliatives. Mercy was incurable. 'Leslie's well out of it,' she would say when he did not appear at Sunday teatime. She did not know how much I agreed. He talked about golf and his new bacon slicer when he was there, he smelt of whisky and beer; compared to Mercy nothing he could think of was harmful. When Mercy went into hospital Audrey cried, but it was relief that she was out of the way. Someone else would deal with her rampaging and undermining, her criticisms of every meal, the sneers at furniture, clothes, accent, vocabulary, occupation, attitudes.

'Too fucking good, that's what you think you are,' she said to Audrey so many times it ought to have been meaningless. 'You were hard to have and harder to keep, that's you.' It never lost its fury.

When Mercy died it was Laura who was with her at the hospital, and it was Leslie who arranged her funeral. The chief reason the ceremony saddened me was that Laura, Leslie, Audrey and I, two nurses and two churchwardens were the only people there and there was nothing we could say to one another about her. Afterwards nobody, not even Laura, seemed to mourn her; her absence seemed more notable because Audrey cleared out her room and the house stank of disinfectant than because any of us were sorrowful. We did not even talk about her; it was not as though she had never existed but as if we wished that could be the case.

In the weeks after she died I went for interviews and I was accepted at Exeter University. It was an uncontentious way to leave home and I had no reason to stay there any more. Audrey was quieter, Leslie still largely absent and Laura could undoubtedly look after herself. I also decided that there was no point in minding about Laura and Mercy, it simply meant that we were more dissimilar than I had believed. I would not argue with her about it, it was not even necessary to discuss it, we would still accept one another, but at a reasonable distance. I must have conveyed the certainty of my decisions quite strongly because neither Audrey nor Leslie attempted to persuade me to remain at home and Laura did not express regret or envy at my departure. Audrey said Exeter was a beautiful place, she believed, and Leslie that he supposed I knew what I was doing. When my exam results came Laura said she'd look forward to coming to visit me. The last few weeks I was at home life was almost amicable; we amused ourselves in different rooms, different places, without parading or demanding reasons. It was not tolerance, but it was approaching a truce.

I did not exactly expect university to be like school, but I tackled it the same way; I left nothing to chance. I joined societies and made friends so I would not be lonely, I studied so I would not fail exams, and I appeared to be confident that the organisation of my life left little to be desired. I was fortunate in that Exeter was not prone to revolution so I did not have to subscribe or even argue about the overthrow of the establishment. I might even have been thought to be in a feminist vanguard because I presented a mind of my own, a determination to follow any course of action I had decided upon. I was not easily deflected; I did not dare to be.

The only disquiet I felt was not when I went home in the holidays, because reversion only demands patience, but when Laura visited me. I had foreseen her scorn, her incomprehension of my routines, her disagreement with my criticism of the outrageous; I should not have been upset.

'We're not alike,' I said to myself and my friends. 'It's absolutely what I expected. It's something I've had to come to terms with.'

In my second year, when I had been to dances, films, pubs with three boyfriends, when I had slept with no one, I went out with Graham. He was a good-looking final-year student. The second time we went out we went back to his room. I could not wait to make love, for ever to make sure of his humour, his sincerity. He told me about his childhood, his day school, his parents' house, politics, ambitions for him; he deprecated, he confided. From Christmas to June we slept together almost every night and in the holidays wrote every other day. During my last year he visited me weekly and when I finished I followed in the same career, and he continued with the same loving and tolerance and passion. I wanted him but I was fearful; without the vicissitudes of exams or separation or reunion to excuse disagreements, I did not see how we could continue successfully.

'You'll have to meet my parents,' I said eventually. 'They're just as awful as Laura says.'

'I'll wait and see,' he said and took my hand. 'Don't worry.'

He hugged me hard after the first visit.

'I know now what I'm letting myself in for. I'll need to eat a very large meal before or after we go there, cultivate a proper respect for doilies and cups kept on saucers, an interest in the British Open and a very blind eye where everything else is concerned. Of course they don't mean well,' he said, and I found that reassuring. 'But who does? We'll visit once a month and that'll be all there is to it. They're tight, tedious and tense, but it's not the end of the world. Everyone,' and he gently shook me, 'survives their families. In the end.'

He adhered to those conditions precisely – every four weeks he was so bland and polite to their faces and so hungry and bored behind their backs that I came to believe that was all there was to it. I could visit without misery, I invited them at Christmas and Anna's birthday without guilt, I treated them as though it was quite normal that they should be left behind.

'Shouldn't you ring her?' Graham said to me the week after Laura and I had argued. 'It's easier for you. You aren't the one who has to apologise. Besides, you'll want to talk to her again soon. You won't be happy with leaving things like this.'

'I'm responsible, you mean?' I asked. I took no notice when he shook his head, 'I'm pregnant,' I answered back. 'She ought to have some consideration for how I feel.'

'That's difficult if she doesn't know.' And he went and stood behind Anna and stroked her shoulder, as if she needed soothing or protecting in the face of irrationality.

'Let's leave it,' I said. 'We don't have to talk about it all the time.'

But I did, every moment I spent alone washing up or ironing or peeling vegetables was to a solitary accompaniment. 'You listen,' I would say to Graham as soon as he came home in the evening. 'You know what she's been like. You've seen the way we've had to make amends for her to Audrey and Leslie. We've had that scene a hundred times over. It's been called different things; when we were

113

children it was picking up the pieces after Laura had broken the rules, since we've grown up it's understanding why Laura has strings of boyfriends, why she calls marriage the suburb of success, why she's too sensitive to go to Henley even twice a year. You look at it too, now. History's a one-way process for Laura. If she thinks Audrey's a bad influence, that's got to be the truth; if Laura chooses to analyse me, she's got the answers, and if she's found promiscuity doesn't work she wants more than ever to destroy what's orderly. What she ought to see,' I would tell him, and he would not ignore me, he would sit in his chair at the table, grave, watching; he would hold out his arms so Anna could stand within them and I would face the pair of them and it was oil and water, they floated quite unmoved over my anger, 'is that what really goes on is this, here in this room, orderly, ordinary and she can leave it alone. I don't want to hear how this is a failure, I want her to look at what really exists, I want her to see beyond her inventions that this is worth having.'

'Of course it is,' Graham would answer. He would stay still for a little while after I had finished talking and then he would lift Anna onto his lap or stand and pull her to him. 'Come on, Annikins, let's see about your story. Let's go and see what's on television.' She would go, not willingly, she would sometimes complain he had lifted her too roughly or she wanted a drink, a biscuit, a bribe to leave my company, but it was not as if she wanted to be with me, there was nothing to be got out of that, but because it was less troubling to watch than to wonder.

'You come, too,' Graham would say sometimes, and we would all sit in front of the television for half an hour, or I would turn the pages of the paper while Graham read aloud.

'Why don't you have a rest?' he would suggest. Then, 'I'll put Annie to bed,' and in the promise of restoration that false calm induced, night after night, earlier and earlier, it was never even twilight, I lay crouched and watched hours of the evening sun, I lay like the embryo inside me, uneasy, temporarily subdued.

'Barbara? Awake?' Graham would say when he came to bed. 'Better?' I would not close my eyes as he took off his clothes. I liked looking at his long arms and legs, the soft pale skin round his hips, but I wanted him to stay like that, statuesque, still, an image I could preserve with as much affection as he gave the photographs of his mother and father.

'Move over. There. Keep still,' he would say; gently, he would lay his hands on my breasts, he would run fingers like dead leaves

114

onto my stomach. 'Barbara, Barbara,' he would say, he would be swollen, huge in seconds, I could feel him. 'Ready?' he would ask and although I nodded, I never was, not as he wanted, not as he remembered. 'Remember with Anna?' he said, and I would say yes very quickly, I did not want comparisons for encouragement. When I was three and four and five and six months pregnant we had lain down on the landing outside our bedroom door, we stood up against the airing cupboard, because all the confidence I had discovered in accomplishing pregnancy and ordering the house coalesced in a sexual energy, and this time all I felt was an ache, a need for assuagement. He stroked, he kissed me, he came and moaned briefly and so did I, and afterwards I suppose he too was grateful for that degree of relief.

Three weeks after Laura and I argued she telephoned, but she did not say that she was sorry.

'It's been awful,' she said. 'Barry, Louise's husband, rang.' When she told me what had happened I asked, 'How's Nicole?' Quite deliberately I put the child before her, and she hardly noticed.

'I'm going away,' she said. 'I've got to get away from all this. Remember Martine? I'll go with her. She's all right, really.' I wanted to tell her that Martine was a whore, that she used promiscuity like a terrorist, she aimed quite deliberately at the most vulnerable point, she ran away from the carnage laughing.

'You know what it'll be like,' I said. 'What's the point in just chasing after other men? You know what she'll do. Don't expect me to pick up the pieces this time,' I muttered. 'Don't come crying because Martine won't play the game by your rules.'

'Don't you ever think you have to be responsible?' I wanted to ask. 'I'm pregnant, I'm not your mother,' I wanted to shout. 'That's how she wants me to behave,' I said to Graham. 'I don't care. I've got other things to think about.' I pushed past him, I washed the floor, emptied cupboards while I spoke. 'She ought to see she can't get away with everything. Why should she say that to me and escape scot free? She upsets me,' I said. 'It's stupid. I feel upset, it's not anger, it's upsetness. I feel sick, I ache, I'm exhausted.'

By the date she was due to leave all I wanted was sleep. I was caught beween turmoil and discomfort, nausea and resentment; I wanted to be rid of them, I wanted oblivion. For days I went to bed. I told myself that I would wake up and it would all be over; I would be calm and forgiving again, rest would have restored my adult perspective.

When she had been gone three days Graham came into the bedroom and said, 'Laura rang. From Corfu, early this morning.' I forced myself not to clench, I watched myself smile at him. 'Instead of a postcard,' he said. 'To say hello.'

'Instead of nothing,' I said. 'She's always got a motive. It's ingratiation, she's doing what she was told not to, she's having her little fling with Martine and she doesn't like it. She's making sure of a welcome when she gets back. She's little-girl Laura, but I suppose I should be able to cope with that. I've had enough practice.'

I laid my hands across my round stomach and slid out of bed. I went downstairs to Anna. I put Laura as far at the back of my mind as I had when I went to school and she stayed behind, when she went to Mercy's room and I stayed with Audrey. I put her back in a world of childhood where I had no attachment any more.

The day after she came back she telephoned. When I had spoken to her I said to Graham, 'I was right. Same old story. Listen to what Laura dreamt, listen to what Laura discovered. I told her that was no good. I told her fantasies were irrelevant, I said Audrey and Mercy and childhood weren't important any more. I told her I was pregnant,' I said, and I had heard her silence; 'I told her about reality. I told her she could come here, though, she was welcome to come and see this if she wanted to.'

The first week she was home she visited twice, and after that she came nearly every afternoon, and although at times it was provoking it also provided an odd degree of comfort. She did not say, 'What's wrong?' when she first saw me, although it would have been a fair question – my face had swollen with my stomach and it was scarlet; it looked bruised and pinched simultaneously. She sat at my kitchen table with Geraldine and Jessica and did not intrude with her holiday stories. She listened to us and then sat nursing a smile instead of a child, raising her eyebrows when we talked about husbands, resentments, discussed our married lives.

'See?' I could hear her laughing.

'You'll see, too,' I would answer back. 'This is the best you and Jas could have hoped for, you leave this alone.'

'How is it today?' she asked almost every time she came, and I said, 'Better. It's just a question of mind over matter,' I told her if I had stopped retching before she arrived, and she did not argue. 'Lots of women go on the whole time.'

116

She nodded, it was so unremarkable as not even to deserve sympathy. 'You don't look too wonderful. What's going wrong?' she could have said if it was important. 'Shouldn't you do something about it?' But she never did.

'Don't overdo it,' was the most she ever said. She did not mean that seriously, it was an excuse to make comparisons. 'Remember when we were little?' she would say as she watched me line a cupboard with fresh paper. 'We swore we'd never do housework, worry about clean teacloths and polished draining boards. Do you?'

'No,' I said. 'We never talked about housework. Besides,' I added, 'she's changed. OK, she overdid it, but she's let up a bit now. If you went you could see for yourself.'

'You could inspect this place,' she said, 'eat your dinner off the proverbial kitchen floor. Spotless; apple pie order; another perfect achievement.'

'If you don't like it,' I said, 'you don't have to come.' I knew, of course, that it was preferable, sitting at my scrubbed table, drinking coffee, to being alone.

'It makes a change,' she said, 'seeing how the other half live.'

'Boring young women, you mean?' I asked, 'discussing child care instead of interesting old women discussing retirement?' She shrugged. 'I know it's not that scintillating,' I agreed, 'Ben and the nursery toilets, Melanie and the sandpit, but you do have the choice.'

'No.' She smiled. 'They're fascinating. Really. Take me out of myself.'

'I'm dropping, I've got to have a rest,' I started to say, and I would leave her to provide tea for Geraldine and Jessica and their children. I let her go shopping. One weekend I let her take Anna out for the day, I went upstairs and left her to discover that the skills I had acquired could not be counterfeited or learnt overnight. I would go to bed and lie expecting to hear her call for help, or Anna cry that she wanted me, but that did not happen.

Often when Graham came in she would still be there, and I would watch her and remember how I used to be welcoming and energetic.

'Let me put Anna to bed,' she would offer. 'You look worn out.' He would deny that with pleasure.

'You have a drink,' he'd say. I would listen to her questions about his work, her attentiveness, the concentration she could apply to events outside her own body. They would sit at the table; words and laughter and drink would skitter around in my head, I would watch

117

them through a haze of heaviness. I would sit and look from them to Anna and she would see and come and ask if I was still ill. I would reassure her but I did not hug or caress her, I found her perfection painful to be close to. It was not frightening, this state, I told myself. If I were to discuss it I would dismiss it with the very words I used, dream-like, abstracted; it would immediately be apparent as no more than the exclusivity of pregnancy. It would go, I told myself, like sickness, like exhaustion; this faint panic of abstraction would vanish. They were not distressing symptoms, all that was distressing was that I had no one to confide them in.

'I worry,' I wanted to say when I went to the clinic each month, to a doctor I had seen before, someone I recognised. 'It doesn't feel right. I'm frightened,' I would say, instead of giving the answers they wanted. I would wait while he nodded, examined me thoroughly, gently, slowly, and at the end of it patted my stomach.

'You're fine,' I imagined hearing, and after every visit I took off my gown and looked down at my body with momentary reassurance. It was too familiar a body to be deceiving everyone; they would have found out if anything was wrong. 'Fine,' I said to myself on the bus home. 'Sickness, exhaustion, they're normal reactions.' As if that was what I had been told.

'Fine,' I replied to Graham whenever he asked.

'You're sure?' he always answered, and instead of his concern pleasing me, it became the focus of all my discontent. I would watch for him from our bedroom window, the long time he took to close the front gate, the fumbling with his key. 'Any one there?' he would say. He did not raise his voice with any enthusiasm; it could not be heard above the television. He would go along the hall into the kitchen, he never came upstairs to see if he could find me.

'Hello,' he would say when I went down into that room. Every time he turned his painless face I wanted to spatter it with torment. He would flinch, it made him recoil that I could so reject the instant of his return, and then he would turn, too. He smiled at Laura and offered her a glass; he presented her with lemon and ice and easiness. When she had gone we sat in silence by the television.

'Being nice,' I would say, 'is easy if you can turn it on and off. If you can choose where to mean it. Laura and Anna are a good audience, they say, "Thank you for taking notice." You perform.' I would raise my voice, wave my hands like a minstrel. 'You like harmonious duets, it hurts you to be involved where you might hear the wrong answer. You like getting it right. You look at me and think, "Barbara feels bad, leave her alone."'

'Barbara always feels bad.' He half-laughed as he answered. 'Barbara always wants to be left alone.' And he would get up.

'It's difficult,' I agreed. I pretended to consider that. 'You don't like watching when it's not going smoothly,' I would say. 'You wish you didn't have to care, you don't like the fact that because you're good enough to ask doesn't mean I'm good enough to give the right answer. You fail me,' I said. 'Every time you open your mouth you mark me down as a failure for needing the question to be put. You pretend, you cheat, you lie, you don't care.'

Then, as soon as I had roused him to anger and scorn, I drew back. It seemed wicked, as though I had forced him into self-mutilation.

'No, leave it,' I would say. 'I'll be better soon, I exaggerate. Understand,' I asked, as though that was all there was to it, and after each quarrel was over I would try to restore equanimity by hospitality. I would invite Geraldine and Paul, Jessica and Laura to supper, and watch us perform as allies. I would see Graham sit back, easy, unrestricted. Until it was nearly time for people to go I would think that it would continue past then, that animosities had been dispelled. But each truce became briefer, each armistice less affable, and only moments after we were left alone the house would become a desert again, I would resume battle for occupation of a single oasis of peace.

'Ask your sister,' Audrey said when I telephoned. She knew I was sick because I had to explain why it was impossible to spend an hour driving to visit her. 'She's always round to see you, it's late to be going on like that now. She works with nurses, doesn't she? Get her to do some finding out for you.'

I was relieved, astonished that I had not thought of that before. It could be quite simple, I would ask Laura why she never commented on my nausea and she would answer, 'Oh, I spoke to Beryl about that, she's a nurse—' 'Is she?' I would nod with admiration '—and Beryl said it's nothing, people just don't talk about it, it might put too many women off,' and we would both laugh, I could see us, grinning like schoolgirls over the kitchen table. It was not difficult after that to say it, I was all ready to smile at her reply. But she shook her head.

'I'd ask someone medical if I were you, I'm no good. I'd call an ambulance if someone got a splinter, I've got no idea about women throwing up past the regulation three months. It's no good asking the nurse we've got,' she said after a moment, 'or Matron, she's hopeless too. St John's Ambulance primary grade certificate is probably the most she's ever aspired to, and that was in nineteen hundred. Is it really still that bad?' she asked after that. 'Perhaps you shouldn't do so much. Rushing around all the time can't help, you ought to sit down sometimes. Ask at the clinic. Why can't they tell you?'

'Maybe,' I said, 'it's not that vital, really.' I could hear her discussing it with Graham. 'We only want the best for her,' they would say. I did not want her there in the evenings any more, I did not want her sipping the gin she brought and assessing me. I lied, I invented an occasion to which she was not invited, I taunted her with details of the food I would prepare, the man I would invite for Jessica. For a week after that she stayed away.

'I missed you,' Anna shouted when she came back.

'How's it going?' Graham asked. She smiled and nodded. She had not even noticed, she had been quite happy with her solitary amusements.

In December she said, 'Six months now, since Jas went. It's helped,' and I waited for her thanks, 'to set myself goals. I think I'll wait until eight o'clock to have another drink, I'll read a book on Saturday evening, I'll go for a walk on Sunday, I won't even try and stay in bed and read the paper.' She sighed. 'Christmas won't be good, though. I dread times when the best you can hope for is to get drunk enough not to notice it isn't over. I'll go out with Beryl, though, that won't be too bad, and there's a party at the Home. I don't mind that usually. It'll pass, that's the main consolation. And I'll watch you do it in style again here.'

I answered that having her and Audrey and Leslie for a day was hardly grandeur. 'Why don't you go to Beryl's?' I wanted to ask. Instead I agreed that she would look after Anna while I shopped and baked and decorated. Two days before Christmas, when I knew she was not likely to come I made myself a new dress, spent careful solitary hours undressed in front of the mirror, bulging, undisguised.

When I tried it on, Anna frowned and said, 'You look like a doll.' It was not untrue; my face was puffy, chalky under powder, there

120

was a resemblance to the smooth, soft plastic effigy I had bought for her present. I woke that night dreaming of it, half-crying because all the effort of transformation was wasted. I turned to Graham and said, 'Listen,' and there had been no one there.

Then I heard the small bell the telephone made when it was put back and called 'Who is it, what's the matter?' He pretended not to hear. I went out onto the landing and said it louder and he looked up as though I was not there, he was not sure who he was talking to.

'It was Laura,' he said. 'She went to see Jas. He threatened her so she ran away, she got a taxi back. She was frightened, she just wanted to talk to someone.'

'You?' I said. 'Now?'

'Of course not,' he answered. 'But I told her you were asleep. Ring her,' he suggested. 'She can't have gone to sleep in two minutes, get her to talk to you about it.'

I walked back to the bedroom.

'What's the matter?' he asked. He followed me as though he had no idea.

'Nothing,' I answered. 'If Laura's fine, that's all that matters. As long as Laura does what she wants, that's the vital thing. Nothing I've said matters, it's fine, quite all right that Laura should use me as long as she wants and then treat my help like so much nonsense. I've failed to console her for Jas, I haven't worked. That's Laura's decision, that's what she rang up to tell me. "I've decided on Jas, you needn't have bothered."'

I got back into bed. I had not looked at him, I did not want excuses, I did not want to hear any justification of her rejection.

'Keep her away from me,' I said, 'that's all. Keep her away from me at Christmas. It shouldn't be difficult, it's what she wants, she couldn't say it more plainly. She couldn't make it any clearer she regards me as useless.'

When she came on Christmas Day she was late. She looked at all of us with her little smile, she walked round the sitting room and gave everyone her parody of a kiss. I got out, I stayed by myself in the kitchen. Even then she came after me.

'Get out,' I said. Even though she knew I meant it seriously she delayed, she pretended and provoked until I thought I would hit her. When it was all ready and we sat down to eat I wanted to order her away from the table.

'You're putting us off,' Leslie said as I turned over a piece of meat, pushed my vegetables to one side. 'The spectre at the feast.'

'She doesn't look as well as she could,' Audrey said. I cut Anna's food and answered that I had been busy.

'None of this bought and cooked itself,' I said. 'I've been at it for weeks.'

Laura looked up from her plate. 'Yet no one else could help, could they?' she asked. I swallowed, and she turned to Graham. 'There were offers, weren't there?'

I stood up, I went away and left them sitting there, I wanted all of them abandoned for ever until I heard Anna say again, 'Where's Mummy?' and Audrey, 'Graham, go and have a look, someone should keep an eye on her.' So I came back downstairs.

Audrey touched my arm. 'All right?' she asked. 'You come and sit down. Come and see what I've got you, eat your pudding and come and look at your present, I went out specially.'

'I'll do it,' Laura said, 'I'll wash up,' and I did not argue.

I would do anything to be in another room from her so I said thank you and went and unwrapped the bedjacket Audrey had chosen, and the kimono from Graham and scent from Anna. When Laura came and took out her scarf, her talcum powder, they could have been labelled second best. She pretended to take no notice and started to read to herself the book she had given Anna. I could not sustain it. For an instant, sitting on the floor, shut out from the rest of us, I thought she would start to rock.

'Have a look at that with her,' I whispered to Graham, 'that Raymond Briggs. It's far too old for Anna, talk to her, I can't yet, you do it.'

'We'll be off in a minute,' Audrey said at intervals after four o'clock. 'When he's fit to drive. Get him some coffee.' At five o'clock I did, I wanted their bags collected, their presents gone. I watched as they got into the car, as it backed and slowly pulled out, their heads side by side, and I turned to Laura.

'Well,' I said, 'I suppose it wasn't really that bad.' 'I wish you'd go, too,' I should have said. She slid Anna off her lap.

'It was appalling, I hated every minute. Lies, pretending, that's all it's about. And you do the same,' she said. I did not answer.

'Go and see,' I said after a minute to Anna, 'if Daddy'll change channels on television for you. Go and get him to read that new book.'

'It's too dangerous, isn't it?' she said. She watched Anna walk backwards to the kitchen door. 'Too dangerous for you to look at what you're really covering up. What you're really frightened of.' I felt my stomach kick and I said I did not want to hear.

'Of course not,' she said. 'You prefer not to deal with anything like that, you like the way you cover up everything wrong inside you. You don't ever look at you and Audrey side by side.' I could have clapped with the relief of Audrey's name; until then I had not known what she was talking about, insinuating, angular, looming over my kitchen. I had been irrationally fearful of hearing any more. Now I was not, I was almost amused.

'Don't be silly,' I said. She came over to me and I did not back away.

'All that matters to you is self-control.' She swayed. 'Secrecy, no matter what's going on, what other people are feeling, what things are really like. Mechanical,' she said, 'blank, void.'

'You've drunk too much, that's all that's wrong,' I said, and then she came closer to me than an embrace could have made us. 'If I'm that unbearable,' I said, 'you'd better not come for a bit.' I held out her coat and waited for her. I opened the kitchen door. 'It's up to you,' I said. I did not push her through it.

'No,' and she tugged the handle away from me. 'You're the one.'

In January when Anna's playgroup began again I was alone and because of that I was frightened. I thought that I would explode, my flesh seemed to be waiting to burst through, I had too few layers of skin; although there was nothing to be seen it itched, intensely. I could not bear Graham near me. Even when Anna held my hand it was an irritant. Geraldine invited us to see her kittens and I could not do it, I could already feel the cat, its fur seething as it rubbed against my leg. Then, and sometimes when I looked at the cot, the nappies and babyclothes I had sorted, washed, stacked in drawers, I would find I had to make an effort to breathe; that I needed to count to remind my body how to continue; that surviving was not automatic.

'Stay with me,' I said to Graham one morning. He did not reason or dissuade. 'No, you can't,' I contradicted myself. 'You'll need all the leave you can get next month when it's born.' He tried to take my hand.

'Why don't I phone Laura?' he asked. 'Why don't I ask her to pop in? If I do it,' he said, 'if I say it's a favour to me, it won't have

123

anything to do with you. She won't mind.' I was too desperate to care if she did.

The next day she arrived at the same time as Graham came home from work.

'I didn't bring you a box of chocs,' she said. 'Giving you that could be open to misinterpretation. How is it?'

'Almost gone,' I said, 'it's given way to heartburn now. Anyway, come and say goodnight to Anna.'

Then she came nearly every day, and I confessed that I could not swallow easily, I showed her brown patches on my skin, I held her hand over my heart while it palpitated. I said, 'It's supposed to be easier the second time.' She listened, she seemed to take me quite seriously but she did not always answer.

'You could tell, couldn't you? Couldn't I?' I wanted to ask. 'If I was all right? You've seen it, what it looks like to die, that's not what's going to happen to me?' and for the last three weeks all of the past months gathered together. It was never out of my head, it was all I thought about and the reason I could not say it was not because I feared to appear ridiculous, but because it would be unbearable.

The very last week before the baby was due I thought I was regaining my equilibrium. When I talked to Anna, or as I cleaned or tidied up, or told Graham who had visited us during the day, I thought I recognised the disembodied commentator who dispensed such a reliable narrative. I thought I could be part of her again, trust in her again, but I could not remember how to do it. Sometimes there were trance-like moments when I could not only remember but re-engage with peace, when I could measure myself between ridicule and encouragement, panic and exhaustion.

'I'm worried about what'll happen to Anna,' I said one day. The thought that, when I went into hospital, Laura and Anna and Graham should remain in the house without me was unbearable; I could not visualise the moment when I would return. I could not dismiss the fantasy of obliteration.

'It'd be just as easy for her to go to Geraldine's. She'd be grateful, she's got her mother coming and it'll keep Melissa quieter if Anna's there. It's difficult, but I do know what I think is best. What she'd like best,' I said very often, and assumed that must register as the factor of most importance. 'That's what I want for her. That's what'll make her happy.' Laura and Graham both kept silent.

When it came to it I had no say in the matter. My waters broke one morning while Laura was pouring tea and half an hour later she rang for an ambulance. I could not stand up any more by then. I remember staring at the particles of cement that obtruded between the red floor tiles, the tiny flecks of black and silver, scarlet and brown bleeding from under the sealed surface. Distantly, receding and booming, I heard Laura shouting into the telephone but all I wanted was the space between pains. I was crawling when the ambulance men came but they pushed and buckled me onto a stretcher. I pulled and shouted against the flatness all the way to the hospital. When they opened the doors and I tried to get back on all fours again I saw Graham in a stiff coat standing against a white doorway.

'It'll be all right,' he said. The hospital walls rose and fell away from me. I had no idea what he meant.

Then, after that, there were no more moments when anything outside of pain existed. On the trolley I believed I was lashed down, all the time I was wheeled along dazzling corridors I called out that it had to stop. I heard my noise as faces swung over and lifted me and I tried to get away, move, because they would drop onto me, smother me. I tried to call out that I could not bear this, it had to be halted, and I fought, fists and screams, pain and arms holding me. I could not make sense of any of it. Inside me there was a tearing, a blackness that pulled me apart, I was consumed with it, all my body destroyed with burning. There must have been Graham, nurses, a doctor, holding onto me but all I knew was that nothing existed outside this and there would never be an end, I could not escape or annihilate it. Then, later, I knew that I was not crying with pain because there was no word of description for the extremity I had come to, but to maintain contact; I wept to keep a hold on reality, not to be killed by it.

'No,' I screamed over and over, because I was splitting open, flayed, I was nothing but tearing and it had no beginning or end.

And yet at the very end there must have been some momentary easing because I have recollections of machines, flat metal bars, heavy dark containers and white masks, but by then I could not place them. I was not recognising any more; the only thought I had, and I knew I must hold onto it, was that the child would experience this too, the namelessness of objects, the sight of things that were bright and disjointed, descending, ominous, an unknown world, alienated from history and function.

The word I probably heard most often was Graham speaking my name, but when he eventually called it in triumph I did not know that it had come to an end, there was no release or joy; I did not seem to realise, I was told afterwards, that it was over, that the shuddering and probing and redness and blackness had ended in delivery, I had gone on arching my back and silently screaming, I could not stop, I could not make sense of relief.

It had lasted for two hours and perhaps because there were no moments of non-pain the lack of contrast made it endurable; there had been no respite but neither had there been any alternative. I had not believed it could stop.

After that, because I continued to call and moan it was decided that I was in a state of shock and that the most suitable remedy would be sedation. It was effective but it was also unfortunate because it obliterated me as fully as pain; I was unable to recognise any difference between the two. Once the pain ceased I could not possibly recreate a memory of it, the oblivions merged together. The explosion where I was convinced that I would tear to pieces became inextricable with nightmares of running, escaping, entrapment; all I knew, everything as far back as I could remember, was fear and the utmost anguish, and all that mattered was to make enough noise, but through all my crying for rescue reality receded further and further; it was no good calling for help, trying to make throat and tongue co-ordinate. I had lost my chance, it was impossible that I would be safe.

When I woke I was in a strange place, muffled, limbs swaddled, stifled with heat, I was in a rocking body apart from mine, and I could not reach out to touch it. Another time, then, later, I repeated, 'Hurts. Water,' and realised that outside of this there was a world where those words had meaning; and simultaneously I was not sure that I wanted to arrive back, if, now that it was at hand, I wanted to rename a world I had forgotten. I would have to recall my period of absence, recover and translate all that unimaginable pain into a recognisable event.

Another time: and yet time was non-existent and I was not sane enough to realise that that mattered; I was not connected to memory, or measures; but later: I knew I did not want to wake up. It was inconceivable that I could remember that distress, describe its place in my life, and it was terrifying that it could happen. I had not known that life was such a fragile cover for torture, that there was no inch of reality under which the reverse was not waiting. And it had been easy, it had taken nothing to fall out of the world into this consuming lake of menace lurking under it; all the time it was that accessible, constantly lying in readiness. Of course I was not sure about remembering: I did not know if I could put up with this knowledge, nor was it something I could persuade myself to forget or assimilate.

'I want a void,' I remember saying, and there being a figure by my bed, nodding.

'Barbara,' it had said, and I recognised not only that, but the person, Graham, holding my hand, agreeing, and then I had laughed, or that was what I meant to do, because it was nonsense to agree, he had no idea what I was on about. I told him that. I sat up and snatched my hands back from his and waved them about, ran my fingers through my hair with his gesture of exasperation. I cried out that he was like someone standing behind a fence on the edge of a sheer precipice, a pit, and a mile below, irretrievable, immured, I was calling that there was no way out.

'And that comes nothing near it,' I said and lay down. I could see quite clearly the deep gash at the edge of the earth, the thin trees around the circumference, the height of their trunks as I stared up, the endlessness of the sky, pale, diminished almost to whiteness.

'Minute,' I said, because he was, crouched on the edge of the drop, his arms wrapped round his knees, frowning with concentration as he looked down at me, and from the bottom of the pit I could hardly see him; the gulf between safety and extinction was infinite.

'It's all right,' he must have said, over and over again; and also, 'It's a boy,' because when I woke again I knew that had happened.

'A boy,' I heard, and, 'That's good,' and then I looked down at the bed and recognised the hands on the blanket and my wet mouth and realised that I was awake and drinking. I looked round and saw that the facts that reality abided by had not changed, that the outside world was still the same.

'Where is he?' I must have said because then Graham laughed, it was an extraordinary sound, harsh, an unlikely way to express pleasure. I turned my head away. I lay still and then, when it was quieter, I asked it again.

'There, look,' I heard him say, because I was not looking at him, I was staring beyond to the door of the ward, the opposite beds, the window, the vase of daffodils and tulips. 'Not over there,' he said, 'look, next to you, they've brought him back from the nursery, look.' I did as he told me. Next to my bed there was a small cot made of thick, grey material that swung, a rocking cot, and he lay inside, still, white wrapping, red head.

'Go on,' Graham said, high, encouraging, talking in the same voice he used to persuade Anna to eat her breakfast. 'Pick him up. Just bend over, it's not far, it won't hurt. Or I'll come round if you like.'

He stood up then, I could see him out of the corner of my eye, hovering, tall against the background beds.

'He's fantastic,' he said. 'Look, he's been here all the time you've been asleep. They washed him and brought him ages ago and he hasn't made a sound. I've been sitting watching him, just lying there, breathing. I couldn't take my eyes off him. Look, let me get him for you.'

'No,' I said. 'I can manage.' I leaned over the side of the bed and took the baby out. I unwrapped the shawl and touched and smelt and looked at the wrinkles, the down, the crookedness, the flatness. Small, immobile, unutterably quiet and light.

'Tim,' Graham said. I stared above the head. He existed, he had been identified, but I could not make sense out of it. There should be something different to show for it, for what had happened, this was familiar, I could have expected this.

'Tim. I've been saying that to myself. Sounds stupid but I hadn't got anyone else to talk to. I can't get over it, every time I look at him I can't believe it, it's fantastic. Isn't it?' he asked, because I did not immediately agree. 'I mean,' he looked at me, his face clenched, too, our eyes level, 'of course I know it wasn't, it was appalling, but it's all over now—'

'Except,' I began, but as though that was that, as if all that dark screaming, the shouts and masks and instruments could be put back in an assignable place, as though they fitted into a scheme of the world, he nodded and went back to stroking the small head.

'Tim,' he repeated, and then he smiled with delight, triumph. 'It's not decided but I thought of it while you were asleep and it's stuck in my mind ever since. It's nice, though, don't you think so? It seems like him. Small and firm and somehow determined. Timothy, I suppose, but Tim was what I thought of. I could tell people, tell Laura when I go back tonight. It suits him. What do you think?'

When I woke again I had not dreamt of anything. The ambulance, masked faces, my screaming body were quite distant. I saw the three beds on the other side of the room, the cup on the table across the foot of my bed, women reading magazines, one nearby talking and taking rollers out of her hair. There was the smell of flowers and antiseptic and milk. I closed my eyes again and slid my hands down under the sheets; there was a space and I could turn over and lie on my stomach. I turned my head from side to side; bed rails, screens, light, slippers in the distance. I sat up. Slowly I wriggled to the edge of the bed and swung my legs over the side. I remember this, I thought, the long way to the floor, legs, cold feet, conversations. I have come back again to the ordinary.

When his cot came back at feeding time he had a red face, a downy head and closed eyes. He was remote, bound up in sleep; he held away from me, reluctant to suck.

'He's just sleepy,' the nurse said when his mouth constantly fell away from my nipple. 'He's not a day old yet. Still recovering. He's had a little try, give him a few hours and he'll be fine.'

Although I could have nursed him, I could even have held him against me and pretended, no one would have come and inspected his performance, I put him back in his cot. Other women looked up at me, shifted babies over their shoulders, continued nourishing.

'He's still tired,' I said in the night, although no one asked me. 'It's too soon for him to be hungry.'

'So how's it going?' Graham said the next day. He kissed my head and pulled up a chair and took my hand. 'I've been watching you both sleep again. I got here ages ago. How are you? Better? A bit?'

'A bit,' I said, and my eyes filled with tears.

'I bought you some stuff.' He tapped the carrier by his feet. 'I took Anna to the park this morning and we got it on the way back. We fed the ducks.' I wiped my face. 'What is it?'

He bent over me. Beyond his blurred shoulder I could see the woman opposite watching.

'Nothing. Talk to me,' I muttered and he leaned over, shielding me like a screen.

'Do you want to talk about it?'

'There's nothing to talk about,' I said. 'You talk to me.'

He squeezed my hand and sat back and rubbed his head and took carnations and chocolates out of the carrier bag.

'I got these,' he said. 'I don't know what to say. Does it hurt still, are you depressed, is that it? What do you want to know?' he asked. 'Everything's fine. Anna is, Laura's coping beautifully. Well, all right, coping all right. Look,' and he stood up, 'I'll put these in water.' He went and filled a jug and placed the pinched pink clusters on my locker and sat and looked at them.

'I forgot,' he said after a moment and almost giggled. He took a brown paper bag out of the carrier. 'I got this for Anna. Laura wanted to get her some comics so I took her to the bookshop by the station. *Topsy and Tim*, it's called, a bit idiotic, really. I waited till she wasn't looking, but I thought she'd like it.'

He took the book out and I stared at the two large faces, black hair, the small neat bodies underneath, the green grass, the blue sky, the front cover full of sunshine and I nodded.

'She's over the moon,' he said. 'Anna. Delighted. What does he look like, does he cry, when can I see him, when can I hold him?'

'I haven't asked about her,' I said. 'I can't bear thinking about her. If I imagine her without me, alone—'

'She's not alone.' He took my hand. 'She's got Laura. You know how fond they are of one another. Of course you can't think about her, you've just had him, you don't have to make excuses. What about him?' he asked when babies started to cry and were lifted out of their cots, surreptitiously fed before their time. 'What time's he due?'

'He doesn't mind,' I said. 'He doesn't get hungry. He has to be persuaded, he's not as eager as them.' He got up and went to look into the cot. 'You can't see anything,' I said. 'He's not wasting away, though.'

'He's sound asleep,' he told me.

'That's right. That's what I said,' he would not take any notice, he stroked his cheek, ran his finger over his lips and said, 'He can suck,' as the mouth pursed very slightly. 'Look, he's starting to move, he's stretching, he'll be awake any minute.'

When the doctor came to see me again I was engorged and he said I would have to stay another day.

'I can't move,' I said to Graham. He had arrived in a flurry, as though he had abruptly stopped running. He scraped his chair, he pulled his hair, his hand scrabbled on the bedcover as he reached for mine. 'I can't move,' I said again. 'I've got to stay on. You'll have to forgive me.' He laughed at the phrase.

'Your parents can come then,' he said, 'and Laura. She wants to. How are you? How's he?' He never waited for an answer. 'God, it's busy, I did the washing, the shopping, took Anna to playgroup, went to feed the ducks. She's over the moon, delighted, everyone is. "Tim, Tim, Tim," she sings his name.'

'Talk to me,' I wanted to whisper. 'Tell me it's over, tell me it's all right.'

He told me about the card for Anna from her playgroup, the television programmes at teatime, her bedtime story.

'What was the rest of the evening like?' I asked. 'What was supper? How did you sleep?'

'Fish,' he said, 'and vegetables. Nothing exciting.'

'What did you talk about?' I asked. 'To Laura, at supper?' He frowned to try to remember, and shook his head.

'It won't be much longer,' I said. 'You'll survive.'

When he had gone I lay still and thought that when he came again I would tell him that other women said, 'Your baby's so good,' and, 'He doesn't know he's born,' and, 'You've got a real gem there.' I would say every time I closed my eyes I saw that image before me, and when I held and nursed him my movements were as deftly automatic as if he had always existed. Soon I would not need to name the distance between us, soon familiarity would eliminate both worry and excitement.

I practised. I got up in the night when other babies were roused, I held him and then put him back. 'Boy,' I whispered sometimes, and his ear moved under my breath, but that was all.

'He's trying,' the nurse said the next day, but I did not see how she could tell. I was the one holding him and I had no idea. I looked all morning from his face to the clock and I covered him up. I turned him over so that it was not easy to see him without getting out of bed.

All morning I thought of what I would say when Audrey and Leslie and Laura came, that all I saw was his body in the cot and my blood in the bathroom, the shadows in other beds, clouds out of the window. That is all it had come down to. They would ask what those other women were like, and the food, and the nurses.

'Beautiful, so small,' Laura would say.

'It was worth it, you can't deny that,' Audrey would tell me, and all day while I waited I could not answer. People juddered in my vision, swirling, ballooning in and out of yawning beds.

They echoed for hours before they came, I could hear them, loud footsteps, shrieking voices in the corridor. When I did see them they walked as if they were joined together, three red figures, Audrey in her pink hat, Laura's scarlet jacket, Leslie's veined face, I could not distinguish them from one another. Then they separated, one by one they bent to kiss me. Each of them put a parcel on my cabinet and I unwrapped the tissue paper round a poinsettia, the striped from soap and talcum powder and tinfoil from an avocado pear.

'Lovely,' I said each time, and did it very slowly as I did not know what else to say.

'Not a lot in here.' Audrey looked round her after a moment and nodded at the length of the ward. 'But that's better. You don't want to get too involved.' I carefully folded each piece of paper. I could ask if they wanted to read my cards, tell them that ten people had telephoned Graham.

'That's a funny thing to bring.' Audrey nodded at the avocado and pushed the poinsettia closer to the centre of my table. Laura said that I loved them, that I hadn't been able to eat them for months; it was the thing, she'd thought, I'd most want. Audrey prodded, pushed, set it rolling across the wooden surface until it stopped next to the fruit bowl, obtrusive beside the grapes and peaches.

'Doesn't it affect your milk? You ought to ask a nurse if it's all right to eat stuff like that.'

'Her milk?' Laura said and got up and walked round the bed to the cot. She bent down and picked him up and held him to face her. 'Her milk's special sleeping milk, anyone can see that, just look at him. He's better at sleeping than any baby in the world, or at least in the ward, that's what everyone says,' and she gave him a little shake.

'You want to be careful,' Audrey said.

'How's Graham taking it, then?' Leslie asked. 'He'll have his work cut out.' Audrey asked why.

'He comes here a lot,' I said, 'but it's not for long. I'll be out tomorrow.' Laura nodded, she jogged the baby up and down.

'Make the most if it,' she said. 'It's pandemonium at home. Anna's social life is like something out of *Debrett's*. I'd stay in for a month, if I were you. And as for you,' and she lifted the baby higher, held him almost above her head, 'as for you, possibly, just possibly I could be persuaded by you that babies were a good thing.'

'Put him down,' Audrey hissed and she half-rose, made a snatch in Laura's direction. But Laura spun, she almost swooped away, as if it was a game they were playing.

'Give him here. What're you doing to him, he's not a toy, he's not yours, leave him, give him here.' Audrey lunged again, and Laura turned to me as if she would give him back but at the last moment held on, changed her mind.

'Did Geraldine and Jessica pop in?' she said and smiled at me, because the names meant nothing to Audrey. 'Graham said Jessica wants to take Anna out when you come home but he wasn't sure you'd want that.'

'I'm not sure,' I said and looked from her holding the child to Audrey and Leslie. Audrey leaned across the bed as if I wasn't there, stretched her arm out to pull Laura's.

'Turn him round,' she said. 'Come on, you're not the only one who wants to see what he looks like. We've made a journey too.'

Laura laid him down on me and I still could not feel his weight; I looked down at his stillness on my thighs, both of us wrapped in white sheets; his eyes were closed, his face was paler than when he was born; wisps of fair hair pulsed on his skull. Audrey leaned closer, not to pick him up, but to stare.

'Look.' She moved her elbow in the direction of Leslie and he stared down. Uncertainly he put a hand on the baby's stomach and it covered over half the body.

'He's like you,' he said to her after a moment, but as though it was unimportant, like the time of day, the bleak weather. 'Same shaped head,' and rocked his hand up and down as if he was testing bedsprings in a hotel.

'Yes,' she nodded, still staring, 'that's what I thought. You'll wake him,' she said and straight away he lifted his hand off and hovered, accidental, apprehensive, and then, 'I told you,' because the baby's eyes opened.

I looked from her to the bed, the baby, and I saw it quite clearly; the stillness, the smooth broad face, the sleepy eyes, the bland flatness and I felt quite cold. I licked my lips.

'Yes,' I said, 'he does.' He did, except it was not a family likeness, an accidental repetition of features; whatever it looked like to Leslie I could see quite clearly that it was different. 'Except in a different way,' I said.

They had asked me about hospital food and told me about the infrequent Tube trains, the cold, how lucky I was to be in the warm. I took him from Audrey and laid him beside me on the bed. Each word they said took minutes, and it hung, meaningless in a space I had to answer.

'Get out,' I wanted to tell them, 'you've done enough.'

'Anna's fine,' Laura said. 'She's like clockwork with meals, breakfast dead on eight, lunch at twelve, tea at five. She doesn't complain about anything as long as they're on time.'

I looked at the clock because I could not bear how long it would

133

go on. 'It's his feeding time soon and that's the one rule they insist on, no visitors allowed while I do that. It's nearly five now,' I said. Audrey started to pass Leslie her coat, she could have slipped her arms back into it as easily and quietly as she had taken them out but she pulled roughly from under and thrust it into his hands.

'We'll be off, then,' she said without looking at me. 'You can give me a ring when you're back, if you like.' I held up my face and kissed them again, one by one. Leslie put his hand on my shoulder. 'I'm over the moon,' he said, 'truly.' He turned to Audrey. 'And so's your mother,' he said, 'we all are, everyone is.'

When they had gone I laid the baby across my knees. He was quite still and I let him rest like that, dormant, dreamless. Then, gently, I slid myself out of bed, out from under him so he rested where I had been, and pulled the curtains right round. They were plastic, and as I pulled them the rings rattled. I thought how long it took to walk round and enclose both of us inside the bed. I sat down, on the edge, and without picking him up unwrapped the blanket round him. His wrist, like mine, like the size of two of my fingers, was circled with an identity bracelet. I pulled it, and then pushed my finger into his clenched hand. Lines, I thought, as I prised it open, an extra line, and stared at the minute pink surface and felt the first intimation of panic because I could not see what I was looking for. I did not know where it should be, what extra puckering I was trying to identify, I could not even remember, now that I looked, where I had read that as well as a particular bone structure, extreme placidity, a particular fold in the construction of the hands was an indicator of mongolism. I put his hands neatly back inside the blanket, adjusted it snugly round him and replaced him in the cot. Then I pulled the curtains back from my bed. I did not find it shocking, nor did it occur to me that I was mistaken; now that it came to it I felt quite calm; I was shivering and it was difficult to walk steadily because my legs felt numb, but I was not surprised, I was relieved that I had found out first, that I had a chance to prepare my behaviour for when I was told.

I put on my dressing gown and then got back into bed and pulled the covers as close round me as I could. I wanted to curl up but I could not move enough to do that so I lay on my back, quite still, and stared at the ceiling. I could not think about the baby; I was thinking instead of the mother of a girl I had been at school with, Esme Waters, whose brother cycled fifty miles every weekend. One Sunday night he had not come home, and at eleven his mother had rung the police and the next day Esme had not come to school. It had taken three days to find his body in a hedge, his bike thrown over the other side. I thought of Mrs Waters sleeping and walking and waking all those hours, freezing with dread, crying that it was too appalling to be true, coldly certain that there was no alternative, knowing there was no part ever as awful as acceptance because after that resistance disappears.

Mrs Waters found out the truth and answered police questions, went to the funeral, stayed with relatives, saw Esme back to school and eventually talked of something else, curled her hair again and went to work. All those hunched silent hours torn between grief and self-ridicule and hope vanished into adjustment. She forgot that the first hours of misery and disbelief and guilt were the most pure time of mourning because afterwards it was impossible to accept that those hours were survivable.

I thought about that, of saying, 'My son was killed,' or, 'My brother died,' reducing the unendurable to assimilated facts. Doubtless it had to be done, but I did not want it yet. I did not think that this was what I had expected: all the sickness had made me fearful, but of death, of emerging empty-handed. That would have been better, I would have preferred weeping and grief because they were noble emotions after a tragic end. Over this I could expose nothing, I was bound to fortitude and concealment. It was not that I would find them difficult, because they were qualities I found easy to display, but that he was not worth it.

'Has Graham come?' I asked later when I opened my eyes to find the Scottish nurse standing by the foot of my bed. She nodded.

'He's in Sister's room right now. Doctor wanted a word. I've come to collect you. The Royal Summons.' She tried to smile. 'And all I am is the messenger,' she said as I got out of bed, because she could not know that I would not ask any questions, she had to try and forestall me. 'Doctor'll tell you. It's not far.'

'Doctor's just come off duty,' she said in the corridor and, 'Sister won't be a minute,' as she opened the door of the room at the end. 'You won't have long to wait.'

It was a regulation hospital room and we were regulation occupants, husband, wife, doctor, nurse; I nodded to the grey carpet and bookshelf and tubular steel chairs, Graham sitting on one and the short elderly man in a tweed suit on another. I knew quite well what we were going to be told.

'I'll introduce myself,' the doctor said and he did not find his statement of business difficult, he had pronounced enough times before not to be dismayed by the diagnosis.

'I knew,' I wanted to tell Graham. 'Listen, let me be the one to tell you. I knew because of the way he looked, I knew hours ago, like Audrey he looked, I knew what that face meant.' I wanted to warn him because otherwise when the words came, *Down's Syndrome*, they would be a shock. When they did and I looked at his face it was like shaking hands after a funeral, there was nothing but estrangement.

'Graham,' I said. He took no notice of me. He turned to the doctor and took his hands instead.

'Why?' he said. 'What can we do?' and questioned and listened and nodded and waited at all the words of comfort and deceit. I pulled at him, tugged his jacket awry.

'Hear me, take no notice,' I wanted to cry, 'he's lying, he's trying to stop you minding.' I reached for the adamant white-coated doctor. I stared at the bristling grey hairs on his short bony neck.

I said 'Graham, please don't listen, you don't want to hear that. It does matter, it's appalling. You tell stories,' I said to the old white shoulders, 'you invent what it means, you want forgetting, you discount abnormality, you talk about imbalances, chromosomes, you can't see reality, you've got no idea what will happen to us.'

He pulled away from me, lined, elderly, courteous and contradictory. 'No,' he said, 'you aren't listening. Give me a chance. Please?'

He soothed and promised and quoted counselling and support. He cited facilities and advancements, talked about affection and attitudes.

'It's not all bad news,' he said, 'you'll see. Give the child help and you'll be astonished. You won't believe what he'll be able to do. With you as parents, with every advantage you can provide,' and he broke off to smile. The world could be his oyster, he meant, he was fortunate, this child, he could be so much worse off.

After a while, after Graham had walked about, reseated himself and moaned and his back had been patted and tea had been brought, I could see it was certain that he would find a way of dealing with this.

'He's not too bad?' he asked again. 'No physical abnormality? He'll just be slow. No spasticity,' he echoed, 'and he'll progress. We've got to learn, too,' he remembered. 'We've got to change our ideas of achievement.' I listened and I saw he could pass the child over to a category, a group for whom provision needed to be made;

he believed good could be dispensed, he had no horror of acknowledging deformity. I stood up and started to say that was not reality, he must not deceive himself and the nurse came out at me from behind her desk.

'Mrs Browne,' she said. 'Mrs Browne, you're not helping anyone, look at your husband.' I could not see any reason to; while I wept he was adjusting, while I raged he was coming to terms. 'Mrs Browne,' she scolded, 'it's not a ruined life. All you need is time and help. He'll be a loving, gentle son, it's the way we label things, that's what's wrong, not him.'

'Society,' the doctor said, and I saw soon they would recite together, it was a professional chorus, 'it's society that calls things right and wrong, all right and not all right, it's not your son. Labels don't have anything to do with that little boy, he's himself. Norms are relative, we have to be sensitive. Wait and see,' he added. 'You'll put this day behind you, I promise. Give it time and all these feelings will be wiped out, erased, I guarantee.'

Graham nodded. He did not frown any more to stop himself from crying; he was ready to look relieved.

'Let's get out,' I said. I stood up because that was not a damaging action, it was not aggressive or provoking or even self-destructive; it gave no grounds for opposition. 'Let's go away.' No one tried to stop me. Nurse nodded, her hand was ready to hold open the door.

'There's a room,' she said, 'a side room, off ward E, I've got a bed ready for you there.'

I said, no, that was not what I meant, it was going home I had in mind.

'Tomorrow,' Nurse said, and I answered that that would be too late.

'We could leave him here,' I said; I said it to no one because as soon as the words were out I knew, I was quite alone in my assessment of a permissible course of action. 'Leave him if we go today. It could be a spur of the moment thing, no one would blame us today, but tomorrow, tomorrow we'll be expected to be responsible. Let's,' I said and I clutched out for Graham. I missed and he did not move to make my undirectedness easier, my hand flailed around like a broken wheel spoke. 'Now, please, let's go now, let's go back to Anna, let's pretend it never happened. All right,' I said. 'Let's go to this room.'

Nurse said, 'I asked Anne Berrington to wait,' and the doctor nodded and looked from Graham to me.

'That might be best,' he said. 'It might be best if she went in now, if she started right away instead of tomorrow. Anne Berrington's your health visitor,' he said to me. 'She'll be seeing you through the first few weeks, she'll be helping you with your baby.'

When we left the doctor behind for long enough to go halfway down the corridor I looked back and he was not even watching, he was walking in the opposite direction. Nurse led us past the entrance to my ward and round a corner to a small cubicle. She said, 'I'll leave you alone for a few minutes. Then I'll bring Anne Berrington and then I'll get baby and your bag.'

The room was cell-like because of the high window and bed, but there was an easy chair for Graham to sit in. I climbed into bed, shaking because the sheets were cold, and then because I could not stop. I pulled my dressing gown tighter and clenched my eyes shut and felt Graham come and sit beside me.

'Don't,' he said. 'Don't. Look at me, Barbara.' He shook my shoulder. 'We've got to talk to one another.'

I turned over to face him and he had not altered; he maintained the discovery he had made in that room, that deformity was not an impossible fact; it was unfortunate, an accident that could be assuaged by mutual compassion. He wanted us to exchange understanding and sympathy, for me to support his display of grief and reveal my own.

'How could it happen?' he asked, and pushed his face into my neck. 'How can we learn to bear it? It could have been worse,' he said. 'It would have been dreadful to have been told straight away. To have known as soon as he was born. I've got an affection for him now, a feeling for him, whereas then I'd always have thought of him as odd.'

I felt his tears against my neck. He put his hair against my cheek, rocking slightly. I looked over his head out of the window and it was quite dark.

'What matters,' he said, and raised his wet face to me and repeated phrases, word for word. 'Lovable, kind'; 'not the way society defines'; 'all right' and 'nothing wrong'. 'It shouldn't be left till now,' he said seriously. 'It should be talked about, the possibility of handicap in ante-natal classes. It's an insight everyone ought to have, it would help you relearn definitions before you came face to face with them. It would avoid such painful reactions. It would help with the moments before you saw you could do something positive with his life.'

I pushed myself away from him, I leaned forward.

'His life?' I asked. 'What life? What help, what place in society? That's rubbish. What will happen,' I pulled my legs up so I was crouched, 'is that people will laugh.' And I did, to show him, I guffawed and shouted. 'They'll be hysterical, rapturous, beside themselves they've escaped, it hasn't happened to them. They know, I know, we don't want to look after the deformed, there isn't a special place for the mutilated in society, they're rubbish. There's helpers, nurseries, toys, pity, pretending, that's what you get for something nobody wants. He's wrong' – I tried to lower my voice – 'and I don't want him. I want the baby I should have had, a proper child, an acceptable child like Anna. I don't want to see other people's Christmas and birthday presents and have you look at that useless boy and say, "It doesn't matter what he can or can't do, we love him, he's taught us love." I don't want to pretend that we live in some fairytale world where it doesn't matter. I don't care,' I said. 'I mean it. I'll abandon him the way the rest of the world does.'

He got up and went away from me, he leaned on the windowsill and I knew there was nothing to alter, I had known all along I would have no ally.

'I'm sorry,' I said. I meant that I mourned him in a way, that I could grieve for his incompleteness, but that was not what Graham heard.

'I'm sorry,' he said, 'but you're not right. That's not what matters, that's not what we're going to believe. You've got to alter. You've got to,' he repeated. 'It'll be all right,' he said at intervals, and after a time, when there was a knock at the door, he was able to turn round and say, 'Come in,' as though he had altered me and we were both ready for anything.

'Anne Berrington,' she said. 'Anne.' I tried to take my eyes off her because she was repulsive. She was short, short-necked, short-waisted, short-legged, and she was carrying a chair for herself.

'Be prepared,' she said. 'There's never enough in this place.' She sat on it in navy coat and shoes and beret and Graham moved so that they were side by side, opposite me. I shifted back on the pillow.

'Time and help,' she said, her head to one side. She had an accent, English underlaid by Australian. 'That's what you need. I'm here to help, not put you right, but help things along. You might want to manage, but don't keep it to yourselves. You've got family, they'll all want to help. A thing like this was a stigma once, you've got to be glad because attitudes have changed. That's a plus,

139

something you've gained.' I managed to look away from her wide thin lips and big brown eyes to her fat little feet in court shoes, small and bulging. 'You've got to think of other people,' she said. 'You've got to take them into consideration. We'll talk it over, see the best way to sort things out. That's what I'm here for, after all, that's what they pay me to do. You're sensible,' she said. 'I can see that. You won't get upset over nothing, you'll do all right. But everyone has their breaking point, that's where I come in, that's where really I earn my living.

'Take it day by day,' she smiled. 'That's the best advice. But don't forget one day you might not be able to, a cry for help's nothing to be ashamed of.' She took out a spiral-bound notebook from her coat pocket and tapped the yellow tip of her pen against her teeth. 'Practical details,' she said. 'Let's get down to business.'

We enumerated the facts of our lives: rooms, bathroom, garden, Anna's playgroup, and when Graham came to his job she nodded with especial enthusiasm. She made notes, her stubby fingers clenched round the Biro. 'Just for the records,' she said, when I asked why. 'Painting a picture.

'Let people know,' she said, 'tell them beforehand. Explain to the neighbours, let the news get about. He's a lovely baby but make sure people realise. You don't want surprises, they just make it harder. Who'll you ask?' she said. 'Who can break the news for you?'

'Laura,' said Graham. 'I'll get Laura and Geraldine.'

'That's the ticket,' she said, 'you have to be practical. That's what we've always found, it's not sympathy that's needed. The more people can do, the better they feel. I'll give you addresses, support groups and meetings; get in touch, they'll be able to help you a lot. They'll tell you as well, they'll say just the same thing, a baby's a baby, you love it whatever. You'll have different feelings, not like your daughter, you'll love him his own way, he'll be just as much pleasure.'

'You've got Geraldine's number?' I said to Graham after a minute. He stared at his closed diary.

'It'd be better to get Laura to do it,' he answered. 'I'll probably ask Laura.'

'Geraldine knows everyone,' I said, 'she'd find it easier. Not Anna, though, or Audrey and Leslie. They can wait.' Anne Berrington raised her head. 'No,' I said. 'I mean it. Anna won't understand yet. And I'll tell my parents. And his,' I nodded at Graham, 'are dead.'

He did not look into the cot when the nurse pushed it in, nor did I pick up the baby.

'I'll see you tomorrow,' Anne Berrington said. 'You'll leave about three, I'll see you at teatime.' Graham held the door for her. 'Goodbye till then.'

'My things are in the case,' I told him. 'You won't forget to bring it. It's by the front door.'

He nodded. 'Is there anything else?' I said I could not think of anything.

'She was vile,' I said.

'She was doing her job. It all comes to the same thing in the end. We've got to learn to deal with it, get over the shock, get on with it. You can ring me if you think of anything,' he said after a moment. 'I won't go to bed early. It doesn't matter if it's late. I suppose it helped, talking, listening to someone being sympathetic and yet realising how ordinary it was to her. She wasn't gushing, as if we had something to be ashamed of. She was practical. Not insensitive but realistic. Don't worry,' he said and I said I would not.

'Go on,' I told him, 'go,' and after a minute he did.

I woke in the night crying, and once I dreamt I had lost him and found I was out of bed, searching for his empty cot. Then I realised it had been wheeled out, he had been put to sleep in the nursery. I went back to bed and watched until it became light. At breakfast I could not hold my cup still enough to drink from and at lunchtime my spoon rattled against my soup plate. All the time in between and until Graham arrived I lay quietly, as without expectation as the child lying beside me, except that for me it was temporary. I knew quite well what was coming, the efforts I would have to make; they were nothing to do with him. I would behave as if nothing had happened, as if I had assimilated it, but as if nothing was altered. I could not bear it, but I did not have to bother with that, all I had to do was show that I could survive it; he was beyond me, it had never been otherwise, but I was under no compulsion to reveal that to anyone else at all.

'I've told Laura,' Graham said, and did not kiss me. 'She's at home waiting. She got Geraldine to do the phoning, last night, it's all taken care of.'

141

'What did you say?' I asked. 'What did you tell her? What did she think?' But then I shook my head because I did not want to know, to visualise Laura hearing, understanding what it meant.

'She wasn't that sure about you telling your parents,' Graham said. 'She thought it might upset you too much. She'll do it if you want.'

'No,' I said.

'What everyone says,' he looked away from me, 'will be the same. They'll say they're sorry, they'll tell us what we know already. Everything that's good about him, everything that's possible in his life. It won't be difficult, it won't be anything to be upset about eventually. It's just the first time, that's all.'

'I'm not bothered about getting upset,' I said. 'I'll find ways of handling that.' I took my case behind the screen in the corner to get undressed. He did not comment or call to me.

When I was ready I took the babyclothes out of their tissue paper and lifted him out of his cot and took off the hospital nightie and jacket and shawl. I looked down at his pale features. Already they looked broader. His head seemed larger, more precarious than I had previously noticed.

When he was dressed we walked outside, the baby over my shoulder. At the end of the corridor the Scottish nurse and the sister were waiting. They walked either side of me to the entrance, asking Graham if Anna was excited at my return, promising that Anne Berrington would call later, reminding me not to forget my post-natal. I watched Graham shake hands with each of them, but I did not transfer the baby to the other shoulder.

'Got your hands full,' the nurse said, because it would not have been difficult, not taken a moment's effort to do that.

'Yes,' I said. I pushed against the door with my free shoulder and walked fast, carelessly down the steps, strode across the car park.

'How's Anna?' I asked as Graham drove carefully to the main road. He told me that she wanted a scooter like Ben's, had refused to share her doll's house with Melissa.

'I was wondering,' he said, 'what the rationale was for not telling her. About Tim.'

'She won't understand,' I said immediately. 'Has she been upset?'

'No.' He glanced at me. 'I've told you, she's been fine. The other thing,' he said, 'is toys. People have brought him presents, bricks, and a teddy from Anna's playgroup.'

'We'll put them in Anna's room,' I said. 'He can share them. They'll look nice. Who's Anna with now?' I asked when the car stopped at the kerbside. 'Where is she?' I did not want to get out, I did not want him to answer; I wanted to go back and begin again but the front door opened and she was there, she ran down the path and I found I had climbed out, as fast as I could, the baby still lying against me, and then she was upon me. Without looking I passed the baby over her head. 'Let Laura have him,' I said. 'I can have you then.'

When Anne Berrington arrived I took her upstairs and every day she came after that I showed her how well I could learn to behave. I could not accomplish destruction simply because I could not endure him, but I found how to stay outside; I discovered a temporary state of immunity where I was free to disregard the implications and consequences. Good, obliging, quiet, I found a place where I was well behaved enough not to have to answer questions, where it was assumed that painlessly, accidentally almost, I had assimilated the event.

On her first visit she had come into the bedroom and looked from the draped curtains to the fitted cupboards and thick cushion covers and carpet.

'Lovely. Beautiful room. Really luxurious. What a place to sleep in.' She ran her hand over the pile on the bedspread. 'What's through there? How many rooms are there up here?'

'Anna's, the bathroom,' I'd said.

'And the lounge?'

'That's the big room on the middle floor. The other one's Graham's. Go and look if you like.'

She did not sit down or ask to see the baby, she scurried, she moved as fast as her bunchy legs could. I heard her calling, 'Look at this, this is really something.' I heard her open and shut doors, up and down stairs, I could see her lick her dry lips and rub her bulging hands, and when she came back into the bedroom she patted my shoulder. 'Lovely, lovely,' she repeated.

'He's there,' I said and pointed to the corner on the far side of the room where the nursing chair and Moses basket were. She tiptoed over to them. I took him out of the basket and put him to one breast and then the other. I laid him over my shoulder, but he did not need winding; he was inert, he did not need anything. When I had changed him and put him back she patted me again, patted my hand.

143

'I'll be here,' she said, 'not every feed, but a good few of them. We'll get it worked out.'

Each day for six weeks we sat while I cajoled and persisted in feeding him with as great a show of enthusiasm as if I had wanted him to be nourished, while I dressed him like a doll, while I laid him to rest with infinite care. I encouraged her to take him from me, nodded when she said she would bath or change him and agreed he was good, he was a lovely boy. In her arms I did not have to recognise him; my eyes could wash over him, he was not imprinted on me.

'Silly boy,' I taught myself to say as he failed to suck, and, 'Beddy-byes,' when he was stupefied with sleep. I nudged her when he burped, raised my eyebrows and nodded in a parody of congratulation. Sometimes she imitated his sound and said, 'A bit more now.' I smiled and gently shook him.

'Come on, do as you're told, you never know what old Anne'll do if you're a naughty boy.' I told her I shouldn't care to get on the wrong side of her. 'If it wasn't for you, though,' I would pretend in utter seriousness, 'I don't know what I'd do.' She would look round the kitchen or the softly lit bedroom and say it was nothing, all in a day's work.

When she left I would stand at the front door for a few moments longer than necessary until she closed the door of her car. Then I would go back to where he lay in his basket.

'She can have you,' I would say. 'You're hers, that's whose you are.'

'Fancy a drink?' she would ask when he had gone to sleep. 'You get yourself straight, I'll see to it.' I could hear her moving about downstairs, I saw her at my kitchen table, looking at my photos and postcards on the wall as she waited for the kettle to boil. I wanted to shout at her to be gone. She would run her fingers over the cups and shelves and the apple-moulded plates that stood on the top, and they would need washing, scrubbing, to get rid of her.

'You're lucky,' she said, whenever the phone rang and I spoke to Geraldine or Jessica, 'all those friends. And that sister of yours, here every afternoon, I see what she gets up to. Helping,' and she would spread a pudgy hand towards the sink, the stove, 'clearing up. Rather you than me, I tell her, but then you're sisters.'

'She likes Anna,' I said. 'She likes it here. She works shifts, the rest of the day's a long time to be alone.'

'You're lucky,' she repeated. 'There's a lot'd envy you.'

'I'm tired,' I started to say but then she brought me a tray upstairs. While she sipped her coffee I left mine to cool. I did not want to drink out of the cup she had handled, I sat turned away from her whatever I did; she could not watch me feeding although I could still see her flat smiling face, her short stretched legs.

'Have him,' I said and put him into her arms. They matched, I could not distinguish between them. They had no place in my house, they belonged to each other.

When she was gone I cleaned the stairs she had walked on, the chair she had sat in. I scoured her cup and waited for the doorbell or the phone to ring and hear her voice. I waited to hear the sound of her car returning and put the lock on the front door, ran back upstairs and watched out of every window to make sure she had really gone, that she was not lingering, waiting for her chance to get back in again.

'All this space,' she said every day, as she walked from bedroom to bathroom, past the doors of Anna's room and Graham's study. 'It's like a mansion, all these rooms. You could have another half a dozen people living here and not fall over one another.'

Every afternoon when Laura came she would ask, 'All right?' and talk about old people, the rewards of caring. She asked questions about Anna's infancy, she tried to make me talk about his future, teething, crawling. She told me people minded, that I should allow them to show it.

'It wouldn't hurt to see friends for five minutes,' she told me. 'You could invite Geraldine and Jessica again. Try, and once you've done it, it'll be fine.'

When she came and sat by me I never said, 'Go, leave me alone,' and when she picked the baby up I never said, 'Take him away.' I listened when she marvelled at how tightly he gripped her finger and told me, 'A woman at work's friend's daughter has Down's Syndrome.' I thought how she must have scrabbled in gossip for that information, all of them swapping relief and platitudes at their own good fortune. 'She goes to a playgroup and they've found a primary school that'll take her, on a trial basis at least,' she told me. 'And she's got a terrific sense of humour. Keeps all the family, everyone, in stitches.'

'You should stay to supper,' I said sometimes, because that would mean that she would cook the meal and talk to Graham. I could listen while she asked, 'How's your work?' and he would chew and swallow and mention a committee, a new work scheme.

'How's the ambulance relief?' he would ask her.

I would watch them on either side of the table and see how they had sat while I had been in hospital, how they had gossiped and drunk wine and interrupted one another. I would not find out what to make of that, but it would be kept at bay; it would not be a ghost I was left with in the kitchen every time she went out of it.

'Let me,' Graham said in the mornings. 'I'll bath him, there's time before I go to work. Look,' he would call to Anna and get her to help take his clothes off and then hold him, dangle him in the water, soap him all over. It took three minutes, loose wet limbs, rinsed, and then his body lolling out of the towel, his eyes shut against the light. When he was dressed and handed back to me and his head moved from side to side he was not searching for my nipple, it was more primitive, an earlier sub-terrestrial echo; monstrous.

'Tim,' Graham said when he came home every evening. He held the baby's face close, as if staring would make those thin eyelids open. He nestled him against his shoulder, walked round the room singing softly, and after a few minutes he rested him in his arms and put their lips together. 'Tim,' he repeated and placed him back in the basket, adjusting the covers round his neck, patting the sides down to keep him warm. 'Good boy,' he would say. 'How's he been?'

I would pick up the newspaper, turn the pages until I came to the television programmes. 'I think I'll go and watch with Anna,' I'd say. She would sit on my lap, in front of the screen, and I would look at her, still watching me, and then we would stare as fixedly at the dancing images as Graham had at the baby.

'He's stopped breathing,' I practised saying over and over again, but I was never too frightened to look in the basket to find out. 'He's got an infection, a virus, a blockage. I found him like it. Anne Berrington's taken him to hospital.' I knew exactly how it should be.

'I know we can't plan ahead,' Graham said, 'but we can talk about the present. I've explained to Anna it'll be a long time before she can play with him, that's not a problem. It's more . . . It's not that he's difficult to love,' and he would go over to the basket, crouch down, rock it, make crooning noises, 'and he's beautiful to look at. I've been thinking,' and he would stare at me. 'It must be appalling, the worst thing of all must be to watch a child suffer. Those babies you read about, half a stomach, heart trouble, lungs that don't work, think of having to keep it still, see it go through operation after operation and know there was nothing you could do. Whereas for us,' and he spread his arms wide with relief, 'we can do everything. There's nothing we can't give him.'

'Don't cry, don't cry,' he would say and try to hold me. 'I feel like that, too. It's shocking, Christ, of course, I mind. When I think what I imagined, what Anna's like, what I expected before we found this out. Yet it's dreadful to feel like that. What is it to him? That's what we've got to concentrate on.'

Every day, every four hours I would stand by the Moses basket and watch how small he was under the covers, how they hardly moved. My hands had made more disturbance to the patchwork when I sewed it than his body did. I looked at the neat folds, the soft sheets, and tried to tear them; he could have been wrapped in sacking for all that presentation mattered, for all that I cared. When I wrapped and unwrapped, suckled and changed, I did it without looking. His limbs, his face had no claim over me. I stared from the door to the chest of babyclothes, to the freesias in a white vase that Graham or Laura had placed by the bed.

There was a lifetime to go, I thought through the days and weeks, to survive, to shut myself away. I had to become as distant from reality as he was, as unmoved by any contact; I was learning, I was forgetting.

One day Anne Berrington did not go upstairs with me when I let her in but asked to go into the kitchen. She sat down in Graham's place at the table.

'The first thing I thought when I came here,' she said, rubbing her fingers along the grain of the wood, 'was that you could have eaten a meal off the floor, it was so clean. You couldn't do that now. The second was how lucky you were to have a sister like that. One who'd turn her hand to anything. She's got a job, she doesn't live here, but she's backed you up to the hilt. But she can't see to all this for months to come. She's done her best, that's not what I'm saying, she's got enough on her plate and she's done marvels. But that's not the point. There's a lot of people who need help. They start off with a relative but often it's someone professional who makes the big difference, someone who can talk things over with you. Once it gets going people really appreciate it.'

'Another thought,' she said. 'How about a support group? A lot of mothers find that's the best thing, practical advice as well as swapping how you feel today. I know you're not much of a one for that,' and she looked sideways at me, 'but I can tell what you need is a bit of companionship, and I could put you in touch. Seeing other people could help you no end. You can't go on relying on family, not when that really means you need proper help. If you can't cope by yourself, that's nothing to be ashamed of, you've just got to face up to it. This girl I've got to go to after you, now,' and she looked at her watch, 'she hasn't got a relative in the world that I know of, she wouldn't have time to sit around like this. "I've had my rest," I say to her when I get there. "I had my sit down at Mrs B's. Into the fray," I tell her. Her kiddy's a real handful. What he does,' she said, as though I could have any possible interest, 'is wriggle. All on his own, all over the place, thump, thump, on his tummy, and then he only sleeps six hours a night, not a wink in the day either. Into everything,' she said.

When she left to go and see him I locked the front door because I would never let anyone else in, I would show that there was nothing I could not do for myself. I would shop and cook and clean, I would put it all to rights so that no one could find any fault. I would telephone Laura, as if I had finished a brief period of convalescence, as if I had recovered.

'Graham must have told you,' I said to her, 'what a fantastic job you've done. He doesn't stop talking about you – Laura this, Laura that. I'm almost jealous. And it's the same with Anna. But now I've got to try, I've got to get on by myself for a while. It's my house,' I explained.

'I could still visit,' she suggested, 'just to see you. Not necessarily to help. Although it's up to you, how you feel about it.' I let her say what she wanted. I did not want to be listening, I wanted to be back upstairs inspecting every room. I wanted to go through the house as if I expected to find some stranger there.

'Come next week,' I said in the end, and for all those afternoons when I was alone I could not stop listening. I was reminded of Audrey pacing up and down, unable to stop until she had found some activity that would eliminate the faint sounds from Mercy's room upstairs.

Every day, as soon as each room was tidy again, I wanted to put a barrier against his door so there were no means by which he should ever bump his way down, straddle and hump across floors, lurch into every area of our lives. I did not want him intruding, but I could not believe in prevention. I remembered Audrey running upstairs to see if Mercy was still shut in her bedroom and I did the same. I banged on the door. 'Wake up,' I called, and waited to see if anything happened. He lay quite still. His eyes were open and when I looked into them they skewed at my shadow.

'Audrey had the right idea,' I said. 'That's what we'll do with you, too. Up here, keep you out of mischief.'

'My sister didn't come,' I said to Anne Berrington each day after that. 'You were right, I do need to manage for myself. What do you think?' I knew she could not look round the kitchen without praising the improvement. 'I feel better,' I said, 'more my old self again.'

When we went upstairs for the feed I asked her questions: whether she had looked for a bigger flat, how her car was running, if her downstairs neighbour still played records too loudly. When I was finished she leaned back so she could see the baby's face resting against my shoulder.

'He's a lovely boy,' she said, 'really lovely.'

'He's fine,' I said. 'I think so too. I'm grateful,' I said as I lifted him up. 'I know what I've got to do. You've helped me see how I ought to approach things. I can manage now. Anyone else,' I added when she did not reply, 'I can't explain—' and I looked up at her as if I thought she might be able to, I laid him away from my breast, left it painfully dripping while I put him over my shoulder, hugged him into closeness, 'would make me feel jealous. I want to do it all for him. You said people took time, you were right; time to get back to normal. I'm glad you told me that. It wasn't easy, but it was the right thing, what I needed. I needed to pull myself together again.'

After six weeks I had to go back to the hospital for my post-natal and Geraldine looked after him. I left her pushing his pram down the road to her house with Anna and Melissa holding either side. And all the way in the bus, whenever I looked down at my lap, I was astonished I was not pregnant, because that was how I travelled on this route. I shifted in my seat as though I was weighted down.

When I got to the hospital I followed the wrong signs, I had to be directed back to the post-natal clinic. There were babies there, though, some people had brought them; as soon as I sat down I could see them. They were small, as small as he was, but focusing, vivid, and they smiled. I read magazines and looked out of the window and thought of the closed view from the ward, and then of the sea, huge stretches where no one would go, where no one would know anything.

When my name was called I undressed and lay on a trolley in a chilly room. The doctor was a young man again. He did not look at my name on my folder. He just called me mother.

'How's your bundle of trouble, then?' He meant it as a joke because when I did not answer he sounded impatient. 'What about your baby?' He picked up my notes and turned over the pieces of paper and then put them down. His face was scarlet.

'It doesn't matter,' I said.

He looked across at the nurse and she came and covered me up so that he could talk to me, person to person. He leant against the end of the trolley. 'Sit up if you like,' he said. A lock of hair fell over his forehead as he fiddled with the pens in his top pocket. 'So how are things?' he asked. 'How are you coping?'

I considered for a moment. 'Fine. People help. You manage. You don't fall apart. I suppose you grow up in a way.'

He nodded and leaned forward and took my hand. 'You're a brave lady,' he said.

The last day Anne Berrington came I made a cake and invited Laura and Geraldine and Jessica to tea. I wiped up every spilt drop of juice and tea, I swept away every crumb immediately. I brought the baby down to be admired, hovering behind everyone who held him as though I was frightened he would jump out of their arms.

'I wish he could smile,' I said to Anne Berrington. 'I'd love him to show you how much you mean.'

'Six weeks,' Anne Berrington said. 'That's my lot. That's all the time you get from me. You've done all right,' she told me. Although I thanked her, I pretended to cry when she shook my hand, I did not believe she would really go. I was sure as I shut the door on her tight navy back for the last time that she was pretending, she would find a way of spying, setting out to watch what I would do.

'I've been thinking about going away,' I said when Graham came in. 'I'd like to be somewhere else. I don't want to be looked at here any more, people staring when I wheel the pram. I'd like to be another person in another place. We could go at Easter.'

He stared at his plate.

'Where shall we go?' I asked. 'Think of somewhere, a place we could go to that would be a holiday. A little one, just a weekend if you like, somewhere where no one knows us. I'll ask Laura tomorrow.'

He did not say that was a good idea, he stared at his plate.

'It'd be nice to take Anna somewhere healthy,' and I pinched her cheek. 'Look how pale she is. She could do with some fresh air. Sea breezes,' and I reached out to pinch her other cheek. 'Do her the world of good.'

'Let go of her.' Graham frowned at me, smiled at her. 'Finish up and I'll read your story. Mum's tired tonight.'

'Imagine it,' I said. 'Sea, sun, stiff breezes. Long walks, exploring.'

The next day I did not wait for Geraldine to come to take Anna to playgroup. As soon as Graham went to work, before it was even time for his feed, I put the baby in the pram, balanced Anna on the end and walked to the library. I borrowed maps, Ordnance Survey sheets with detailed miles of coast and footpaths of the west of England and when we came home I pushed all the furniture to one side and spread them out over the sitting-room floor. They covered all of it, white and uneven. I took off my shoes and trod over them, delicately, minding the folds. I was testing them, I told Anna, to see which place felt right, where it would be good to visit.

After a while I left them and went upstairs to Graham's room, it needed to be bare; it did not want history for the baby to refer back to. He could lie in here thoughtless, with nothing to answer him. I started to shift everything into a pile in the middle of the room, I heaved boxes and books until I heard Anna call and I ran downstairs to the maps again. I did not put them away, though, I crawled all over them, reading, reciting names. When I heard a knocking at the front door I did not even suspect Anne Berrington; I knew I had found a way out of all that.

'Fancy you coming,' I said to Laura. 'You've come and I'm going. We're going away, at Easter.' I watched her standing in the doorway, Anna suddenly beside her, staring at me. 'Graham can't say no, he can't. It'll be a holiday. I won't let him say no.'

Laura drew Anna back from the door. 'We'll go and get you a drink,' she told her. 'We'll ring Dad to make sure when he's coming back. Would you like a drink?' she asked me.

151

'No,' I said. 'I've got to do this. I've got to see where looks right. No, I've got another idea.' I reached out for her hand. 'You come upstairs. There are things there, too, things I've got to see to. Graham's room, I've started to clear it, junk, all of it, it should have been thrown out years ago. Everything he kept about how things were, family, school—'

'In a minute,' Laura said. 'I'll see to Anna first.'

'It's all useless,' I explained. 'No one'll ever use it now, it's rubbish, that's all it comes to.'

'We'll go and see what's on television,' she said. 'There might be a film Anna could watch for a bit, we won't be long.'

When I opened Graham's door it was more disorderly than I remembered. The heap of photos I had rammed together and tied with string was uneven; some protruded and others had fallen to the floor. In the centre of the room was a pile of clothes and the drawers I had tipped them from stood empty on their sides.

'Laura,' I called, and she came upstairs straight away. 'This is it. I want to get rid of all this pastness, parents, grandparents I never knew. They're nothing to do with us.'

'But won't he mind?' She looked as uncertain as Anna.

'It doesn't matter, it's for the baby to go in. He's got to have a place, I can't keep him with us. There's got to be somewhere for him to go. Anna can come in here,' I said. 'She'll need to come up and downstairs to him. But he'll want his own room, a separate place so I can look after things downstairs. That's the best way to arrange it.'

She stood there not moving, while I filled the bags. Then I heard the front door.

'Graham,' she called. 'Up here!' He ran up, two at a time.

'I've sorted it all out,' I said and there were four bags to prove it, spilling onto the floor. 'Nearly, anyway. I'll finish tomorrow, and paint it before we go away. When we come back it'll be ready, he can go straight in it. Isn't that good?' I bent down again, I started to burrow through all the rest of it, all the old possessions I had heaped on the ground, throwing them aside until I was surrounded by them. 'You can't put anything back,' I said. 'I've cleared it all out.'

In the evening while he was reading papers from his case I sat at the table and wrote a letter. 'Dear Audrey and Leslie,' I wrote. 'Dear Mummy and Daddy, Something has happened that I have to tell

152

you about. Some tests on the baby have shown there's nothing physically wrong with him, but it seems likely he's going to be slow. He has Down's Syndrome which is not serious or disabling, we simply have to come to terms with it. Six weeks seems a long time now, and it's long enough to adapt . . .'

Except that each line I wrote I crossed out, thick black smudges of cancellation. I looked at the sheet and at Graham sitting still and I slid it into the kitchen drawer. After he was asleep I got out of bed again and came down and smoothed it so I could read under the markings. I copied it out, I wrote it very clearly again so there was no possibility they would not understand.

After a week Graham agreed we would go away. I was not surprised, all that time I had unpacked and repacked and organised. I did not see anyone, I set myself tasks: cupboards to clean, clothes to mend and the cases to attend to. When Graham was at home I practised friendliness. I leant against him and whispered funny phrases Anna had used during the day; I waited for him to smile before I asked what he would like to eat. I reminded him of other holidays, Anna floating shells in rock pools in Cornwall, walks he and I had taken over Dartmoor. I bought him new shirts and did not protest when he would not try them on. I showed him the guide books I had found.

'Look,' I said to Anna when the day came for us to leave. I thought of Laura and Geraldine and Jessica lined up to wave us off. 'Look at it now, we're going,' but all there was to see was the grey sky, the supermarket, the florist's, the library, packed pavements, queues, and all there was for me to do was close my eyes and rock and rest. It was travel that was nothingness, I thought, I had not realised it before, it was that I wanted, I did not want to arrive anywhere.

'Keep driving,' I wanted to say, but that was stupid, that was not what I had asked him to do. When I woke to feed the baby, Graham took Anna out into a field. They climbed over a low fence and I looked out of the window as they stood beyond the bleak road. He pointed to thin muddy lambs tottering up to broad sheep. They were all small, everything I could see, animals, Anna, Graham, all dwarfed by the pale sky, the streaming fields. I knew that all that was safe was this, inside, locked away, watching.

'Look,' I said sometimes, as we passed a river or a church, and then I slept again. When Graham said, 'This is it,' I did not want it to be. It was raining and the town was full of families with push-chairs, people wrapped in macs and scarves staring into gift-shop windows. I did not want to be there long enough to consider why they preferred to do that rather than sit in their hotel lounges and watch television. I did not want to imagine that indoors it was stifling, desperate beyond this cold and disappointment.

'It should be near here,' I said as Graham drove along the front, 'not far, it's very close, keep looking for the name.'

'Seaview,' Graham said. 'Does that sound right? It's a joke,' he said when we were in our room. I joined in laughing because that was nearly right, it felt like an exaggeratedly humorous passage in a dream, and we were experiencing it together. Without animosity I could look out at the rain and back at the two beds with shiny eiderdowns, the oversized washbasin, the wardrobes, our bags; we were locked into the room by them, there was no space to sit or to put the carry-cot except on the beds. I emptied all the cases higgledy-piggledy over them, opened drawers of the dressing table and thrust everything away.

'I can see my parents here,' I said. 'Audrey and Leslie thumping up those narrow stairs, knocking into the sailing boat in the hall. We went to the seaside once and it was like this. It's a time warp, we've gone backwards, all these people here in this town are part of it. We should buy a newspaper and see what date's printed on it. We could go out on the town,' I laughed again, 'and see what the latest style of miniskirt is. And bouffant hairdos. And there'll be boys riding motor scooters. Where we went,' – I lay back on my bed and the pink satin slid around beneath me and the clothes I had not put into drawers fell onto the floor – 'there were tea-rooms too, and tennis matches, and huge cardboard cornets outside one tea-shop. It was dreadful, the disappointment of having an ice-cream and it being an ordinary size. It seemed even smaller than usual when you looked out of the window and saw that huge yellow cone oozing vanilla cream. The landladies weren't that different. From this one,' I explained. 'Eternally aged forty-nine, hair that's just out of curlers, feet that hurt in shoes. And they never listen, they're always on the run, they've always got something, someone, waiting. Yours must have been different,' I said. 'Nice little *pensions* in the middle of French provincial towns, cabbage-rose wallpaper, bidets, nice weather. Did you join in?' I asked. I raised my head on one arm and regarded him as he and Anna stood side by side between her bed and the window. 'Did you become a group that was you and your parents? Did you all get together because everyone else was so different?'

'I don't remember,' he said.

'Did you enjoy them?' I asked. 'Or is that too difficult to remember as well?'

'I remember boredom,' he said. 'Having to sit around in rooms waiting for my parents to finish reading, talking. Feeling strange. We'll go and take a look around,' he said to Anna. 'When he's had his feed we'll all go for a walk before supper.'

We ate supper, we slept, we ate breakfast in a dining room that shone with fluorescent light. Our table was next to a middle-aged couple who were Audrey and Leslie's age, and the woman had the same tight curls and hard waves and thick legs. I could not see her face properly but I knew it would be long and wide and blank, and the man's nose as red as Leslie's. I stared hard at them across the aisle.

'What is it?' Graham asked.

'I was wondering who they were,' I said, 'they look familiar.' But behind their plates I could not really distinguish properly, all I could see clearly were egg and bacon and cornflakes and plates piled dangerously with toast. For a moment I thought the heap would topple, yolk and rinds would splatter all over their laps. 'Mind,' I wanted to shout, but they were all right; they chewed, they cleared their throats and swallowed. Gradually I could see their faces again.

'They're like them, but it's not,' I said and looked down at my plate.

'Finished?' Graham leaned across the table to Anna. 'We'll go and see the sea if you have.'

We went along the front, past shop windows and families, all pushing, all with children in carriages, all of us trudging like some defeated army, pointlessly moving on. There was a rhythm, a unity of exhaustion and inconsequence, ice-creams, funfairs, fairy lights, hopeless diversions from the tide and the wind and the cold. I could have walked for hours looking out to sea, snatching and rescuing; I was mesmerised.

155

'Think if you were in a boat,' I said, 'in that wind. You'd never make it. And look at the cliffs.' Even to tilt my head made me giddy. 'The height. The distance.' I shook myself but I still did not feel quite ordinary again. 'It's terrifying.'

We took the carry-cot up and down steps to tea-shops, we drank coffee and milkshakes and hot chocolate and bought nuts and crisps and magazines. Twice a day we went back to the hotel for steamed fish and jam sponge and soup and lamb and trifle. I was getting better, I noted, I was able to see the woman pushing the carry-cot, I could watch the woman feeding who could not arrange the baby's limbs properly. When she put the child back in the basket, I looked at him, a waxen parcel under the covers. I nodded and said to Anna, 'Shall I read you a story?' Or asked Graham, 'Where would you like to go this afternoon?' I was nearly ready, it only wanted a little more time before I could bring all this to an end.

'I'll manage,' I said to Audrey. 'I won't end up consumed by hatred. There's this idea, the idea you must have had, too, that it needn't go on. Maybe,' I ventured, 'it made things worse for you because you couldn't do anything. With a healthy old woman like Mercy there's only poisoning. And there was Laura to consider – she'd have been held to blame as well, taking food to her, it would have looked bad from her point of view. Except here,' I said, 'no one else would be involved.'

'If you stop feeding them,' I said, 'you have to watch them doing without, listen to them. It's happening in front of you for a long time. Or even something quick, a pillow, it means putting it there. Picking it up and standing with it in your hands, aiming so you don't have to look at them as you do it. An accident,' I said, 'where it just happens, that's the only way I can imagine it.'

In the afternoon it was still windy and we walked along the front and looked into shop windows.

'What now?' Graham said when we came to the end. 'Walk back again?'

I pointed to the sign over the road. 'You and Anna could go there.

'Army ranges,' I read. 'Unexploded mines. This is stupid, this can't be right.' But Graham did not answer. He stopped the car quite suddenly and I grabbed his arm. 'What for, here? We can't stop here. It's nowhere, this is nothing, nothing.' I pointed to the stunted trees around us, the grey horizon miles away, the level miles of wasteland. 'We can't stop here, it's flat. It's not right.'

'Don't be ridiculous.' He wound down the window. 'It's ideal for walking. You don't have to take notice of those signs.'

'But it's – flat.' I clenched my fists and stared out. 'I'm not coming.'

'Christ.' He started the car up again and drove, quite fast, towards a large board. 'Look,' he said, 'go and look at that map and tell me where you want.'

I did as he said. I did not look very hard, though. I closed my eyes as I had when I walked over the maps in the kitchen and contour lines swirled until I could see where they were tightest, the brown plateau they pointed to. I stepped back and followed the path with my finger.

'To the left,' I said and closed the car door. 'All right?' I turned back to Anna. 'And then at the crossroads go right. And then it's a couple of miles further on.'

At first I almost said, 'This isn't right, either,' because I could see other cars and groups of bright anoraks, but then I looked further and there it was, a level cliff top that fell away to nothing underneath, grey and green against the sky, the sun shining on it.

'Listen,' and I helped Anna out of the car and took out the carry-cot and wheels, 'listen to the wind.' Even though I shouted it was difficult to hear. It was behind us, pushing and buffeting. As Anna stood there it could almost carry her. I looked from her face to the other children, whipped with pink and excitement, and the flattened grass and swaying bushes, bright and brown and purple, and barking, scurrying dogs, toppling adults. I laughed, but that was impossible to hear as well. I pointed ahead to Graham and Anna and he nodded and Anna took his hand. I pushed the carry-cot against the car. I bent to make sure the brake was firm, and I shook it. It was obvious the car broke all the force, not even a breath lifted the sheets inside.

'Come on,' I mouthed. 'Race you to the top.'

I was quite far ahead of them, it was like sailing, caught, helped all the way through tussocky grass, fast, and not ever panting, but halfway I stopped as if to let them catch up with me.

'I've just thought,' I cupped my hands round my mouth and put them close to Graham's ear, 'supposing it changes direction. I'm going down to see the pram's all right.' I ran past him, into the gale this time, so I could not hear any arguments.

It was difficult, I was pushed back, hoarse and gasping. I was level with the car almost before I realised, undoing the brake with as much relief as if I was rescuing it. I stood still beside it for a moment and then without looking at anyone round me, shading my forehead against the sun, walked slowly over towards the edge of the cliff. I stopped on the way by another noticeboard and stared at the information about the preservation of bird and plant life and looked from striped and dotted patches that indicated rock strata to words jumping senselessly in front of me. I was not really looking at them at all, I was trying to see beyond, to the very edge where the bushes stopped and the ground fell, to find the place where it sloped most and where there was least shelter. I could see one spot, it was just out of sight of the car park and there was a path between the bushes and I strolled, gently guiding the pram, and when I reached it I stood still and looked back and round me. I was almost invisible. I could hear voices but I could see no one and the wind, when I faced the sea, was strong enough to blow me over. I turned the carry-cot sideways and straight away a gust caught it like a sail, the hood bellied out, it could almost have been swept from my hands there and then except I heard a noise, I heard a child. It came from above me. As I looked up I could see Anna at the very top of where I had climbed and she was running, arms wide and shouting, that was the noise I had heard, she was running in circles, faster, swooping, blown as hard as the carry-cot was and Graham was below her, looking another way, and I screamed. I jammed the brake onto the carry-cot and wedged it against the tree and screamed, 'You've gone too far, bring her down.' He did not turn round and then I started to run back up the path, across the open car park, falling, shouting, and past the noticeboard to the foot of the hill, and that was all I could get to because I could see her waver and teeter and there was not time enough for me to go any further before her body was falling, and I could hear the noise, the splattering, the soft screaming as her bones burst through the skin, and I screamed again and again until there were people all around me.

'Look,' they said, tugging at my hands, trying to pull them, one after another, from my face. 'Look, it's all right. No need to cry. Just look and see.' Eventually I did and Graham was holding her.

They were coming down, slowly, carefully so she did not over-balance, and she was waving, scarlet-faced, laughing and frightened.

'Here,' another voice said. I took the handle of the pram. 'Although it would have been all right where it was. I could hardly lift the brake, you've done it so tight.'

'Are you all right?' they asked.

'It affects children in the playground like that,' one man said, and then lowered his voice. 'It's panic, I suppose, a kind of madness. Extraordinary. Primitive, really.'

'Like the mistral?' another woman asked. There was a silence then and I did not look up. I did not smile round their faces and apologise and explain, I kept looking at the ground and I saw the shape of Graham's trousers and then they were foreshortened, closer, closer still and then he was touching me.

I took Anna's hand and held it. 'Let's go back,' I said. 'Let's go and get back in the car.'

'I want to go,' I said when we were back at the hotel. 'It was a stupid idea, coming here. It's no different. There isn't anything else I can do.'

As soon as I was back in the house I could see it would do me no good to be there again, either; none of it held me together any more.

'We shouldn't have gone,' I said, 'or come back. It's not the right thing—'

'Where will you feed him?' Graham asked and offered me the carry-cot. I walked away to the window.

'Look at this.' I ran my fingers over the glass. 'You can't see where you are. And this,' I picked up a cushion from a chair, held it distant, dropped it onto the floor. 'Look at the dust,' I said. It seemed a cloud of it was rising, obscuring, distorting.

'Here,' Graham said and put the cushion back. 'Sit here, that'd be best. We didn't stop after Basingstoke, he must be starving.'

'He doesn't say so.' I waited for Graham to take him out of the carry-cot and put him onto my lap and stared ahead, round the room. 'Tawdry,' I said, 'half the things we've got. Tarnished old junk. I'm not talking about hi-tech,' I said with sudden passion, 'but this,' and I kicked the table and the fruit bowl on it rattled, 'and that,' and I shook my head. I could have bared my teeth at the dresser, 'Need a clean sweep. They're relics, like Catholics keep, guarantees of the past against the future. Candles on a worn-out altar.'

'He's ready,' Graham said, and stood in front of me until I had unbuttoned my blouse. Then he bent and took the head in one of his hands and put it to my breast.

'Don't you see what I mean?' I tried to pull his hand away. 'Things we should forget about?'

'He's waiting.' Graham held the head there until it began to suck. 'He'll be all right now,' he promised.

'Let's put these away now,' he said to Anna, and carried her bag of toys to where she sat on the floor. 'Come and show me which cupboards.' She got up, she had been quite still there, her hands splayed wide on the tiles, her head drooping, rocking slightly from side to side, and held onto him, pulled the bag, wound her legs round his. 'We won't be long,' he said and picked her up.

'Supper?' he asked when they came down. I laughed.

'Salami?' I said. 'Bread and cheese?'

'We'll have a look,' he answered, 'see what the fridge has in store.' He drew Anna beside him. 'Look,' he said. 'Choose.' She turned over packets of hamburgers and chips and pasties. 'You lay the table,' he said. 'Get the bread and butter, put the knives and forks out. These'll only take ten minutes to cook. Ketchup, mustard, get those and I'll open a tin of beans.'

'You should look at this place,' I said. 'Look at it now. This is what could do with altering, this house, all these rooms, but especially this. I've seen too much,' and I scraped my chair on the tiles, 'of this, and the bedroom, they don't work any more. Don't you think?' I persisted when he was silent. 'Don't you?' and he shrugged.

'They've been all right up to now. But if that's what you want.'

'One of the things,' I said, because I had seen it on the journey home, rooms without carry-cot or clothes, clear, light, but now it had escaped me, I could not begin to prepare for it, I was away from it again.

'Anna can go to bed,' I said, and it sounded rougher than I meant, 'when she's finished.' I looked down at the baby. 'He has.' I took him away from me and walked over to where Graham sat. 'You look after him,' I said, 'this is nothing to do with me any more. Food, meals, making a scene out of this. This isn't what should happen, it's not what I see here.'

He stared for long enough for me to know what he saw. I was out of place. The solid floor and the plates on the table and smell of sausages and Anna staring from her chair, clutching the back, all meant that the room had not changed for him.

'Give him to me,' he said, and laid him over one shoulder, uncoordinating, unresisting.

'He's getting bigger,' I said. 'Look, Anna, he'll be a big boy soon. Big enough to—' and I stopped. 'I don't know what he'll be big enough for.'

Graham shifted the weight on his arm. 'Why don't you go up to bed?' he asked. 'It's no bad thing, once in a while, to admit defeat. Exhaustion. Why don't you let me—'

'All right,' I sounded agreeable. 'Except I might not go to bed. Not straight away, that is. I might look round a bit first at the rooms.'

'I should try and rest. I'll bring them up soon, we won't be long.'

'I've got things I've got to read.' I walked towards him, lightly touching the table. I took a piece of bread but it crumbled. 'I've just remembered. You stay down as long as you like.'

All the time I climbed the stairs I remembered, because after yesterday I had known a different thing that I would have to do.

I closed our bedroom door tight and put a chair against it, took the right telephone directory from Graham's desk and sat on the chair, my back to the door. I turned through Hackney, Hamley's, Hammersmith and Fulham Social Services and I memorised the numbers. I sat watching the window get dark and said the numbers over and over again. I saw my fingers dialling them, but I could not hear another voice. I could hear my words, 'I've got a baby I want adopted,' but not the answer. I could hear Graham laughing and Anna's high voice, I could see the silent baby, I could see them all in the kitchen, but I could not be there too. He had made that impossible and it could not go on. I went back to my picture. I practised the words that would make it happen.

'I was thinking,' I said to Graham when he pushed against the bedroom door, and moved the chair away.

'Here,' he said and held the baby out to me. 'Will you put him down? Anna's getting undressed, he weighs a ton to carry round.' I took him ungently and put him into the cot.

'I don't need to be made to touch him,' I said. 'You could have done that. I don't lack contact with him.'

'I'll read her story,' he said, 'if you want to go to bed.'

'It's not that I need to be bonded to him,' I said. 'It won't change. You might change, you might think of that, years of wordlessness, lolling, dribbling, vacancy. They might alter you, but I'm not like that. You know how to be good, you've learnt that, that was one of your childhood lessons.'

He turned his back on me.

'I've thought of something else,' I said when he came back in, but he did not take any notice.

'She's asleep,' he said. I could not understand, because I was thinking of the morning, of how soon I could phone. 'I need a breath of fresh air,' he said, 'I think I'll go down the road, somewhere for a walk.'

'Trust me?' I said but it was too dark for him to see if I was joking.

'Trust you?' His voice was difficult, he was not frightened, it was defensive. 'Why trust?'

'Why not? Am I safe without you watching? What might I do if you're not here? Think of it, where I could go, who I could phone—'

'Give it a rest,' and his shadow pushed itself back and forth against the door frame. 'Go to sleep. I won't be late.'

When I woke I thought it was crying but it was Graham moving, settling to sleep. It was late, he must have been out for hours.

'I turned him over,' he said. 'He was restless. I didn't think I'd woken you.'

'Restless?' I pushed myself up on an elbow. 'Waking up? Needing to be settled? Him?'

'OK.' He lay down, his back to me.

'He's quiet now,' I said. 'Couldn't you sleep?' He did not answer. 'You probably thought you heard him,' I said. 'He's never done that. He can't. You thought, that's it, in your sleep you imagined you heard something and when you woke up you thought it was

164

him. It wasn't Anna?—' and I sat up to get out but he shook his head.

'Definitely not.'

'What time is it?' I said and leant over to hold his arm up, let his watch shine, but he pulled back. 'Four,' I said as he folded himself under the duvet and I lay down again. 'You can't have lain awake ever since you got in, that would be ridiculous. You must have imagined it. That's what it must have been. He's never woken,' I said. 'He won't do things like that.'

When I woke again it was morning and I could not wait.

'Come on,' I said to them as I watched their soft-haired heads bent over the table. I wanted a spell to cast them instantly outside, the half-hour until they were absent eliminated. I wanted to sit by the telephone, my words rehearsed, shrouded. I thought that my voice would sound dry like dust. 'Hurry up,' I repeated, insistently. I stood on my toes to watch them eat, but they sat quite still. I watched the telephone as well, as if with the weight of my expectation it might start up by itself. If it had rung I would have believed straight away in transference. 'I've got a baby,' I would have said. 'I want you to have him.'

'What's the rush?' Graham asked. 'What's your hurry? Mind,' he said when they were finished. I thought he meant myself.

'How?' I asked. 'Why?'

'So she can get her coat.' I moved from where I had been waiting by the door and looked back into the room. I saw the order and light and Anna's round arms sliding into her anorak, her feet astride and cheeks puffed with concentration. Graham's face was turned down, all the planes were softened as he bent to help her. Only the three of us there.

'I want them to have him,' I said.

But Graham said, 'Who's having Anna this afternoon?' I turned.

'Having Anna?'

'To play,' he answered. 'Geraldine or Jessica? She said last night she wasn't staying here after lunch. I assumed you'd fixed something.'

'Anna?' She did not look up at me. 'There's nothing happening. We've been away for days, how could I fix anything?'

'Last week,' he shrugged. 'Before we went. I don't know, it's just what she said.'

165

'She could,' I considered, 'she could go wherever she wants, anyone'll have her. When you take her to the playgroup you could ask, you could say, Who'll have Anna this afternoon?'

I leant over the table and picked up dirty plates and cups but I did not stack them, I pulled them together, a spattered, stained group.

'We'll see.' He reached across and pushed Anna's mug over to her. 'Drink up.'

'How will you let me know?' I asked, 'who's having her, if someone will? I've got people to phone,' I said. 'It might be engaged. You might not be able to get through.'

'I'll keep trying.' He smiled as she gulped the last of her milk, wiped the drops from her chin. 'Good girl,' he said.

I had rehearsed all of it except that I would not get any help.

'They'll collect him,' I had told myself, practised the parting. I had gone to stand at the front door, looked at the path, as I would when the pram was wheeled away, promising to visit in a month. Except I would not go. A month after it would not seem as though he had not existed but as though it was right to forget.

I dialled and talked and heard other voices consult and papers rustle, but it did not turn out as I meant it to. I could be visited, they said. I could be interviewed, but there was no other promise.

'I'll come this afternoon,' the woman had said. 'It doesn't matter if your husband's not there, I'll just talk to you first.'

Because it was not what I had planned I thought she would not keep her promise, and when I saw her I wished she hadn't. She was not ugly like Anne Berrington, she did not offend me. I looked at this woman and I saw Anna advanced by twenty years, pale, blonde, incapable of horror, unaccustomed to dealing with it.

'Come in,' I said. It should have been, 'Go away,' but she followed me, sat opposite me at the table. I watched her uncertain blinking, her effortless swallowing.

'Do you want to tell me what's happened?' she asked, and her voice was quiet, it was hers that sounded like dust.

'Tell you?' I said. 'Again? Why? I told you on the phone.' I looked away at all the room stretched round us. We were bounded in by it.

She nodded. 'I'd like you to.'

'I had a mongol baby. Down's Syndrome. I want him taken away, into care, adopted. I don't want him, that's all. It shouldn't be difficult. I haven't neglected him,' I assured her. 'He's fed, he gets washed and dressed, you can go and look, I don't mind what you inspect about him. But that's all he ever needs, that's what I'm not prepared to do. Those things don't mean anything, they're functions. He's nothing apart from that and I don't want just that. Is that enough to tell you?'

She did not answer. She spread her fingers and looked at them on the wooden table, flat, pink on brown, whorls, scars.

'Where is he?' she asked. I pointed to his place, the space by the corner, out of all the draughts. She walked over to where the cot was, carried it to the chair next to her, and leant over and looked, wondering, touching.

'Sweet,' she said and tried to think of other words.

'Not to me,' I said. 'Silent. I don't want a silent baby. What I want,' and I spaced the words as she stroked his cheek, 'is for you to take him away. Not today, maybe, or tomorrow, but to say you'll do it. Otherwise,' and I let her see me clench my hands on the table, 'I'll have to do it, make him out of the way. I can't have him with me any more.'

'I see,' she said. She did not look at me but down at him, rocked him. 'But the thing is, he's not just yours. Other people have a say – your husband, for example. What does he think about it?'

'He doesn't come into it,' I said. 'He's nothing to do with him.'

'Nothing to do with him.' The rocking stopped.

'He's not the father.' I held my hands now to stop them shaking, I could not believe I could be so clever, invent so quickly and exactly to defeat her guidelines.

'Not the father,' she repeated. 'I see.' She turned to me as if she thought she did.

'He's gone away,' I said, 'the real father.' Then I remembered Jas, his width, his blunted nose. 'He was a man my sister knew. He was leaving her, he was going to Manchester and I thought I wanted to see what she saw in him. I thought I had the chance. He rang me up, he needed someone to drink with. I dressed up, I practised small talk all the way there and when we came out I couldn't walk, I was drunk, reeling. I couldn't have stopped him if I'd wanted to. It was in an alleyway, a turning-off by Gunnersbury Park. Every time I opened my eyes I could see headlights flashing in the car park

167

opposite, and it was over as soon as it happened. And straight away afterwards, as soon as it happened, I told myself it hadn't. I got a train, he got a train, it wasn't even a night out. I said I'd been to the cinema with Geraldine when I got home. Do you know,' and I leaned across the table as though I was going to take her hand, 'it never occurred to me I'd get pregnant. And then, when I found I was, that it wasn't Graham's. I put it out of my mind completely, it wasn't until the clinic checked dates that I remembered that night. Do you believe that?' I moved my fingers closer to hers. 'Do you believe anyone can be that stupid?'

'Have you told him? His father?' she asked. 'Have you tried to get in contact at all?' I shook my head. 'Or an abortion?' She did not flinch her little face at the word. 'Was there a time when you considered that?'

I bent away from her. 'It was too late. I said to myself, "It's Graham's, Graham knows it's his, he doesn't sense anything else." I thought there'd be some sign, something telling me whose it was, what to do. I thought something would intervene and nothing did. What it was,' and I looked up at her, 'was that I was a bit crazy. When I think back, that's what it seems like. Don't you think so? Isn't that how it seems to you?'

She looked down at the baby again, back up to me. 'I'm beginning to see what you mean,' she said.

'I could make some tea,' I said. I wanted more time to get used to that idea, Jas inside me, outside the pub, instead of inside the pub with Graham and Laura.

'Old women and the unemployed; fun-bunch,' he'd said and I'd laughed, it was the nearest I'd come to excitement. 'Doll's house games, kids stuff,' he'd said and then I had turned away, so angry I'd spilt my drink.

'Yes, please,' she said. She did not look at her watch, perhaps she found it exciting, too.

'What I'm frightened of,' I said, 'is Graham. Not just finding out, but what it'd do to all of us.' I waited with my hand on the teapot. 'You should see Graham with Anna, what she has to live up to, take an interest in, what she has to do in return for him as a father. He expects. He finds it easy, he gives, but he expects us to find it easy to respond. He doesn't see they're two completely different things. Do you see?'

She no longer leaned across the table like a child eager for a story; she sat back into her chair, judicious, considering.

'Look,' I said, 'at all the generous attention he's going to give to that baby, and me watching and knowing it's my fault. I can't do that, there are things that are impossible, no one could be expected to do them. I'm not saying I want a reward,' I said, 'but I do want you to see I'm not taking it lightly.' I leaned towards her, closer to her eyelashes, hair, fingers across her mouth. She could not back away, she could not get up and leave me without answering. She stood up to it, though; she regarded her hands in her lap, the cups on the table. She did not shift or laugh or fidget.

'Do you see?' I asked eventually. She nodded, eyes still downcast. 'So will you do something? Can you?'

I wondered if she was silent because it turned out, put like that, that I was not asking for a lot, not a wrong thing, or even a very difficult one; if it upset her that it was not impossible or unreasonable to bring adultery, deformity, to a satisfactory conclusion.

'When I go back,' she said, opening her handbag, 'I'll have a talk to my senior. He'll talk to you – maybe,' she added, because I shook my head.

'No,' I said. 'No one else. I've told you, I've said it all once. You can report back, you're the one they sent to find out.' But she was not looking, she was turning the pages in a diary, huge, dark blue velour, big enough to write a book in.

'Next week,' and she ran her finger down the side of a page, 'we've got a case conference. I could bring it up then.' But I would not let her go on, I pointed across the table.

'What was the point of you coming if it was just to make notes? Get hold of a story and take it back for other people to judge, what are you there for?'

She still did not look at me. She was not moved by anger or mistrust. She was writing in the book, putting it back in her bag.

'I've told you,' I said, 'and now you're going. Is that all there is to it?'

She sighed. 'Of course it's not,' she said, 'but one person can't make a decision like this. It's too important.'

'So what happens?' I asked. 'You all get together, a committee of you, and examine the evidence. What I did, what I deserve. All for a fuck.'

She did not look away at the rude word, she noted the dresser past my shoulder, the pottery, the pinboard with soap coupons, and she stood up, but she turned towards me.

169

'I'll phone to let you know,' she said. 'After Wednesday I should have some news. At the latest by the end of the week.'

I stood in front of her; I wanted to push her back, to ask at what point I had lost her, when she had withdrawn from my kitchen to her office and turned my story into a case.

'I feel as if I've told you this for nothing,' I said. 'I didn't expect it to happen immediately' – you and that pram going, this door closing – 'but I didn't see it like this. I thought something would start to get better.'

She looked from the carry-cot to her watch. 'It will,' she said. 'It's just a question of time. Whatever the outcome, it will get better. Waiting's the hardest part, but you have to try and see it in stages. Don't think of an end result yet, take it step by step. Think of next week and after that—'

'Oh, yes,' I nodded. 'I can see endlessly, that isn't difficult, even since he was born I've thought of that. Isn't that why you're here?'

'There just isn't an easy way.' She put her bag on her shoulder. 'I can't give you easy answers. This is stage one, we've got to wait for the rest. Come on,' and she smiled, 'it isn't so bad, waiting. You've done the hardest part, telling someone, the rest is just patience. Give it to the end of the week,' she persuaded, 'set your sights on that, getting through till then. Then we'll have another look. See where we're going. We'll talk again then.'

I waited and she was right, it became easier because it lasted so long; it lasted three months and even then it was not over, but instead of the waiting defeating me it became acceptable. It was like an affair, I thought, diminished by time from the obsessive to the comforting, something to rest at the back of my mind as a promise. And like an affair it still engendered panic, days of disbelief and faithlessness, but I overcame them, I learnt to return to it as a reliable state.

At first, every morning when Graham and Anna had gone, I had sat by the phone. I had allowed ten minutes when I willed a ringing, and then I had gone away from it, I walked away but I had not let it out of my sight. In our bedroom was an extension, but in Anna's room, in the sitting room, although it could be heard I could not be certain of reaching it in time. I did not go in those rooms any more; I ran when I went up and downstairs to the bathroom and I dragged the extension to follow me outside an open door. I did not go out to visit, I did not invite people to come and see me; when Graham was late because of meetings, or when he sat upstairs at his desk I did not mind; I was busy with the future.

'Such a nice couple,' I would say to Audrey and Leslie when my different version travelled to see them, another woman sprung from my groundwork, calm, adult, competent without effort. We would sit down and I would be gentle with them, pour tea when Audrey's hand shook, touch Leslie's shoulder when he turned away from me.

'A large family,' I would explain, 'very happy until three years ago when the eldest child was run over. They wanted – not a replacement, I suppose, but to do something to make up for that. Compensate instead of mourn.'

'I can understand that,' Audrey would say. 'You can't keep crying over spilt milk.'

'They'll have to change his name,' I remembered. 'Ironic, really. Their son was Tim, so he'll have to be different,' and as I said it he would be altered, a laughing boy with only a low hairline, a flat face, nothing else to distinguish him. 'Johnny,' they would call, and he would lollop obediently to answer, grinning, pawing with affection.

'I see,' Audrey would say and fold her arms and look beyond the tea table, the net curtains without spite or anger. Leslie would put a hand on her arm and it would rest there, unresisted.

Even when I shook myself from that, when I saw Audrey shrivelled on her kitchen stool, Leslie swaying by the bedroom door, I thought that by that time it would not matter, I could withstand what they were because I would be announcing that it was over.

'She won't come back,' I said to myself. 'We can't,' I said to Anna when she wanted to go out, and asked for her to be collected and taken to other houses. Although I spent days alone I was not pleased to see her back, it was an intrusion, a breaking into a world where I was waiting for someone else.

After a week she did telephone. 'It's Carmel Summers,' she said, 'we met last Tuesday,' and ten days later still she came to see me.

'We've had a lot of discussion about it,' she said, 'around the different views. It's a complex area; there isn't a straight line out.'

I tried to concentrate on what she was saying, because now she was here I did not have to listen for the phone. I had taken her into the sitting room because then I could not watch it either, she would not be able to detect I needed her verdict. She stooped from the armchair to look at the bookshelves, slipped her neat sandals on the rug.

171

'I talked to my senior,' she said and I nodded. 'He's inclined to let me decide on some aspects, initially, but the group decision is that there are a number of possibilities for you to consider and then we'll be in a better position to help you. You and Graham.' I hated her then because it meant she would not help, they would let him into it and he would never agree.

'That's not what you said before,' I said. 'He's got nothing to do with it. You know that,' but she took no notice.

'What I'd like to talk about today,' she sat up straight, eyes downcast, 'is help. Who, when and where. I don't mean vague promises from friends that you feel too embarrassed to take up but professional help. Everyone thinks they're alone in this, that's what makes you feel so desperate, but it's not the case.'

I studied the rug, too, marooned on the polished boards, I heard Anna's singing and the blur of the television from her room; I could see Carmel back in her office, betraying, satisfied. They would have told her what to do, an older woman, plump, desperately prying, and two men, one little, wispily bearded and the senior, bulky-waisted, tired eyes. Humane, they would call him. 'Like a killer?' I could hear Jas ask. 'Money? House? Husband?' they would have asked. 'She'll be all right. She doesn't need to get away with it.'

'You're wasting your time,' I told her. 'You know the only help I want.'

'One day next week,' she said, 'we could go along to the Wisden Centre. It's not only the nearest to here, it's one of the best, purpose-built, swimming pool, playground. It takes three-year-olds to start with, it's a feeder for the special schools. If we could fix that now—' and she took the big blue book out of her bag.

'No,' I said. I saw the pages stop turning. 'There's no reason to go on. I told you, I don't want him in a special school, I don't want him in a centre, I don't want him. You, the council, whoever gets him, they can put him where they like, but it's of no interest to me, nothing to do with him is of any account at all, except him going. You knew that, you're lying otherwise—' I stopped. 'You know what I want,' I said more quietly.

'And what does Graham want?' she asked, quiet, too, sly, but I was ready for her.

'Nothing,' I said. 'I've got nothing to tell him until I know what you'll do. I'll tell him then, I'll tell him what's happened and he'll believe me. He won't say, "You can't," because if he did I'd say, "You have him," and we know that couldn't happen. That baby's mine and he's going, he can't stay a punishment for ever. He's not yours, no one will stare at you taking him out, taking him to places to play idiot games with idiots' toys. Don't pretend.'

I sat back in my chair because she leaned towards me.

'Barbara.' I would not look at her. 'It isn't wrong to feel like that, but feelings change. I want to show you how they can, get you to give yourself a chance. I don't want you to have regrets afterwards. And I want you to see what he could be given, how he could respond to that. No one,' and she reached out to touch me, 'wants you to decide yet. What we want is for you to find out what's best.'

'I know what I want,' I said.

I was frightened when she left because I thought she might declare me irrational, abandon me as unsuitable. Still I would not change, I was more frantic. I told her I was glad to see her go if she could not help.

'I want a decision,' I said. 'I'll find a private place, they must exist, some people must have got desperate enough to want someone like him. I could do that.'

She perched herself on the kitchen table. 'Tell me,' and she looked round the room, 'what you mean by a happy childhood. A happy family life; how you see that?'

'How it was before him,' I answered straight away. 'How it will be when he's gone. You've seen Anna,' I said. 'That's what I can do.'

'I'll call in,' she said, 'later in the week. Or ring again.'

Every time she came she found a reason to go and look at him. I waited for her to come back. She did not comment or question, I supposed she checked that he was uninjured. I did not care enough to ask.

'This is taking a long time,' I said. It had been three weeks and I was frightened of losing my anger, becoming lulled.

'Mothering,' she said. 'We all think we know about it. We've all been mothered, we'll probably all do it—'

'What I do,' I said, 'is leave his pram outside one shop while I go into another. Then people don't know he belongs to me. And I can watch them, I see them look into the pram and nothing happens, he doesn't smile. They wait a minute and then they look round to see if anyone's spotted them, and then they back away. Would it make it easier,' I asked her, 'if I was there? If I stood next to the pram and said, "Don't bother, he's got no idea"? Would that help, do you think?'

She visited, she telephoned, regular, docile, calculated because the longer it lasted the less desperate I would become. But that was not what happened; I did not come to feel I could live with him; it was something else, a more immediate opportunity for activity. I thought that for six months I could leave his future in abeyance. I also thought that I would progress, that by the end generosity would have earned me a reward.

'Tell me about Graham,' Carmel asked. 'What's he like in everyday terms?' I answered her. 'What about friends?' she said, and I imagined a ghostly procession of them round the kitchen, but I did not refuse discussion.

'Graham's what you'd call moral,' I said. 'And busy. He goes to work all day, he goes to meetings in the evenings and we don't talk, not about him or the baby or his job. Sometimes he asks me, "How was he?" or, "How was your day?" but he knows the answer, every time he looks in that carry-cot he can see. I don't mind,' I said, because to sit in different rooms, to dress and undress in silence, to converse through Anna at meals was easy. When I went upstairs to bed and he stood up to stack his papers, align them with as much purposeless care as I had just applied to the breakfast table, level spoon by central plate, and then he turned to hug me, to extract some signal of comfort, that was worse, that was unbearable. 'We don't have anything to do with one another,' I said. 'Not really.'

'Friends?' she reminded me and I nodded.

'I send them away,' I said. 'Geraldine rings up and invites Anna, collects and brings her back. I say hello and goodbye. What should I ask them in for? Jessica's ex-husband, the playgroup rota, to talk about those?'

'Your sister,' she asked, 'your family?'

'Laura's busy, too,' because that was what she had said when she'd rung. 'Over-run with old ladies, filling in for people with flu.

She's got no reason to come. What you don't seem to understand is that no one's got a reason to come while he's here, I won't let them have one.'

'Except me,' she said.

'My parents wouldn't, anyway, they never have. They like their own safety, too, you can explode in that, you don't dare in the outside world. Control, habit, they grant you a lot of leeway. Besides,' I hesitated, 'he frightens them. He's an underbelly, he's what you cover over, hide in the spare bedroom, what you get drunk not to see. Both of those to both of them,' I said, 'adaptable.'

'What about you?' she asked. 'Do you think that too?'

'He doesn't represent anything to me,' I said. 'I know exactly where I am with him, I want him gone.'

On the day Laura came I did not answer the phone. I never did after five o'clock because by then the Social Services office was closed and they could not ring to tell me that they had decided, someone would come to take him away.

'I took a chance,' Laura said. 'Teatime.' She bent as if she was going to kiss me. 'I thought you could only have popped out.' She pulled one of the kitchen chairs over to where I sat by the window. 'Maybe it's out of order,' she said, 'if you were here all the time. It's been ages, nearly a month.' She touched my dressing gown. 'Aren't you well?'

'Tired,' I said and looked at the clock. It was still an hour until Anna went to bed.

'Look.' She dragged her bag off the table. 'I brought a bottle, for us.'

'No, thanks.' I got up, away from her and went over to the door, opening it as though I needed to listen. 'You can't when you're feeding,' I said. I watched her find a glass and corkscrew, pour, sit back in the chair and tip her head, close her eyes.

'That's better.' I wanted her gone, I did not want to watch that letting go. 'How've you been?' she said. 'Graham said Easter was a good break. I rang one day, you must've been asleep. I never know whether to ring and ask, I suppose I think if you want to talk about it – except who would you talk to?' She moved her head sideways to look at me. 'I saw Geraldine the other day and she asked how you were.' She dangled the glass from her hand, she had drunk it very quickly. 'As if I ought to know.'

'There isn't anything to talk about,' I said. 'I know what people think. They feel relief because it's not them, and I don't blame them. But that doesn't make me pretend it's all right, it can be put right.'

'It could be worse.' She poured another glass. 'There are other things. He could have been perfect and died, he could be badly injured, his life could be in danger.'

'That's a help,' I said.

'No one's saying it's fair.' She shook her head. 'Only bearable. There's Anna,' she said. 'She's got to develop an attitude towards it.'

'No,' I said. 'He's nothing to do with her, nothing to talk about to her, you, Graham, Audrey, anyone. We can talk about other things if you like, your job, walking sticks, bedpans, I'm quite happy to hear about that—'

'Because they don't make any difference?'

'Because you want to.' I shrugged. 'It's up to you.'

'All right,' she said. I suppose she thought she was performing a therapeutic exercise, drawing me back into the world, because for half an hour she talked about those things. I could see the corridors, bent figures on slow frames, purposeless, waiting to pass.

'Once upon a time,' she said, 'people used to pay money to keep them out of sight because they wanted them out of mind; now if they're out of sight the next step's elimination. They really could die,' she said, 'for all anyone cares. Relatives, the state, the whole world. It's a waste of money, keeping them going, surviving for no one except themselves.' She giggled. 'They do enjoy their food, though. I find that quite cheering. What I'd do,' and she poured another glass of wine, 'is take to food and drink. Get sozzled, eat to sober up. I couldn't see any point in surviving except for self-indulgence. And I'd make a fuss, drive around in a wheelchair with a placard saying, "My pension's sixty-five pounds a week, what does the Queen Mother get?" You have to be sensational to get people to sit up, take notice. It matters. They're lonely,' she said. 'That's the worst because it's not their fault, nothing to do with them.'

'It's half past seven,' I said when it was. 'Anna's got to get to bed and I've got to feed him.'

'I'll come up,' she said, 'you can still listen. What gets me about it is the harm everyone's doing to themselves. You can't cast people out, cut them off because they're not convenient to have around any more. Our family cast one another out and look at the efforts we've made, you and I to get close again. If we have. It's all you can rely on, you've got to rely on that, on the next generation down.'

'Like Audrey?' I asked. She stopped walking around my bedroom. She picked her glass off the dressing table and looked in the mirror. 'I've got to think about that. All right,' she said after a minute. 'Mercy didn't find Audrey, but she did get me, and all right, Audrey won't have me, but she's got you—'

'Something for everyone,' I said and took the baby from over my shoulder, put him to my other breast.

'You feed him,' Laura said. 'You could give him a bottle. You could give him away. See.' She smiled and raised her glass and came and stood by the bed and then turned away from me.

'If I'm feeding him,' I said, 'I can't be tempted. You can put aspirin in a bottle, it can't be intravenous in my milk. It's me I'm protecting – I don't have to decide every four hours I'm going to let him live, it's not for him.'

She started to walk round the room again and fingered the bedspread while I changed him. When I had put him back in the carrycot I said, 'I usually have a rest now if that's all right?'

'If I was going, you mean,' she said and stood still. 'No supper, no coffee, even? Come on, you'll have other evenings to have a rest in—'

'I'm out of practice,' I said. 'People make me tired.'

'Stay awake five minutes.' She went over to the door and leaned against it, as though to keep herself in the room, to stop me opening it for her. She took hold of a dressing gown to steady herself and then kept hold of it, held the black skirt of Graham's kimono over her like a shield. 'I haven't said it yet. I haven't said what I really came for.' She pulled the silky sash loose, wound it round her fingers. 'I had a party last week because I wanted to celebrate. I had it to show people I'm pleased. I'm not getting married, I'm not even telling him – I want it just to be mine. I'm having a baby,' she said. 'I want you to be involved. I want you to be part of it. Will you?' she said.

Laura

Once I'd got over my chagrin at Barbara's pregnancy and once she'd decided, although I couldn't quite fathom why, that I was all right to have around the place, it was difficult to remember what I'd done before. Then I remembered it was Jas, so I concentrated on the new routine, and I was grateful for the diversion.

Living with Jas had been a very exclusive business. He wasn't interested in spending time with any friends I made at work – an evening once every six months with Barbara and Graham was the most he'd allow. When he left Barbara was the only person who had the faintest concern about what had happened. Also, as soon as I was back, the weather was appalling, cold and rainy. Every day I heaved myself out of bed and looked at a grey sky as I drank my coffee. Every day as I went into the red building to work, and smelled disinfectant, I felt like going home to sleep and, once I'd been allowed my statutory fifteen minutes' holiday re-cap the first day, it was as if I'd never been away. So I thought it would be nice to go to Barbara's and reminisce a bit more, revel in Martine's awfulness, play with the idea that – to see Debbie and Marie, of course – I might go to Birmingham, even go further back and discuss more of the whys and wherefores of Jas. But the first day I went Barbara said, 'Geraldine and Jessica are coming, it'll be rather child-oriented talk, I'm afraid, not a lot of interest to you probably.' That still didn't deter me, I didn't mind at all as long as I was with other people.

I could draw a picture of those afternoons, the kitchen warm and smelling faintly of damp macs and hot children, thin cross Geraldine smoking and fat resigned Jessica trying not to chew her nails, Melissa and Ben and good Anna watching television at the other end of the room or running up and down stairs; squeals, disagreements, tea and biscuits.

Some nights the last thing I thought of before I went to sleep wasn't Jas but what had happened that afternoon. Geraldine and Jessica were at home in that kitchen and I was an onlooker, but I altered that, I reran scenes where I changed the whole shape of things.

'That's not fair,' I said to Geraldine when she smacked Melissa, or to Melissa when she teased Anna. Instead of letting Jessica put words in Ben's mouth, I'd say 'We're going to learn some new talking today.'

'You're so patient,' Geraldine and Jessica would start to tell me. 'It's so nice to be with someone objective.'

I imagined days I might be late arriving. Everyone would be expectantly looking up from the table when Barbara ushered me in.

'You're a breath of fresh air,' Geraldine would smile.

Sometimes I laughed, there were certain words none of them would ever utter. On the whole, though, I didn't mind sitting at my end of the table watching them all, listening to talk about subjects I thought I was familiar with – desertion, disillusion. All I wished was that I'd known them ten years ago when I was an adolescent, because then I'd have been thrilled to hear the secrets of married life; I wouldn't have been expected to contribute, whereas now I just wasn't asked to.

There were some subjects we never talked about, though, difficult ones that stood out a mile: like the way Melissa whined and Geraldine snapped, Ben's silences, Jessica's overeating. They were never raised, and the most obvious of all, Barbara's health, was always avoided. I supposed it wasn't polite to say, 'You look awful,' to your hostess, but as she got more pregnant and more sick it ought to have worried people. I could see that she found it physically troublesome, but it was because it was a blow to her activities that it most upset her. She didn't admit that it might have more significance than preventing her doing the housework.

'What does Graham think?' I asked.

'Does he notice?' she answered. I said that wasn't fair, he always wanted to know how she was. He'd come home and hug Anna and give me a little wave.

'How's Laura? Tending the sick again? You're a very good sister to have.'

'She doesn't have to come,' Barbara would say. 'I managed before.' He and I would ignore that.

'Have you mentioned it at the clinic?' I asked. 'What does the doctor say? Can't they give you something?' But she always had reassuring answers quite pat, it was nothing to worry about. Everyone told her it was unusual but not extreme, she couldn't bear a fuss, and although maybe I should have challenged her, forced to keep on at the doctor, I didn't. I didn't argue and I helped, I went out of my way to be useful.

'Has Barbara said how grateful we are?' Graham asked, when I'd altered my shift to the early-morning one so that I could come and give Anna lunch.

'It's all right,' I said. 'It's convenient for both of us.' I told myself it was, we both needed help, her to rest and me to recover, that although the holiday had done me good I still missed Jas and if I could help Barbara instead of feeling miserable that was the best thing all round.

When Jas first left it hadn't hit me that missing him wasn't just an immediate reaction. It had taken a couple of weeks before I started to realise it meant the end of a lot of other things, too, and that miserable feeling still hadn't disappeared. Jas going meant he and I weren't going to live anywhere together; I could wave goodbye to all the dreams I'd had of him oiling my pregnant stomach, of the warm and welcoming kitchen we'd have in the house we'd buy – not as big as Barbara and Graham's, not as tidy and well decorated, but not dissimilar. I could forget every picture of holding his babies, entertaining his friends, gossiping with other mothers. I knew all the time they weren't very admirable pictures, but they were still cherished and desirable and unattainable.

By November it was getting better, though. I was beginning to have days when I saw myself six months, a year hence, sitting calmly on the couch learning a foreign language, and occasionally it didn't seem too unrealistic to think of starting evening classes next term, even eventually meeting someone else. The adult thing, I told myself, was to wait until I was feeling better and then to back gracefully away from Barbara, demonstrate my independence without losing her goodwill. I couldn't go on substituting her home for mine, and it wasn't the same anyway, the dramatis personae was different; in my house I would have been in charge, and in hers I was accidentally included.

I'd started to think of how to introduce the idea – 'I won't come tomorrow, I'm going shopping and then for a drink with Beryl' –

when Barbara started saying, 'Could you take over for a bit? If I don't lie down, I'll fall down.' I'd think, 'What a good job I'm here,' and happily send her upstairs.

'Let's make a cake,' I'd say to Anna and spread Barbara's ingredients round me and bask in that warm kitchen. When Geraldine and Jessica arrived it was up to me to make tea, find the straws, sort out whose turn it was for Anna's Wendy house, and the effect of that was what I wanted more. Even though Geraldine and Jessica said I didn't need to, I liked marking off their next visit on Barbara's wall calendar, rushing out for extra milk, organising when Anna would visit them. If Barbara wasn't up to it, I told myself, it was only sensible; except I knew underneath that she should have been getting better and I should have found it a chore. But I ignored that, I deliberately went out of my way to extend the tasks she gave me.

'How does Graham cope at the weekend?' I asked her one Friday before I left. She was still in bed. I felt a little in awe of that room, as if I ought to knock, wait at the foot of the big dark bed. 'I could take Anna out if you wanted.'

'It does Graham good. He'd only work if she wasn't here. If he used to spend all day teaching children he can spend the weekend with his own.'

'I thought he was dotty about her,' I said, because that was what everyone was told, and I'd seen it for myself; he'd always played with her, read stories, answered her questions.

'In his way.' She punched the pillows and then lay back again.

'What's his way?'

'Oh.' She shifted her head. 'He provides total attention for half an hour then switches off. Then she comes and finds me. He's got no idea of what it means to look after her all day.'

'I thought he took her to the park. Read to her. Put her to bed.'

'One of those,' she said. 'He spends half an hour a day. Time it, you'll soon see.'

'Still,' I said, 'lots of children don't even get that. Look at Leslie, he never spent a minute with us, we didn't get any attention at all.'

'Don't exaggerate.' She closed her eyes. 'Anyway, Geraldine or Jessica will have her, that's what she likes.'

When Graham came in I said, 'Barbara's not feeling very good.' He dropped his newspaper on the kitchen table, took off his coat and dropped it on a chair.

'So much for the weekend,' he said. 'She's usually exhausted, this time she'll be sick, too. Sorry,' he rubbed his forehead, 'that sounds awful. But I do a full week as well, I'd quite like not to have to spend the weekend failing to conform to her high standards. I'm a bit tired of orders from the sick bed, despair if I leave the bathroom floor dirty—'

'I could help.' I picked up his coat. I could hang that in the hall as I left. 'I'd like to. You don't have to have a lousy weekend. It's no trouble, I wouldn't mind.' I smiled at him.

I wouldn't be doing anything exciting, anyway. Since Corfu I'd led a very quiet life. I picked up his paper and turned over pages until I found the 'Weekend' section.

'I don't seem to have got into my stride again since Jas. I could easily take Anna out.'

'Really? Really? That'd be fantastic. She'd love that. Look,' and he glanced at his watch, 'time for a drink?' I hesitated.

'Perhaps tomorrow,' I said. He could offer me one when I brought Anna back, we could chat together while Barbara put Anna to bed. 'It's time for Anna's story now. I ought to be going.'

'See you in the morning, then,' he told me, and all the next day I waited for it to be over, for Anna to stop complaining and the shops to close, and when we went there he was asleep in the bath.

'Tea? Coffee?' Barbara said. 'Or are you rushing off somewhere?'

'No, I can't stop,' I said. I pretended I had to meet Beryl, but I still went back, the next weekend, and on Monday mornings, I thought at least I had that to do in the afternoons.

After a month or so I also thought it was going well enough for Barbara to discuss more than the best place to buy navy tights or cotton socks. I thought we could get round to the part we'd played in one another's lives, even make the part I had in hers now a bit more established. So on the afternoons that Geraldine and Jessica didn't come I'd get there early. Quite often I'd take her something, Earl Grey teabags, kiwifruit. I'd wander round her kitchen finding a place for it while she settled down to the ironing or cleaning cupboards.

'Can't I help?' I'd ask, and sit down at the table. 'How are you feeling? You seem a bit better. What've you told Anna about the baby?' I asked. 'Have you told her when it's happening?' Barbara shrugged.

'I expect she's picked it up.'

'I could tell her. Say that's why I'm here so much, that it'll be nice when it comes. Were you told?' I slipped in. 'Were you told Audrey was having me?'

'I don't remember,' she said. 'I don't expect so.'

'How awful.'

'Why?' She looked up at me.

'Not to prepare children for what's happening, not look forward to it together. I don't think you should let them find out by default, as though it doesn't matter what they feel. Although it didn't,' I added. 'What do you remember best about it?'

'I don't,' she answered. 'I hardly remember anything at all.'

'Liar,' I wanted to say. 'It was unforgettable. You just don't want to discuss the way Audrey did it.'

'I tell you what I do remember,' she said. 'You had chicken pox.' She put down her iron. 'I remember that.'

'What happened?' I was agog. 'How long, how bad was it?'

'Not very, I was only about four, it was before school because I was at home all the time. Really,' she said and tested the heat against her cheek, 'what I remember is being bored. No one to play with.'

'Nice of you to miss me,' I said, 'even if there wasn't ever anyone else to play with. That was awful, that was one of the worst things, wasn't it?'

'I saw her point of view sometimes.' Barbara considered the pleated skirt in front of her.

'I saw her point of view too and it was appalling.'

'No,' she said. 'You didn't see her point at all. You didn't care. It didn't matter to you what mood Audrey was in or if Leslie was tight as a tick—'

'Was he?' I interrupted. 'I never noticed that.'

'Exactly. You were just intent on what you wanted to do. Rows didn't alter anything. You might just as well wait until things are over and done with of their own accord. You never let anything alone.'

'I think that's hypocritical,' I said. 'It's just another disguise.'

'Pragmatism,' she said. 'I do it all the time.'

'I know it's a long way off,' I said, 'but who'll look after everything while you're in hospital?'

'Anna? Graham, of course.'

'But what about when he visits you? Of if there's an emergency?'

'What emergency?'

'At his work,' I said quickly.

'He can ring Geraldine or Jessica. It'd only take them five minutes to be here.'

'I could come,' I said. She didn't look surprised or thank me, but nor did she laugh.

'I suppose you could.'

'I have thought about it,' I said. That was certainly true. 'I'd like to. I'm sure I could – not necessarily like you – but I could manage.'

'Anyone can manage,' Barbara said. And then the next day she said, 'I've been letting things slip. We used to see far more people at weekends. I'll have a supper party instead. I'll have Geraldine and Paul, and Jessica and you must come, too. What about Saturday?'

'Saturday's fine. Saturday's quite a good day,' I said, 'I'm already looking forward to it.'

She said, 'Nothing too elaborate but it'll do me good to get back into practice.' All week I helped her shop and amused Anna while she cooked, and stirred sauces while she rushed upstairs to be ill. On Saturday I dressed up as though it was a special occasion. When I arrived Graham asked me where I was off to afterwards, I looked far too glamorous for an evening in Hammersmith. I was introduced to Paul and I tried to remember all the things Geraldine had said he designed, and when I sat at the dinner table I listened to Geraldine and Jessica talking about puppets and theatre design and children's workshops. I watched while Barbara talked to Paul about purpose-built primary schools. I sat back while Graham passed plates and poured wine and all there was to do was eat my prawns and chicken and drink as quickly as possible, except the fourth time I passed my glass to Graham he didn't fill it straight away.

He asked, 'How's work?' and put down his knife and fork.

'Mine?' I raised my eyebrows. 'Do you really want to hear? You wouldn't rather talk about children's artistic potential?'

'No,' he said.

'Why not?' I asked. 'My work isn't relevant to all this. Problems about dancing classes don't exist for old people.'

'They don't for the unemployed kids I deal with, either,' he said.

'I don't do it for fun,' I said. 'I think it matters. What's supposed to happen if no one'll look after them. Forcible euthanasia?'

'Of course they matter,' Graham said. 'I wouldn't question that for one minute. Or how it affects you. It's bound to alter your perception of everything else.' He hesitated. 'Like this,' he said. 'I think it's admirable.' He handed me my glass and I felt myself blush. I drank half of it straight away. 'Doing that,' he added.

'I'm grateful to it, really,' I said. 'Work. It takes my mind off Jas. It's ridiculous,' and I pretended to laugh, 'how you just miss people. Even though it's pointless, even though you know it had to end, you still regret that experience ending and you wonder why it has to. Why people do behave in a way that makes sadness inevitable. Why we are cruel—'

'What I wonder,' Graham said, and he leaned far back in his chair so we weren't level any more, 'is why he'd leave someone like you. It gets better,' he added. 'You get over it.'

'It doesn't make sense, though,' I said. He nodded and stared into his glass.

'But what does? These people, all this effort, I don't know if it's worth considering. It's rather like trying to explain to Audrey why you or I do the jobs we do; or to Barbara, even. Or Barbara to me.' I didn't answer, I kept still. 'I don't know why Barbara does anything any more. Once upon a time I could have said, "This effort on my part will be positive, that will be negative"; now I've no means of guessing. I've got no idea why some things happen. I don't even know if you can tell me.'

'No. I don't know either,' I said after a moment.

'Anyway,' he said, 'we'll talk about it another time. Later.'

I couldn't wait. I watched the clock until it would be time for everyone to go and I could offer to wash up, because that was what used to happen, after everyone had gone Graham and I would do the dishes and argue about the Green Party or unilateral disarmament. But Barbara said, 'No, that's fine, I'd rather you had a good night's sleep.' All the way home and half the night I wondered if she'd heard what he said.

'We'll talk about it, later,' he'd promised, and the more I went over it the more likely it seemed that he'd give a lot to talk about her. That was the last thing she ever wanted.

I stayed away for a week or two after that, I didn't want to rush the things that he might want to say. Also, he had a series of evening meetings, but every time I was there I'd start to think, at the time that he came home, of the conversations he and Barbara had when he arrived.

She'd sit in her wicker chair, sipping Perrier water. As soon as he said he was tired she'd snap back, 'I don't know why you do it, then. There's no need to take on such exhausting work. You're not

186

even the right person for it. Young unemployed boys don't trust middle-aged, middle-class men like you. They see through you, they don't have confidence in you. You don't like them, either, you only do it because of social conscience.'

It was just the same as hearing Audrey hiss, 'Useless. Fool.'

'You might as well not bother,' Barbara said, rather than, 'Pack it in, you're an idiot.' Because she didn't rant and stamp round the kitchen that was supposed to make it different.

I used to watch Graham as he listened, building Anna's bricks on the floor, and wonder why he pretended nothing fundamental was involved, that they were both just pursuing an intellectual exercise.

'I'm glad you've told me that,' he said to her sometimes. 'I appreciate the benefit of your insights. I don't agree,' he'd tell her, 'but that doesn't matter. As long as you've put your side.' He thought that was answer enough.

'Laura doesn't want to hear this,' she'd say then. 'Let's talk about something else,' and we'd listen to her talk about repapering the hall, rehanging Graham's family photos.

I wondered what he thought of her sitting there in judgement over everyone, and I guessed that really he'd had enough of it, but he needed an ally if he was going to try and change anything.

After that, I started arriving when Anna had finished her lunch and staying after tea. When Graham got home on time and asked if I'd like a drink, I always said, 'Yes, please,' and I'd see Barbara frown at him. At six o'clock I knew she wanted visitors to be gone so she could begin her orderly preparations for the next day, and that was still how she saw me, an afternoon caller.

I bought a bottle of gin so that I didn't have to say how guilty I felt about always drinking theirs.

'Look,' I said, taking it out of its carrier bag and waving it like a white flag at Graham.

'You shouldn't have,' he told me, 'but thank you.'

'Drink, Barbara?' he would ask and she'd shake her head. 'Bad day?' And she would shrug. 'So how was your day?'

He'd look round for glasses – he never remembered where they were kept – and I'd hand them to him.

'Old ladies, mothers and children. And tonight I'm going to varnish my toenails,' I would answer. He'd laugh and pour quite a lot of gin into my glass.

'Stay to supper,' he said sometimes, 'and I'll tell you about mine.'

'If the afternoon was that boring I don't suppose Laura'll want to

187

extend it.' Barbara sat down and put her head back, closed her eyes. 'Perhaps you could see to Anna. She's almost ready for her bath.'

I could meet him as I was leaving, I started to think. He'd be coming home and he would say, 'Come back and have a drink – no, let's go to the pub,' but I could see it so clearly I knew it wouldn't happen.

We'd sit in corner seats and he would ask, 'What does she talk to you about? What is it that keeps her going?'

'Stamina,' I'd say. 'Look at Audrey.' He'd laugh.

'I'd rather not. Do you understand?' he'd ask. 'Is it just me who finds her behaviour irrational sometimes? Does it have to be like this all the time?' I'd pretend to consider, I wouldn't say no straight away. 'How would it be with someone else?' he'd ask with his third pint. I'd wait before answering that one.

'Aren't all marriages the same, eventually?' I'd suggest. 'Aren't they like any family tie, other people's always look better. Besides,' I would add, 'people change. Look at Audrey. Barbara says she's altered a lot. Talk to her,' I would urge. 'Talk about that. Get her to look at things too.'

'That supper party,' he could say – he could say that in their kitchen if that was the only place we could meet. 'Have you thought any more about what we discussed?'

And Barbara would say, 'What was that, then?'

'Work; feelings; you,' I could answer and then he would have to tell her, 'I don't understand why you do things,' and she would be forced to account for herself.

'You can't go on covering things up,' I could add and he would nod.

'Stay and have another drink. Stay and listen.'

But he did not. He waited for Barbara to take Anna up for her bath and then he waited for me to drain my glass and saw me to the front door.

'Thanks for coming,' he'd say and I would tell him it was my pleasure.

'See you,' Barbara always said.

And that was it; I went and spent days that never altered with her and Geraldine and Jessica, I stayed for weeks of early evenings to see Graham and eventually I began to think there wasn't any point in going back, I wouldn't be able to alter anything.

I didn't want to know, every time I looked at him, that he'd never stop making himself agreeable to her. I didn't want her calling, 'Anna, come and say hello' when I arrived, and whenever I asked, 'How are you?' I wanted her to say, 'Deathly.'

'I must dash. I'm not sure about tomorrow,' I started to say when it was five o'clock, as though I had to fit in a bath and change into a ball gown by seven, and I'd go home and watch television and once a week go out with Beryl. When Barbara asked what I'd done I'd smile and say, 'Well, it wasn't talk about whether Anna's vocabulary was larger than Melissa's, or if Graham ought to redecorate the kitchen.'

Whenever she decided to have a rerun of her supper party I didn't want her to think that I had to be included; I didn't want to spend any more evenings like Anna's birthday, Ben's birthday, Bonfire Night, when I was asked along like a depressed recluse. I turned up with boxes of presents and fireworks and might as well not have bothered, I didn't have any place playing with sparklers or helping blow out candles.

'Let's talk about Christmas,' Barbara had started to say and that was worst of all, it was the first I'd be spending without Jas. I didn't want to think of Graham saying, 'You'll get over it.' I'd got no reason to believe anything he said; I'd thought I'd had a place in her house and I hadn't. I'd thought Graham wanted me to point things out to her about their marriage and that had been wrong, too. I didn't want them any more. I had to find a way of getting better without them because they didn't help.

'At least you can get out and about,' Barbara said to me when I did drop in one afternoon a couple of weeks before Christmas. I'd spent the weekend between the television and my bed and hoped the shadows under my eyes looked as if they were from exhaustion rather than insomnia.

'Jessica's the person I really feel sorry for,' and she sighed in sympathy. 'Nothing exciting ever happens to her. I had an idea though, supper, Saturday night, with Andrew from Graham's work. They'd get on, I'm sure, it's certainly worth a try.'

I didn't answer straight away. I'd thought that in a way it served me right, I'd talked convincingly about my exotic evenings. Before I'd thought of a way to say that I wasn't totally occupied every night, that this very Saturday there might be a space, she said, 'Graham likes Andrew, and he's very fond of Jessica, of course. He says they're quite similar. It was his idea, really, he's highly enthusiastic. I won't ask you too,' she said, 'otherwise Andrew won't know who he's meant for.'

I still didn't answer. I picked up one of her recipe files and read it until it was time for Graham to come home. 'Look,' I thought I'd say, 'I've got a bone to pick with you. I could do with a bit of immoral support in my social life, you know that.'

He'd look embarrassed and say, 'I wish Barbara hadn't told you.'

'Why didn't you think of me?' I'd insist. 'You know how much I miss Jas. It was you I told, why couldn't you remember that?'

'I don't know,' he'd say. I wouldn't ask why then, I'd wait until Barbara took Anna up to bed. Then he'd answer, 'I'd be too jealous, seeing you chatting all evening to Andrew. He'd try to say that was because he liked talking to me. He didn't want me to spend all my evenings out of his house with a new boyfriend, he relied on my company too much. 'You're a bit of a lifeline at the moment,' he'd confide, and I'd be content to leave it at that.

'I hear you've taken to matchmaking,' I said when he came in. 'Andrew and Jessica.' He threw a small parcel at Anna.

'Catch,' he said. 'It ought to be for your stocking really, but I couldn't resist it. Go on, open it.' I had to sit there while she painstakingly undid the brown paper and folded the tissue.

'What is it?' she asked.

'A yo-yo,' he said.

'Show me,' she told him and hung on his knees while he wound up the string and fitted it between his fingers.

'It took me years to get the hang of one of these.' He started to play it up and down, smooth, as easy as swimming. We all watched, none of us could take our eyes off it.

'Is that why you bought it for a four-year-old?' Barbara asked. 'To give her years of practice?'

'Of course.' He smiled.

'Frustration,' Barbara said. He shrugged.

'Don't worry.' He stroked Anna's head and opened her hand and closed it gently round the toy. 'It'll keep. I'll do it for you every night until you can manage it. That's how I learnt.' Then he turned to me. 'I wouldn't call it matchmaking, Laura. More socialising.'

'I wouldn't know,' I said. 'I won't be invited to see it.'

'I've explained that,' Barbara said. 'Come on.' She stretched. 'All I do is mention Graham wants Jessica to meet Andrew and it becomes a cause for complaint. From what you say you've got enough outside interests. Jessica's not like that. It's not easy to be a single parent, especially with a child like Ben.'

'Why doesn't Laura come too?' Graham asked.

'I'm not invited,' I repeated. Graham stood up.

'You come,' he said, 'it's not an either-or. If Andrew likes Jessica, fine, if he doesn't, it won't matter. I don't see the problem.' He turned to Barbara. 'I don't think it's unreasonable to try and accommodate what people want.'

'Is that a bone of contention, then?' I asked, and for a minute I thought I had got her, I could see him exposing every moment of frustration and annoyance she provoked.

'No,' he said. 'I'll tell you what the trouble is.' Although I was watching him like a hawk I didn't know which of us he was talking to. 'The trouble is that I'm not a good patient man who's preserved his humour and sense of proportion. I'm a cowardly man who doesn't dare get angry.'

'Because of what you might reveal,' I suggested after a moment.

'So are most people,' Barbara said, 'except most people don't think that's unusual.'

'Laura does,' he could have answered, or he could have looked at me.

'Anyway,' Barbara said after a minute, 'come about eight, then, if that's what you've both decided.' She finished her Perrier water in two mouthfuls. 'Anna wants her story read,' she said to Graham. I stood up too.

'I'll give you a ring,' I said and scrambled into my coat and almost ran out of the front door, all I wanted was to get away.

For a fortnight after that I didn't lie when I said I was too busy to visit. I made new curtains. I put up shelves in the kitchen, read two volumes of the *Raj Quartet* and went back to drinking every night, except I managed with wine instead of gin. I volunteered for extra duties at work, I got the prospectus for next term's evening classes, and except that at the end of every five days there was a weekend, I could have survived. Every Saturday morning, while I ate my toast and stood by the window looking at the grey streets and the cold day, drinking coffee and looking forward to nothing, I thought that all this bleak weekend, and as many more as I could imagine, I'd spend either walking round this room or at Barbara's house. I could go back and offer to babysit and take Anna out, and then stay for tea and hope to be invited the next day; I couldn't put the clock forward and find the whole new group of people I'd meet when I started to learn French. I couldn't get through two days with the prospect of going shopping and to the library, I wanted something else. Not Jas, suddenly to alter. I thought of getting undressed again and pretending depression was flu; I looked at last night's paper to find out when I could start watching television; I thought about Martine going into pubs and bars and clubs alone and ringing up phone numbers in lonely hearts columns, and old people who weren't in homes sitting by themselves in cheap cinema seats eating boiled sweets. Because that was a nadir I kept for very special occasions it worked. I put on my coat and picked up my shopping bag and library books to go downstairs.

When it happened I didn't realise at first. I stood by the front door, I opened and then half-closed it, I stared and stared at the handwriting, the postmark, I could hardly bring myself to pick up the envelope. He'd written to me and I couldn't bring myself to read it. I couldn't believe the black marks on the white paper. It was impossible that I'd been rewarded like this, I couldn't believe that what I didn't even dream of could actually happen.

Sorry about the silence, Laura Jas wrote, he didn't put Dear or the address or the date; *but I thought, given Barry's phone call to you, it was the better part of self preservation. Nicole's fine now, and Barry's come more to terms with Louise's departure. Does it work? I'm not in the business of passing judgements, but six months on we're having a quite accidental but possibly fortuitous brief separation – Lou's got four old friends coming for Xmas so I said I'd make tracks too. And the point of this is that it's ridiculous to come to London and not meet you, isn't it? Have a think and I'll give you a ring (unless everyone's plans here alter). Till then – or always – take care, Jas.*

I shut the front door and went back upstairs and read the letter three times. I screwed it up and unfolded it. I wanted to see him and shake the paper in his face and say, 'What's this, then, are you saying you want to come back?' or, 'What do you mean?' Except I knew he'd never answer that, that was why he'd written this letter.

'It's not fair to me,' I told myself. I knew at the same time I was ready to grin at his slyness, start visualising him in my room again.

'You can't go back,' I told myself, because I didn't dare believe he'd ask me. 'I'd better talk to someone.' I looked out of the window, I took off and put down and picked up my coat and bag, I walked to and fro past the phone. 'I can't explain it,' I said to myself as I dialled their number. Graham answered. 'Is Barbara around, can I come over? I need to talk,' I said. 'Something extraordinary's happened, I've got to tell someone. Are you going to be there for a bit?'

'Now?' he asked. 'What's happened, are you all right?'

'I'm fine,' I said, 'I think. I think that might be it. Can I?'

'Come? Of course.' He sounded relieved. 'Come as soon as you like.' When I arrived he opened the front door so quickly he could have been watching for me.

'Hello,' I said. 'Look.' I held the envelope out so he could see the postmark. 'This came from Birmingham. I just found it. It's a letter from Jas. Read it, go on.' He frowned. 'Go on,' I said. 'You can, it's all right.'

'In a minute.' He didn't take it from me, he went into the kitchen. 'I'm making some coffee,' he said. 'Go upstairs, I won't be a minute, go and sit down.' So I went and walked round the sitting room and smoothed the letter ready for him.

'Where's Barbara?' I asked when he came in with the tray.

'Asleep. And Anna's at ballet. Black? white? sugar?' I nodded because when I spoke I kept wanting to clear my throat as if I was at a job interview.

'Sit down,' he said again and poured and fussed about where to put the cups. Then I passed him the letter and he read it. He put it on the arm of his chair as if he didn't want to touch it.

'It upsets me,' I said and picked up and put down my cup. 'It's insulting if he thinks he can walk in and out of my life when he pleases. It seems to make nothing of the time we were together if it can just stop and start. As though it was always a casual thing. I don't know what to do.' I waited while Graham sat with his elbows on his knees and looked up and down, up and down the page.

'It could be fondness,' he said eventually, 'or good old-fashioned guilt – wanting to put things right after behaving badly—' and he stopped, as though trying to decide whether to offer a third explanation.

'He wouldn't. He wouldn't think of that.' I turned so he couldn't see my face. 'Jas never admits he's wrong. Forgiveness doesn't come into it and nor does fondness. He wants to walk in, cocky as you please. He wants me to say how wonderful it is that he's back, and of course we can be friends.'

'Say no, then, you don't want to.' He twisted sideways to look at the paper again. 'Say no.'

I twisted my hands. 'Except he might not mean it like that. He might be upset Louise wants to spend Christmas with other people and he thinks I'll understand. Or he and Louise might be coming to an end and he wants to test things between us. It might not be manipulative, he might be quite seriously reconsidering . . . Mightn't he?' I asked. Graham sat quite still.

'So, say you do want to,' and then he said very quickly, 'except I wouldn't. You can't trust him, you've got nothing to gain. I think he's being extraordinarily inconsiderate and selfish.' He looked back at me. 'But then I always did. Always.'

'You don't know,' I said, 'you only see him from your point of view. The way he felt things was different. If you think people discriminate against you, you do get defiant—'

'Discrimination?' Graham sat forward in his armchair. 'But you can't be held responsible for that. You can't help the way other people behave. If you let him play that game with you, if that's what he's banking on, that's appalling.'

'Is it?' I asked, and sat and thought that he was right, and it had been.

'People manage,' he said. 'You have. You haven't become deceitful because of the way he treated you, why should he blame you for how he's been treated? If you can manage to stay generous and honest, why can't he?'

'I'm a soft touch,' I said. 'As soon as I think of him being in London I have a fantasy of going back to how we were. It's that person I lived with I don't want to be unhappy.'

'I think that sounds very generous,' he said. 'It doesn't mean you're an easy touch.'

'I don't know.' I picked up my cup of coffee and it was half-cold.

'All right,' he said, 'but think about it. Think about what to do. But remember what it was really like.'

I said I would and refused a drink and asked how Barbara was feeling and then said I wouldn't wait for her to wake because I ought to go. I had a lot to do, I said, weekends were busy, weren't they?

'Remember what it was really like,' he'd said, and from that minute I couldn't wait to leave; it was the permission I'd been waiting for to go back to a whole series of pictures of Jas I hadn't dared look at for months – Jas in bed, in the dark, in the shower, at the cinema, in the pub, buying candyfloss, stretching, laughing. For two weeks I ran and reran every one of them until they almost seemed to be real again. I went to work and went out for a drink a couple of times, I watched television, I visited Barbara, I bought Christmas cards, I window-shopped for Anna's present and it was all only half-happening. I couldn't concentrate and I couldn't relax, the only thing I could do was not imagine meeting Jas again, or the moment when the phone rang and it was his voice, because if I did, that would never happen.

'Laura,' he said when it did and I was as surprised as I'd ever dreamt. 'Is that you, Laury?' I couldn't answer. 'Laury, it's Jas.'

'Where are you?' I asked eventually. 'How are you?'

'King's Cross, I'm fine. How are you? Did you get my letter?'

'Yes,' I said.

'And did you read it, about meeting? Laura?' he asked. I swallowed.

'Now? Come here, you mean?' I looked round the room. It wasn't possible that in an hour he would be sitting looking at me.

'Now?' He hesitated. 'Why not? If you like. How about Tottenham Court Road? Go for a drink. Or if another evening's better I could ring again—'

'How long are you here?' I asked and immediately regretted it. 'No, let's make it tonight, Tottenham Court Road'd be fine.'

'I'll see you at eight,' he said, 'my money's running out.' And for four hours after that I watched the phone in case it rang to tell me to stay at home. I tidied the room and washed my hair and ironed my clothes, and by seven I was dressed in my new trousers and boots and checking my bag for keys and change for the tube as though it didn't matter, as though I was meeting Brenda, anyone, as though I was just popping out for a quick drink. I wanted to stay quite blank, I didn't want to think what would happen by the end of the evening.

When I arrived at the Tube I realised I'd allowed forty-five minutes for the journey. I read the map and walked up and down. Every time a train pulled in I walked up the platform, pretending to want the front end and when the fourth one came I heard a shout and he was leaning out of the carriage. He was behind me, two coaches back, tall, in a new black overcoat that made his face lighter, holding the door to stop it closing. He looked exactly the same, and I ran, I got in as all the doors reopened and tried to close again.

'What were you doing?' he said. I was immediately sure he'd known that I'd been killing time.

'I'm not sure,' I said and looked away from him because it wasn't the ticket barrier, having my arm taken as we went up the stairs, walking to the pub with the empty corner table. Here it was too noisy, all we could do was try and catch sneaky glimpses of one another. He strap-hung and leaned over me, so I had to be careful, but when the train stopped and he stood up straight I could see him properly; he was still handsome, big eyes, straight nose, quite thin lips that he tried to turn down when he smiled to make it seem cynical, but he hadn't shaved that well and he'd had a haircut that was just too short at the front.

'You got here all right, then?' I said at Marble Arch. He nodded to himself in the window. 'Where's your luggage?' I looked round for his black canvas bag. 'Did you leave it at King's Cross?'

'I'm travelling light,' he said.

'No, where is it – you haven't lost—'

'I didn't bring any,' he said. 'I can always borrow a toothbrush.'

'All over Christmas?' I said. He didn't answer. 'But you're here for Christmas. That's what you said in your letter.' I could hear my voice, worried, shrill, checking his arrangements.

'Not definitely.' He still smiled. 'I thought we'd wait and see. Like I said, if necessary I can always borrow a toothbrush.'

'I see,' I said, and clenched my back against the door. 'Not mine you can't,' I should have told him, because I knew what 'Wait and see' meant, that I'd be on my best behaviour to make sure he wanted to stay and he'd be the one to decide what happened.

'You mean, you're just here for a night?' I asked. I might as well get it straight.

'I thought I'd see how it went,' he said. 'Christmas is a long time.'

'And after Christmas?'

'Louise's friends go Boxing Day,' he said. 'That's no problem.'

'I suppose not,' I said and looked out of the window and saw we were coming into another station. 'Oxford Circus. That was quick,' I said, because it had been, five minutes to find out what I ought to have guessed all along.

'Nearly there,' he nodded, as though I meant I was looking forward to it.

'Can you walk in those things?' he asked when we got outside.

'Those heels don't look very safe on ice.' Instead of leaning against him or taking his arm I asked where we were going.

'There's a place near here Carlos told me about. Wakefield Square. A club, where all the Spanish go. It's by a community centre. Or maybe a church.'

'I haven't heard of it,' I said. I didn't ask who Carlos was and why we had to go to a Spanish club.

'*A to Z*?' he requested. I shook my head.

'You could ask,' I suggested, as though that was a perfectly normal procedure, as though he could be like the thousands who did that when they needed directions. I counted it as the biggest success of the evening that he didn't shout at me not to be stupid. 'I will if you like,' I offered, because I couldn't bear standing on that freezing corner any longer.

He shrugged. 'Ask who you like.'

After five minutes I finally got the information from a paper seller and I said 'Straight on,' and, 'Left next,' and, 'Half right at the next junction.' Apart from that we didn't talk, so I understood that he was angry. I didn't believe he'd really expected me to agree to one night on approval. I thought that he probably hadn't imagined how I'd react at all. Then I stopped worrying because he walked very fast and I had to run to keep up with him. I couldn't remember if I'd got the directions right, and when I stumbled twice and he hadn't waited or even turned round I was ready to give up. But then we came to another corner and opposite us was a church and on the railings outside it actually said Wakefield Square.

'So where now?' I asked. He sniffed and hunched his shoulders and I looked at the almost totally dark square. He jerked his head towards me and crossed the road and opened the gate that led up the path to the church. There was a faint light coming from the back. I followed him along the gravel and when we reached the end I said, 'Where have all the gravestones gone?' He didn't answer.

'Is this it?' I asked. He went down a flight of steps and in front of us was a door with a sign *Estudiantes*. He pushed and we went in.

The first thing I noticed, even before the dismal overbright lights, dingy green walls, was the cold. It was as freezing in here as outside; everyone – all ten people, that is – had their coats on. They were mostly young men, and none of them smiled. They looked up and stared and then went back to their cigarettes. Next to the door was a small bar. When Jas turned to me I said, 'Something warming.'

Before I had time to add whisky, ginger, the barman turned on the espresso machine.

'Vodka and tonic,' Jas said very quickly.

'Quite a place,' I wanted to say when we sat down but I drank some coffee instead, bitter, non-alcoholic and I cupped my hands round it. Then I said, 'Look, I didn't mean coffee, actually, could you get me a Scotch?' When I sipped that I felt slightly better.

'You recognise the games he plays,' Graham had said, 'but you don't have to go along with them.'

'So who's Carlos?' I asked.

'This bloke in Brum. He said he always comes here because he can feel comfortable.'

'Miserable bastard,' I wanted to say, but instead I nodded.

'It must be the weather that makes it seem different tonight.'

'Was it cold there?' I asked, and drank half my glass in two mouthfuls. 'Did it take you long to get here? Is the coach fast? Why did you write that letter? Why did you come?'

'I told you.' He drank too, put his glass on the table, looked at people's backs. 'Lou's got friends down, I was in the way. I could've stayed with people there but I thought I'd see if I preferred a couple of days here.'

'I thought you said Christmas.' He looked round, as though he wondered who I was talking to. 'Anyway. How is it, Birmingham? How's it going? Do you like it?'

'All right.' He sounded more enthusiastic. 'All right.'

'All of it?' I prompted 'Or what's good and what's not? And what about working in the the law centre?' He drank some more.

'I can do without white management committees,' he said. 'I thought law centres represented their clients. This one seems to be stuck with every white liberal who hasn't moved out to Warwick University. I'm not a sore thumb, though,' he said. 'In some places there are even more blacks than whites.' I nodded, although Shepherds Bush Market hadn't been exactly a white middle-class enclave.

'Good,' I said. 'And are there a lot of Spanish? In fact,' I gradually warmed to the subject, I could remember an article I'd read, 'what are all the immigrant groups? All you hear about are Asians, West Indians, but presumably there are more.'

'You read too.many newspapers,' he said. 'You can't divide people into racial groupings any more. You've got to look at who's

where and why and how long and employment and tenure groups –
it's nothing to do with how many blacks and how many Spanish.'

'I see,' I said after a moment. I waited for him to explain more but
he just turned his glass round. I drank the last of mine and looked at
him, and he didn't look up, so I stared at his wavy hair and his bent
head and the hands I ought to remember every particle of. 'So how
are you?' I asked. 'You still haven't told me that.' He did look up
then, and smiled with his mouth turned down.

'I'm a bit regretful,' he said. 'Maybe it was warmer in
Birmingham.'

'We don't have to stay here. We could go somewhere cheerier,'
but he picked up both our glasses.

'I quite like it,' he said. 'Another?'

'Where do you and Louise go? Do you argue? Do you miss me?' I
didn't say.

'Does Carlos work at the law centre? What does he do?' I asked
and started to sip again.

'It's a collective,' he answered. 'Collectives don't divide work up
like that.' I tried to think of another article I'd read.

'Aren't they supposed to work better when people have areas of
special interest, though?' I did remember. 'Isn't it difficult
otherwise to see all the boring bits get done?'

'You should go up and tell them,' he said, 'they'd appreciate your
opinion.'

'I thought of changing jobs in the summer,' I said. 'I thought I
needed jolting, but then I had a holiday and that seemed to do the
trick. I went to Corfu – I didn't send you a card, did I? It was good,
though. Sun, sea, sand, we could all do with that once every ten
years.'

'Could we?' he asked but I took no notice.

'Mainly, though, I did a lot of thinking, that was what I used it
for. About family, mostly – awful things like Mercy dying – I
wanted to see what I had a right to be angry about and what had to
be accepted and how it affected the way I behave as an adult. And I
decided that you can't expect everything to be pleasant, you do have
to use unhappiness as well as happiness. It's changed how I feel
about quite a lot,' I said. 'I don't get manipulated by other people
into going along with them. I'm not looking for rewards any more.
In everyday terms,' I went on when he didn't even nod, 'Barbara's
the most obvious example. I've really seen a lot of her and it's
stopped being a competition. I've decided what it's honest to accept

199

and what I can't stand. I don't necessarily say, but I know in my own mind. I can be with her and yet not feel I've got to please or defy her all the time. It's give and take.' He took his time over examining the drop of vodka and piece of lemon left in his glass.

'Moved in?' He said and looked over the rim.

'Moved in?' I asked.

'So you haven't moved in yet. It's what I expected of you. Adjusting events for security. Getting someone to look after you.'

'I don't see what you're getting at,' I answered, as though it might be a friendly thing he had to tell me. He tipped his chair and pushed his hands into his coat pockets. I looked past him at all the dark figures, still talking, still smoking, light glaring down on them, draughts from the high windows whistling under the tables.

'Come on.' He leaned forwards. 'Isn't it obvious?' I shook my head. 'It was what you wanted from me, it's what you want now, it's what you'll want from everyone. You haven't found anything out, you've just found an excuse for being even more tolerant. You'll take anyone, so long as you can cling, you'd be happy in an everlasting blizzard if you could cling to a mountain top. You're not unnatural; but don't kid yourself you've altered.'

'No,' I said, and it didn't sound like a word at all. 'That's not true, I do see things differently, I mean it.'

'I've seen things differently too.' He smiled again. 'Not all women revolve around one man, one man and her sister. Getting free of all that has taught me it was pretty constricting, even if it was nicely dressed up. Evenings out with Barbara and Graham, come to supper, fit in with the family. Ties, apron-strings. You loved them and the next thing in line was a wedding ring.'

'I'm going.' I tried, I clutched the table. 'I don't want any more of this. Stop it, I'm not listening. You're lying, you're warped.'

'You don't like the truth,' he said. 'That's all you mean by lying. What did you come for?' he asked and he leaned back in his chair and held onto the table too. 'Old times' sake? Don't give me that. You're not really here to tell me about the new-style Laura, you're here to see what you can get out of it again.'

'What did you ask me for, then?' I said but my voice wasn't too steady. 'Because Louise got bored, because Louise kicked you out? Has she found someone else?' I asked. 'An old friend? Is that why you wanted to meet? And because I took it seriously, because I thought there was more in it than a one-night stand, because you won't get away with that, you'll say anything to get your own back.'

'I made a mistake,' he said. 'All right. But it's got nothing to do with anything except you. The minute I saw you on that platform, the second I even opened my mouth and you turned that cringing little face round I realised I should have stayed away. I can't take it.' He shook his head. 'I can't stand how you are.'

'Or how Louise is,' I said. '"Not all women revolve round one man", she's two-timing you, that's what you mean, so you want to do the same.'

He moved, brought his chair back upright and stretched right across the table and put both his hands over mine.

'I'll have you,' he said, 'she's no more a whore than you were. Move,' he gestured with his head to the door and I sat still, 'you heard me.' I pulled my hands away.

'It wasn't my idea,' I said. 'I didn't ask to see you again, I'd got over you. It was easy, it was easy to do without you. The only reason I saw you was because I felt sorry for you, poor, lonely Jas in London for Christmas. You seemed pathetic, deserted, nobody wanting you and you couldn't manage. That's why.'

'Get,' he said, 'get out before I get you.' I didn't look at him.

'Sit down,' I said, 'wait. I'll go. I'll go if you wait. The last place I want to stay is this creepy nothing. The last person I want to be with is you. But if you come too, I'll scream. They won't stand for that. You let me alone and I'll go.' I pushed the table towards him. 'I'm going,' I said and stood up and walked quite steadily across the floor.

I waited for him to shout or grab me, or one of the other men to bar my way, but I was out, I was up the steps and past the gravestones along the path. I was all the way out of the place and on the pavement without thinking. I ran again, any minute he'd be out and catch me, I couldn't believe he'd let me off, the only chance I had was if he couldn't find me. I grabbed the railings and swung myself along them and when I got to the corner I heard a noise, a door bang, a car backfiring, and then I couldn't move, but I made myself, I stamped my feet and then I took off my boots and started to run, only a little way, skidding all over the place, until I was into the next road. But although it was well lit it was a nothing street, second-hand bookshops, a travel agent, flat glass fronts, blank, the whole road was empty, so I started to run again. My feet were sopping wet and I was just starting round the next corner when I thought, No, he'll expect me to go this way back to the station, so I went past the offices with ships in the windows and the row of dustbins and took a parallel street. That was busier: sex shops, arcades, a light going on and off that said Funtime. I put my boots back on and walked on the edge of the pavement, making sure I didn't catch anyone's eye. When I got to the end I immediately turned left so I couldn't be seen dithering. In that road there were restaurants, I walked very fast, my coat hugged round me, all I thought about was keeping moving, how cold I was and suddenly it was Shaftesbury Avenue and my legs went limp. Even if I hadn't seen a taxi and it hadn't stopped I wouldn't have gone any further.

All the way back I looked out of the window at Marble Arch, Holland Park Avenue, and thought, Two hours ago I wouldn't have believed this could happen, but it has, believe it now. When I was nearly home I thought he might be waiting there, so I knocked on the glass and said to the taxi driver, 'If I give you an extra pound, can you wait while I go up and check if my sister's arrived? If she has we'll both want to go to Hammersmith to see our parents.' He nodded and I gave him a ten-pound note.

I walked straight ahead to the front door and no one shouted or lunged forward. I unlocked and relocked it and walked upstairs and when I went in I looked around as if I really expected to see Barbara. I went and opened the window. 'No,' I called, 'but thanks very much.' He raised his hand and waved the note. 'Keep it,' I said. I didn't see how I'd ever go downstairs again; I couldn't even move away from the window.

I stood and watched for ages, but apart from the usual drunks, there wasn't anyone else to be seen. Then I lit the fire and the oven, put on an old blow heater, took off all my soaking clothes, threw my socks in the rubbish and put on a nightie and dressing gown and sweater. I put the television on, too, and took the gin bottle out of the kitchen cupboard and drank straight from it, two swallows, and then poured about half a glass and filled it up with water, because if it tasted awful I wouldn't drink it too fast. Then I picked up the phone.

'Graham,' I said when the ringing stopped. 'Can I talk to you? Can I tell you something?'

'That's appalling,' he said when I'd finished. 'That's awful. I'll come over.' I said, no, I'd be all right, if Jas wasn't here now he wouldn't come at all. He wasn't like that. 'I know that much about him,' I said.

'Not necessarily.' Graham sounded angry. 'You didn't guess how he'd be tonight.'

'I just wanted to tell someone,' I said. 'I don't want you to fuss, I don't want anyone to do anything, it was just to talk about it.'

'Do you want to talk to Barbara?' he asked. I hesitated because when I thought about what Jas had said, I didn't.

'Is she asleep?' I asked. 'Then I won't,' as though I was making a sacrifice. 'It's not worth waking her for this. If she's heard, make some excuse, say I rang because I was fed up over doing overtime at the weekend. I'd like to be quiet for a bit, alone for a bit, actually. I don't really want to have an inquest over it.'

'All right,' he said. 'Fair enough. I'll tell her that. But we'll see you on Monday. Christmas,' he reminded me. 'You can't spend that saying, "No inquests," and staying alone all day.'

'All right.' I tried to laugh. 'Audrey and Leslie should be quite a distraction.'

'I tell you what.' He suddenly spoke very quickly. 'I'll give you a ring in the evenings, find out if you're OK. I won't ask questions, and I'm sure you're right, he won't come back, but just to make sure. For my peace of mind, not yours. OK?' he asked and I agreed.

When I went to bed it wasn't that late, twelve o'clock, I'd been back indoors by ten, and I thought the gin'd make me sleep like a log. But I woke up every half-hour because someone was there where Jas used to sleep, shouting at another Jas to go away, to stop peering in through the window. I burrowed into the pillow for the warmth of that person and when I woke up again Barbara had been ironing all my clothes, pulling paper off my walls. 'You can't stay here,' she'd said. 'I don't know where you can go.'

When it was light enough to get up and have a shower I had one last look at Jas; I looked round the room and quite deliberately remembered where and how he sat, legs out, book held at a distance, in an apron in the kitchen, creeping up on me and kissing, making love, pale and dark parts of him, two ghost bodies entranced, transfixed where I was still lying. I waited until I couldn't cry at those any more and put them on one side.

Then I thought of his furious face and that I'd run away from him, and that from the moment I'd got on the train I'd known that although he'd come back love didn't enter into it. And I remembered all the times he'd threatened to leave and when he did finally disappear all he left was a letter about Louise, and I put those pieces on the other side. 'That's that,' I said and got out of bed.

'Better?' Graham asked when he rang in the evening and I said, Fine, wasn't gin wonderful. We both laughed.

'I've been quite worried,' he said. 'I did almost drive over last night, but then I thought a ring at the bell'd probably frighten you even more.' I thought about that for a minute, him standing on the doorstep, his hands in his overcoat pockets. He'd rock on his heels and smile when I opened the door.

'I'm all right,' I said. 'I've been thinking things over. Being gullible. Being made a fool of.'

'Christmas depresses everyone,' he said. I laughed. 'Is that supposed to make me feel better?'

'Really,' he said, 'it's to try and put it in proportion. It's Christmas that's making you fed up, as far as Jas is concerned it was a misunderstanding and you've forgotten it.'

'How's Barbara?' I asked.

'Looking forward to Christmas,' he said, 'I suppose. Busy. A bit frenetic. What are you doing?' I said the next few days were quite full.

'Staff parties. Mince pies and punch, it'll be a real rave-up.' He laughed but the next evening it wasn't too bad, carol singing and back to Matron's idea of a festive meal, then a fairly drunken staff party, and on Christmas Eve Beryl got merry enough to invite me on to her boyfriend's party and after three hours in the fire station canteen I never again wanted to see another bunch of mistletoe or imagine 101 uses for a fireman's helmet.

Ten hours later, on Christmas morning when I arrived at Barbara's, despite the orange juice and paracetamol I still wasn't in very good shape.

'OK?' Graham said as he took my bag of presents.

'I'll get better,' I said. 'Where are they all?' I looked round the hall as though they might be hiding under the carpet. I couldn't hear any noise upstairs or from the kitchen. I even started to wonder what had gone wrong. 'Don't say they didn't come?' He slowly shook his head.

'I would if I could. But I'd be lying. Wait a minute.' I looked in the mirror over the table to see if I was blotchy or becomingly flushed after last night's excesses.

'Yes?' He looked nice; his hair shone and he had on a dark blue shirt and darker sweater and jeans.

'I mentioned the Jas business to Barbara,' he said, and still looked me in the eye. 'I hope you don't mind.'

'Not really.' I smiled and waited to go upstairs. 'I was thinking of doing the same myself. That's OK.'

'Not exactly.' He rested my bag on the table. 'It's just that I wouldn't say anything now, if I were you.'

'I don't understand.' I looked in the mirror again, rubbed my hair until it stood on end. 'If I was going to tell Barbara, if you did tell her, what's wrong with mentioning it?'

'She was upset. She said she thought you'd be ridiculous starting it all again. I think, in a way,' he hesitated and I couldn't tell if he was deciding whether to tell me or pretending it wasn't a very significant point, 'Barbara thinks she went to a lot of – not trouble – but tried quite hard to be helpful when it first happened and if you and he get together now it'd somehow negate that. Which I can see is irrational—'

We both looked at the floor and I thought it was a good job I had a hangover or I'd be furious.

'She minds a great deal,' he said.

'About her,' I answered. 'About how things look to her.'

'I just thought I'd better mention it,' he said.

'Fine.' I took a last look in the mirror. 'It's all over now, there isn't anything to discuss. Not with anyone. Come on,' I said. 'Let's get it over with.'

When he opened the sitting-room door the room was glowing; it was full of flowers and the tree smelt fresh and there were silver and gold decorations hanging from all over the ceiling. It was as enticing as a funeral parlour. Audrey sat like a trapped animal, hands fluttering on her lap, deprived of a teatowel, kept at bay from the brussels sprouts; Leslie was reaching for a glass; Anna perched like a hen on an egg, rustling and stroking her tutu, and Barbara wasn't looking at anyone. She was sitting bolt upright, eyes closed, swallowing.

'Happy Christmas,' I said and walked in a circle round them, planting kisses on all their cheeks, and after more cheerless words Graham asked who wanted a drink and Barbara got up to do some more cooking. I said 'I'll give you a hand,' and I was out before anyone could argue, running downstairs after her.

'Nice,' I said when she opened the kitchen door. The table was laid with a white cloth and gleaming glasses. 'Very impressive.' I leaned against the door. 'Do you feel noble,' I asked as she looked into the oven, 'having all of us? It's not my idea of a fun-packed Christmas. But then what is? My idea of fun doesn't seem to work out any more.'

'I can manage,' she said and kept peering into the steam, 'you didn't need to come and see.'

'Anyone can manage,' I answered back. 'I didn't come to see, I came to help.'

'Why?' she asked.

'Because you look worn out. Because you've got a lot to do. Because you've looked rough for the last six months, if you want to know. Because I'd rather be here than up there.'

'And that's to help,' she said. 'You've found a funny way of showing it, then.' She shut the door but she still stayed bent over.

'OK, tell me what you want done. I can't tell by looking. There aren't notices up saying "peel cabbage", "make bread sauce".'

'What would help,' she said, 'would be if you'd stop this, "You can't cope, you look awful."' Slowly she stood up and walked past me to the fridge, her hand in the small of her back. 'I don't particularly need help now. I don't need you around. I'd like to be by myself. Why don't you go upstairs and talk to everyone up there? Go and keep them company. Help them out.' She uncovered a bowl from the fridge and put it on the dresser, took down a clove of garlic and the salt cellar. 'It's not working up there, it's always difficult before lunch. If you mean it, if you're serious about giving a hand, go and divert them.'

'Upset them, you mean,' I said. 'That's what you think I'm doing. That's not true, I did come to find out if you were all right.'

'Did you?' She turned again, concentrated on lighting the gas under a saucepan. I watched as she measured and stirred, her lips pursed.

'All right,' I said. 'I won't any more. I won't upset you.'

'Given your marching orders?' Audrey said as soon as I went back in. She'd get her hands on me if she couldn't get them in the washing up. 'I could've told you as much. Two women in a kitchen. You'll see when you get your own place, you can't stand other people messing it up.'

'I have.' I sat down on the arm of Leslie's chair, I did not want

206

Barbara's empty one, and I stared at the rug and the polished floor. I did not want to look at any of them. 'You know I've got a flat.'

Straight away Audrey turned her head. She didn't like to be reminded of the way I lived, she'd always pretended to know nothing about the existence of Jas. Last Christmas, when I'd insisted on talking about him, she'd shut herself in the bathroom. 'Ready when you are,' she'd called out to Leslie. As it wasn't even lunchtime I'd offered to drop the subject.

'I've helped Barbara for months,' I said. 'I know her kitchen as well as mine.'

'Helping?' She turned her head. 'That's nothing. That's her letting you, that's when she feels like it. She wants you out of her way now, that's the difference.' She nodded and smiled to Leslie and Graham looked up.

'Anna,' he said, 'come here.' He lifted her from a chair and sat her on his lap next to Audrey. 'Tell Grandma about your ballet classes. Tell her about the playgroup. Tell her about you and Mummy and Laura going to see Father Christmas.' She fidgeted with the frills of her skirt and Graham loosely held her, his chin resting on her head, his hands stroking her arms.

'She isn't listening,' I wanted to tell Anna, because whenever she paused for breath or to wait for an answer to a question, Audrey said, 'Such a little chatterbox,' or, 'What a long tongue she's got.'

'See what's on television,' Leslie told me after a bit. 'There's a film starting about now.' Graham did not say Anna was not supposed to watch this early, he offered us all another drink. This time I accepted and sat and watched Anna again, curled up on Graham's lap, wriggling against his thick sweater, dragging her toes into his jeans; I watched his hands stroking her blonde hair, long fingers slowly lifting it from her neck and occasionally he blew in her nape and she giggled.

'That's nice,' she whispered.

'Seasonal,' Audrey said when the film was over and looked at her watch. 'Another ten minutes. Not long to go now.'

At two o'clock we were called downstairs, put on paper hats, pulled crackers and said, 'Leg, please,' or, 'Just a little stuffing.' When we all had our plates and glasses full Audrey leaned across the table to me.

'How's that job?'

'About the same,' I said. 'Some people've died and others've taken their places. That's about all that changes.'

'I suppose you think that's funny.' She screwed up her eyes and I looked at her red paper hat.

'I wouldn't if I were them,' I said and passed Graham the cranberry jelly. 'But I have to get used to it.'

'I don't know why you do it. When you feel like that. There must be other jobs.'

'Belly dancing,' I said, 'road sweeping, milk deliveries; typing, that was pretty fulfilling. The possibilities are endless.'

'You know what she means.' Barbara sliced one of Anna's brussels sprouts in half, then into four. 'Eat these, too, good girl.'

'No.' I put down my knife and fork and drank; it was probably quite expensive wine, Graham cared about things like that, but I didn't taste it. 'I do a job I like and every time we meet we have an inquest; what career prospects have I got, why don't I work where I'll meet rich young men instead of poor old ones?'

'It'd help my old age,' Leslie said; he'd finished his glass and nodded to Graham for more. 'See it that way, Laura.'

'No,' I said, 'I don't. I don't see why I'm expected to defend what I do all the time. Barbara taught in an infants' school; that wasn't impressive, but that was fine because it was Barbara. Status isn't relevant to some jobs,' I turned to Graham, 'it's not something you think about in jobs like ours. Did you?' He took a deep breath and swallowed. Although he hadn't spoken much he hadn't been eating in his spare moments because his plate was still almost full.

'It's not the most important factor, no.'

'Not to you,' Barbara said, 'but that's not the only way of looking at it.'

'What's your way, then?' I asked. 'Come on, give us a treat, show us something that matters to you. Or is it still the same, what his job looks like? That must have been difficult for you.' I turned to Audrey. 'A butcher. What does that look like?' I picked up a piece of meat on my fork, I'd have waved it in her face if she hadn't got there first.

'You,' she said and across the table she was mottled and shaking, but it was Leslie who answered.

'That's enough of that,' he said. 'You don't have to go out of your way to be unpleasant.'

'I'm not,' I interrupted. 'I wasn't trying that hard.'

'Come on, then.' Leslie caught Graham's eye again, touched his glass. 'You tell us, then. You tell us what a butcher looks like.'

I could have, I could have shouted, 'Bloody, fleshy, brainless,' but I looked at his overflowing red face, his fat fingers clutching his knife and fork and I knew he'd heard it all before, he wasn't the target I wanted.

'Her,' I said and pointed at Audrey. 'She's the real family butcher.' Graham put down the bottle he was holding.

'That's enough,' he said. He'd put more wine in Leslie's glass and his own, but mine was still empty. 'We aren't here for this.'

'Then what?' I wanted to ask because he was smiling at Audrey, turning to Barbara and Anna. He started talking again, not to anyone, but as he started eating his meat.

'When I was a child it was my ambition to own a shop – butcher, baker, candlestick maker—'

'Candlestick maker,' Barbara joined in. 'Who'd do that now? When Anna's grown up we probably won't have candles, her children won't have any idea what it means.'

'What what means?' Anna said and altogether Audrey and Barbara and Graham began to repeat the rhymn and I started to laugh, the three of them were reciting like a nursery class, chanting away as though that would alter anything. When they stopped Anna shouted, 'Again.'

'That's enough,' Graham said. 'Quiet now.' He pointed to the dismembered turkey. 'A spot more? Leslie? Laura?'

I looked at my half-full plate and Leslie's empty one and Barbara did the same and for a second I saw what she did, the dangerousness of food, all that fatty weight lying taunting her.

She stood up. 'I won't be a minute,' she said. We all listened to her going upstairs.

'Eat up for Mummy,' Audrey told Anna. 'Finish your dinner, empty your plateful. She's gone to all this trouble.'

'I never learned to cook,' Graham said when we'd heard her safely descending again. 'I've always been sorry.' He looked at all the leftover food, too, he started to put plates on top of one another, Barbara's last because her potato and white meat were almost untouched. 'It's good to learn while you're young, you're more adaptable.'

'Pity we missed the chance,' I said. 'I couldn't boil an egg when we left home.'

'You could have.' This time Audrey didn't look up at me, she picked up her pudding fork and dragged the prongs hard across the tablecloth. 'You watched. You could have helped. I didn't stop you.'

'No.' I waited a moment. 'Everything you can learn by watching someone who keeps their back to you and says get your fingers out if you go anywhere near them, I learnt. That's true.'

'That was you,' Audrey said. 'That was the way you acted. Barbara helped: birthday cakes, Christmas puddings, you're forgetting them, how did they get there?'

'You know that as well as I do,' I answered. 'I remember them perfectly. They weren't home baked, they were Lyons chocolate sponges that came in a box and Mrs Peek's Christmas puddings that came in a wrapper, that's how they arrived, that's the effort you made with them.'

'Ice-cream,' Leslie said, 'that's what I remember. A vanilla block because it was a June birthday. That's what I had.'

'So did I.' I leaned across the table to him. 'I got ice-cream, too. Not a block, though, on my birthday we had individual portions, brickettes, that's what they were called, one each. We'd each unwrap our own paper and put our own little block in a glass dish and eat it. That was what I got. What birthday cake?' I said to Audrey. No one answered. Graham stood up.

'Ready, Barbara?' he asked. All the time she'd been standing by the door, she hadn't corrected or altered one word. Then she opened the fridge and gave him a frosty bottle. He refilled Leslie's glass and his and mine. 'Pudding,' he said. We all looked round to see it.

'You were the one,' Leslie said and raised his glass to Barbara as she walked across to us carrying the steaming plate. It rested on her stomach and it glistened and there was holly round it and I could see it the next moment in flames, I could see the whole table on fire. 'You were the one who got cake. January. Yours was the first and we had cake for you.' He sounded almost triumphant. He turned to Audrey. 'And you were the one who made it.'

'I wonder,' Graham said and looked at the mountain in front of him; he waved a match over it and almost straight away blew the flames out, 'which is the lucky piece?' He cut a small slice and put it in front of Anna. 'I wonder if this is it? I wonder what Anna will wish for?'

We all behaved a little better after that. Graham answered Leslie

210

no, it was a real shame, there weren't the openings nowadays for boys in the retail trade. Barbara told Audrey she'd probably got enough jackets left from Anna, and Anna asked if she could get down and when could we open our other presents.

'Now,' I said, 'but only if you let me make coffee and wash up. Only if you all go upstairs now while I get on with it.' No one tried to argue.

I filled and emptied and refilled the sink and finished the wine left in Barbara's glass and poured another from a half-empty bottle at the back of the fridge and a brandy from the bottle by the stove. By the time I went upstairs with the tray of coffee I didn't want to argue with anyone any more.

'Wonderful,' Graham said and seemed to back me into an armchair. 'Black?' he said and put the tray on a stool. He hardly waited until I'd finished one cup before he poured me another.

'You've got all your presents to open.' Anna jumped about in front of me. 'All, all.'

'You help,' I said. When I bent to pick them up my head spun but I thanked Audrey and Leslie for the scarf and talc and tights, and Barbara and Graham for the indoor herb garden, and Anna for the chocolates.

'What did Laura give you, Anna?' Graham asked and she pulled the Raymond Briggs book from under Audrey's chair. 'Have you read it?' he asked me and came and sat on the arm of my chair. 'I've sneaked a few moments in Smith's, I've been dying to read the whole thing.'

Anna came and stood the other side of me and went away again and Graham and I read silently but in synchronisation because we laughed at the same times and by the end I could even focus again.

'Let's see what's on television,' Barbara said. 'Let's relax for a bit now. I looked in the paper, it's supposed to be quite a good film.'

'If he's fit,' Audrey said when it finished at five o'clock, looking at Leslie's closed eyes, 'we'll have to start making tracks.' No one argued.

Barbara helped them pack up their presents and pressed lukewarm turkey and pudding on them, she'd have decorated the tinfoil if it'd made left-overs more acceptable. I waited until the last minute before I went downstairs and stood waving at the front door.

'Thank God they never stay the night anywhere,' I said. Barbara shrugged.

'I wouldn't mind having them. It wasn't too bad.' She went back into the kitchen, as though all that mattered about the day was that she checked I'd washed up properly.

'Not too bad?' I said and followed. Anna took my hand and I put her on my lap. 'What are you talking about? Whatever are you pretending now?'

'Go and find Daddy,' she said wearily to Anna, but I wasn't having that, I held onto her for a moment. She almost had to struggle to get away.

'She mustn't listen, she mustn't hear what's as plain as a pikestaff to the rest of us, you're going to go on just like Audrey, always pretending everything's all right, send her away so she doesn't realise anything's wrong— This whole place is a sham,' I said. 'All you care about is how it looks. All you care about at all is how you cover up, underneath, what's really going on, you'll do anything to avoid that.'

She sat down with such appalling patience that I didn't confine myself to Christmas, I marched up and down and accused her of self-deception over everything, from the day we'd just spent to the way she dedicated her whole life to a surface gloss.

'Perhaps,' she said after a while, 'if you dislike it here so much, you'd better go. Perhaps you'd better not come for a bit.'

I got my coat and refused to ring for a taxi and didn't say goodbye. I slammed the door and walked all the way home and thought the only thing I really regretted was that I was too hung over to do any serious drinking. I was past analysing or pitying or even self-pity, it was a day that had lasted forever. All I wanted was to obliterate the whole hateful lot of them, but all I could settle for was the film on BBC2 and more black coffee.

'Yes, what?' I said when the phone rang. My first thought was that it'd be Audrey ringing to tell me off.

'Whatever happened?' Graham asked.

'Christmas spirit,' I said and he laughed.

'We could do with more of it.'

'It was hangovers, really,' I said. 'All the usual hangovers of family gatherings. I'm sorry, though, it couldn't have been too wonderful for you.'

'I'm past caring,' he said.

'How is she?' I asked. 'Was she very upset? Or was it just the awful end to an awful day?' He didn't answer. I imagined him shrugging, his eyes sad, his mouth straight. 'I'm watching television again,' I said. 'What are you doing?'

'Wondering what to do.'

'Have a look at *Giant*,' I said. 'It'll make you feel better.'

'Is that all it takes?' and he laughed again.

'Not at all. Coffee helps and having a hot bath and sitting in front of the fire.'

'Sounds wonderful.' I wondered, I just wondered if I could say it, say, Come and see for yourself.

'I'd better go and try it,' he said, 'hadn't I? I'll let you know how it goes. Don't worry about it,' he said. 'We'll all get over it.'

The next day I couldn't believe how cheerful I felt. I made the unprecedented effort of ringing Beryl and invited her and her boy-friend over for a drink. In return she asked me to her party.

'I thought you'd be tucked up with your family,' she said, 'otherwise I would have before.' Then her boyfriend invited me to the station party on New Year's Eve, and on both occasions I congratulated myself because I was entertaining, I gave good value, and I didn't get drunk or maudlin or rashly into bed with anyone.

'I've been to some very civilised gatherings,' I rang to tell Graham. I was just returning the compliment but I telephoned at seven when I knew Barbara would be reading to Anna, or resting.

'Not too dull?' he asked. I giggled. 'Not in the least. Quite eccentric. I'll tell you some time.'

'Ours were,' he said. 'Dull. Geraldine and Paul and Jessica for drinks, going to Geraldine's, going to Jessica's, three separate oc-casions, all exactly the same. You should have come,' he said. 'Livened things up a bit.'

'I wasn't asked,' I said. 'I'm not a great social success in your house. Still,' I sighed, 'I should come back and say I'm sorry.'

'She misses you.'

'She says that?' I asked. 'But you can tell,' I added.

'That's what she means,' he answered. 'It's not easy. Try, it'd be nice to see you soon. Come one evening,' he said. 'About six. We'll walk in together, if that makes it easier.'

'Meet me on the corner, you mean?' I suggested. He laughed, overloud, an unfunny joke.

'Not exactly. But you know what time I get back. Just come around then.'

At the end of the week I did. He opened the door to me and took my arm. 'Well done,' he said and then called, 'Look who's arrived,' and Barbara came into the hall.

'Laura, how nice.' She smiled. 'Come and see,' she called to Anna, 'come and see who's here.'

I watched Anna's bath and read two stories and Graham gave me a drink and we all chatted about cold weather and hypothermia. When I said it was time to go Barbara said, 'See you soon, then?' and I answered, 'Tomorrow.'

For the last month she was pregnant I went two or three times a week. What I waited for was Graham coming back from work and saying, 'Stay and have a drink.' The rest of the time I tried to shut my ears because I didn't understand what she wanted.

'I was looking at my skin,' she would say and thrust her arm under my face. 'Is yours like that? Has it got those marks? Those patches? I was reading about . . .' – and it could have been anything from cervical cancer to brain tumours – she'd describe ailments that would never affect someone of her age. I didn't have the patience to disentangle them. If she wanted to worry about brown blotches, warts, blurring of the vision, that was her affair; I didn't have the expertise to reassure her or enough interest to find out what she was frightened of.

'I can't think properly,' she'd say and press her hands to the sides of her head. Half an hour later she'd announce, 'I think I'll get Geraldine to look after Anna when I go in. I'd like her to be with other children.' I would grit my teeth and nod.

Every day I wanted to say, 'Get on with it, hurry up,' because every day she seemed to sink into such a state of doubt I couldn't believe she'd ever rouse enough energy to give birth. She still made the effort to keep the kitchen shining, the sitting room warm and tidy, the bedrooms and bathroom clean and organised; she washed, dressed, cared for Anna, she functioned. I couldn't wait to take her place. I don't think she knew, though. As far as she was concerned I gave placatory answers to her irrational questions, I went on helping and I waited alongside her; I was someone to unite with in boredom and quiescence, I sympathised that she wanted it over and done with.

When her labour did start the first thing I realised was that I couldn't have been more useless.

After ten minutes she was crawling round the kitchen floor. Even watching her I'd found it difficult to believe she'd been driven to that, that it could be that bad, and I phoned for the ambulance and for Graham.

'You'd better go straight there,' I told him. 'You won't be here in time to go to the hospital with her, I hope,' I added because she really was a horrible sight, panting, putting her head onto the floor tiles to rest. It seemed as if she'd gone back into some primeval state where the only way to deal with pain was by animal means. All the time I waited I didn't dare even touch her; in case she attacked me, biting or scratching I suppose I imagined. When the ambulance men came they seemed quite wary, too. At first they talked to her in soothing voices but she took no notice. She crawled away from them and they practically had to corner her. When they picked her up it was upside down, they had to turn her over onto her back to put her on the stretcher and then strap her on, hold her down.

I sat and watched all that. I had made some tea and I sat at the kitchen table with the pot in front of me, a cup I held and didn't drink out of, as though I lived there and I was watching a mad stranger being removed. I was grateful, I thanked the men quite profusely for the speed with which they'd come and their help; I didn't speak to or touch or go near Barbara. I stood at the front door and watched them carry her down the path.

When I went back inside the house I felt like cheering. She was going to hospital and I was deposited in that smart house. I inherited her friends, a child, Graham; all I had to do was demonstrate how easy it was to make life enjoyable.

'It may take ages,' I told Anna when she came back from playgroup. I hoped it would, because after that my days were numbered. 'You play with your farm and I'll make a casserole for Daddy. We'll have a nice afternoon and not worry.'

It almost came as a shock when Graham rang at five o'clock. I couldn't at first make out what he was saying. 'Distress' was the word he used most often and then he said, 'Well, it's all over, anyway, and he seems fine—'

'He?' I waited.

'He,' and he laughed. 'Him, the baby. It's a boy.' I tried to say that was wonderful.

'It was appalling,' he said. 'It only took three hours, it was catastrophic. When it was over she wouldn't believe it, she was still screaming, so they gave her a tranquilliser. She's not making any sense now. It'll be better tomorrow,' he said after a moment. 'Don't tell Anna,' he said. 'I want to do that. Just stay there, I won't be long.'

'Daddy's coming back,' I said to Anna and bundled her into her coat and made her run to keep up with me to the supermarket. I bought Spanish champagne and burgundy and made her run even faster back, in case he'd arrived. I wanted to be there waiting, smiling, comforting.

'I'm exhausted,' was the first thing he said, he hardly looked at me, straight away he turned to Anna. 'You've got a brother,' he told her. I smiled and nodded and she jumped and shouted and swung on his arms.

'Why not ring Audrey and Leslie and Geraldine and Jessica and tell them,' I said after a little while because all she did was hang onto him, wrap herself round his legs so he couldn't move.

'I'm too excited,' she kept saying. 'I'm too excited to stop.' I could see she would decide it was impossible to go to bed, she'd have to stay up. All evening she would sit on his lap, turn his face to hers and repeat, 'Baby brother, baby brother.'

'Listen, Anna,' I said, 'ring everyone up and tell them. Then I'll tell you something. A secret.' I looked round as though making sure no one could overhear me. 'I'll tell you when you're in bed,' I whispered, 'after supper, after your bath.'

All the time I waited for them to be over I was patient. I said, 'Not yet,' and, 'It won't be long now.' I waited for hours until she lay down. 'All right,' I said, 'now listen. If you go to sleep quickly we'll buy three presents in the morning. One for Mummy, one for baby, and one for you.'

'Is that it?' she asked. She sat up.

'No,' I answered, 'that's what happens if you go to sleep. If you don't –' and I paused, 'if you don't, we won't buy any. Especially not for you.' She lay down again. 'Think what you want,' I said. 'First of all think about Mummy, then the baby, then you.'

'What I like?' she asked.

'We'll see,' I said. 'You keep thinking.'

'Look,' I said when I went back downstairs. 'Surprise.' I took the champagne out of the fridge and unrolled the burgundy from its green paper. 'I hope you like them.'

He sat up in his chair and rubbed his eyes as though he'd been asleep. 'They look wonderful. I couldn't think of anything better.' He yawned and his whole body seemed to curl. He hung onto the arms of the chair.

'Do you want a rest?' I asked. He sat and looked into space.

'I'd like to go somewhere else,' he said. 'Let's go upstairs.' Quietly, not to disturb Anna, I followed. He shut the sitting-room door behind us. He stretched out in an armchair and sat so that his head was low, I could look down on him. He stared at his feet.

'Anna wasn't like that,' he said. 'She took all night, but it was quite civilised. Listening to Anna saying, "I've got a brother," ringing people and telling them, "It's a boy, yes, they're fine," doesn't seem to have much to do with what happened. I was useless, I didn't exist for her; she was in another world. When he was born I was almost shocked, as though that wasn't what we were waiting for. And before that I was petrified. I feel a dead loss.' He leaned his head back and closed his eyes.

'So do I.' I wanted him to have sat on the sofa so I could be next to him; all I could see was his knees. 'When it started I just rang the ambulance. I couldn't help at all, not even talk to her. Although she might not have wanted anyone near her while she was dealing with pain.' I shifted slightly back so that if he sat up we would be level. 'She hates being seen *in extremis*. Being sick, feeling ill—'

'I know,' he said. 'I know she doesn't want anyone anywhere near her. But what do you do? When?' he asked. 'Now? Ever?'

'Why should you, what is there to make you?'

'A couple of weeks,' he said, 'and they'll have been home so long I'll have forgotten. All these ideas about the distance between us'll seem like a toothache that's only there if I think about it. Sometimes I can't feel a thing, other times it nags and other times it feels like an abcess about to explode. It's neuralgic. Everyone says, "Imagination," but something imaginary isn't necessarily unreal. Do you see that?' he asked. He sat up and I nodded and said yes and he sighed, twice. 'I don't want to lose her. I want us to get back together,' he said and then shook his head. 'She's not in danger, I don't mean that—' He stopped and looked at me. 'God, I feel worse than ever.'

'No.' I leaned forward then, I took his elbow in my palm, held it quite gently, warm, big enough to fill my hand. 'You've had an awful time. It's no fun watching people suffering, it doesn't bring out the best in anyone, it brings out fear.' Before he pulled away I let go. 'You could ring the hospital, that might make you feel better. You could see how they are, that would set your mind at rest. And then we'll have some food, that'll help too.'

'They're OK,' he said when he came downstairs, and that seemed to be that. He ate his casserole quickly and we talked about my job, NHS cutbacks, when Geraldine and Jessica wanted to visit. Neither of us referred to pain or distance, we concentrated on the arrangements for shopping and cooking and I made sure he knew how much I wanted to help.

'I'll stay overnight,' I said, 'sleep in Anna's room, then I'd be here to give a hand in the mornings.'

'Anna's no problem,' he said, 'not yet, anyway. When Barbara gets home it might be different—'

'But she'll be here to deal with it,' I said, because I couldn't make it any better for myself. He yawned.

'I'm grateful to you,' he said. 'We couldn't manage without you.'

'Yes, you could,' I contradicted. 'Look at Geraldine and Jessica, they're always here to help.'

'But not the same. Not family,' he added. I looked at the bottle of burgundy and thought of the champagne I'd left in the fridge. He yawned again and again.

'Family isn't necessarily a recommendation to me,' I said and started to put the dishes together, 'or hadn't you noticed?'

He smiled and his eyes watered. 'You're a survivor,' he said. 'Don't underrate yourself. I'll make some coffee in a while, I'll drive you home.' I took no notice.

'I'll get a taxi,' I said. 'You're much too tired.'

I took my time about arriving the next day because obviously all I'd have to do would be housework; I would cook and clean and amuse Anna while he visited the hospital. 'How do you do it?' he might ask me. 'How can I get close to her again?' I wouldn't even ask 'Why?' or, 'Do you really want to?' I'd just listen.

'I've got something for you,' he said as soon as I went in the front door. 'Come and see.' He hurried in front of me to the kitchen. On the table was a large square package. 'Undo it,' he said. 'It's a bit of a selfish present. Us more than you,' and before I unwrapped it I could see what it was.

'A winebox,' I said. 'That's nice.'

'My contribution to this evening,' he said. 'Make it a bit more celebratory than I managed last night.'

'That will be nice,' I repeated. Then he gave me a paper bag.

'Look in there,' he said, and turned away as though it was salacious, wrapped up for disguise. I took it out and saw a bright picture of two children, black-haired, slightly out of proportion, big-headed, short-legged, sitting on a hillside. '*Topsy and Tim*,' he said. 'I'd thought of Tim already and this sort of clinched it. What do you think?'

I nodded judiciously. 'Tim's all right. Tim's certainly all right.'

'I'll take it this afternoon,' he said and half-laughed. 'It's for Anna, of course, but I'll show it to Barbara. I got Anna some beads,' he said. 'She told me you said she and Barbara and the baby all had to have a present, so I got Barbara and the baby some flowers and Anna did rather better than anyone. That was a good idea. I'm going after lunch,' he said.

I nodded and found the tin opener and tipped soup into a pan. While it boiled tasteless I watched him walk round the kitchen, humming, leaning over Anna's shoulder as she threaded the glass necklace. I thought of him spending the morning shopping, choosing, thinking of his family, and then I remembered he'd thought about the evening too. I sat down and read all the small print on the winebox, vineyard, year, preparation, flavour, and thought of us drinking it; Anna in bed and two litres of alcohol and food and talk, and I thought I could tell him about Jas, we could talk about love and commitment and jealousy and agree and smile at one another, that at least he wanted company and friendship from me.

'Nice stuff,' he said while he ate the soup.

I said, 'It's rubbish,' because that was obvious.

'Everything's nice,' he admitted and squeezed Anna's shoulders. 'Isn't it?'

All afternoon while he visited Barbara Anna and I watered and dusted the plants and Geraldine came and said, 'Jessica and I thought we'd pop along tomorrow.' All the time I watched television with Anna and made her supper and promised Graham would be home in time to put her to bed, I watched the clock, I counted the hours until he came back.

'Much better,' he said when he did. 'She's a different woman.'

He smiled and swung Anna over his shoulder, he sang while he bathed her and when he came downstairs into the kitchen his fine hair stood on end.

'He's fantastic,' he said and grinned. 'I can't say too much in front of Anna, of course, but I can tell you. He's so good. He sleeps like a log, hardly even wakes up for a feed. He's the ideal baby.' I didn't smile back; after the first glance I didn't want to see how much pleasure he'd had in his afternoon.

'That winebox,' I said, as though buttering the trout I'd got out of Barbara's freezer took all my attention, 'how does it open?' He jumped to his feet and unlocked the vacuum tap and poured glasses. When I put the fish in the oven he set the table and all the time he talked, the relief, it was a feeling like nothing else. He could not stop smiling.

'Cheers,' he said, and ducked behind his glass with pleasure. 'To Tim.'

'Geraldine came,' I said while we waited for the food to be ready. 'She and Jessica want to visit.'

'Fine, fine. What about you?' I made a face.

'I played the Good Samaritan and said I'd go with Audrey and Leslie. I didn't mention there was an ulterior motive, of course, but I reckon if I see them now it'll let me off for another six months.'

'Is it that bad?' he said.

I shrugged. 'Maybe it's only me. I remember when Barbara first took you to meet them, you said it wasn't that awful. Was that what you really thought? What did you think, honestly?' I tried to put that first time back in his mind. 'The hostility? The irritation?'

He frowned. 'I can't remember. It's sort of blurred into how I see them now.'

'And how's that?'

'That they're not worth worrying about. Not for me, at any rate. But then other people's parents are never that appalling.'

'You mean you won't bitch about them?'

'I'm feeling too generous to bitch about anyone,' he said. 'I'm finding everything delightful at the moment.'

I checked the oven and the vegetables and warmed the plates and talked about Italian food and markets and he filled our glasses again.

'What were your parents like?' I asked, as we started to separate the fishbones from the flesh. 'Is it OK to talk about them?'

'They seem a long time ago.'

'But they were nice while they were alive?' He nodded. 'When did it happen?' I asked. 'Or don't you want to?'

'I don't mind at all,' he said. 'It's rather nice to remember them at a time like this. They died years ago, actually, before any of this, before Barbara, even. They bought this house, though, well, their money did. When it happened I was at university, just in the first year. Possibly because of that, because I wasn't at home any more, it didn't seem to make that much impact. Or I didn't let it, you can't tell at that age. I was upset, I cried for them, I missed them, but I told myself I was independent, I kept reminding myself they were quite old and it would've happened soon, anyway. I suppose I behaved as if it was all for the best.'

'What happened?' I asked. 'Is it all right to ask that? Barbara just said it was an accident—'

'It was a car crash,' he said. 'They were going out to supper and they must've been late because my father drove straight into a lorry on the North Circular. It was instantaneous.' He looked down at his plate, he'd kept taking very small mouthfuls; he didn't stop eating, but he didn't stop talking either. 'That's what I was told, anyway. Actually, I didn't even think of questioning that – it took years before I thought it might not have been quite that conveniently swift—'

'It can be,' I interrupted. 'Multiple injury, shock, heart failure, it can all happen in seconds.'

'Really?' He leaned forward. 'Really and truly?' I nodded and looked away from his sad face to my plate.

'Someone should have explained it,' I said. 'That's the trouble with doctors.'

'You tell me,' he said. 'Multiple shock—'

'Multiple injury,' I corrected, 'followed by shock, followed by heart failure. One, two, three, it's as fast as that, the body can't cope, it just gives up, stops. You don't feel a thing.'

'I see.' He drained his glass. 'That helps. I don't think about it all the time, hardly at all really, I don't think you can bear to. What non-instantaneous death could mean in circumstances like that. But it did bother me on and off. How you'd feel in the minutes before you faced extinction. And it seemed appalling to accept that, their pain and horror and confusion and me going on living and not thinking about it—'

'But you did,' I said. I put down my knife and fork and waited for him to pour some more wine. 'And you don't need to any more. Instantaneous does mean instantaneous, you can think of other things about them now.' He rubbed his hands over his eyes. 'What else about them? Tell me some more,' I said after a minute.

'Barbara's given me a sort of picture – elderly impressive relatives

221

whose pictures hang on the stairs—' He looked up then and half-laughed. 'You mean, that's not how you see them?'

'Did she say that? Was that what she told you?'

'No.' I tried to sound uncritical. 'But it's obvious, isn't it? They're so different from our parents; she can quite safely be proud of them. No one can contradict. And even if she likes to show them off that doesn't mean—'

'No,' he nodded. 'I'm sure she means well. And my picture isn't necessarily that trustworthy either, I got them wrong quite a lot of the time. When I was younger I called them armchair socialists because all they talked was politics – Suez, Hungary, strikes, CND, you name a cause and they'd have an opinion on it – but that wasn't fair. My mother said once, she was washing my pram to give it away to a jumble sale, "Over this pram of yours most of the burning issues of the world have been discussed. It was the only place left to us to do it." When I was born they were quite old, forty and nearly fifty, and she stopped all the meetings she used to go to. She made it quite plain it was no sacrifice. "The world didn't miss me, but I like to think you would have," she said. "The only thing I couldn't stop was thinking," she told me, "even being a besotted mother didn't alter that."'

'What a nice woman she sounds.' I offered him my glass. 'More?' He filled it up.

'She was. Really nice to be with. They both were. They probably took everything I did too seriously, they wanted to put a stop to all the fierce games, any competitiveness, but what I chose to do, woodwork, stamp collecting, cross-country running, things they couldn't have given two hoots about, they'd be interested in, and they'd talk about them till the cows came home.'

'Extraordinary,' I said and looked into my glass and couldn't think of any answers, and it was extraordinary because I couldn't see any more where the words were coming from, his mouth was quite out of alignment with the rest of his face, I couldn't make anything around me come into focus.

'They were well off, of course.' He looked down as if he couldn't help but apologise. 'And they were proud of their own families – well, they were both only children and I was their only child, so I got to know my grandparents' life stories really well. My father's were a Liverpool sea captain and a lady of the manor, and my mother's were a Manchester school teacher and the Honourable gent whose children she went to teach. They had very similar backgrounds – half-skilled middle class, half-unskilled gentry – and money and brains made a quite extraordinary combination in both their cases. They didn't abuse, they weren't supercilious. They felt responsible.' I nodded, I still couldn't see him well enough to answer. 'They made me what I am,' he said and made a face. 'That's what Barbara's got against them, really. There they hang on the stairs, imposing, impressive, and what have they bequeathed to me except what she calls an overworked sense of social responsibility? Overworked because I put all my energies into jobs that don't provide equality but consume all my waking hours. A born do-gooder, she calls me,' he said. 'Born unsuitable. She says people only want support from their equals, not their social betters. She says they can tell where I come from.'

'Yes,' I answered. That was all, I couldn't marshal a single word of disagreement. 'Tell me some more,' I said after a minute. 'Did you have a big house? Lots of toys, scrap-books, photo albums' – once I got started it was surprisingly easy – 'a nursery and a study, like your study upstairs? Holidays abroad before package tours started? Conversation over supper, newspapers,' and I suddenly felt so near to tears that I covered my eyes. I heard him move, I heard the plates rattle as he leaned across his fishbones and shook my wrist.

'What is it, whatever is it?' I picked up my glass.

'Nothing. I just hate mine so much. Envy, I suppose, except you shouldn't envy people for having happy childhoods. I don't Anna, or even friends of mine – it's just made you—' I stopped. 'You're nice,' I said. 'They made you nice.'

'I've got faults.' He sat back and looked over our glasses and then refilled them. 'I'm sure you're well aware of them.'

'No. Yes,' I contradicted, 'but if we start on that – no.' I smiled. 'Tell me about when you were young.'

I closed my eyes while he talked about it, and I heard the civilised voices, discussions, debates, and I saw the holidays, shrimping, swimming, going to France.

'Bayeux,' he said. 'I found history then.' I watched while he was growing up, putting up tents, camping, playing, boys who came to stay, learning to fish. 'Beach holidays,' he said. 'Hours lying in the sun, lying on the water, rocking, dreaming, building a raft.' I knew that I, too, wanted to lie flat. I could not think of any way to do that, I could not see how to stand or talk or ever move again and I could hear him asking me, 'Laura, Laura.'

'A little rest,' I said. I put my head on the table.

'All right?' I heard him ask later. I could smell coffee. 'Sit up. I've made this, come on, you'll feel better then. Laura,' he said, 'won't you?'

I lifted my head. 'You don't look too wonderful either,' I said. He put the cups down and sat opposite.

'Christ,' he said. I sipped very slowly.

'I can't move,' I told him. He nodded.

'I've made up the bed in Anna's room. That is,' and he considered, remembered what he'd done, 'I put the duvet on the other bunk. It took ages—' He shook his head and held it. 'Christ,' he repeated.

'Have I been asleep ages, then?' When I looked at my watch it was too small to see properly. 'How are you?'

'Don't,' he said. 'Coffee, that's the thing.' He drank his cup and poured another. 'Go on up, take it upstairs. Go to sleep. Drink it in bed. Sorry,' he said. 'I can't talk. Coffee and sleep, go on.'

In the night I thought I was on a boat, I could hear the creaking of Anna above me and I was desperate for water. I woke very early and looked for a porthole and then lay wondering if he would be angry or abrupt or silent, but he sounded quite cheerful when he called that breakfast was ready. It was gentle and familiar, we didn't talk, we passed butter and milk without asking, and when we'd finished quietly planned the day ahead.

'I'll go in to the hospital this morning,' Graham said, 'and maybe stay until after lunch. It's this afternoon that Geraldine and Jessica want to go, isn't it?'

'And Audrey and Leslie. And then she's back home. It's not long to spend in hospital when you think of nine months before and years and years after. I liked hearing about your family,' I said when he kissed Anna goodbye.

'I liked talking,' he answered.

I washed up, took Anna to playgroup, bought steak and salad, early daffodils, and in case we could face alcohol again two bottles of Bordeaux. I swept the kitchen, I watched the sun shine on the plants, I studied the room full of food and drink and flowers, and although I was less sure of the rest of the house I walked through

224

that, too. I stood at the door to Anna's room and smiled at the bed I'd slept in, and then I looked into their bedroom: Barbara's neat dressing table, Graham's clothes on the floor, the baby's basket and chest of drawers in one corner. I went to the sitting room and lay down on the sofa, and then I walked again, up and down, rooms, stairs. I was waiting, I didn't think.

'Laura,' he said when the phone rang at lunchtime, 'do me a couple of favours, it's taken me nearly half an hour to find a box that works. Ring Geraldine and Jessica to say tomorrow not today, and put Audrey and Leslie off, too.'

'What's happened?' I asked. 'What's the matter?'

'It's nothing.' His voice was tired. 'Nothing to worry about. She's just got to stay another day, she's sore, a bit tired, tomorrow would be better for visitors. Can you do that?'

'Straight away,' I promised. 'What time will you be able to get back?' As though it didn't matter, that there was still another day after today, an evening after this one.

'Not late,' he said, 'teatime.' I could spend all afternoon looking forward to it.

'I want Mummy,' Anna said when Geraldine brought her home from the playgroup and I explained what had happened. 'You said she was coming.'

'Tomorrow,' I reminded her, 'that's what I said. But it won't be long, just one more day.'

'I want Daddy,' she said. 'You go. I don't want you here instead.'

'Let's make a nice pudding,' I offered. I did not want her hiding under the kitchen table when Graham came back. I wanted to mix the sauce for the steak and scrub potatoes, I wanted him to see happy smiling faces.

'I'm going to bed,' she said and crawled across the floor. I followed. I tried to coax her out from under her bunk, I cajoled and pleaded until all I wanted was to hit her.

'No, go away,' she said.

'All right,' I answered eventually and went downstairs and let her sulk.

'Laura,' he called as he opened the front door. Straight away Anna began to wail. He did not look to find out where I was, he raced upstairs. I heard him crooning and walking about. When I went into the hall he was sitting on the landing with her.

'She's upset,' he explained, and he carried her into the kitchen. He sat her on his lap and built Lego, coloured pictures, stuck shapes on paper.

'I want Mummy,' she said whenever I went near with tea, biscuits, coffee. She flung herself against him as though I would forcibly separate them.

'Come on, Anna,' he said at intervals, 'you're not like this. Look at all the good times you've had with Laura. Look,' but when he stood up she clung to him like a monkey. He walked bow-legged round the kitchen, upstairs, down. 'Look at this,' he said and carried her up to his study. He came back holding an album. 'Look at all the pictures of you and me and Mummy and Laura.' He slowly turned over the pages but she hid her face.

'Make her go,' she said.

'She's just upset,' he mouthed. Her face trembled, her thumb quivered by her lips.

'No,' I said. 'I'd better leave, that's the only thing.'

'I'm really mortified,' but he patted her back, the thin spine through her jumper, all that tender flesh besieging him. 'I was looking forward to this evening.'

'So was I,' I said, but I waited until I was out of his house.

When the telephone rang I'd been in long enough to pour a glass of gin and turn the television on.

'I can't apologise enough,' he said, 'and Anna's sorry, too.'

'Good,' I said. 'Ring me again in the morning and tell me how she is.'

'How are you?' he asked.

'Having a drink. Watching the box. Bored. How are you?'

'About the same. You wouldn't like—' and he hesitated, 'Once she got to sleep I could come and pick you up, she'd be OK for ten minutes. I was looking forward to that steak—'

'No,' I said.

'She didn't mean it.'

'Then she should be congratulated on a very convincing performance.' I balanced the receiver under my chin and picked up my glass.

'She's unhappy,' he said. 'I'm not pleased with her. But try and see it from her point of view.' I pretended to think about that. 'She's never done it before,' he said, as though that made it better. 'Tomorrow she'll be fine,' he promised. 'I'll talk to you then.'

I didn't go to the hospital until the last possible minute the next afternoon, in case he rang and said, 'Anna's desperate to apologise, how soon can you come over. Now?' Or, 'I don't care what Anna behaves like, I want you to be here.' I needn't have bothered, the telephone was silent all morning. When I did finally leave I realised I hadn't bought Barbara a present. Outside the supermarket was a tray of avocados, soggy and overpriced, but I asked very nicely and they wrapped one up in tinfoil. At least she might think it was appropriate. I couldn't bring myself to think about what I'd missed, or what I'd got to look forward to; I didn't care if I was hours late for Audrey and Leslie. I drifted along the road, cradling my little parcel as though my hand was some warm jungle environment, and quite deliberately let bus after bus sail past me. They were standing by the bookstall.

As soon as I walked in Audrey called across the whole foyer, 'Where is she? What happened to her? What are they keeping her in longer for? Why couldn't we come yesterday?'

'She's tired,' I said. I waited until I was close enough not to shout. 'I told you. Today was more convenient.'

'Not for us it wasn't.' She pushed up against me. 'And you could have come another day. You're close enough, you didn't have to come the same time.'

I looked back at her. I supposed she meant to look festive in the pink hat but it clashed with my red jacket and turned her face a muddy yellow.

'I'm looking after Anna,' I lied. 'I had to get Geraldine to have her. This was easier.'

She pulled herself round to look at the noticeboard. 'It's ward C,' she said. 'We'll have to look for it. I'll manage.' And she strode ahead as though it was a minefield she had to negotiate singlehanded.

At every corner she barked, 'Come on,' as though we were deserters. Barbara's was the bed nearest the door and although that was why we'd come, it still gave me a shock to find her. She didn't look her old self, she looked vulnerable, wiped out, as if she'd survived a motorway pile-up rather than given birth. She was like a stranger, I thought, nothing to do with me.

'Sit down,' she said. I found chairs and we all handed over our presents.

'This one was late, of course.' Audrey pointed. 'Took her as long to come two miles as it did us fifty.'

'Were you working this morning?' Barbara asked. I said, come on, surely she remembered, I'd arranged leave this week because of looking after Anna.

'You?' Audrey said. 'You, keeping the home fires burning?'

'Me,' I said, 'and I told you, I'm doing all right.'

'What's that?' she asked when Barbara unwrapped the avocado.

'Barbara understands,' I said and smiled.

Audrey pulled her chair away from mine. 'She doesn't want too many people round her. She needs a bit of privacy.'

I stood up as though I might go, but I didn't mean that, I was waiting to pick the baby up. I went round the side of Barbara's bed to the cot and lifted him close to me; I looked into his tiny sleeping face and all I could see was Graham's. I joggled and nursed him and told Audrey how wonderful and good and quiet he was. I couldn't wait to put him down.

'Let's have a look. That's what we've come for, too,' Audrey said. I passed him over like a shot.

'Geraldine and Jessica came earlier, then?' I asked Barbara. Now I did want to leave, I wanted to get rid of the thought of him in my arms. 'They asked when they could have Anna, take her out, did you get it sorted out?'

She nodded, but as though it'd never happen, as though she'd never get out of that place. 'I'm going,' I wanted to shout. 'You lot get on with it, I'm leaving,' but instead we all sat there and played pass the baby and examined flowers and cards and talked about visiting hours and food, anything to pretend we had things to say to one another.

'Look,' Leslie said, 'look at that.' He had managed to lean over the barricade of Audrey's arms. 'It's you that he takes after,' and he looked from his wife to his grandson. Then I did stand up, I wouldn't listen, I couldn't bear to contemplate that, but Barbara could, she looked from one to the other of them and for a moment I thought she'd snatch him away but she only stared. When Audrey handed him back to her she hardly seemed to notice. She let him lie

228

across her stomach as if he'd never been born, as if she took no more notice of him outside than inside. I suppose we'd only stayed half an hour and perhaps because I was standing up Barbara started looking at the clock, saying it was nearly feeding time, how kind to make such a journey. Audrey put her coat on and the chairs under the bed as if she was being given five minutes' notice that she was to be out of the place for ever.

'We're thrilled,' Leslie said, 'we both are.' Then he bent and kissed Barbara goodbye.

'I'll see you, Barbara,' I said. No matter how long Audrey stood watching I wasn't going to embrace anyone. 'I'll see you tomorrow,' as though it was something I was truly looking forward to. I gave a cheery wave. 'Take care.'

'Satisfied?' Audrey said. 'If you hadn't stood up she wouldn't have noticed the clock. Dragging us all this way and pushing us out as fast as you could?'

'I'm not in charge of when she feeds the baby,' I said.

'You could tell.' She pushed ahead of me in the corridor, pulled Leslie's arm to keep up with hers. 'You knew what you were up to, you'd worked it out already. I could tell from when you arrived late you were up to something.'

After Audrey and Leslie had fought their way onto the bus to the station I couldn't decide where to go. 'He might be expecting me,' I thought. 'He should have let me know.' I went into Hammersmith and looked round the shops. I went and had coffee. I wasted two hours before I caught the bus to their road.

'Here I am,' I'd call as I went in. He'd come and take my arm. 'There you are,' and I'd have nothing to worry about. But as I turned the corner he was already out in the street, standing by their car, struggling to pick Anna up because she was fighting and kicking. I could hear her shouting, 'No, no.' I shouted and Anna started screaming and he looked up at me and let go of her.

'Where've you been?' he shouted. I ran to him.

'Seeing Barbara, why, what's the matter?' He grabbed hard at Anna, he caught her arm again.

'What happened, what went on there? Was she all right?'

I put my hand out to him. 'Nothing,' I said. 'Barbara was fine.'

He pulled away, he shook away my fingers. 'What's happened, then?' He wrenched Anna upright.

229

'What are you talking about?' I asked, trying to stroke Anna's head to stop her crying.

He stared at me. 'Barbara. I don't know what's happened, I got a phone call from the hospital, half a bloody hour ago now, I was waiting for you to come, there was no answer from your place. I was taking her to Geraldine's, I couldn't wait for you any more—'

'What did they say?' I sounded much calmer than I felt. 'Who rang? Didn't they give you any idea?'

'There's no urgency' – he imitated someone else's voice – 'just someone wanted to see me, a paediatrician. Of course I said was there anything wrong with Tim and they said he was just as I'd left him. I didn't think of asking about Barbara then—'

'She was fine,' I repeated. I bent down in front of Anna. 'I'm sure it's OK, you go, it'll be nothing, it's something really routine and they'll apologise for worrying you. We'll go indoors.' I took Anna's hand. 'It's cold out here.' I couldn't begin to imagine anything about it, I didn't want to. I held on to her tightly. 'Daddy's just got to pop out for half an hour, we'll go and wait.'

First of all I rang Geraldine to say I'd arrived. Then Anna and I played with her doll and her doll's house and her stencil set and picture shapes; we made a card for Audrey and Leslie and one for Barbara and also, while I pretended not to notice, one for me. By then it was an hour past her bedtime and I was worried to death. 'He'd have rung if it were awful,' I told myself, because if it concerned Barbara and the baby he'd tell me about it; that was all we'd ever been to one another. I listened to him talk about Barbara, he advised on Jas, that was all there was to it, and that was infinitely preferable to nothing at all.

'Come on,' I said to Anna. 'Let's get you undressed.' She even agreed. I walked up and downstairs, in and out of the sitting room for her book, Barbara and Graham's bedroom for her dressing gown. I wanted never to have dreamed through those rooms, I wanted to be out of the house, not to see any of it again.

It wasn't until nine o'clock that I thought of ringing the hospital myself and then I was even more frightened because I might be told he'd left hours ago, but when I finally steadied myself to dial I heard the car. I ran to open the front door and stood waiting, welcoming. He didn't move, he was staring at the wheel. I called, quite softly, and he turned very slowly and he was crying, his shoulders were shaking and tears poured down his face. I couldn't move. He wiped his eyes, twice, while he fumbled with his keys and the car door and then he walked up the path and past me into the house as though I wasn't there.

'What is it?' I said. 'What's happened?' I followed him into the kitchen and I held onto his arm. 'Tell me, please.' I tried to guide him to sit down.

He shook me off. 'I'd like a drink,' he said and stood with his back to me, staring out of the dark window. I pumped the last stuff out of the winebox.

'Here,' I said, 'come and sit down, come and tell me.' I waited and then he came and sat opposite.

'She's my sister too,' I said. 'Tell me, Graham, please.' He still wouldn't. He shook his head and covered his mouth. I went and stood over him and he crouched, he cowered as though he was frightened of me and pulled his hands away and held them tight. I couldn't bear that.

'Graham,' I said. 'You've got to tell me.' Perhaps it was more difficult for him to refuse when my face was forced up against his. He started to, he tried to keep his mouth steady and bit his lips and then he said, 'Sit down, get a chair.' I pulled it up close to him and then I took his hand. He looked at our fingers together, he turned mine over for a minute and then he said, 'It's Down's Syndrome. That's what they wanted to tell us.'

After a bit I asked questions: who had given them the news, what had they said, how did they know, what advice could they suggest.

'Tell me about it,' I'd said. 'Explain exactly what happened.' What about Barbara, what about you? I'd thought. I couldn't imagine the answers to those.

'A doctor,' he said and let go of me and drank all the wine in his glass, 'and the sister. They just told us. They tried quite hard, they tried to be nice. It's not their fault. Afterwards they left us alone to talk about it. They sent us a health visitor. They gave Barbara a room to herself for tonight. They're trying to be thoughtful.'

'It's no one's fault,' I said, 'no one's fault.'

'I can believe it,' he said. 'That's the worst part. At first I didn't, and possibly tomorrow I won't, but at the moment it seems quite plausible. I can believe every word they said. I'm quite convinced. I can see him for all the years of his life with far more clarity than I

231

can imagine Anna growing up. Anna having boyfriends, doing exams, that seems utterly unlikely, but with him it's like imagining an accident – far easier to believe in what's dreadful than a calm rosy future.'

He looked past me, picked up his glass and walked over to the dresser.

'We used to have some brandy,' he said, 'duty-free from some final Continental spree Barbara and I went on before Anna. We brought five bottles back, way over the odds because she was pregnant and we knew it'd be a few years before we went again. We went to loads of places. Tours, Avignon, Perigord, Rheims; we bought so much stuff that time we even declared it at Customs. It must be somewhere.' He looked at the plates and bowls and salt cellar and jelly moulds. 'Maybe I put it upstairs.' He didn't move. 'I know,' he said after a minute. 'That stuff you bought last night. I didn't open it, we could have that.'

He wandered around trailing his hand over the dresser and the draining board until I pointed to the corkscrew and bottles where I'd left them.

'Not what you intended,' he said and frowned, he made an awful face of difficulty as he pulled the cork out and filled our glasses.

'Nothing's what I intended,' he said. He kept frowning, harder and harder, and he tried not to, but he started crying all over again.

This time I didn't go near him, I let him walk up and down and wrap his arms round himself. I went to the fridge and looked rather sadly at the steaks and got out cheese and cold meat and pâté and started slicing bread.

'Have something to eat,' I said when he was quieter. He sat down. 'Pickle?' I asked. 'Tomato? More wine?' On the other side of the table he nodded and chewed as if he hadn't eaten for days, as if it was all he'd got on his mind.

'You look starving,' I said. It sounded like a rebuke but it was right; his eyes were glazed, his shoulders were hunched, all he wanted was to wolf food.

'I've got to telephone Geraldine,' he said, mopping bread round his plate.

'I did. I told her you'd gone to hospital but I was staying with Anna.'

He shook his head. 'About this. That's what the nurse, health visitor said. A woman called Anne Something, you'll see her tomorrow. "Tell people first," she said. "People will still come and say, what a lovely baby, but you ought to let them know." I volunteered you and Geraldine to do that.'

'Give me a list,' I said, 'and I will.'

'A list?'

'Of people to tell.'

He stared at me. 'I've got no idea. It's just what she said. Friends, I suppose, people at work. Not Audrey and Leslie, Barbara said. Or Anna, of course. Ring Geraldine, she'll know. Get Geraldine to do it,' he said after a minute, as though once that was done everything would be OK. 'I'm going to lie down.'

'How's Barbara taking it?' was the first thing Geraldine asked. I told the truth, that I didn't know. 'You'd better find out before she comes back.' I said of course I would.

'I can think of the locals,' she said. 'If Graham wants me to let other people know he can give me a ring. Or you can. What about Anna?'

'Graham'll tell her, too,' I said. I wondered how he could describe it; I looked at our food and wine glasses on the table and thought of the basket and rocking chair and clothes upstairs. There couldn't be descriptions because it shouldn't have happened, it was something to escape from, something to try and pretend out of existence.

'I can't stay,' I lied. 'I said I'd ring you and then Graham wants the phone. I'll speak to you tomorrow.' I arranged a time for her to call and then I arranged all the food back in the fridge. I washed and wiped up as carefully as I ever had for Barbara, I cleaned the table top, I scrubbed the draining board and I couldn't help myself, I was delaying, as though if I left it long enough I might alter something, I might be helpful, and then it was unbearable to think of him alone, there was nothing left except seeing how much it mattered. I went upstairs but the sitting room was empty. From the doorway to their bedroom I could see his shape under the duvet; he'd gone as far away from me as he could.

'I've rung Geraldine,' I said. 'She'll see to it.' I walked very gently round the bed to the window.

'What are you doing?' he asked. He half-sat up. 'Leave them alone.' Then he focused on me. 'Sorry.'

'Leave what alone? The curtains? No one can see, the light's off.'

'No.' He sat up properly. 'I thought you were touching the cot and stuff. No, I didn't, I was asleep, I thought—'

233

'That it was Barbara?' I asked. He didn't answer. He pushed the duvet off and got out of bed.

'I'll do that,' he said, and came across and drew the curtains, reached out across me and pulled the needlecord together.

'I rang Geraldine,' I said. He didn't move or answer. 'She'll do everyone she can think of, but if there are other people – at your work, I suppose she meant, she'll call tomorrow.'

'Shut up,' he said. 'No.' Without looking he put an arm round my shoulders. 'Don't talk. Don't go. Stay here tonight. Sleep in Anna's room again. If you would. I'd like that.'

Once I was in the bunk I fell asleep straight away but it was like being drunk, I was awake again without any time passing, I was sitting up; I'd pulled myself over to the wall, as though I was frightened of something coming into the room.

'Are you awake?' I heard him whisper. From the shadow I couldn't see anyone, everything was dark.

'Where are you?' I whispered back. 'Come here. You'll wake Anna.' I listened but there wasn't any other noise.

'She has,' he said more loudly. 'She woke up half an hour ago. I put her in our bed. I wanted to see if I'd disturbed you. She's asleep again now.'

'Is she? Good.' I pulled the duvet up round me and moved to the edge of the bed. I could see him standing against the wall.

'Come here,' I said again. He sighed and walked across the room and sat on the edge of the bunk, not quite beside me but close enough for me to touch. His head almost touched Anna's mattress above us.

'Were you asleep?' I asked. He had his pyjamas on, dark blue, they weren't very different from his jeans and sweater. 'Or couldn't you? It's funny, I didn't hear her wake, was it long ago? Did she cry? Couldn't you sleep?' I asked again. He didn't answer but put his head in his hands. 'Don't,' I said, 'please don't be so unhappy.' I leant towards him.

'I can't stand it,' he said. 'That's why. I can't stand it.'

'I know,' I said. Although I didn't care about the reasons, I just wanted him resting on me.

'It's unbearable. It's unbelievable.'

'Don't,' I said. 'Don't cry,' and all at once he was, he was sobbing

234

and pushing his head against me, leaning right over me as though he was falling. His whole body leaned against mine. 'Don't,' I said. 'It'll get better, everything has to, you know that. Even if it's awful getting used to it, that does make it better.'

'No,' he said, 'no. Don't talk. Don't tell me.'

I wrapped my arms round his shoulders and rocked him and rested my chin on his head and then I put my lips against his cheek.

'There,' I said, 'there,' and pulled him tighter against me. 'There, hush, be quiet,' and he altered, he didn't cling any more. 'Graham,' I said when he was quite quiet, 'lie down.' Then he was absolutely still. 'Not because of this, but because I want you to. Lie down,' I said again.

He didn't move; I could have toppled us both backwards.

'Come on,' I said. 'I want you to.' He looked at me.

'What do you mean?' he asked; I could have laughed.

'I want to lie down with you,' and I did put my hand on him then, I laid it on his jacket and where the buttons ended my fingers touched his chest. 'Don't you understand?' I said. 'I don't know how else to ask you. I want to go to bed with you. I want us to make love.' He didn't say anything, I couldn't believe it, without speaking he could stand up and walk back to his own bedroom. I leaned forward and put my face against his.

'Don't you?' I asked and let my tongue trail his lips as I spoke. 'Don't you want to?'

He sighed, he shuddered as though it was afterwards, over and done with, not beginning.

'Laura,' he said.

'Don't,' I said a little while afterwards and took his hand and stroked his palm. I could begin there. 'It doesn't matter, it was bound to be quick. Don't,' and he didn't move, his hand was inert, his head was like a monument. 'Please don't mind about it. There's nothing to mind about,' I said after another moment. 'It was bound to be quick, it wasn't like doing it properly, it was just a reaction. It was nice,' I lied. 'Let's just lie still,' and I let my fingers creep up to his palm, I laid them inside his hand and he didn't move a muscle.

'I'll get up,' he said after a long time. 'I can't stay here, I have to go.'

'No,' I said, 'you don't have to.' I stroked his face. 'You don't

235

have to at all. Stay a bit longer. Don't go, not for a bit.' I slid my leg closer to his. 'It'll be all right,' I said, 'really.' I moved my hand to his hip and felt his skin contract as if I was cold. 'Really it will, I promise.'

'It couldn't be worse,' he said.

And that next time it wasn't quite as quick, but that only accidentally made it better because what was obvious was that he didn't care; it wasn't that I might as well not have been there, or that it could have been anyone, it was quite definitely us because we said one another's names, but for him it was gasping and moaning and plunging about in a world of grief or fury or disbelief. While that went on I couldn't see any prospect of improving it. I couldn't say, 'Let's do it more like this,' or, 'Let me lie this way instead.' I just held him tight and when it was over I hugged and stroked him again. I looked at him, I stared at his straight nose and closed eyes and brushed his hair back from his forehead, drew lines on him.

'I must go,' he said when I thought he was asleep.

'Don't,' I whispered. 'Stay here. Let's stay like this,' but he rolled away. He hovered for a minute on the edge of the bunk as if he was falling into space but he didn't pull himself back to me.

'Graham,' I said, and put out my hand. But he wasn't looking and I shut my eyes so I wouldn't see him go. When he was out of the room and I heard the door close I burrowed under the duvet, and stayed as still as he had. I wouldn't look at it any closer than he had, I wouldn't come anywhere near it again until it was morning.

'Anna,' he called. 'Laura. Breakfast.' I wanted a bath, I wasn't ready for him to see me again yet. I lay huddled quite still and then he called again and I pulled my jeans and sweater on and ran upstairs to the bathroom. I could hear Anna say, 'I'm ready, where's Laura?'

'Coming,' I called.

'Tea, toast, coffee?' he asked. He was wearing a suit that put him at a distance and talking without waiting for answers. 'What shopping do we need? Aren't we nearly out of teabags? Or did Geraldine get those for us? Maybe it was coffee. Maybe—' He stopped, frowning. 'The health visitor's coming this afternoon; maybe I should get a cake.' He turned to Anna. 'Whose house are you going to for lunch?'

'Here,' I said. 'She's staying here. I'll be here. I'll cook lunch.'

236

He took no notice, he walked round the table drinking coffee, he didn't eat, he kept right away from where I was.

'What time are you going to the hospital?' I asked.

'Three,' and he put his hand on Anna's shoulder. 'We'll be back for tea with your brother.'

'I know.' She got down from the table and put her arms round his leg. He picked her up and kissed her.

'I'll be here,' I said but it sounded like a question. 'I can help. I could make a cake, if you'd like.

'I'd like to.'

He tried to put Anna down and she started to pull his hair. 'Give me a ride,' she moaned and then grabbed at my arm. 'When's Mummy coming, when will I see them?'

'Later.' I pulled away, I didn't want her body linking the two of us together.

'And we'll make a cake for them?'

'That's right,' I said. Graham shook his head and slid Anna to the floor.

'That's enough,' he said, and then to me, 'That's not possible. You can't do that.'

'Why?' I asked.

'Because,' and he stopped. 'I think you should go,' he said quietly. 'Let's leave it at that.'

'No,' I said. 'Why? Barbara'll expect me to be here, she'll be worried if I'm not. Or upset. What's wrong with that? What's wrong with me seeing her?'

'Don't be stupid,' he said. 'I'll tell her you're doing an extra shift at work.'

I stood up and made a pile of the cups. I emptied his crusts and Anna's eggshell onto one plate very neatly.

'No,' I said. 'Why shouldn't I? Why shouldn't I stay, too? You'll be seeing her, what's the difference between you and me? I'll behave as well as you will. It's the same for both of us. Isn't it?' I taunted. 'I don't see the problem. It's separate things,' I said. I put knives and spoons into two piles. 'Barbara and I don't have any connection with you and me. Surely you can see that? I thought you'd realised that? Hadn't you?' I said.

I looked at him then, I tried to smile, to put things onto that footing but he picked Anna up again.

'No,' he said and kissed her. 'Bye-bye,' he said. 'I'll see you later, Anna.'

When he brought them back from hospital Barbara put the baby upstairs and then sat with Anna on her lap in the kitchen. I cut the cake I'd spent the morning making and ate the crumbs. Graham watched out of the window for the health visitor.

When she arrived he made her tea and talked non-stop about bus routes and playgroups, neighbours, his job, and she perched on the edge of her chair pink-faced, eyes bulging with concentration, as though that was all she'd come for. I sat on the edge of my chair until she took Barbara upstairs.

'I'm sorry,' he'd say, 'I didn't mean it, of course you had to stay,' but as soon as they were out of the room he said,

'You could go now. I don't think she'll mind. There isn't a lot to see, no weeping and wailing for you to comfort. He hasn't got any identifying marks yet. Nothing to stay for.'

'I stayed to help,' I said, 'you know that.'

He put two cups and saucers into the sink. 'I can probably manage this lot. And I think when it comes to supper I can fry eggs. Or there's all that food you bought, we never ate that. That'll do. We could eat grass, fish and chips for weeks for all I care, it doesn't matter. And Barbara's not going to complain.'

'Barbara won't notice anything.' I did pick up my coat because now I'd seen her I didn't want to be anywhere near her; I didn't want to be close enough for that cold misery to rub off. She was miles away inside herself, relying on years of practice. 'I can see through you,' I could have said and she would have looked blankly past. 'See what?' she'd have asked. 'There's nothing to see.'

'What do you want her to do?' His voice rose. 'Is she supposed to fall on your shoulders, too? Is she meant to weep with gratitude because you're here, because of what you think you can do to help? Or am I supposed to do something, is that what you want, me to make an announcement? Leave it alone, leave it.' He banged the spoons on the sink and turned the hot water on full, faster and faster, until the sink steamed. 'She'll be all right,' he said, 'just leave it, go, please.'

'Right.' I banged my chair under the table. 'You don't need to ask, I would, anyway. I can see she doesn't need anyone at the moment and that's the only reason I stayed. But she won't be all right, she's got to look at what's happened. And that's the only reason I'm coming next week and the week after and the weeks after that, because then she will need someone. Is that clear as well?'

He shot round. 'Next week? The week after? *No*.' He shook his head very fast. 'There's no question of that. We've been through this, we've talked about it—' he stopped for a moment. 'I told you. She wants to be left alone.'

'That's right,' I said. 'That's why I'm coming. I lived with that for twenty years in our house and it mustn't happen again. You said it.' I pointed at him. 'We have talked about it, her distance, that's what I'm talking about now. Her. She mustn't get away with it. It's got nothing to do with you, it's her. The reason I'm coming is to make sure she doesn't get any worse.'

For a week I believed that and I tried not to wonder if he did. I went to work and talked about Barbara, I read books on mongolism as though my life depended on it. I found out the best ways of coping, dealing, improving on it; the only motive I had for going to her house was to help. I cared about her present state of mind, I said, to Beryl, to Geraldine and Jessica and to Anne Berrington.

'Someone's got to interfere,' I said. 'Someone's got to get her to be positive about it, she can't be allowed to hide like this.' None of them disagreed.

If she went back to bed after lunch I made her get dressed; when she stayed indoors I told her she should visit people again and let friends come and see her. I didn't say, 'Graham minds too, think of him,' or, 'Anna misses how you were, the old you'; or 'It's not the end of the world, other people survive it.' I was more sympathetic than that. Whenever I wanted to say, 'I'm unhappy, too,' I was firm with myself as well.

'Geraldine and Jessica are coming,' I said, 'that'll be nice. I was talking to a woman at work and she knows someone who's got a Down's baby into a playgroup and she's doing really well. It can work out all right. You have to give it time. Let yourself get used to it. Give him time, too.'

As soon as Graham came home in the evenings I left.

I didn't have to account to him or explain or apologise; he didn't want to hear I'd made Barbara come downstairs and cooked Anna's lunch. He picked Anna up and put her on his lap and I said straight away, 'I'll be off, then,' and he always said, 'Right.'

He didn't get up and tell Anna to stay and watch television. He didn't come to the front door with me and say, 'Don't go, talk to me, let me talk to you, let me ring you later.' He took Anna's hands and waved them as I went. If I ever looked round to see if he was watching at the kitchen window the only person I saw was Barbara, upstairs, arms folded. Then I thought of all of them in that house, for the evening, the night, years, and I walked as fast as I could to the bus stop. I didn't mind going.

'Barbara's resting,' I said one evening, 'but she was up this afternoon.' Even if all she'd done was sit in his chair and stare into space. He nodded. 'I bought some pizzas for supper, they're in the fridge. Anne Berrington came of course—' I stopped. 'I was in Anna's room this afternoon,' I said. 'We were playing a game. It reminded me. I sat on her bunk bed and thought back. I thought that I couldn't understand.'

He looked up then and he did lift Anna to the floor.

'Where's your new doll, Anna?' he said. 'Go and see if you can find her in the sitting room. Go and see if the *Radio Times* has come and we'll see if there's anything you can watch later. Go on, go and have a look.'

I waited until she had dragged her way to the door.

'Couldn't understand what?' he said. 'What are you on about?'

'Nothing,' I said. 'What is there to understand? What could be the matter? I come here every day, look after Anna, make sure Barbara eats and Barbara feeds the baby, leave as you arrive and go home to an empty flat. What I don't understand is that we don't speak to one another. I don't see why what happened has to make us loathe one another. I didn't loathe you afterwards—'

'Don't pretend,' he said. 'It's not like that. You coming here has nothing to do with me. When Barbara came home you wanted to see her. That was what you said. I thought that was what you wanted. You were quite clear about that.'

'I did,' I said, 'but it has to do with you, too. Not as well, not connected to Barbara. I did want to see her, but I don't see why we have to behave as though we hate one another. Completely leaving Barbara aside, whether I see her or not, I don't understand why we have to be like this.'

'What do you want, then?' he asked, but he seemed quite incurious. He stretched his fingers and examined them one by one. 'What am I supposed to think, that you want to see me too?'

'Why shouldn't I?' I answered, and his fingers stopped moving. 'I don't see why you should think that I don't want to see you.'

'Because of what I thought I'd observed,' he said. He gazed at the table and I watched his shoulders; he was so hunched his face was invisible. 'The next morning all you said to me, was, "I'll do the shopping, I'll cook," and when I make it plain that's too painful you take no notice. "I've got to visit her," you tell me, and for two weeks you come every day and the moment I get in you can't wait to go. Except for bulletins about Barbara and the baby you've not got a word to say to me.'

'You're pretending,' I said. 'You told me to stay away, it was you who said I wasn't needed. Didn't you? Truly? So what did you mean, what did you want?'

He looked up. 'I mind about you,' he said, 'that's what I meant. I can't help it, I don't like it, but I mind.' I laid my hand on the table beside his. It was quite steady, it was only inside that I was shaking.

'I do, too,' I said, 'and I mind about her, but they're quite separate things. You're not connected with anyone else except you. I've been here all week and seen her and there's no connection between that and you and me. It's nothing to do with anyone except us. It's separate.' When he didn't contradict me I slid one of my fingers between his. 'You used to go to meetings in the evenings,' I said. 'Don't they happen any more?'

'I thought I ought to be here.' I ran a finger over his. 'There are meetings,' he said, 'every so often. Not tonight, that'd be difficult, Friday, maybe, that could be a possibility. I'll ring you,' he said.

'It's only to do with us,' I repeated to my face in the mirror all evening. I recited it for two days and it was the first thing I said to him when he arrived and then I didn't care.

'Laura,' he said. I never asked and he never confided what excuse he'd made, what he felt about leaving her, what he thought about before he arrived and after he left. When he was with me I found it difficult to recognise the person I'd known for years. The person who came to me was quite different.

'You,' he said. He would hug me until I was breathless and then fling himself down on the bed, hands under his head, feet crossed and stare up at the ceiling.

'What?' I asked. I would go and crouch beside him. 'What is it?' He'd put an arm round me. I lay beside him. Every time he rolled onto me it was as though he was unconscious.

241

'Don't move,' he'd say, 'stay like that,' but it was not passion, or even desperation, it was because he couldn't alter it.

He would lie almost still and take off his clothes, he kept as still as if he was too weak to stand and I would be the one to pull down the duvet, straighten the sheets as he climbed in.

'Laura,' he would say then, 'oh, Laura,' and he made love as if he couldn't bear to think of it finishing, as though when it did he would be angry. He groaned and pushed himself away from me and I let him, I wanted him not to but all the time he was out of my hands.

'You,' he said afterwards and then it was easier. He lay beside me and stroked my face and arms, he was quite open, almost adoring. Yet I sometimes felt anonymous, as though while his hands moved about his mind did, too; I sparked off sensations he wanted to follow up and he did that regardless of whether I was lying there naked beside him.

'Tell me,' he started to say, 'tell me about what's happened to you. Tell me about your life.'

'Not childhood,' I said. 'Even if you haven't heard it already, I'm not going to talk about that now.'

'I don't see why not. She doesn't have to come into it. And if she does, I don't see the problem. You still go and see her—'

'I can't,' I said. 'I don't think about you when I'm with her, I don't see why I have to talk about her when I'm with you.'

'Don't say that. She doesn't talk,' he said, 'you know that. Understand, tell me. I want to hear about you. You're the one who insists on bringing her into it.'

'I don't want that,' I answered. 'This is only to do with us. If talking brings other people into it it won't work. I'll tell you about something else,' I said. 'I'll tell you about later, when I left home.'

He considered a moment. 'All right.' He lay back; it was like Anna after she said, 'Tell me a story.'

'What happened when you left home?'

'I went to learn how to be a secretary.'

'What was it like, what did Audrey say? Where did you live?'

'It was awful,' I said. 'Utterly boring. Audrey screamed – with relief, I expect – and I lived in Hackney, I rented a room there.'

'That's not enough.' He frowned. 'That doesn't tell me anything. I want to know where, how it looked, what happened. Wait,' and he

242

got out of bed. I heard him whistling in the kitchen. If I sat up I could see his naked shadow on the opposite wall.

'Turn the light off,' I called, 'the neighbours'll notice. I'll put the fire on, we can see by that.' In the dark I watched him come back, balancing a tray on his bare hip.

'Tea,' he said. 'Move over.' He put it in front of me. 'Come on, I want to know, I want to hear everything.'

'Awful,' I repeated, 'it was vile. Audrey made scenes about ingratitude, and moving, the room was bleak and Hackney was cold and ugly.' I shivered and he hugged me in the warm bed.

'That's more like it,' he said.

'There were high-rise estates all round, windy shopping precincts and the only people left seemed to be immigrants and racists. The course was the worst thing of all – the people on it wanted jobs in Ford's, a wedding, a semi and a couple of kids, and they didn't believe in virginity but they did believe in stag nights and going steady. I left,' I said, 'except that was a bit stupid, really. I had a row with one of the teachers over a quiz on "What Makes A Good Secretary" and I put "Liking boredom". So she asked me why I'd bothered to come and I said that typing was useful. Then she asked, "*Your* typing?" and put her hand over her mouth and raised her eyebrows. Everyone laughed and I walked out.'

'And didn't go back?'

'Only for my coat.'

'Tell me about the room,' he said. 'Where else can I picture you? What were you like in that place?'

I considered.

'It was a little terraced house near a park, and in the park were three benches, two swings and a shelter where all the local yobbos hung out. There was another girl in the house, a nurse; she had the back room upstairs and I had the front one and the old woman who owned it was in a wheelchair. We didn't talk much at all – the nurse, Joan, worked odd hours, and the old woman, Mrs Cranley, wasn't into confiding. It was quite a silent life. We talked about the weather when I paid my rent, the time when I went out and came in, that was about it.'

'Vile,' he nodded. 'You were right. So what happened?' he asked. 'Were you very lonely?'

'Not for long,' and I smiled. 'I had a boyfriend. Every day I went past a building site and after a month Evan, the student who was working on it, put on a shirt and asked me out for a drink. He'd just finished at university and was doing it for six months to save up to go to India. Everyone wanted to go there then. We didn't go out a lot because he was saving, but the landlady didn't mind him coming to see me. We spent a lot of time together, evenings and most of the weekend. There wasn't a lot else to do.'

'What about you?' he said. 'Why didn't you go too?'

'To India, you mean?' I pretended to try and remember. 'I'm not even sure he asked me – I don't think we ever discussed it. It had always been what he was going to do. He was nice, I liked going out with him, but that was all there was to it. We weren't crazy about one another. What I minded was that he left just after I walked out of college. It was a bit daunting to have to think about what to do next and find a new boyfriend at the same time.'

'So in theory you could have gone. You weren't at college. There was nothing to keep you?'

'In theory,' I sat up, 'I could go to Katmandu tomorrow. OK, now. I've got a job but it's not just a question of ties or the money to get there, it's if you want to. If you're adventurous, I suppose. I don't think I am.'

'So you're just adventurous with people?'

'Not very,' I said. 'I don't think that's true either.'

'Don't ask me again,' I told him.

'What about before you left?' he'd said. 'What about home life?'

'There are things I don't ask you. I don't say, "I was remembering you and Barbara when I first knew you, what was that really like?" I don't say, "What was it like when Anna was born, having that child together?" I don't tell you how I try and forget about you once you've gone because it's too difficult, I can't bear seeing you in that house, thinking of you at home instead of here.'

'You've seen me in that house,' he said, 'and that house is like a morgue.'

'Is that why you come here?' I asked. He moved away from me. 'You're not the only one who cares,' I told him. 'I do, too. I mind about things to do with you.'

'You don't know what to mind about,' he said. 'I don't sometimes. Going back sometimes I realise I've forgotten all about it and then I think, "I should go away more often, if I did that it wouldn't be so bad."'

'You mean you'd forget more often.'

'That'd be a start,' he said, 'that'd be a possibility, wouldn't it? I did that once,' he said. 'Went away. Ran away from home. When I was a child, fourteen, not really a child, a schoolboy.'

'Was that the only time?' I asked. I tried to remember if Barbara had ever said, 'I've got no idea where Graham is,' but she'd always been able to say, 'Graham's coming this weekend, Graham's written, we're meeting Graham,' that was all I'd heard from her before I knew him.

'I found other ways after that,' he said.

'Other ways of what?'

'Coping with things, I suppose. No, of managing not to take on things I couldn't cope with. I learnt not to do that.'

'Except now.' I asked, 'Is that what you mean?'

'I could always run again,' he said. 'I didn't say it didn't work.'

'Why did you?'

He shook his head. 'More about you. That's nicer. Who was your first boyfriend?' he asked. 'Seriously, that is. Evan?'

I looked down at his face, waiting, his blue eyes staring. 'Why?' I asked, and stroked his mouth.

'Because I can't get enough of you any other way. Who?'

'Evan, then,' I said 'I suppose. Well, there was one in Henley, George, but he went off to university – he came back, of course, but the first holiday the opportunities wearing a college scarf and doing the Christmas post presented outweighed the thrill of me in his father's garage. Then in the summer I left school, anyway.'

'You slept with him while you were at school?'

'You've been to Henley enough times,' I said. 'It's incredibly dull.'

'And after Evan?'

'Hundreds,' I said. 'Is that what you want to hear – promiscuity run riot in the Home Counties and E.8?'

'I've told you.' He stroked my arm. 'I want to hear everything, everything that made this happen now. What did you think about?' he asked. 'What did you want?'

'Enough to live on. Not to do a pointless job. Somewhere I liked living. Someone to live with. I've done fine on three out of four.'

I leaned back against the pillows, his fingers left me.

'Where did Jas come into it? I knew he left you,' he said, 'what about the rest?'

'Tall, dark and handsome, it was the usual story, love at first sight, living together after a month. By the time I'd definitely decided on names for our children he'd decided to go to Birmingham. End of story.'

'That was it?' he said. 'The love of your life in three sentences?'

'Except for afterwards. Getting used to it being over, realising the future I'd thought of, us together, us and children, a child, wasn't going to happen, either. I'd lost more than just his friendly face.'

'The first time you fall in love,' he lay and thought about it, 'is that the best, then?'

'No, but it's the first,' I said.

'What did you and Jas do?' he asked. 'When you'd got past spending all your time in bed? Or didn't you get past that?'

'You tell me something,' I answered. 'You talk about running away.'

'It's too long ago,' he said.

'That's not fair. So was learning to be a secretary.'

'This was at school.'

'So. Tell me a school story.'

He folded his arms and looked ahead over the sheet.

'School stories are all the same. Bullying, friendlessness, opportunism. Heroes and villains. Except you can't judge which is which. I can't, not any more.'

'I can,' I said. 'I'll tell you.'

'It's about a boy called Emil,' he said. 'German, he came on a school exchange. He was goggle-eyed; he had shorts that were too long and hair that was too short, he was like a dog waiting to be kicked, and that was what we did to him.

'There were four of us and we stood him up against a wall and threw sticks at him, we stole his letters from home, we teased, lied, everything we could think of. We called it a game. We kept it up for weeks and then one day, when it was coming to an end, because even torment does, it can lose its novelty, I opened a lavatory door and he was sitting there, wanking. He wasn't even enjoying it; he looked as terrified as he did all the rest of the time. I couldn't stand it. I blocked the door so he couldn't get out and gave this great shout: "Emil's found a new game, come and see." But before anyone could there was a sort of crash, and when I got the door open again he'd cracked his head on the wall. He was half-propped on the loo, with blood starting to come out of the back of his head and his willie hanging out of those awful long shorts. So I ran.' He turned to me then, he sat up straight as though it still mattered. 'I went out of

246

school, back home, took a tent and sleeping bag and five pounds and I ran, I ran and walked as far as I could, ten miles probably. I swore out loud the whole time – "Fucking Emil, shitface Emil" – and when it got dark I stopped and tried to put the tent up. It took hours. Then I got inside and I cried.'

I tried to take his hand but he edged away, he moved as though I was unwelcome.

'Then my father came. He'd got the police out, he was in a car. They took me home and that was that. More or less. Nothing happened. Emil went off to Casualty and then back to Germany, no questions, and no one asked what I'd done, nothing. Wiped out. I told my parents I'd run away because a gang was bullying Emil and I couldn't decide whether to tell. Forgiven and forgotten.'

'Until now,' I said. He got out of bed.

'Time to go home,' he said. 'I'd rather have a tent.'

Every evening I sat waiting for him to come, waiting while he took off his overcoat and walked round to remember the room. I sat and watched him pick up a book, draw the curtains, and the shapes of furniture changed, the table and chairs and bed became different because the two of us were there; and afterwards I was always lying, waiting for him to go, stoop as he went out of the door, watching the shape of the room flatten because I was left alone in it.

'I wish you could stay,' I cried and kissed him all over, stroked every soft inch of him, hung and stroked the brown wisps of hair out of his eyes. He would clutch me and bury himself. 'I want you.'

'Don't be unhappy.'

One evening he didn't take his coat off. He took my hands and said: 'Barbara said you came round today, and you and Anne Berrington spent a pleasant time talking about where to go and what to see in West London. "He's a good boy," Anne Berrington tells her and Barbara tells me that too. She doesn't say much else, but she always remembers to tell me that. We could go out,' he said. 'How about a pub? I'd like that. I'd like to take you out and see people look at you and go and buy a gin and tonic and a packet of crisps and know it's you I'm giving them to.'

'Why?' I said. 'What's wrong with here?'

'Nothing. I just felt like a change. Come on, where shall we go?'

'Bed,' I wanted to answer. 'The one on the green?' I said.

247

Because it was Friday night it was crowded. We sat in a cramped dark brown corner and I thought it was an uncomfortable and unnecessary outing.

'If you ever had Saturday free,' I said, 'we could go and hear the Irish band play in Fulham. That's really good. I know people who go there – well, they used to. There might even be a party afterwards. There often was.'

'You went a lot?' I nodded.

'With the friends. And Jas? He was there, too, of course; the perfect partner.'

'We'd have asked you and Barbara,' I said, 'except Jas said you wouldn't like it. What's the matter?'

He said, 'Nothing.'

The music was loud and it was difficult to talk.

'I can't hear you,' I said.

He shrugged. 'I thought we'd come for a drink, come on.'

'You come on.' I reached out to stroke his neck.

'I want to think,' he said.

'That sounds ominous. And difficult,' I said, 'in here, in this noise.'

'We'll have a couple more and then we'll go.'

I watched him swallow and go to and from the bar. When we left and got in the car he didn't say 'Let's hurry,' he drove sedately back. I thought of him every evening, remote, always coming or going.

'I won't come in.' He looked at his watch. 'I'll see you after the weekend.'

'You're sure?' I asked. 'You won't pack your rucksack and disappear?'

He smiled. 'Don't put ideas into my head.'

'What will you do?' I couldn't remember him and pretend it didn't matter he wasn't there; I wanted specific events, a supper party, Sainsbury's, so I could picture his absence.

'I told you, I've got to think.'

'About us?'

He shook his head, opened the car door for me. 'Don't worry. Go on, I'll be late.'

That weekend I put up two kitchen shelves, took apart and failed to reconstruct a skirt that needed altering, started on the third book of the *Raj Quartet* and bought an extra half-bottle of gin. I drank a lot and cried and slept. As I woke up on Monday morning the phone was ringing.

'Laura,' he said. 'Stay there. Don't go. Take the day off. Wait there for me.'

An hour later he rang again. 'You're waiting, you're not going, are you? You'll stay at home?'

'What is this?' I asked.

'I told you,' he answered. 'I was thinking, I've thought of something nice. Wait and see.'

'I can't not go to work. I can't pretend to be ill, it wouldn't be fair. I'm ready, I'm dressed.'

'Wait there,' he said. 'I'm on my way.'

I walked up and down the room, to and fro across the window; I looked away and back until I saw the car stop outside and he got out. He waved up at the window and beckoned, leapt onto the pavement and opened the passenger door with a great flourish.

'Come down,' he shouted. He made a trumpet with his hands; all the road must have heard. 'Come on down. I've come to take you away. I'd had enough,' he said. 'I couldn't stand it any more. I thought we'd get away from it all.' He closed the door on me and got into the driving seat and put a finger to his lips. 'It's a secret.'

'Why aren't you at work?' I asked.

'I couldn't stand it,' he said. 'I can't do it. Seriously. No.' He grabbed my hand. 'I couldn't live without you. Unless I spend a day with Laura, I said to myself, I'll be done for. That was it. I wanted to see you in the daylight again. I want to have a proper time with you.'

He drove with his arm round me all the way through South London.

'Ever been to Brighton?' he asked. 'Dirty weekends?'

'Only one,' I said, 'and it wasn't that dirty.'

'I know it quite well,' he said. 'I went to school near Lewes, just outside, really, it's not a big place.'

'Is that what we've come to see, then? Childhood haunts? Back to your roots. The very downs where you pitched your tent, the paths you ran, the rivers you fished. Is that what today's about?'

'So what happened when you came here?' he asked. 'What did you see?'

'Not a lot.' I said. He raised his eyebrows.

'No time for the pier and the pavilion, even? Jas too busy doing his stuff?'

'I had flu,' I said. 'Jas spent most of his time getting the landlady to make me hot lemon and honey and buying paracetamol. I got better by Sunday, though,' I added, 'and we didn't leave till Monday. So it wasn't entirely wasted.'

'Did the landlady mind?' he asked. 'You not being married? Or did you wear a ring? Did you pop into Woolworth's first to make it look legal? You were lucky,' he said, 'to find such a generous landlady. One who didn't mind you being ill. And him not being white. Even in this day and age.'

'Ah,' I said, 'you're forgetting. He faded in the winter. He didn't look too bad at all. Where it showed.'

'Sorry,' he said, as the road went over the downs. 'I'm not being fair, am I? It wasn't a very good place to come really. Tell me where you've never been.'

'Most places. Where I have been is easier. Paris and Wales and the Lake District and Amsterdam, and Corfu, of course. That's about it. The rest of the world's my oyster.'

'We could go to Italy,' he said, 'or Spain, Basque country, live dangerously. That'd be a start. That's a possibility, isn't it?'

'How about stopping soon?' I said. 'We could have a drink.'

'There's a map in there.' He pointed. 'Look up the road for Rottingdean. There's a nice place about five miles away, you won't ever have been there.'

'Look,' I said, when he came and sat beside me on the green plush seat, 'don't let's play games. Other people don't matter, other places don't matter. This is it, now, you and me, coming here, going back to Shepherds Bush. This is what we've got and this is fine. It's what we reckoned on, isn't it?'

'Not any more,' he said. 'Not now we've got this far.'

'This far?' I laughed. 'Sixty miles from London. Come on.' I put my arm round his shoulders and pretended to shake him. 'One half of lager and you've forgotten where we are. It must be the sea air, it's gone to your head.'

'Don't misunderstand me.' He moved away. 'You know what I'm talking about.'

'Let's go for a walk,' I said. 'We can't come all this way and sit in a pub.' We went up and down the front and back and down to the car.

'I do realise,' I said, 'that it's difficult dividing yourself in two. Perhaps you should talk; perhaps you ought to tell me what you feel about her, about Tim. Perhaps it's easier for me to listen than it is for you to keep quiet.'

'No,' he said immediately. 'That's not it at all. All I feel, all I want to talk about is you, nothing else is bearable.' He stood still. 'Surely you can realise that? Barbara hardly remembers how to talk,' he said, 'there's nothing to discuss. It's nothing to do with us. You're different from all that. You're all I've got.'

'I can't make up for what's happened, though. I'm not a distraction, I want something too,' I answered.

'What?' he said. I thought of going to that house, of arriving and knowing she didn't mind if I cleared up the kitchen or did the ironing, she didn't tell Anna to leave me alone, she looked the other way.

'What can I do?' I always asked, and I polished or scrubbed or dusted. 'Any shopping?' I said because that was best, out of the house. 'I'd better feed him,' she said at five o'clock and went upstairs and I waited until I heard Graham's key. 'There's Daddy,' I said to Anna and put on my coat.

'Let's go back,' I said. 'We'll get a sandwich on the way. I don't want to stay here, I don't feel in a holiday mood any more. I will tell you, but not now, later.'

He drove fast and I was glad to get away, it had felt unsafe there; the outside world promised too much, it made us open to more than one another.

'Upstairs,' he said as soon as I opened the front door. He put his hand over my mouth. 'Upstairs, quick, no talking, now, now' and he started to take off his jacket, he was unlacing his shoes as I unlocked my flat door. 'No more. It's four days, it's been that long since we went to bed, we've wasted all that time.' He was undressing as he spoke, fumbling his shirt with one hand and mine with the other. 'Come on, help me,' and he pushed himself against me.

'You haven't taken your trousers off—'

'I don't need to,' and he wouldn't. 'Lie down, here, never mind the bed.' He pulled me down on the floor next to it. 'Keep still. Stay like that. This. This is it,' he said, 'this is what—'

* * *

'We could be anywhere' – he raised himself and we were at right angles to one another – 'we could be going anywhere, we could be anywhere in the world, anything could happen,' he said. 'Couldn't it?'

'Stay at home tomorrow,' he said. 'All week. It's a holiday,' and the next three mornings he arrived at nine o'clock and said, 'Be ill. Don't go. Tell them you're ill. I am.'

We sat side by side on the bed. 'Where to?' he asked. 'Get the atlas.' He traced his finger from London. 'Oxford? Cambridge?'

'It can't be far,' I said, 'if you've got to be back by half six.'

'I can't leave her all the time,' he said. 'You go there, you see her.'

'I'm not asking you to do that,' I answered. 'It's fine, I'd like to have another day out.'

On the way we didn't talk, we listened to the radio or I counted off the miles and gave him chewing-gum. I never asked what he'd decided at the weekend, I didn't want to find out he'd given us that week or a month. I didn't want to know, either, that Barbara had some suspended sentence hanging over her.

'The open road,' he said sometimes, and then he'd smile at me and my heart went out to him, he could look sad and as if he was determined not to be at the same time.

The first day, every day we arrived we bought a guide book, and then food for a picnic and a bottle of wine, every time we did that as though when I said, 'Hungry yet?' he wouldn't answer, 'No, let's go back to the car.'

'Whatever for?' I'd ask. 'Don't be silly, what've we come for, we've only just arrived.'

'Stay, then.' He would clench my hand and then fling it away. 'You stay and do what you like.'

'What's the matter?' I asked. He always gave the same answer.

'We've got to go, don't you see? I can't stand it, I hate leaving. If we go now,' his voice would drop and he'd take my hand as though he was being reasonable, 'we'll have done it, got it over with, we won't have to think about it all the time.'

'But I don't mind,' I'd say, and hold his arm and wait for him to be calm enough to look at a museum or a cathedral. 'I don't think about being back until it happens. All the time we're together is just that; even going back is time together. If we let it hang over the whole day we might as well not have come. Don't think about it.

This is Oxford,' I said. 'We've come to look at it, we've come here to be together. You can be in love with me, or you can be at odds with her. But I don't want it to overshadow everything.'

'You don't have her,' he said. 'It's not up to you.'

'Don't,' I said. 'What do you want?'

'To go,' he said, 'for it to be tomorrow now.'

The next morning when I got in the car next to him I said, 'We could stay in London. If you don't want to have all the bother of travelling we could go to Kew, or the Tower, we could have tourist days out. If you count it up, I did once, it's amazing how few places you've actually been to.'

'With Jas,' he said, 'finding places to take him round.'

'Jas was born in London,' I answered, 'and I had a life before Jas.'

'London's dangerous.' He shook his head. 'People could see us.'

'At Kew?' I asked. 'Who do you know who goes there on a Wednesday morning?'

'It'd make it easier for you, of course.' He sat forward and examined the driving wheel minutely and scraped some white specks with his fingernail. 'If it got back to Barbara. If it was common knowledge without you being responsible for it.'

'It's not just my responsibility,' I answered. 'And I don't want that, anyway.'

'What do you want?' he said. 'What are you doing this for?'

'You.' I tried to smile at him. 'You know that.'

Then he put out his arms to me. 'I'm sorry. I get panicked. Spies round every corner. People I work with, Geraldine, Jessica, Audrey, even, absolutely impossible coincidences. I spend all day dreading them, I ruin all the time we have together with spooks.'

'You don't ruin it,' I denied. 'Yesterday was lovely.'

'I didn't mean that,' he said. 'I was thinking of something else.'

'What?' and he shook his head. 'In the evening? After you got back?'

'Leave it,' he said. 'Let's move, come on, where do you want to be?'

'What did happen?' I could have asked again. I could have slipped it in as we went along the motorway, I could have put my head on his shoulder as we walked along the Backs.

I said, 'It's spring, look at the blossom.' He squeezed my shoulder. 'It's the sap rising,' I couldn't have done anything if he'd told me, I couldn't have altered it for any of us.

253

'Sad?' I asked when he sighed. I took his hand. 'Come on, we've got hours yet.'

'No,' he said. 'Let's go.' And then, 'Where could we go, where could we run off to where no one would ever think of coming after us?'

'Would you like that?' I asked.

'Where?' he said. 'Tell me a place.'

'Nowhere would be perfect' – I meant to sound sensible, not pessimistic – 'there'd always be a few ghost women with prams, little girls with skipping ropes, playgrounds.' I pointed to one over the road. 'Schools. Look,' I said, 'we can have one another wherever we are, we can be together wherever we like. Whenever, too, within reason,' I added, because we hadn't spent an evening together all week. He looked at his watch. 'I'll be late,' he said.

'Where did Jas take you? Why didn't you travel with him? Why didn't you and Jas go abroad?' he asked as he drove back.

'We did, to Paris.' I said. 'But neither of us had that much money. And he didn't like the hassle at Customs.'

'Waste of money too, I suppose.' He slowed down.

'How?' I asked. He nodded at an old woman to cross the road.

'Paying to spend time in a hotel when you'd got a perfectly good room here.'

'Why? Why was that all we'd have done? Why is that all you think we did? Spend time in bed?'

'Didn't you?' he asked. 'More than we do. Wasn't that what was good, wasn't that what it was about? What's this about?' he started to shout. 'What am I supposed to do about this?'

'It wasn't about that,' I said. 'We argued and he was insulting. Quite often he picked a row to put me in the wrong and spoil things. I hate that.'

He put his hand out. 'I'm sorry,' he said. 'I've got to go. I told you that, didn't I?'

The next morning he was so late I wondered if it was worth ringing work and saying I would do the afternoon shift. Anything was better than looking out of the window and counting minutes.

At eleven he telephoned and said, 'I've got an idea, let's meet

254

somewhere else. I'll see you on platform nine at Victoria station, we'll decide then,' and hung up before I could argue.

When I got there he was nowhere to be seen. I bought a newspaper and read the arrival and departure boards. I realised I had no idea where he'd phoned from; the call-box could have been anywhere. He could have left home at six a.m. and I wouldn't have known that. I didn't want to know about Barbara or Tim or Anna, I didn't want any part or discussion of the rest of his life. He and I were quite separate, but I'd never been frightened by it before. I'd worried about what he might decide, but never about what had happened to him. Standing there, with people milling all round me and announcements being shouted at me, I couldn't believe I ever would see him again. I knew I'd stay half an hour and then I'd go back to Shepherds Bush, everything I half-thought could happen, everything I pretended I didn't dream about in five years' time would be over. It would be Jas all over again. Then I thought that at least I would see him, he couldn't, as Barbara's husband, disappear into thin air. I didn't believe that, either. I could quite easily imagine their house without him, Barbara and Anna and Tim going up and downstairs, in and out without missing him; it was as though he could be completely blotted out by everyone, all these anonymous people with suitcases were more real than him. 'Five minutes,' I said to myself, and as it was up he put a hand on my shoulder.

'Sorry I'm late.'

I fell on him, I cried that I hadn't believed he was coming, that it was too late now to go anywhere, that I could have waited at home, he could have told me why I had to come here.

He shook me and said, 'I told you, I'm sorry. You can't have everything you want. I can't divide things up, I can't flick a switch from one person to another.'

'That's not my fault,' I said.

'You didn't choose this?'

'Don't,' and I took his hands, I put mine over his on my shoulders. 'What shall we do?' I asked. 'Where did you want to go?'

'I wanted to think,' he said. 'I wanted you to come here and look at express trains and think of Berlin and Madrid—'

'Why?' I asked.

'To see them. To see what it could feel like. To see if it could happen.'

255

'All right.' And I looked all round the station at the engines and dirty coffee cups and tired passengers on seats. 'I think anywhere would be better than here. Any other city.' I looked at my watch. 'Except we haven't got much time today. It's one o'clock already.'

'We'll make plans,' he said. 'We'll go for a drink and have lunch and decide where to go next.'

'Tomorrow, you mean?' I asked. I really didn't know what he'd answer.

'That's up to you,' he said.

'Not entirely,' I argued.

In the pub he sat with his head in the shadow of a case of silver cups, the place was full of trophies and shields. 'I can't decide for you.'

'You did,' he nodded, 'when you came back, every day after he was born and you said, "This is only between you and me." When you go and see her now, that's your decision.'

'You're not passive,' I said.

'You don't know what happens.' He finished his drink and stood up to buy another. 'When you go home you've got no idea. You should feel it. You go back and watch television and read your library book and think about where we'll go the next day and what we'll do when I come in the evening.'

'Don't you?' I asked. 'Don't you think about those, too?'

'I try to think of nothing else,' he said. 'I look round my house and those thoughts outside are my lifeline. It's you.' He sat down beside me again. 'I don't believe in you. It's you I can't always keep hold of when we're together. I take you to – ' and he held up a hand 'where have we been? Oxford, Cambridge – I can't remember, four days of buildings and parks and I can't believe I'm in them with you. I'm waiting to look down and see that flat round face looking up at me from his pram or feel Anna take my hand or see Barbara turn her back. I find it difficult; every day I find it more difficult to believe.'

'Let's go,' I said. 'Come back. Come back with me, now. It's ages, you said, it's four days ago, it's nearly another weekend and we've spent every minute not in bed. Or go back now and come this evening; it's because of that, it's because you haven't touched me.' I pushed myself into him, I felt him take hold of me. 'I'm bound to be unreal if that happens.'

'All right,' he said, 'maybe. This evening, I'll try.'

256

'Let's go for a walk,' I said. We went through the park and caught a bus and past Earl's Court I said, 'This is it, we'll go to the graveyard. It's private.' As we got off I said, 'It's somewhere you'll meet no one you know. You can stop worrying for five minutes about being found out.'

'Why did you need it?' he asked. 'When did all this happen before?'

'All what?'

'Don't be naïve.' He didn't go in, he ran his fingers up and down the iron railings outside. 'There was George in Henley, Evan the student and then the next one you mention is Jas; who filled up the years in between – another married man? Is that where you learned not to ask questions about home life, how you pretended it didn't concern you? Is that where you found discreet dumps like this?' He nodded at the place. It had changed since I was last there; it was seedy, there were men drinking and couples staring into space with bottles beside them.

'It used to be nice,' I said. 'I used to come at lunchtime when I worked in an office off North End Road.'

'With?' he asked. 'Who was it then, who were all of them?'

'Let's go,' I said. He shook his head.

'Tell me the names first,' he said. 'No biographical details, just names for me to conjure with.' I shook my head. 'I need something sometimes,' he said, 'when I look at Tim in the bath or Anna eating her tea, I need something to get me through that.'

'They were boyfriends,' I said, 'that's all. Nothing serious. They lasted three months or six months and none of them meant anything.'

'And that was all right,' he said. 'That was how you got practice in. Nothing meaning anything. Until Jas, of course,' he added.

I started to walk away from him, I didn't cry, I didn't think, 'This is the end.' When he caught up with me I said, 'We can't go on like this. We've got a choice, but it can't be like this.'

'Laura,' he said, 'don't, please, please, don't. I want you so. Go home. I'll come, I'll see you later.'

I said yes then, I didn't have a moment's doubt. 'Yes,' I said. I didn't look back at him but I caught another bus and all afternoon I tidied my room. At six I went down the road for wine and put it in the fridge. Then I took off my clothes and got into bed and waited.

When he came I made him keep quite still, I laid him down and made sure of every inch of his body.

'I do know what happens,' I said. 'I can't bear it, either. I do feel it. I want you.'

'Don't cry,' he said, 'don't.' I lay still, too, on the pillow and he kissed me. 'Tell me the best times you've ever had,' he said.

'This,' and I hugged him.

'What did you used to dream of; what do you long for?' he asked. 'Tell me those things. What's not a Jas story?' he asked before I even began. 'What else? Tell me what I really want, tell me that.' He leaned over me. 'What's made this happen, you and Barbara? Keep her out,' he said. 'Make her, make it all, everything go away again.'

'Again?' I said.

'I want you, I want nothing except this. Don't forget.' And he traced my eyes and lips with his mouth.

'What do you want?'

'Tell me,' he said, 'tell me your dreams, come close to me.'

We lay still under my scarlet cover and I told him about Mercy and the fire.

'Audrey was a child,' I said. 'Imagine being told about it, or finding out. I can feel sorry for her when I think of that. Worse things happen to children than death.'

'I dream about fear,' he said.

'You can make things better, though, you don't have to be frightened.'

'Hiding and escaping,' he said. 'Discovery, someone finds you and me.'

'Who finds us?' I asked. 'What happens?'

'Anna. She's watching, and then she's lost, too, and I have to look for her.'

'You leave me, you mean. What happens to me?'

'You go,' he said. 'I have to find Anna and take her back, I have to make sure the house is still standing and Barbara and the baby are in it. Sometimes,' he said, 'I dream I rebuild that house, like a Lego model. I have to reconstruct it before I can go and then when I try I know it's useless to hurry to where you are because you'll have gone.'

'Gone where? With whom?' I tried to sound interested, not angry or defensive; it was only a dream.

'How should I know? I don't take you.'

'You mean you don't find me?'

'That's right, too.'

He lay back on my pillows when I got up, watched me crouch by the fire and pour wine. 'One day we'll hire a château. You can, I've seen them in the *Sunday Times*. We'll go by boat and by caravan and I'll arrange firework displays every night. And a funfair, a perpetual fourteenth of July. I could,' he said, 'I've thought about it. Where could we go?' I didn't answer. 'It wouldn't solve anything,' he said, 'but we could do it. Look.' He swung himself out of bed and took his wallet out of his trousers. 'Look.' He pulled out three rolls of notes and dropped them, one by one, on the bed: a bundle of lire, a bundle of francs, hundreds of pesetas. 'I mean it. I could.'

I looked at him standing there with nothing on, at the rolls of money, his eyes moving from them to me. Then he picked up his trousers and started to put them on. It took no time at all; in a minute he stood there in his clothes ready to go and I sat there undressed ready for him to leave. I tried to see what had happened before this, what he had become.

'Graham.' I got up and put on my dressing gown. 'You're not serious. You got them just as a joke. You went past Thomas Cook and thought, "That'll make her sit up." That's what happened, isn't it? They're lovely, they're like a promise, a dream, but we can't. I hate saying this, but just in case it's not a joke, we can't. You do see that? You've got to.'

'Of course.' He buttoned his jacket and picked up all the notes. He flicked through them and put them into his wallet, put it in his inside pocket and patted it, put on his coat and pulled it tight over the top.

'You look dangerous,' I said, 'as if it's some illegal transaction.' I smiled. 'I should get you a fedora, you could be a gangster when you stand like that.'

'I don't need you to tell me,' he said. 'I don't need you to tell me that. You don't realise, either. I was trying to show you something. You don't see what I mean. You've got no idea about me.'

The next week I expected every phone call to be from him. I found his absence unbearable.

'He'll be at a meeting,' Barbara said because I went there and wondered aloud if he'd be home that evening. 'He's never in. Or in and straight out. He's like that. He likes Anne Berrington,' she said.

'I tell him she's vile and so he likes her. And he likes the baby, of course, he spends hours picking him up and putting him down. More than I do. Or you,' she added. 'I don't blame you.'

'Give him my best wishes,' I said because now I could not wait; he might even be waiting at my flat.

'If I see him,' she said. 'I might not.'

'Laura,' the matron said the next day at work, 'there's someone in reception for you.'

He was standing reading an old magazine. I ran across the shiny parquet.

'What's happened?'

He put a hand on my shoulder.

'I've got the afternoon off. I wanted you.'

'But I'm at work.'

'I've said I've got a meeting straight after work. We'd have hours. I missed you.'

'You frightened me,' I said. I felt my heart shake, was terrified of what he'd come to tell me. 'I'll have to say you wanted to make an arrangement about this evening, that you were passing.'

'You mean you're not coming?' He dropped the magazine on the floor.

'I can't.' I took his hand. 'It's too difficult. I'd have to invent an emergency, I'd have to pretend it was life or death. It's too complicated.'

'Suppose Jas had rung,' he said. 'You'd go flying off there.' I turned to go. 'Wait.' He bent and picked up the magazine. 'What time do you finish, five? I'll see you then.'

'You shouldn't do this,' I said as I got in the car. 'You shouldn't have come this afternoon. What will you do to me?' I looked at his anxious face; his hand on the wheel was clenched white at the knuckles.

'I couldn't stand it,' he said, 'waiting for you. I'm taking chances. I ask Barbara if you've been, I ask Geraldine and Jessica if they've seen you. "Where's that book Laura used to read?" I say to Anna. "Maybe Laura will come at the weekend." I go into that house every evening and look at that child and go downstairs and look at Barbara. I try, I do try to talk to her. "I've got work to do," she

260

says; she means she can't talk and iron simultaneously. You,' he said.

'We'll go back,' I promised. 'It's all right, I understand.'

'I'm going back,' he said. 'We're not going anywhere. Get out, you can walk from here. I'll come tomorrow. I can't stay with you any more.'

The next day I cleaned the flat until he came, I scrubbed the stove and bath and Hoovered and changed the sheets and when I opened the door to him he hugged me.

'Wine,' he said and gave me a parcel. It was the same box he'd bought before Tim was born. I wanted to cry.

'Who came?' he said, and pointed to the laundry bag. 'Why don't you say, "So-and-so stayed," and let me guess who so-and-so is. I don't have rights over you. If I stay away you can entertain who you like. People can come when they like here. As long as you clear it away afterwards.'

'Stop it,' I said and covered my ears. He put his arm back round me. 'Stupid.'

'Tell me,' he said. 'Don't lie. Let's have a drink.' When I gave him a glass he looked into it. 'What do you think about this?'

'Now? This moment? Nothing. That you frightened me.'

'What do you see happening?'

'Going on, just as it is,' I pretended.

'Tell me the truth,' he said, and put down his drink. 'What am I supposed to do?' Gently he took hold of my shoulders. 'What am I supposed to change? Why couldn't you leave it, leave it alone as we were?'

'Graham,' I said, 'I don't understand. I don't know what you're talking about. You promised me holidays, fireworks, and disappeared for a week. I've got no idea what's happening except that you went. What do you want?' I asked.

'I could stay at home,' he said, 'and be silent in the same room as someone else. I don't need lies from you.'

'I don't give you lies.'

'Then what do you give? What do you need from me?'

'Why did you tell her?' he asked. 'What did you say to Barbara? That was where you went wrong. What did you do that for?'

I shook my shoulders away from him. 'Tell her? You must be out of your mind. What would I do that for?'

'Tell me. She rang you up, she rang you two weeks ago, she told you she didn't want you to come any more. But you did, you went

261

back to her. She said she wants to manage by herself, she says she has to because of Anne Berrington, but that's not true. I want you to tell me, I want to really know what you said.'

'Told her,' I said it again. 'Told her? I don't understand you. I don't see how you'd think that. She's told you the truth, she's told you exactly what happened. A week, two weeks ago, Barbara rang and said she didn't want any more help. She didn't say why and I didn't ask, you know what she's like, she'd say anything if she wants to be by herself. It's nothing to do with me, truly. Why would I?' I asked.

He held his head and whispered, 'Because of how you are. Because you don't want me. To send me back to her.'

I looked at him. 'I'll tell you something,' I said and took his hand; I held it as though if I kept it calmly in mine we could be restored to one another. 'The last thing I'd do is tell her. The last thing I'd want is to send you back. I'll give you the best possible reason why the very last thing I want is for her to suspect. I couldn't possibly tell her about us because of what's happened.' I took his other hand. 'I'll tell you,' and I swallowed, I wanted to whisper too. 'I'm pregnant,' I said. 'That makes it an unimaginable thing for me to do.'

'Pregnant?' he said. 'What for?'

I stepped back, I tried to smile. 'Because I wanted to.'

'Whose is it?' He looked at me. 'Whose?'

I squeezed his hands and said very slowly, so he would completely understand me, 'I don't love anyone else. I love you. It's your baby.'

'You should have told me,' he said. 'You should have mentioned that. You should have said you wanted to get pregnant, that that was what I was for. You shouldn't use people,' he said, 'except you always have, haven't you? What are you going to do now? What's supposed to happen next? Have you thought of that?' He walked away. 'Think,' he said. 'Go on, tell me.'

I shook my head.

'You should have,' he said. 'You should have tried a little fore-thought at the very least. I should have known. If I'd known then I could have told you. I could have said not to. I could have said, "You never get over it, it lasts for ever."' He stood still then, he stopped walking up and down. I stayed where I was, too, I was too cold to move. 'But you didn't. You only thought what you wanted.'

'It's your baby,' I said. 'That's what I want. I didn't do it on purpose,' I lied.

'No.' He shook his head, his shoulders, almost his whole body. 'That's no good, I don't care what you want, it's what you've done, you've used me. How you've had me here and what I've wanted doesn't matter, it's only you who counts.'

'No,' I said, 'it was because of you, you were the cause.'

'Anyone would have done,' he said. 'You wouldn't care, anyone to make up for Jas, anyone to get your own way. You never tried to see beyond anything except that; consolation, distraction, selfishness, that's all you understand, you've got no desire at all to see what happens, what matters to anyone else. You can see this,' he said. 'I don't want it. I'm not having it and nor are you. You can't have a child I'm not father to, you can't do that. You can't appear at my house at Christmas with it, have birthday cards that Barbara sends it, parade around with it for everyone to admire, force it in my face as your victory.'

'No,' I said. 'That wasn't what was going to happen, I wasn't going to do that. That wasn't what I thought at all, I never meant it was just mine, it's ours.'

'Ours?' He looked at me with utter disbelief. 'Whatever would I want that for? What did you think I could do? I don't want its existence,' he said, 'it lasts for ever, that's what you want. Something to hold over me for as long as you like. To get even, to make me look a fool for trusting you, to show me I was nothing except fatherhood, show me there was nothing in it.'

'That's not true,' I said, covering my ears. 'That's the opposite of the truth. I loved you, I told you.'

'You never listened,' he shouted. He dug his hands into his pockets, rocked harder to and fro. I remembered how I had first imagined him outside my door and ran across to him and tried to drag his arms around me.

'I do listen to you, I thought you loved me. Listen, please, I didn't think this would happen, it's because of you I want it.'

'I don't,' he said. 'It's nothing to do with me. You sort it out. It's not mine and I don't want it there.' He pulled away.

'Don't go,' I said, and tried to get in front of the door. 'Stay, stay and listen, please try and understand like you did.'

He took my arm. 'You understand. You're not having it. It's nothing to do with me.'

'It's yours,' I said. I was crying. 'Ours.'

'No,' he said. He put his head in his hands and shook it and then made a megaphone with his hands like he had outside the house two weeks ago. 'No,' he bellowed, and the whole street could have heard again.

I backed away, I couldn't answer, I couldn't touch, there was no way near him any more. I sat down on the bed and covered my eyes again. He didn't try to speak, but I heard him move. He walked round the room. I thought he was touching things; he went into the kitchen and over to the window. He wasn't just picking up his coat, he was going over old ground. In a moment he'd sit beside me. Then I thought I recognised the sound of the door but I waited to un-hear it, I waited for his voice. I sat there as long as I could bear without seeing anything, but when I did open my eyes he was gone.

I let him go, I let him come back; he told me I was evil and selfish and I pretended I could argue him out of it.

'Don't cry, don't do it,' he said every time.

I repeated, 'I'm having it. You can't stop me. It's mine, it's nothing to do with you any more. Go home,' I told him. 'Go where you belong, get out, it's nothing to do with you.'

He left, he telephoned, he returned twice in an evening, he threatened and pleaded and none of it had any effect.

'Whose is it?' he asked. 'Tell me the truth about that, anyway.'

'Mine,' I shouted, 'just mine. It wouldn't want you, nobody would. It doesn't have to be like this.' I wept. 'I want you,' I said. 'I wanted it for you, not to hurt you. I want you to see it, I want you to like it.'

'I hope it'll hurt,' he said. 'I hope you go over and over everything you've done and it makes you weep. I'm sorry any of this ever happened. I regret you. You were a mistake. I want you sorry,' he said.

After he left that time I started to treat myself very gently. I stopped waiting on edge for him to come, instead I gave a running commentary on what I was about to do. Every morning I said, 'Let's get dressed, time to catch the bus, nearly there now.' At work I didn't volunteer for taking people to hospital or clearing up after lunch, I found lots of small tasks no one usually had time for. Some days I wanted to stay buried in bed, and a couple of days I thought, Do that, then, and slept almost twenty-four hours. After that I was reasonably calm again. The thing I didn't find difficult was not thinking about him because there was nothing I could mind that I'd lost. It was a relief to be without him, I said to myself, and it wasn't

264

as if I'd be alone for ever. What was less easy was thinking about the baby, because although I never thought of getting rid of it I couldn't look forward to it either.

Sometimes I thought, 'I'll make this baby disappear and another one take its place, start afresh,' and then I'd feel desperately sorry for the one I was casting out; what had happened wasn't its fault. 'Leave it in peace for a bit,' I told myself. I kept very quiet and detached and sewed patchwork cushions and watched television. At the back of my mind I let it be decided that it was too unbearable to think about him, but that I had to tell Barbara I was pregnant. I'd wait until I missed my second period. I never thought of not doing that; he didn't have any part in it any more, but telling her did.

It wasn't a premonition, it was just a very strong feeling of unease one afternoon a couple of weeks later that made me catch the bus to Hammersmith after I left work. When I got to her house the front door was open and I heard Anna crying. I ran into the empty kitchen and then upstairs. Anna was standing in the sitting-room doorway and all the furniture had been pushed to the walls. The carpet was covered with paper and Barbara was crawling forwards and backwards over it – head down, hair flopping all over her face so she couldn't see properly, muttering what could have been gibberish.

I suppose I could have said, 'Let's bend down too and see what Mummy's looking at,' make it seem a silly harmless game, but I asked, 'What are you doing?'

'Going away,' she said, 'with Graham; I'm finding the place.' I ran again. I took Anna downstairs and gave her some juice, and telephoned Graham, leaving a message that Barbara was ill and he was to come as soon as possible. I could hear her calling, 'Come here,' so I told Anna to see what was on television. When I went back up she'd moved on to Graham's room. It was ransacked; all over the floor there were heaps of photos with bent frames, upturned drawers, clothes, annuals with pictures of cricketers on the front, a stamp album, everything he'd preserved from that peaceful childhood, all turned upside down.

'He might want it,' I said, but she screeched. 'No. I want to get rid of this, this is for the baby, the baby's got to have somewhere to go.' Because I couldn't see any way of putting everything back where it'd come from I pretended to agree.

'Let's do it this way,' I said, 'books in one bag, clothes another.' I thought he could then sort them out later if he wanted. For half an hour we packed up plastic bags, wordlessly; we were like a film of women clearing up after bomb damage, silently sorting possessions from rubble.

When Graham came in he ran up the stairs three at a time and when he saw me I said straight away 'I came to see Barbara. I thought you ought to be here.' Barbara just smiled at both of us. She sat on the floor rooting through everything that was left, burrowing, really, like an animal trying to find a lair. I couldn't watch; I said, 'I'll go and see Anna.' I didn't want to hear him deal with it, I didn't want to watch them together.

'What happened?' he asked when he came down. 'What were you doing here?'

'I was coming to tell her,' I said, 'about me. I was going to tell her I was pregnant.'

As though I hadn't spoken he started to fill the sink with water and put in the dirty plates from the table and draining board.

'She wants a holiday,' he said. 'That's what the maps are about. Wasn't that clear? And she wants me out of it. I thought you'd be the first to understand that. She wants space for the baby. I'm surprised you didn't cotton on straight away.'

'She's not well,' I said. 'Anyone can see that. I think you ought to talk to a doctor.'

He turned from the half-cleared table.

'No,' he said, 'I think you ought to go. I don't want you here any more. I don't want you talking to her now. It must've been a blow,' he nodded, 'all prepared to make your grand announcement and finding her incapable of listening. That doesn't mean she's round the bend, it's just a temporary aberration. You'll have to try to tell her again, keep coming back other days.'

'I will,' I said. 'I'll ring to find out what's happened. I'll come back later on.'

As I left he could have taken my hand and promised we would talk about it; he could have said, 'I need to know about you, I need to know how you are'; but he didn't come anywhere near me, and after

266

that I didn't think about him any more, or her. The only thing I thought about, the only thing I wanted was sleep. I wasn't anxious any more, I didn't get pangs from hunger or sickness, I was only exhausted. I sat with my eyes shut on the way to work, on the lavatory; I stood with them closed as I washed up. I came into my room like an addict in the last moments before satisfaction. I scrabbled with the switch on the fire, fumbled with my coat, kicked my shoes anywhere and lay down; it was nirvana, I thought, it beat anything in the world.

I ought, I thought very occasionally when I woke, to tell them at work; to think about money; to tell Audrey and Leslie. I wondered sometimes if it would be all right or what I would do if it wasn't, but it was like giving myself instructions in a foreign language when I'd only learnt that one phrase. I knew I was safe from having to answer.

I still stayed sensible underneath, though. I arranged to go to the clinic and went into the director's office where I'd only been once before, when I was interviewed, and made a formal request for maternity leave from the end of September for a year.

'That's right,' I said. She stared at me, her white curls drooping, eyes popping. 'Maternity leave.' She told me to sit down and made tea with her electric kettle. I looked at the wheelchairs on the lawn outside her window and tried to keep my eyes open. She asked if I was getting married, was it a wise decision? 'Whatever will you do?' she asked, when I'd refused another two biscuits. I woke up enough to say that I'd saved a bit, lots of people managed on Social Security, and there'd be my pay for a while, wouldn't there?

'But later on?' she asked. 'When the child's older?'

'It'll be easier then.' I was surprised how confident I sounded. 'Nurseries, play activities after school. Besides, this job's pretty flexible—'

'But telling it,' she said, 'explaining why you've done this.'

'I won't have to,' I said. 'By then it'll just be a fact. It won't think of questioning it.'

'You're a dark horse,' Beryl said when I told her. 'Three months! Whose is it? That bloke you used to have, the Indian one—'

'No,' I said. 'It's nothing to do with anyone else.'

'That's what you think.' She grinned. 'You wait and see what the old dears'll say to you.'

267

'They'll come round, they'll have to.'

Beryl shrugged. 'Look at it this way,' she said. 'It gives them something to talk about till then. Some of them might even hang on out of curiosity to see it. You'll be doing them a favour. What does your sister say?' she asked. So after work I went to the off-licence and bought a bottle of wine and telephoned. Even when there wasn't any reply I still caught the bus.

'Have a good holiday?' I asked when Anna let me in. 'I thought you were still away, or out. There wasn't any answer when I rang.'

Barbara was sitting in front of the dresser, hands in her lap, so firmly ensconced in her dressing gown, so still, it was difficult to imagine when she'd last left the house.

'Aren't you well?' I asked.

'Why?' She didn't look up.

'Geraldine was asking after you,' I lied. 'I met her in the street. She said no one'd seen you for ages.'

'The reason people ask how I am,' she said, 'is because they're glad it's not them.' She still didn't look at me; she watched the shadows on the wall opposite. 'I don't blame them. But that doesn't mean it's all right for me.'

'But that's not the only reason,' I said. 'People care as well. If all they felt was relief that they weren't you, they'd just steer clear. Wouldn't they? Look' – I was beginning to feel a bit desperate – 'let's have some wine.'

'You can't if you're feeding,' she answered. Although I was sure that wasn't true I didn't argue. I drank some quite quickly and began to feel more confident.

'They don't steer clear,' I said. 'They try to help. All right, they don't see it the same as you do, it hasn't happened to them. It could have been worse. There are a lot worse things that happen. He could have been your only perfect child and died. . . We don't have to hide what we don't like,' I said. 'People might be frightened of it, you're probably right. But you don't have to react like this. You can have different feelings.'

She stood up. I watched her close down the shutters, turn off, pile papers instead of looking at me.

'What about Anna?' I asked. 'And Graham? What about their feelings?'

'I don't want to talk about it,' she said. 'It's got nothing to do with anyone else.'

'I don't agree,' I said. She took no notice, she moved round the

268

kitchen as if I wasn't there. 'What shall we talk about, then?' I asked.

'Your job. Bedpans, the usual thing. I don't care.'

I started to talk about some of the old people, and what I'd do when I was one of them. She stood facing the dresser, pretending all her attention had to be directed towards going through a folder of bills, sharpening pencils. I began to feel nervous again, the wine wasn't helping; I wanted it to be over and I couldn't say it.

She said, 'I've got to feed him,' and walked out of the room.

All I could do was follow her, but once I was in her bedroom, and she lay down with him in her arms, I walked round, and picked things up, and none of the things I touched felt as if they belonged to her. They were mirrors, brushes and pots that she'd accumulated, furnished from Graham's parents, furnished for Graham's son. I thought again about passing things on, about retaining important people in your life.

I said, 'You can't cast people out. There are some people you can't pretend about, you have to have them in your life. You can't pretend some people aren't convenient, we all rely on the next generation.'

'Like Audrey does?' she asked. 'And Mercy? Like they relied on one another? Is that what you're on about again?'

I drank a bit more wine and said, 'Audrey's got you. Mercy got me, that was all right in the end.' I looked down at her lying still, the child sucking. 'You feed him,' I said. 'You don't have to do that.'

She almost smiled. 'If I feed him I can't be tempted. If I didn't, I'd have to decide every four hours not to doctor his bottle with aspirin.'

I went and looked out of the window.

'He's finished now,' she said after a bit. She got up and took him into his little corner, laid him down and changed his nappy. She never spoke to him and he didn't look at her. She said, 'I'm going to have a rest now,' and lay down again in the middle of that big bed. It was obvious I was expected to go.

'Don't I even get a cup of coffee?' I said.

She shook her head. 'I need to rest. People make me tired.'

I wasn't going to be told to go like that. I leaned against the bedroom door, partly for support, partly in case anyone wanted to come in and I found something to hold onto, a strip of material.

'I still haven't told you what I really came for,' I said. 'I had a party last week,' I'd thought I'd say that to demonstrate positively how pleased I was, 'to celebrate my new status. I'm having a baby. I'm not getting married but I'm having a baby. I'm not telling him, it's nothing to do with anyone except me, but I'd like you to be involved. I want you there too. I want you to be part of it.'

I might as well have announced I was growing mustard and cress on blotting paper for all the excitement she showed.

'Are you?' Her eyes were open. 'Are you all right or are you sick? Do you rest?'

'So far so good.' I thought, that's it, I've done it, it was that easy, she knows.

'Who knows?' she asked. 'Audrey and Leslie? People at work? Or am I the first?'

'More or less,' I said. 'I've been to the clinic and I did have to mention it at work, because of arranging maternity leave.' Maternity leave made it sound real.

'And its father?'

I leaned harder against the door. 'I'm not telling him. The baby's got nothing to do with anyone except me. He isn't important,' I said. 'He didn't intend it, it'd be nothing to him if I didn't have it. Why should he have any say in what I do? It's my choice, it's my child.'

'I don't believe you,' she said. She put her hands behind her head and stared at me. 'You make him sound unmentionable: criminal, lunatic or married.'

'No,' I said, 'but I'm not going to be cross-questioned about it. I'm not going to tell one person one thing and one another until everyone puts the pieces together and thinks they've got the answer. The baby's father's the equal of a test tube, functional—'

'I still don't believe you,' she said. 'You aren't like that.'

'I am now,' I said. 'I've decided to be.'

She stared at the ceiling. 'And you've thought about it?' she asked. 'It knowing,' she said. 'The baby? You won't tell it, presumably, or it'll tell other people. It'll never know, that secret will stay, it won't know its father from anyone.'

'There's nothing wrong with that,' I said. 'It'll be all right. Children don't ever have any say in deciding what parents they'd like, or what they're like, or why they were born.'

'Because two people create them,' she said, 'that's why. Children are obsessive. You need someone to share. It's not good dealing with that obsession alone.'

270

'I won't,' I said. 'I want you to be part of it.'

She turned over the other way and pulled the covers round her ears. I was left holding the doorknob so hard my hand hurt. In it I found the long piece of cotton that I had pulled from one of the kimonos on the door; I realised it was the belt Graham tied round his waist every morning and night. I let it go and it was creased from where I'd clutched it.

'Give me ten minutes,' she said, 'and I'll get up.'

I went and sat quite still in the sitting room and read the paper. When I heard their bedroom door open I went down and waited politely in the hall for her, let her precede me into the kitchen.

'Audrey and Leslie will be terrifying,' she said and filled the kettle. 'Tea?'

'I crave it.'

She looked at the empty glass I'd brought down. 'It's better for you than wine.' She washed up the cups and wiped the teaspoons and draining board and table.

'Why?' she said. 'I never knew you wanted one, I never knew you were even considering, not marriage, let alone motherhood. I never thought they appealed.'

'Nor did I.' I sat and waited to be waited on. 'Not until I got pregnant. Then I couldn't think why I hadn't before.'

'So you didn't choose him, the father. It was an accident.'

'If you keeping talking about it,' I said, 'I'm going. You make decisions and expect me to respect them, what's different about this? Why can't you respect mine?'

She poured milk into a jug, measured it into our cups.

'It's intriguing. You know that quite well. Is that why you did it?' She stared at me and poured tea quite accurately at the same time. 'Is it?'

'Don't,' I said. 'I really mean it.' I drank some of the hot tea. 'Besides, there are much worse things like Audrey and Leslie to think about. It's them that's appalling, I go over it all the time, should I write or should I go? Should I phone? Or should I let them get over it before I appear in person? Think about it.'

'Maybe I'll ask Graham, he's always dealt with them quite well. He'll be surprised,' she said, and poured more tea for herself as if she'd forgotten I was there. 'I was imagining,' she said. 'It was odd, I could suddenly see it living with them – Audrey and Leslie; or us, even. I couldn't see you with the baby. I assume you don't want it adopted, but the hospital'll talk to you about that; if it's all right you can't give it away fast enough. If there's anything wrong it's another story. Or if you're married, it's difficult then. You're in quite a good position if you want to be.'

'I'm not having it adopted,' I said.

Immediately she shook her head. 'Of course not, I was getting mixed up. Forgetting.'

'Mixed up with who?' I asked. 'Jessica didn't ever think of that, did she?'

'You don't think of it,' she said. 'It's suggested to you. It's something you have to go through, it's incredibly difficult. It takes a long time.'

'It sounds like pregnancy,' I interrupted. 'Anyway, it's irrelevant. I'll concentrate on having it.'

'I could tell you.' She frowned.

'I'd rather you didn't,' I said straight away; I remembered her crawling and screaming. 'It's different for everyone.'

'I know.' She stood up and smiled. 'I'll give you things. He won't need them. I'll sort them out, I've been meaning to do that. I'll get them all ready. I could do it now,' she said after a minute. 'When is it?'

'There's plenty of time.'

She laughed. 'It always seems like that, then you're sorry when it's over.'

A week later, after I'd been to the hospital I went back.

'I hear we've got cause to congratulate you,' Graham said as he opened the front door to me. He led me into the kitchen and said it so that Barbara heard. He took my hand and leaned forward and kissed my cheek. 'All the best,' he said. Barbara sat by the window and the sun shone on her. She nodded.

'I won't stay.' I wanted to bury my face in him. 'I was on my way from the clinic. I was just hot and tired, I wanted a quick sit down.'

'How's it going?' he asked. 'Everything all right, no problems? You can go on working, can you? Have you talked about that?'

'You should go with her.' Barbara lay back in her chair as if sitting still in that warm kitchen was all she wanted in the world. 'Do you think she's that incompetent? They love men like you.'

'Laura's not incompetent,' he said. 'Laura knows exactly what she's doing.'

'I do feel stupid there,' I said. 'They treat you like—'

'Defectives,' Barbara said. She looked up at the motes of dust round her head, squinted, pulled a strange face. 'When's your test? she asked, putting her hand up as though to catch the light, shading her eyes. 'I thought I'd sort you out some baby things after you'd had the results. There's no point in counting chickens.'

'I don't suppose Laura's worried. I shouldn't think she loses sleep over that,' Graham said to me. 'Do you? She's sure it'll turn out for the best.'

'It's in about three weeks,' I said. 'I've got to be at the right stage. I know when it happened,' I said. 'About a week before Tim was born. So they know when to test it.' Still she looked at me, or at the dust, or at Anna out in the garden. My mouth was dry. 'If I tell you this,' I said, 'it'll just be because of the test, not because I want to tell any more. It was—'

'I don't want to hear,' Graham said, 'and I don't think you want to tell us. If you decide something you've got to stick to it. Hasn't she?' He turned to Barbara, then back to me. 'Although you can do what you like. It's entirely up to you. That's what you like, isn't it?'

'Where's Anna?' I asked.

Barbara nodded over her shoulder. 'Out there. Didn't you see? Looking after the pram. Not the most vital of tasks, but she seems to think there's a point to it.'

'I'll go and see her,' I said, 'tell her she's having a cousin.' Anything was better than staying in that room with both of them. 'It's a lovely day for sitting outside, even the path's hot.' I started down it, burning up through my sandals, to where Anna was sitting.

'Are you coming often?' I heard him say. I jumped and looked round. Through the open door I could see Barbara watching, squinting against the sun, frowning or smiling. 'Just so as I know what to expect. So I can construct a few reliable excuses to go upstairs or out whenever it happens. You don't expect me to go through this every time, do you? Concerned enquiries about your state of health?' He pointed to the weeds around the bushes. 'We need more ground cover,' he said. 'Because as far as I'm concerned you could spend the next five months as sick as a pig, laid out flat, it's of no relevance. If the end result isn't anything to do with me, nor is the interim. You can't have it both ways. Barbara, of course,' and he shook his head ruefully at the weeds again, 'is delighted. It's what she's been waiting for: a reason to organise again, clothes parcels, cots, prams. She'll be in her element. It'll be a God-given distraction.'

'What do you want me to do?' I asked.

'You've known that all along. You mean, "If I won't do what you want how do I make up for that?"'

'All right.' I stopped by a rose-bush; Anna and the pram were on the grass in front of us, Anna rocking and talking to the dolls she'd spread out in front of her, the pram quite still.

'Stay away, I suppose,' he said. 'And now you'll say you can't do that.'

'She'd suspect,' I said.

'You could suffer from exhaustion. You can use the telephone to talk. You could easily find a reason.'

I shook my head. 'There's not really anyone else—'

'I wish I'd realised,' he said, 'how selfish you were. Totally. Getting your own way's the only thing that motivates you. You can't have changed since you were a year old.'

'Doing the wrong thing and calling it difficult,' I said. 'Wasn't that always your speciality?'

'Look,' he said, pointing at Anna, 'come and sit on the grass, play let's pretend. Let's pretend it's you and me and Anna and Tim and new baby—'

'Stop it.' I bent down to take off my sandal as though a stone had made me uncomfortable. 'I'll come when you're out. I didn't know you'd be home on a Thursday afternoon.'

'I take time off.' He held his arm out to balance me. 'Remember? Quite often I think, "I'll stop and go—" but there's nowhere I can think of any more so I come back and sit in the garden. You sit down,' he said. 'Shouldn't you try not to stand about too much? 'Anna,' he raised his voice as I slowly got down onto the grass, 'tell Laura what we've found. You remember.' He took my arm. 'Come and see, stand up again, it won't take a minute,' and led me over to the pram. Not in there,' he said, and as though it was a joke squeezed my elbow, 'up, past the top of the fence, that roof opposite. It's a nest. Not ours, I grant you, but I spotted it. And it's a real rarity. Why is it a rarity, Anna? Why are they?'

'Because they're swifts,' she said, and fed grass into the mouth of a doll.

'Not a London bird,' he said. 'Migratory. They have an extraordinary life-style too, entirely on the wing – if they're grounded it can be really difficult for them to get going again. Extraordinary.' He looked at me. 'Eating, sleeping, fucking, doing all that while you're flying. Think of it. Extraordinary,' he said. I wanted to cry.

I didn't go there again until after my test. Barbara rang and said, 'I've got loads of things I want to give you, you'd better come.' 'There you are,' she said, and all over the kitchen were neat little piles of underclothes and nightclothes.

'I bought a lot,' she said taking a packet of plastic bags out of the dresser drawer, 'far more than I needed, but I used to like deciding what Anna would wear, what sort of picture I wanted for that day. Red for the sandpit, blue for shopping in King Street. I liked the idea of her choosing later on, too. "I'll wear my yellow shorts today." You can have all her Babygros.'

'Are they good?' I asked. I didn't know if I'd ever be able to use those vests and jackets; they'd had too much invested in them, I was too superstitious to take the risk.

'All right.' She patted the pile of nightgowns. 'I prefer these. You mustn't worry about them, not now your test's done, you'll be quite safe to use them. Besides, think of jumble sales. You never know what someone had before they gave away their shoes or coat.'

'But you don't know them. They're at a distance.'

'So's he.' She spun each bag round, fastened it with a plastic tie. 'I'll get a carrier for you. I was thinking,' she said, 'about telling Audrey and Leslie. Perhaps best to write and then phone. Forewarn, leave in peace, half-confront, then ignore till it's born. They'll come round.'

'It's putting pen to paper,' I said.

'I did. I wrote and told them about him.'

'What did they say?'

'Nothing.' She opened the doors to the garden; it was grey and chilly but the pram was at the bottom of the garden. 'But then nor do I. We understand one another over that. They might be quite understanding about you, too.'

'Your flat,' she said when we were drinking tea, 'is it big enough? I was thinking, maybe you should try and buy. Or rent something larger – or one of these rent and buy schemes – you should go to a building society, apply to a housing association. They'll be able to tell you.'

'It's fine,' I said, 'and I like it. And at first when I'm not back at work it won't be too cramped and I'll be able to afford it. When I'm back at work I'll think then.'

'You shouldn't leave it too long.' She shivered in the breeze and

275

closed the doors. 'You've got to think ahead. What we could do,' she said, 'is look at places together. I could get lists from agents, go through them and mark what looks possible and what doesn't and then you could have a look. There's quite a lot to take into consideration – schools in the area, which ones are good as well as where they are, secondary and infants. Nurseries, too, although being a single parent you shouldn't have too much trouble with that. But you don't want to travel miles to and fro, especially in winter, and you'll need to get to work easily. I'll just get a few, I could ring some agents later on, get some preliminary lists, then I could let you know what it looked like, couldn't I?'

For three months Barbara and I walked almost every morning or afternoon through Hammersmith and Fulham and Barons Court. She balanced Anna at the foot of the pram, the baby lay still and we went up and down streets where she knew no one and she read estate agents' details aloud to me.

'I can't afford it,' was what I usually said. She brushed that aside, it was unimportant beside the itinerary she had planned for us, the distances we had to cover.

'Say if you get tired,' she told me, but I did not. I did not enjoy these outings, but they used up time, and I thought that was probably how she saw them too. I would have let it go on until the end if it had brought us closer, but I never made contact with her.

'I suppose you're getting tired. I suppose you've had enough,' she said in August. 'It's the close season in house-buying now. This is when people go on holiday. It starts up again in the autumn.'

'I'm quite happy where I am,' I promised her. 'I don't mind my flat.'

After that I hardly moved. I got up to eat and each day I went to the park for fresh air. Every evening I watched television to send me to sleep. If I thought anything at all it was that I was communicating peace and serenity to the baby, resting for its future.

I packed a case to take to hospital, but I did not believe I would use it. I went to bed and, even when my waters broke, I didn't bother to get out. It was more difficult to wake up and drag the wet sheets off the bed than stay asleep.

When I finally did, I was ready to climb back onto the bare

mattress and go to sleep again; the pains were there, but bearable. I didn't need to alert anyone to deal with them. Then I woke up properly, for the first time in days, because I realised that the reason I'd been able to sleep had been that I didn't have anyone to alert, that in the last month Barbara had asked me to tea twice, and in the whole nine months never said, 'Will you be all right by yourself? Do you want me to go with you?'

After a couple more hours I put that out of my mind. I put everything except breathing and waiting into the background, dialled 999 and waited for the ambulance. When I got to the hospital I gave my name and address and waited for my admission card, and after five hours I got a bed. After another three hours I was waiting for a space in the delivery room.

Between pains I was aware something else was going on, but if I thought about that, about being alone except for nurses, that no one knew where I was or what was happening, the pains either disappeared or I started to cry. Instead I talked to the nurses, to other women and especially to myself.

'We're in this together,' I said to the baby. 'This is how it started, this is, just the two of us,' I thought, because I gave up any ideas about anyone else intervening, that it wasn't lonely, that this was what I'd envisaged, there was no need to feel nostalgic or sentimental about what I didn't have. It was the child and me and until the pains got worse, that was sufficient. Then I couldn't believe in any complicity between that battling thing inside and my body because we were completely at odds, I didn't want it to go on, I didn't want to stretch that far.

I don't remember the birth very clearly; I was useless, I didn't have any control over what happened. It was only because the doctor said, 'It'll hurt a bloody sight more if I use forceps at this stage, just push,' that I did, and then there she was, and that I do remember, red and squashed. I didn't feel love at all, or relief, or pleasure or gratitude; what I felt was more like terror.

I cried a great deal of that night and the nurses were very kind to me because they thought I was missing the father.

'You could have had a friend with you,' one kept saying, 'I'll ring someone for you,' but I said it wasn't that, I was . . . but I didn't have a word for it. The baby slept beside me in a crib. I kept looking at her, not to make sure no one had taken her but because I thought

I could wake up and find myself back in the flat, that none of this had happened; that only when I got used to the sight of her would the feeling of her being there be more real than her absence. I picked her up, I fed her, she sucked, she opened her eyes and hands and clutched. I did not imagine for a second that there was anything wrong with her; she was too independent for that. I was frightened to death of her, I was responsible for her and she was absolutely separate from me.

The next day I rang Barbara and she came in the afternoon. She and Geraldine and Jessica all came in the evening, and the next day Geraldine came and in the evening Jessica. They made up a rota, twice a day, for all seven days I was there, and brought me babyclothes and scent and flowers and food.

'God,' Geraldine said, 'it's half-empty. Only you and those two up the end. Why don't you move beds?'

I said no, I had the nurses if I wanted someone to talk to, I quite liked this, sleeping, feeding, listening to the radio.

'I've got used to it,' I said, and stroked and kissed the baby while they watched us.

When Barbara came she always sat on the side opposite the crib and said, 'Everything OK?' I always said yes and waited for the evening or the next afternoon to tell Geraldine or Jessica my nipples were sore, or that Cathy had been sick or gained two ounces.

'Look,' they would say to me and one another, 'extraordinary eyes, quite blue, quite beautiful.'

'Those finger nails. Perfection.'

'Aren't you lucky to have her?'

'I rang Audrey and Leslie,' Barbara said on the last day. 'Give them time and they'll come round. They asked what you'd called her, so I told them that. Audrey said, "It's a pretty name," as though you'd been in danger of choosing Clytemnestra.'

'Or Audrey,' I said. 'They come to the same thing. They can take all the time in the world to come round, it couldn't matter less to me.'

'She won't have any other grandparents,' Barbara said.

'She wouldn't, anyway,' I answered, and bit my tongue, but she didn't ask why that was.

'Look who wanted a look,' Geraldine said the last evening. 'Well, he said he was going to a meeting so he'd give me a lift and then he said he might as well come and see.' I wanted her to say it again so I could believe he was there.

'She's in that cot,' Geraldine said. 'Can he pick her up?'

'I'd rather not. I'm not confident with small babies,' he answered. He sounded exactly the same as when he reminded Barbara he preferred Gruyère to Emmental. He looked the same, too. I couldn't believe that this image of him next to my bed was real. I thought he must have been altered by what had happened, but most of all that he couldn't be here. I couldn't make sense out of it.

'Have a look, then,' I said. That sounded sensible enough and he went closer. I didn't watch, I suppose he saw her.

'You pick her up,' Geraldine said to me. 'Nice for Anna to have a girl cousin.'

'She's asleep,' I said. 'I won't wake her.'

'So how's the food?' he asked, and sat at the end of my bed so that Geraldine's chair was between us. 'What times are the meals? Still two hours ahead of the rest of the outside world? At least it's warm,' he said. 'It's freezing out. And you've missed Bonfire Night. Jessica had a party this year, fantastic fireworks, you'd have liked those, but it was perishing cold. That night,' and he nodded to Geraldine, 'Barbara asked me to say, Anna did get a cold so she won't be going to playgroup. You don't need to collect.'

'You'd better stay away too, then.' Geraldine patted my hand. 'The last thing you want with a new baby is a cold. Who'll take you home?' she asked. Straight away I said I was sharing a taxi with another woman at the end of the ward.

'She only lives a couple of roads away,' I said, 'it's really convenient.'

'And you can see one another after you get home, too,' Geraldine said eagerly.

'What time's your meeting?' I asked Graham. 'I thought they started at eight.'

He looked at his watch and the clock on the wall.

'I tell you what,' Geraldine said, and I thought, she'll go, she'll say she's got to get back early and I can get out of bed and take him to the empty television room and . . . and I had no idea.

'If Laura doesn't mind I'll cadge a lift back as far as the Broadway, the buses last night were appalling. It was nine before I got back.'

'You've been really nice coming,' I said to her and held her hand and pretended I wasn't crying.

'Whatever's the matter?' She put her arm round me and Graham walked backwards, away from the bed, in a semi-circle until he faced the door.

'Nothing,' I said. 'I'm just a bit worried.'

'About Cathy? But she's the picture of health, they'd have told you by now if anything was wrong.'

'Not that,' I said. 'Nothing, really.'

'We'll all come and see you,' she said, 'and Audrey and Leslie won't keep it up. And there'll be people from work, and once you get into going to the clinic and mother-and-baby mornings – that's how we all got to know one another. You won't be lonely at all. Really, really, Laura, it'll be fine.'

'I know,' I said. 'That was what I thought.'

When I took Cathy home from hospital and went back to my room it got worse. Not missing Graham, because after that night I reminded myself that he'd said, 'Whose is it? You're not having it?' and, of course, I'd not expected to get away without some regrets. Being frightened was what got worse.

I lay in bed at night almost laughing at myself for thinking we'd have some immediate and spontaneous trust between us, that baby and me. I couldn't have been further from the truth, further from anyone. I fed her, I knew I could manage that, and she didn't cry and wasn't sick; I wasn't frightened of her dying in her sleep or smothering. I was quite sure of her ability to survive, but I had no confidence in my ability to look after her. I imagined the future, the years of protection from accidents, slights, fears, questions; I saw her at nursery, at school, with friends, on holidays; and I could not believe I would be able to keep her going through all that. I took precautions. I went out and bought a cat net, fitted a double lock for the front door against burglars, put a fireguard against the gas fire before she could even sit up. I held one of my hands over the other on the pram when I took her out, for reassurance that it would not run away from me.

'I like it, really I enjoy being indoors. I don't mind if it takes all day to seem not to do anything except look after her. I don't particularly fancy mother-and-baby clubs, I like it like this. You come here, when you can borrow the car, it's easier than me getting on a bus,' I told Barbara, and I quite understood when she could only come once a week.

At Christmas when Audrey and Leslie were invited and accepted – it was supposed to be a family reunion – I had flu. Barbara came one day and heated me up some soup and the doctor came another with aspirin and to look at Cathy. By New Year's Eve I was convincingly exhausted; I didn't have to go anywhere.

'I'm just an obsessional case of motherhood,' I joked, but it was not that. It was not that I liked being alone, or staying at home, or that I missed Graham. I did not think about him. I did not care what Barbara said or that she did not mention Tim or that Anna never came with her to see me. Isolation, abandonment, loneliness were nothing. I was appalled; I could not believe, I could not bear what I'd taken on.

Barbara

I miscalculated the effect of Laura's baby, not through lack of sympathy but optimism. 'Think what it'll mean,' I said, only half-truthfully.

'I'm pregnant,' she had said.

All afternoon she had followed me around; I had shut my ears to her, made it evident I did not want her to stay. She had pursued me, declaiming and provoking. It was a history of the outside world I could do without. I had gone to feed the baby, put myself away with him. She followed and stood in my room.

'Look at me, listen.' She could have skipped with self-importance and frustration; capable of any invention, she would have concocted the most outlandish plot to gain my interest.

'I'm pregnant,' she had said. 'I want you to be part of that.'

I had lain quite still, I had put the child away from my breast so that all my attention focused on her words. I had felt myself sinking, falling; there had been an immense descent where time had slipped and I had lain as still as twenty-five years ago. I was back in another bed. I had to fight against grabbing her, reaching out from the sheets and holding and pulling her hard down with me. I had wanted to pull her into my bed or put her back in her cot and climb in with her; I wanted to go back to a time when, from within that cot, inside those bars, I was powerful. I wanted that room again, I was desperate, yearning for whispering and nestling in the twilight and the mornings, all the days when I had devised our whole lives and she had never disagreed.

'I'll tell you,' I had said. 'Listen. No, pretend, look, do . . .'

I had never needed to insist or persuade; I always knew the right thing and she had always believed me. For years I had made our lives as smooth as any could be in that house; I knew how to take care of things for both of us. Ever since, all the years without, I had missed it. For twenty-five years I had been deprived of every pleasure childhood had contained for me and now she was giving it back, it was starting again. 'I want you to be part of it,' she had said. I could see it, I could believe it was beginning again. I could hardly bear the excitement of it.

'Are you?' I said. It took minutes to find even those words. I did not say, 'A baby! Your baby! Oh, Laura.' I did not trust myself. I had to hold those words back, I must be as dubious and cautious as she would anticipate. I could not for one moment risk that she would take it away again.

'Whose?' I asked. 'Have you told the father? Will you tell Audrey and Leslie?'

I held tight and asked polite questions that had nothing to do with affection. My voice felt hoarse but I was pleased with the phrases; the prurient tone, the lack of nervousness was what she would expect. I was doing it well.

'What about the father? Criminal, lunatic or married? What's the matter with him?' I asked, as suave, as careless as she had been. 'You'll need him,' I warned her. 'Don't pretend to yourself you won't.'

I started to annoy her, to disconcert her independence, and it became easier. In five minutes it was clear that she was trustful, that I had blinded her to the pleasure she had given me.

'Leave me,' I said after a bit, 'I'll get up soon, let me rest a little while.'

When she left me alone I repeated, 'I want you to be part of that,' close to the pillow. The other words, 'a baby,' were secondary; all I was aware of was the occupation she had given me, the months she had promised of structure and activity. I would take over for her, I would plan and accomplish. Both our lives would enmesh, I would manage both of them, lead each of them for both of us. There would be no room for any other preoccupation.

'Come downstairs and I'll make some tea,' I called to her, when I could speak clearly again. She followed me into the kitchen and waited while I waited on her.

'What will you tell people?' I asked. 'What will you say at work? What will you tell the father? What about Audrey and Leslie?'

I repeated the questions until I was certain she was not secretly planning a return to the father, that it was my help she needed.

'Adoption?' I asked.

'No, there's no question of that. Not a chance. Never.'

I believed her, I relaxed with relief because she was too vain to alter her mind. I drank the tea I had made for us and sat and watched her. I had accepted involvement in a style she had found characteristic; I had got what I wanted and I had not let her know; I must not spoil it now.

'Have some more, have a biscuit, stay to supper,' I wanted to say, but I was restrained. I looked at her, healthy and uncertain, and I knew I must not force or overwhelm her before she was ready. She would need to be alone before she wanted attention from me again.

'I'll sort out some babyclothes. I'll get them ready before you come next time' I said. That helped, it gave us a place in the future. 'There's a test to make sure it's all right,' she said. I smiled because I knew it was unthinkable that anything could be wrong, and that both of us knew this baby would be perfect.

I shook my head. 'It's a formality. Have it if you want, but it's fine. I know.'

She smiled back. 'I know, too,' she said. 'I'll come again soon,' she added after a minute.

I held my hands back because I wanted to stretch out to her, to clasp and praise her for what had happened, for all she had given me to look forward to. But when she stood to go I only touched her shoulder. I stood still, stayed there to watch her go down the path and smiled again, quite to myself. It was as though she was wheeling him away from me, as though a substitution had taken place.

When I went back in I did not go upstairs to look at him, back to hover over his cot to watch, to see if by my will his breathing would stop. I called to Anna, 'Come down for a bit, we'll clean up the kitchen.' All the time I was anticipating the moment I would tell Graham. I fed the baby and put Anna to bed and walked the kitchen. I knew that after the months of her pregnancy my waiting would also be over. After that I would not have to look at his lolling head, his unsmiling eyes again, adoption and birth would coincide. He would be taken away and she would have another child, a real child would come into the house again. When I heard his key in the lock I was smiling, I almost ran to greet him.

'Laura came this afternoon,' I said. He looked round the room, as if he still expected to see her there. 'Surprised?' I meant because I was not in bed, to be met by my voice instead of silence. 'She had an announcement to make. She brought some wine,' I said, 'look,' and I lifted the bottle off the table, found glasses and polished them. I was flushed, a hostess dipping over a welcoming table. 'Sit down,' I urged him. 'Sit down and let me tell you.'

He did not argue or question, but sat in a hard straight chair and stared at the space in front of him.

'She came to tell me she's pregnant. And to ask me to help.' I slid to sit opposite him, to lean chin on hands, and titillate him with my story. 'She's pregnant. Astonished?' I asked.

He looked past me as if he was fragmented; he looked round the room as if he had never visited it before.

'Except,' I said, 'it would be more astonishing to find after all these years that she wasn't. Don't you think? Considering? She's lucky to have escaped for this long.'

He looked past me; I might have been a strange woman he had encountered in this familiar place. He reached out for the wine and filled one of the glasses, as if the other did not exist.

I looked down at myself then, I put myself under the same scrutiny: dressing gown and bony ankles and rolled sleeves. I covered up my bare thin chest, I pretended that all that was to be seen was my face. I smiled and offered him the bottle and my glass to fill. This time he shook his head as though I had no chance.

'What do you mean?' he asked. His face looked different, too, as though it was all there was about him to notice. It was altered, distorted, white and crumbled, fallen-mouthed, hollow. 'What do you mean about her getting away with it?' He seemed to have difficulty with the words.

I filled my glass and considered the pale trickle against the stem. I appraised the liquid as if we were united in a tasting ceremony, as if words were nothing. 'Come,' and I laughed. 'You know what I mean. You know as well as I do. You've got as good an idea of Laura's sleeping habits as I have. Well,' I drawled the word, I grinned to show a difference in the extent of our information, 'you came on the scene somewhat later, so not quite as good an idea, but you've got a fair one. You know what I mean.'

'Came on the scene later?' he said. 'How much later? Later than who? How do you mean?'

'I've known her longer,' I explained.

He took a deep breath and nodded and let it out.

'You've seen five years of it. I saw ten. I mean . . .'

I stopped because suddenly it was a surprise, this conversation; it

286

was unsettling that after months of separation to different rooms, hours of silence at opposite ends of the house, we were sitting opposite one another, talking about someone else as though it was a normal activity. It was as if our baby was already put aside, as if all the time he had shut us off was already past. I thought about what I was saying so that I would not risk destroying reconciliation by narrow-mindedness.

'There's nothing wrong with the way she goes on,' I said, 'not wrong. But you can't take so many chances without there being consequences. You can't sleep around for years and emerge unscathed without being very lucky. So many people hope they'll be safe, men and women, just hoping, not bothering, not taking care.'

I swallowed some wine, I hoped it would steady me, fortify me.

'It's not the end of the world,' I said. 'You can at least say that. It's certainly not the end of her world. Audrey and Leslie may feel different, but there's no reason why she should suffer unduly. They'll be awful to tell, there's no doubt about that, but they're not all that matters. It might be best,' and I considered my glass, I tipped it the way he did when he was considering, uncertain whether this was the right moment to speak, 'if I—'

'Is she?' he interrupted. I looked up, startled; I could not think what he was talking about. 'Suffering?' he asked. I shook my head. 'So how was she, then?'

He said it so urgently I put Audrey and Leslie and who would tell them to one side and considered his question.

'The same. The same as usual. Intransigent; thinking about herself; convinced of her rightness. How she always is.'

He looked away but he did not accuse me of intolerance. 'I'm not as harsh as you,' he might have reprimanded me, but he let my opinion stand.

I leaned forward, I wanted to express appreciation that he too was avoiding disagreement.

'Most of all,' I said, 'what she's most obstinate about, especially, is the father.'

'What about him?' he asked. It was dragged out, he meant he would not care about such a person.

'Nothing, she won't say. It's not a subject for discussion, she's not telling. She's not letting it be known if it's Jas or someone new or someone casual. A man at a party, anyone, anywhere, a man in the park—'

'In a park?'

287

I shrugged as though such encounters were commonplace, as if, because of their very frequency, he might have forgotten the details I had provided.

'Why not? Why shouldn't she? She's free. Ideas of morality' – I would have tapped his arm reprovingly if I could have reached him – 'have changed. We slept together.' I found I was reminding myself of that, it was not something I recalled with any familiarity. 'Nowadays you sleep with lots of people. You do it because you feel like it, that's all there is to it. Except, sometimes, like now, when there's consequences.'

'Tell me what happened,' he said and emptied all the rest of the bottle into his glass. 'Tell me when she came and what she said. Tell me what she's going to do.'

As I did I was not a person who had been sitting alone and undressed at five o'clock, I was Laura's sister who had listened and helped. I was not weeping and climbing into bed at the end of the afternoon, I was making Laura tea, encouraging and questioning not silent and powerless. I was making plans, organising what had to be done.

'What is it,' I asked from time to time, 'that you object to so much? Children without marriage? Not naming the father? The irresponsibility?'

He shrugged as though I had missed a vital link of reasoning.

'She's always been like that,' I reminded him. 'One for the moment, not long-term implications. She leaves other people to see to those. But she can't do without help,' I reassured him, 'from everyone. She'll need everyone. With Leslie for a grandfather, no father, no brothers, you'll be needed too.'

He put his hands flat on the table and loosed and clenched them. 'It's what she chose,' he muttered.

Then I was relieved because I thought I had located the trouble.

'Is that what's the matter?' I asked. 'The assumption the father can be cut out at her convenience? Is that what you mind?'

He stretched and yawned, turning away from the table as though he was uncomfortable with boredom. I looked for another way to pursue it.

'But she's always behaved that way. Used where it suited, abandoned where it didn't. People have functions for her, they fall into categories. People are useful,' I explained to him. 'You and me, people she works with, people she meets, we've all got different advantages. She doesn't waste energy on useless involvements, emotions that go nowhere. She sorts out what she can get and who she needs. It's not an unreasonable way to behave.'

I did not say that to provoke, I said it to be fair, to give a perspective to the picture I drew.

'If you're alone,' I said, 'you have to develop self-preservation. She doesn't pick and choose who to favour. I get used as much as anyone else. My skills, organising, helping, she regards them as a gift – she'd never believe I've taken pains to acquire them. She believes in accidents, they're unavoidable, they can justify anything. What they justify for her,' I expanded, 'is not caring that people are affected by what she does. Is that what you mind? How people are used?'

'Me?' he asked. 'No. Why should I? I'm not one of the people who's affected.'

'I handled it quite well,' I said, 'I didn't judge either. I said I'd give her babyclothes, and help, that's all. I didn't force things. I accepted it as natural, I wanted her to feel comfortable about it. She'll need me, you see, because she isn't going to do much about it. It's me that's going to have to do things.'

'What things?' he asked.

When I explained that we would have to look for a place for her to move to, he did not argue, or ask where I would find the time and energy. He sat quite still as though it had washed over him, as though it was a temporary event without consequences. He stared at the table as though he was trying to recollect, to resume progress with whatever had been on his mind before this intruded.

I let him be, I did not attempt to pursue the topic against his inclination. I cleared the glasses off the table, I washed the dishes that were in the sink and put away the pans and cutlery that had dried. I finished sorting the papers from the dresser drawer, I read and discarded old recipes and invitations, and all the time I hugged the future to me, I held it as a talisman against all the time since he had been born. I waited, too; I watched Graham to see what he would do, what indication he would give that he noticed a change in me. When he stood up I did the same, and followed him upstairs.

'Don't be long!' I said.

While he went into his study I read, I listened to the radio, and when he came back into the bedroom and started to undress I pulled his pillow close to mine and turned on the lamp by the side of the bed.

'You're not tired?' he asked, but he did not look at me; he did not trace under my eyes to find if there were shadows, put his hands on my shoulders to see if I would be lifted to meet him. He lay down beside me, still.

It was I who reached out a hand to touch him, and then he moved immediately, he clambered, he hoisted, he was without thought of distraction, concentrated pumping and groaning, and it was not that I was unresponsive, it was simply surprising. I had not comprehended, I could not begin to remember how to react, I did not have any way of feeling about it.

'Better?' I asked afterwards, though, and touched his head and thought that it could be. It had been an unfamiliar encounter, it did not bear any relation to previous routines, and I thought of Laura in this bedroom, of hearing, 'I want you to be involved in it.' I did not mind waiting for the day to come because it would be different.

By the time Laura came back again I had made all the necessary alterations. It took a short while to adjust because all my attention had been focused on achieving his adoption, but now I could put that to one side. I would carry him all the time Laura was pregnant but I could afford to forget him, I could move him back to a place at the end of things. I could allow myself to be diverted until he went; my attention could be directed on Laura's needs and organising her life. I could anticipate an ending because when her child was born he would have to be gone.

'Tell her I'm busy,' I said to Anna each time the phone rang, whether it was Geraldine or Jessica or Carmel Summers.

It was not untrue; I was digging, I had found a place for him; it meant that the garden had to be altered. For a week I made a long level drive and then laid stones all along it. I excavated and constructed a path from the top of the garden to the bottom and at the end, where the stones stopped and the grass began, where there was a little hollow and some shade, I put him in his pram.

'It's a nice place for a pram,' I said to Anna, walking backwards to the house with it in full view, watching it recede, shrink. When I was back inside the house I saw I had found the right place, because the trees were camouflage; in the shadows, out of the sun, it could hardly be seen at all.

I went out to the chemist and bought tins of milk powder,

because I was not going to feed him any more. I was going to mix bottles that could be cooled and sterilised and refrigerated and reheated, that anyone could prepare.

'I was drying up, anyway,' I told Graham, 'and I want to go on the pill again.' There could be no reason to argue with that, it was evidence of the other alteration, of another change which he could only welcome in our life. 'My breasts don't even hurt,' I said. 'I hardly notice it.'

For the baby there was certainly no difference between rubber and flesh, he did not distinguish. He lay propped on a pillow while I ached and turned away from him. I put him in his pram and sat in the house and did not think of the distance between us.

At the end of the week, when the telephone rang, I spoke to Carmel Summers and found I was prepared with what to say.

'Other things are more important,' I told her. 'I haven't changed my mind, not at all. It's just that I can wait. My sister needs me, she's pregnant; I can't ring every day for the next seven months. That's how long I'm giving you,' I said. There was no reason to make excuses for the ultimatum. 'You haven't been in such a rush. We've been over the same ground every time we've talked. It's your turn now to do something practical. I'm giving you time. In seven months you can arrange who'll have him, can't you?'

She did not argue with that. 'I'll be in touch,' she said.

It was at the end of the next week that Laura did come and I was waiting, calm and prepared, rocking in the chair by the window. It was the last quiet time before activity had to begin. She did not stay to take up my attention, but went out to look for Anna.

'I'll go and talk to her,' Graham said as I watched her go down the new path. I smiled at his generosity in realising we should not stay inside and leave her out there alone.

'That's a good idea.' I sat back. I could see them with my eyes shut, laughing with embarrassment, silent with constraint; I could see them going up to that pram where he slept. I did not mind, he was quietened in my mind like an old panic. He had become of less importance than the clothes I would parcel up for Laura. I could sit with the sun silvering my face, look up and see her nodding at the couch grass Graham was pointing to, both of them intent, agreeing. I could put aside that baby; all the time they talked he was nothing in their minds and nor was he in mine. I could wait for Laura to return to me. I could stay here and plan and be quite certain how I could use time up in the future.

I sat like that for a long while because they stayed out in the garden almost until it was time for her to go. I did not mind because when she came indoors and said she would have to leave she promised she would be back another day. All the time she had been near me that afternoon I had stayed quiet and relishing, near to happiness. I did not have to mind what happened any more.

'What have you done?' Graham asked that evening. 'What is it you've arranged with her?'

Although I was surprised she had not told him I was more than willing to; I was glad of a topic of conversation to carry us through the time while I cooked and we ate.

'She'll have to find somewhere to live,' I said. 'I've just offered to help. She can't stay where she is now, it isn't right. It's a tiny place, you must remember. She'll need space, they both will. They'll need to be separate. It's not easy,' I said. 'It might sound it, flat hunting, but there are so many factors. Location, access to work and nurseries, price. Everything's got to be taken into consideration. It'll take months, it always does. The more you look at the more there is to be considered.'

'Why?' he asked then. 'Why you? Why are you helping?'

He said that over and over until I was ready to cry and then suddenly he stopped as if he had been struck dumb. When I spoke of other things, how long she would be able to continue to work, whether she would return once it was born, he listened without seeming to, his face turned to his plate, closer to disdain than interest.

'I'll find some good agents,' I said, 'someone reputable so we don't go off on wild-goose chases. We've got ages, at least three or four months, that's the best thing, isn't it?'

The next day I telephoned all those the local directory listed and the next week I telephoned her to arrange when we would meet.

'We're starting tomorrow,' I told Graham. 'I might be late back. If it goes well we might take our time considering their respective merits.'

From that first afternoon I saw it was not an occupation that would absorb her; I had her attention from momentary curiosity, but she was not motivated. It would not last nearly as long as I needed it to, it would mean an effort to keep her for any time at all.

Every day, after the first half-hour, she said, 'Let's go and have a cup of tea,' and at four o'clock, 'Anna must be tired. Haven't we seen them all yet?'

I cajoled her with as much skill and determination as if it was Anna complaining.

'It's not far,' I lied. 'This one sounds good. We might as well go on now we've got this distance.'

She sighed as if it was a quite pointless outing I had organised, as if it had nothing to do with her future. 'Isn't this a trouble? Are you sure you don't mind?' she ought to be saying. I could have replied it was no bother, that although I did not have time on my hands I was prepared to organise my life around this. But she did not ask.

'We've only just begun,' I said instead. 'We can't expect miracles.'

'I don't mind staying where I am,' she answered. I would not allow that, I could not let her back out of providing me with this use of time.

'It's not practical,' I said. 'It's not fair. You mustn't give up this easily. You haven't just got yourself to think of.'

She sighed and I knew my only advantage was that she did not care enough to oppose me.

'I'll see you on Thursday or Monday,' I said each week.

I was more determined and less certain every time. As she dragged up and down stairs, as she waited for me to consult maps and roneoed lists, I could see that she was tired, but I ignored it. I behaved as if her reluctance would be overcome like a child's, I plied her with cakes, pretended we would soon be going home.

'You can't expect to find what you're looking for straight away. We've got months yet.'

'I'd rather live in a shoebox,' she said. 'It's too much trouble. It's too difficult.'

'It's worth it,' I said. Whatever it cost her, I needed all those trudging hours for barter; I could trade streets and stairs for the work Carmel Summers was doing. In the morning when I wheeled the pram to the end of the garden, in the afternoons when I left it propped against for sale signs, I was able to go beyond the limits of his existence; all the time I was alone with him I could easily foresee his departure. Now I had tasted diversion it was all I wanted. I did not ever want to go back again to that waiting. I wanted all the time it took Carmel Summers to arrange to pass without my notice; adoption and birth would be simultaneous.

'You could even live with us, we could buy somewhere bigger,' I suggested.

She smiled, it would not work but she was grateful. There was nothing more I could offer.

'It's not going badly,' I said. I told that to Geraldine and Jessica if they asked, and I told it endlessly to Graham. 'It's more expensive than I thought. And flats are more difficult to get loans on, and more complicated to buy. And she changes her mind about what she wants. It's such a long process.'

He nodded over his book. 'That's fine, that's understandable.'

It could have been relief that I did not say, 'He's got no place in this house, that baby, it's empty with him in it. Get rid of him.' I thought he preferred me to be too tired, asleep at night before he came to bed and reluctant to wake in the morning. I thought this was why he did not mind that for three months we behaved as if it was reasonable to discuss nothing but surveys and conversions. I thought that I did not mind either. If for days and weeks he did not seem to notice that we walked and shopped and played with Anna and fed the baby, worked, entertained, lived and slept apart, I preferred that as well. Once, I would have screamed that it should impinge upon him that we were only biding time, passing it mindlessly, living in a limbo like that baby, that this was what he had brought us to, but now I did not want any discussion beyond routine; I was grateful for acquiescence.

'Maybe,' I said at intervals, 'we should think about a holiday.' Or, 'get the car serviced; see about the window catches.'

We vacillated and divided tasks between us and did not comment when they were not performed. 'We should go to Henley,' I said, too, but I was not insistent about that either.

For all that summer I must have been peaceful to live with, undemanding, equable. In the daytime I was out, because even when Laura did not come I searched out houses myself. I hauled Anna and the pram through hot streets on humid days, in the evenings I read brochures and at night I lay and thought that she had turned to me and said, 'I want you to be involved,' and I had been. I could not have tried to give more to it. All I was frightened of any more was that it would stop.

'We're going to see Audrey and Leslie soon,' I said one afternoon when she came to visit me. Straight away she turned in her chair and leaned over the back of it. It was as if she was behind bars.

'You tell her,' she said. 'You tell her for me. She won't shout at you, she won't call you a whore. She'll be sorry you're putting up with me, you'll get pity not blame. You do it, please, I can't. And they've got to know. Please.' Although I nodded every word made me more uncertain. 'I can't, I know what she'll say, you tell her I want it, she'll listen to you. Tell her it's the right decision, make her see. Will you? She frightens me.'

'It'll be all right,' I said. 'It won't make any difference to me.'

I knew that would not be true because once Audrey and Leslie knew I would be lined up on their side. Through all of childhood she had done that, got the better of my shielding, dismissed me to the sidelines with the adults; I was frightened that was her intention now. Whatever she said, however many times she came and sat in the garden or agreed to visit a flat, that was what she wanted. Underneath she had had enough, she had enough confidence to manage by herself.

'I'm tired,' she had started to say. 'I think I'll decorate my kitchen instead. I know where I am here.'

I could see past it, I could see beyond immediate need into months ahead when she would not want me there, where nothing I did would be of any influence and I would be lost.

'You'll feel better,' I told her. 'You can rest at the weekend.'

'You'll tell them,' she had asked and scowled and kicked her heels and stretched her stomach against my table. I had seen her shape alter. 'Someone's got to.' She yawned. 'I never want to walk another step. I could stay indoors and sleep until it's born.'

I held out until July, and then I packed us into the car. When Audrey opened the front door I wheeled the carry-cot away into the garden and she boiled the kettle and arranged biscuits on a plate.

'Let me, I'll take it, Anna loves those, look, I'll put it here,' I'd said.

We all sat down together, arranged to eat and drink. After ten minutes Leslie invited Graham and Anna to watch television and she carried the tray back to the kitchen to wash up. I followed her.

'I'll give you a hand,' I said, and closed the door behind us.

'Laura been over?' She waited while I wiped tea-cups so that she could return each to its proper hook. 'Still doing that job?'

'At the moment. Until September.'

She stood still.

'What's happened, then?' she said sharply. 'What's she done?'

I could see her add the months up in her head and discover it was too long for working out notice. 'Waiting for the sack, is she?'

She thrust the crockery roughly into the cupboard. I watched the delicate patterns swing dangerously.

'It's not the sack,' I said, 'it's leave.'

'That's what they call it,' and she pushed the cupboard door. 'She's lucky they let her off that lightly, they'll make a lot of fuss in some places. She'll have a job finding something else.' She grinned, to encourage me to tell her, or at Laura's difficulty, I couldn't tell. 'Golden handshake more likely,' she said. 'That's what it is. Have a good long break, Miss Harris, and don't come back, that's what they're telling her.'

'No,' I said. 'She is going back afterwards.'

'So what's the mystery?' She started to rub at the shelves. 'What's going on that's so peculiar? What's it all about, then?'

'She's having a year off,' I said.

She turned and let the sponge drop into the sink.

'What's she up to?' She stared at me. 'What are you saying?'

I didn't answer.

'Look,' she said and she turned to face me, apprise me of the ways of the world. 'She's done something. Fiddled the books or killed someone off or cheeked the boss. They're hard up for people in those homes, they won't get rid of someone for nothing. Come on, what is it?' I was still silent. 'What's she done? I'm not asking again.'

I was quiet for as long as it took her to draw a conclusion, and when she did, and it did not take a moment, her choices were limited – crime, pregnancy, and I denied the first – she became rigid. I could have pushed her over, stiff and staring like a wooden doll. She was clenched, from her teeth to her fists.

'Pregnant.' She shook and spat at the word. 'That nigger. She's had him back, she'd go with anyone. I'll kill her.'

She hit one hand against the other, three times. Her whole body trembled.

'Whore. Filthy bitch, she loves it, she'd crawl for it, she revels in it.' She drew her breath in. 'His?' she asked and it was like a scream. 'His? That man's—'

I shook my head.

'Whose, then?'

I said I could not tell her, I did not know.

'I'll find out. I'll make her tell.'

I believed it, she was poised, ready to stretch Laura against the white wall and beat her, pummel and torment her into confession.

'I'll have her, she won't get away with this. I'll kill her.'

She wrapped her arms round herself, crouched; clutching with pain she half-ran to the window and back across the room, stamped and shrieked in front of me, 'Whore, filth, bastard, trash, all her life, hear me, all her life, I hate her, I hated her, I saw what she was, from the moment she was born you could tell, you could see what she'd turn into. You know what,' and she grabbed me, 'she deserves what you've got. That's all she's fit for. That'd teach her. Doesn't she? Wouldn't it? That'd show her. That's what she ought to put up with, give her that to look at, give her that to look after every day and she wouldn't be so keen on it.'

Although I pulled away from her she took no notice.

'I want her here!'

She hit the top of the shiny kitchen table and glasses and a jug jumped on the shelf.

'Tell her that's what she's got to do, that's what I want. Let her see what it does, I'll show her—' and I nodded because that was impossible. 'Get her to me, I mean it.' Her teeth gleamed. 'Filth,' she said, 'that's what it is, that's what it's about.' She raised her fist. 'I'll make her sorry. You tell her,' she told me when we went, she was calmer now she had cried. 'You get her back here. You do that. Promise?'

I did not make any but when I met Laura the next week I wished I had, I knew certainly now that she had altered, she was evading me.

'I've been thinking,' she said. 'I've got to be more independent about this. I can't keep thinking about what Audrey'll say. I want to be free of all that. I'm not doing what I'm told any more, I'm not house-hunting, I'd rather stay as I am.'

'Don't mind her,' I said, 'you know what she's like. She'll come round. She'll feel different when you've seen her. She'll change when you've had it.'

'See her? Change when I've had it?' Laura laughed, she leaned back against her sunny room as if it was a joke. 'I wouldn't let her near me if she was the last person left on earth. If she could cast spells she would. She'd like it if it went wrong, if I ended up – hurt,' she added. 'I don't care, I don't need anyone. I don't need daily visits either.' She looked sideways at me. 'You've got your own place to take care of. You don't need to keep coming to see if I've done the shopping and Hoovering. I don't care.'

I could see that, too; in the sun the windows were dusty and it smelled of late breakfasts.

'That's not why I come,' I answered. 'I'm doing it because you can't go on living here, for ever. Think how cramped it'll be when there are two of you.'

'There used to be.' She shrugged. 'It wasn't too bad. This one'll be smaller, it won't take up the room a grown man does. I don't have to look,' she said and stared into the carpet. 'I can do what I want.'

'You're tired,' I offered. I would agree to anything to avoid losing her. 'You need a rest. I want to be involved. That was what you wanted, too,' I reminded her. 'It was your idea in the first place.'

'Who's looking after Anna today?' she asked. 'And Tim?'

I said Geraldine had taken them with Melissa to the park.

'What time are they due back?' she asked.

'A walk would do you good,' I said. 'It isn't good to stay indoors all the time, you'll end up forgetting how to walk. You don't really need to sleep all the time.' 'I miss you,' I tried to say, but she was already yawning, breathy and distant. It would not have made any difference, she had already decided she had had enough of me.

I went home after that because I did not dare press her; until her baby was born I would have to abide by her rules.

I would not say that I survived that time, those last two months, or that I took it day by day; I would say that it became a block of weeks I fought myself through, intractable, implacable. Whatever things I tried to rely on, housework, shopping, dressing, areas where I knew my way, all the rest was waiting. Each week had its prearranged excursions: Geraldine to tea, a visit to Jessica, a phone call to Audrey and Leslie, intervals of habit that would dispose of time, but washing him, putting on his clothes, feeding, were always superimposed. Talking, I would still be trying to fit his legs into trousers, drinking tea I would be drying his wet body from the bath;

every day his face, his needs, his limbs, became the entirety of my world. All that autumn, the grey chill mornings when I dressed Anna in a cardigan and long socks, the astonishing heat when I took the pram into the garden at mid-day, I thought it would never come to an end. I counted minutes while I cleaned or led Anna to and from the park. I laid the baby down, picked him up and only let him stay because soon I would be free of him.

In the evenings while I could settle to nothing I looked at Graham and thought that I did not care what he saw, I did not care what he made of it. It mattered least of anything that he did not ask, that he kept to himself, because I wanted a shadow to live with; it suited me absolutely that he had become no more substantial than the clothes he wore. I could look at him and know he was sad, I would never have denied that, and because what I felt was different I was able to recognise that I had never seen such sadness. He was hollowed by it, insubstantial in conversation, uncertain in activity, halting, hovering like an old man, but I put that to one side. There was no help I could give him, I had my time cut out with waiting.

'Look, Anna,' he would say, and beckon her to the cot to pore over that expressionless head. I would turn my back and force silence. I did not want her touched by his blankness, I wanted to pull her across the kitchen to my side.

'Leave him,' I said, 'he's tired.'

Graham would put him down, cover him as gently as if he was capable of noticing.

'Is he?' he asked, but I could not be bothered to answer. I was unlocked from everything in that house, all I was tethered by was promise.

'I'm tired,' I said at night. I could not sleep, I could not move, but I did not have to make an excuse. As he turned away from me I could feel it was a relief not to be challenged by my dry body, not to listen to my lying silence. We were united in avoidance, we were conspirators, accomplices in estrangement.

For all the last month I thought I should remember the exact date the baby was due. I did not want to find out. It was almost time but I preferred uncertainty to the knowledge that it was imminent, that within days she could turn and say, 'I've changed my mind, this baby's only mine.'

Nor did I telephone Carmel Summers. I dreaded that, too, to hear her say, 'Adoption? You should have got my letter, we've decided we're not able to help.'

Every time the phone rang I sent Anna to answer it; I preferred to continue in suspense for even two minutes.

When it happened, when she called, 'It's Laura,' and I heard her voice, 'I've had her, I've had a daughter,' I did not answer. I could not speak because I was waiting for her to tell me to stay away.

She said, 'I've got her, she's here with me, come and see.'

I could not believe the words. I made her tell me again, I was suffocated, smothered with relief; I was to be rewarded, I was to achieve the end I had been waiting for.

'Anna,' I called. 'You've got a cousin.'

I took her and the baby to Geraldine's house, thrust them both into his pram. I tried to run but I tottered, I was even glad of the chrome handle to hold to. I left them there and waited for a taxi, and while I sat and looked at the traffic lights I thought that not immediately, but at a foreseeable point in the future, I would push Laura's pram while she was at work. After each outing I would take the child to be in my house with Anna.

'Look, Anna,' I would say as Laura's child looked up and smiled as she recognised us.

'Look,' Laura said as soon as I arrived by her bed. I was almost frightened to, in case of imperfection, but there was nothing wrong at all. She was pale and a pulse beat in her forehead and a fine down of hair covered her scalp. Her mouth pursed and relaxed as she breathed. I felt nothing at all. I did not want to clasp her to me or carry her off; I did not care about her, she made no difference. She was one and the same as any other baby. There were cots at the other end of the ward I could have looked in with as much enthusiasm. I could have counterfeited engagement and astonishment with the same alacrity and lack of pain to their mothers, to anyone in that hospital. I felt nothing at all and there was no comfort. I was blank, devoid, there was nothing there; the months of expectation and suppression and substitution had no result, it was like an expected death, there was no hope of grief or release.

'She's beautiful,' I said. I did not touch her but I stared for long enough to be convincingly entranced. I turned my head to see her from other angles, to remark on her lips, her eyelashes and fingernails and I nodded and listened while Laura talked about how hard she could suck, how light she felt to hold.

'Beautiful. Wonderful. Lovely little baby,' I repeated and then sat beside Laura. I gave her the scent and flowers and magazines I had bought in the entrance. I asked about the other women in the ward, and how long she would stay. I told her that I would arrange for Geraldine and Jessica to come tomorrow, and in the days after that we would all take it in turns. I did not say, 'What happened?' or, 'What was it like?'

She told me that she had not wanted to go to the hospital.

'I was so tired,' she said. 'I'd have had her at home rather than make the effort to get here.'

I read the headlines on the paper beside her. I jumbled words up, isolated letters, upended, reversed them through all her account of pain and anaesthetic.

'It was worth it, though,' I said when she stopped. I smiled, and looked at her. I listened to the account she gave of the meals and night feeds and strictness on numbers of visitors. I did not look into the cot again until I left and when I did she was the same; small, desirable, faultless. I had not the least interest in her.

'Beautiful,' I said to Graham when I got home. 'She's lovely, just what you'd expect.'

He nodded and continued to transfer notes from a pad to a letter.

'Good,' he said. 'I've got to get this done for tomorrow. Good. I hope that's what she wanted.'

'I'll have to visit most days,' I said, 'and Geraldine and Jessica will as well. We'll take it in turns. She's only in for a week. After that she's on her own.'

He nodded and frowned.

'That's what she wanted. You're doing what she's asked.'

The next week I rang Carmel Summers again.

'He's still here. I've still got him. I suppose you'll tell me you've been busy all this time?'

'So, haven't you?' she answered, but I was not having that.

'My sister had a baby. I told you that, I said I'd be helping her, but nothing's changed, my baby's no different. He's the same, and what I want, that's the same, nothing has altered. Where've you got to?' I asked. 'What happens now? Who've you got lined up as parents?'

'What we'll do first,' she said, 'is make a couple of visits.'

301

'We?' I waited. 'I'll come with you?' My heart jumped. 'Do I have to agree to them? Do I have to approve?'

'I mean we'll go to the Wisden Centre,' she said. 'That's the next step.'

'Is that a place to meet?' I asked, envisaging cups of tea, mixed declarations of commitment and regret over swiss rolls. 'Neutral territory?' I foresaw a mountainous range of negotiation. 'Is that what happens, I see if I approve of them as his parents?'

'Maybe I haven't explained it properly,' she said after a minute. 'You have to be more aware of all the options. That's why we're going there. You don't meet anyone, you don't meet anyone there about adoption. The Wisden Centre is purpose-built for Down's children, it's where you'll see what help you can get. It's specially designed, you'll be able to see all the ways we can help you to look after him.'

'Me?' I said. 'I don't understand. I don't think you understand. I don't need to go there, I don't want to see any centre. I don't want him, I thought I'd made that clear.'

'That isn't how it works,' she said. 'You have to be aware of all the options. You can't see all the possibilities. You're approaching it from the wrong angle. That's not how it is. It's a question of adjustment,' she said.

I could have torn the words out of her voice.

I asked, 'What have you been doing? Six months, I've given you half a year and all you suggest is a day trip. You're a fool, you're lying, pretending. You understand what I'm saying, why don't you do something?'

'I am,' she sighed. 'I'm doing what has to be done. You won't alter anything by getting angry. We have to work within a system. I'll try and visit,' she said after a moment. 'We'll work something out.'

'I'm busy,' I answered. 'I still go and see my sister now she's had the baby,' although it was hardly true. I visited but she slept. I offered to take Cathy out and she refused, sometimes I knocked and she did not answer. 'I might not be here,' I said. But I had nowhere else to go.

'I'm not going anywhere,' I said when she arrived. 'No tours of inspection, no discussions, no support systems. It's not a condition of sale, I'm giving him up. I don't want alternatives.'

'It's not a condition,' she said. 'It's a request.'

'Which I'm refusing.' I did not even open the front door wide enough for her to come in. 'What do you want?' I said. 'I can let you in, but all I'll tell you is that nothing's altered. What will you do?'

'It's not my choice.' She shifted her briefcase from one hand to another. 'It's a procedure. This has to happen, then this, then the other, visits, consultations. There's an enormous amount to go through before there's any question of making a decision. I'm not making it up, it's the guidelines we have to follow.'

'Not to me,' I answered. 'Listen, I'm not unreasonable, I'm just not interested. I don't want helping to care. I want it over.'

She leant against the porch. 'Let me in,' she said. 'Reasonably, look at it objectively, what do you expect to happen? You to say, "I don't want him," and me to reply, "Here's the adoption papers?" Is that how it's supposed to work? You look at it too. It's not that simple, it's difficult.'

'It's difficult,' I nodded. 'I agree. He'll be difficult, that's the problem. I'm not unsympathetic, either, I can see the position you're in. Who wants him? That's the root of it, that's the difficulty, isn't it?'

She shook her head and looked down at her briefcase.

'I'll leave it for now,' she said. 'Give me a ring if you want to talk again, though.'

I took no notice.

'You can't leave me,' I said. 'You can't just walk off and forget you've got to deal with this. You've got to keep tabs, he's your problem too. And me, I'm your responsibility as well now. You've got to do things about this, you'll be in trouble if you just abandon us.'

'I'm not,' she said. 'I'd come if you'd let me in.'

'When you can help,' I said.

After that I did not wait to hear from her again, I wrote letters. Instead of going out or answering the phone I imagined addressing her senior, the newspapers, radio and television programmes. I thought how I would expose her ineptitude, her laziness; in return I would be given immediate understanding and every promise of relief.

I planned phone calls to the Samaritans, to adoption societies and they unanimously condemned her, marvelled at my determination. Yet all of them, I realised, would also have advocated patience.

'Wait, give it until after Christmas,' they would have advised. 'It's not the best time to publicise deformity. Wait until the festivities are over.'

I took account of that. Well in advance I began to make plans; the longer I had to discuss it with myself the more certain I became that I had not damaged my chance of success. As long as I was prepared to adjust my timing, the New Year would guarantee a solution. In the meantime, in advance gratitude, I would arrange a Christmas, I would manufacture a seasonal celebration that would ensure an equivalent well-being for everyone else.

For all December I telephoned Audrey and Leslie every day and went to see Laura again. I did not let complaints or silences deter me.

'Send her to someone else. We don't have to put up with her coming,' Audrey argued. 'Get rid of her. She's got other friends, let them take care of her. What do I have to be in the same house as her for?' she asked.

I said because I wanted them together again.

'She won't,' she told me, 'she won't dare face me. You can say what you like, ask till you're blue in the face, she won't listen.'

When I went to see Laura I knew that, but it did not worry me that she and Audrey would not be reconciled; I hated it because no matter what I said or did she obliterated me from her room. I could forgive the lost dream of her child, I could bear her motherhood if she would allow me diversion, but she would have nothing to do with me. I was not to extract any relief from her at all.

When I stood by Cathy's cot she never said, 'Pick her up, see how she is, what do you think?' There was no possibility at all that she would ask, 'You can't have her for a day, can you?' I could not ever imagine a time when she would deposit that child with me as she departed for work, or a night out, a weekend off, a holiday. She did not need to confide everyday details of feeding or bathing Cathy, nor did she confess to any disquiet; it was as if this role so naturally fitted her abilities there was no need for any consideration of it. She sat by her window, nursing, and hardly noticed the world outside; she did not ask how Graham or Anna or the baby were. She drew away from me when I walked past.

'Any shopping?' I asked. 'Shall I clean the stove? What did you cook yesterday evening? You must look after yourself properly.'

She looked as if I was haranguing her, berating and insulting. She did not nuzzle her daughter, though, she did not concentrate so exclusively on her welfare and existence that she was blinded to other people, that was not the root of her distance. Quite often she looked past her as well, she was looking for someone else to appear, to alter all of her life again.

'Do you want to tell him? The father?' I asked. She didn't answer, but fixed the guard more securely round the fire, turned the pages of another book on childcare. 'He might be glad to hear,' I suggested.

She said, 'Don't be stupid. Don't interfere. I told you, she's mine, I'm the only person responsible, she's nothing at all to do with anyone else. Do you understand that?' she asked me, and put down the book and went and stood by the cot. 'I'm the only person who'll ever look after her.'

'I want you to be involved,' she had said, and it had not been true, it had only been placatory. I should not have let myself be fooled. I should not have trusted in her again, but at least I had not lost more than that. I had not exposed my belief in substitution to anyone else, there was no question of public ridicule; I had simply failed to ensure the necessary progress on the part of Carmel Summers. I had been misguided, I had been delayed, but the loss of her child did not mean the permanent imposition of my own. I had to wait longer for escape but I could find an activity to make it bearable.

'I'm looking forward to Christmas,' I said to her. 'Audrey and Leslie have quite come round. It'll be fine.'

I could see it, I could see them turning to me, hugging me gratefully before they left. I could see rewards for all the time I would devote to it.

'I enjoy it,' I said to Graham. 'It's worth making an effort for.' I cooked as though for a siege.

'It's got to be done,' I insisted. 'It's no trouble.'

Every day it became a celebration in its own right, and it was also a breathing space. It allowed me to resist the temptation of confiding, of telling him, 'A woman came to see about taking him away. I told her to come back.'

Sometimes when it was late and I stood to go to bed and he said, 'I won't be long,' I almost stayed. 'Listen,' I almost said, because in the long run I would not be able to keep him out of it. Instead I stretched and put away the tinsel and wrapping paper.

'It'll be fine when it happens,' I said. 'We should start looking forward to it. I'm not even tired, I love doing things like this. It gives me energy, it makes me feel better.'

For all the time beforehand, for all that month, it did.

When everything was ready, on Christmas Eve when the house glowed with preparation, Laura rang to say she was unwell. I found tears on my face. I began to cry with frustration at the decorated tree, the presents, the food, that everything it meant could be dismissed with such ease.

'You must come,' I shouted, 'I want you here. Why do you think I've done it? Come anyway,' I said. 'I'll come and get you. It'll only take ten minutes.' I would have brought her any distance to stay.

'No,' she said. 'I ache. I can't move. Not anywhere, not even to sit in a car.'

'You can't stay by yourself,' I argued back. 'You'll have to move, to cook, pick Cathy up.'

'I can manage that,' she said. 'I know what you think,' she added, 'you think I'm getting out of seeing Audrey and Leslie. Cheating. But it's not, it's genuine. I tell you what,' she offered, although I had not been able to ask for anything, 'if I feel better Boxing Day I'll come then, if you can put up with them staying overnight.'

'I want to see how you are,' I said. 'I'll come and see how you are.'

The next day, when Audrey and Leslie had arrived, when Graham and Anna sat facing them in the quiet sitting room I left. I let food stay unattended in the kitchen and I took soup, magazines, a nightdress, flowers, a thermometer. I drove away from a house that required me to return, rushed along silent icy streets because I had nothing else, and all day I kept it up, came and left, to and fro. Each time I went home I invented complications: feverishness, emergency numbers, locum visits. On every journey I ignored what I was going to, I remembered what I had managed to leave behind, and at the end of the day, when all the wasted time was over I went home and sat with their annoyance.

'It couldn't be helped,' I repeated. I did not look at Anna's crying or Audrey's anger or Graham's boredom. 'She was ill, they needed me.'

On Boxing Day I put aside all the stagnant expectations, the sad hours of resignation and television, I let Audrey and Leslie leave without interest, parcelled them off with Christmas cake. I side-stepped Anna and Graham as though there was neither grievance nor recrimination, I pretended nothing had been spoiled. I could not care about all that effort, uneaten food, unopened presents; the sick couple took all my time.

'It only needs organising,' I said.

For all the time they were ill I did that, I cut up my time so that there were no spaces. I engineered all the days I could make it last so there was no room for any other considerations. I did not think about anything outside or write any letters of complaint; I threw away my notes, I did not look up the telephone numbers, I did not even wait in to hear from Carmel Summers. I had found an alternative occupation again.

I sat in Laura's room and watched them sleep. I sat and wished I had no reason to leave, and when they woke I lingered. I was not needed; their warmth and idleness required nothing outside of themselves in that room. It was the place that glowed, all of it reflected in the red bedcover; all of it was as desirable as lying wrapped within that. I had to tear myself away.

Every day when I returned home I was not welcomed. I was resentful and displaced. I wandered about through meals; I forgot my words, I was an absentee, tested and disliked. I fetched and carried, arrived and left, I was outside of all their lives. Nothing came of it, no promises or future occupation, I could find nothing in it to take me further. For all that time I was dependent upon separation, waiting upon feverishness. I had no expectation beyond it. I could not pretend what would take its place next. I knew she would not say she was grateful, but I did not think she could discard me; she would acknowledge that I had a right to be with her. I did not plan activities or try to see how we would link together. I said to myself that I was waiting until she recovered her strength, that when she was quite better we would talk about it.

On the day I expected that, on the day I planned to take her back to my house to convalesce, I went to her room and it was empty. She had run away laughing, and I could not bear it. I hit her door, I tore up the note she had left, the lies she had written about recovery and independence. I cursed her for surviving and wept because I did not know where I could find anything else. She had been my last chance of distraction, she had sent me away and I would have to go back, nothing could keep me away from him any more.

I went home and the next day when I woke I was not resigned or sad or determined, I was numb, immune to sensation, immobilised; it was exhaustion, Graham said, but it was not to do with tiredness, it was to do with pointlessness, impossibilities. It was to do with the blankness of the child I went back to, and it took over, that blankness, that mindlessness, it shut out every other sensation; it was a draining, a preparatory desperation. It felt like the destruction of everything I had promised myself, empty and deprived and accepting. It was acclimatisation, it was grief and it was bitter and angry, it was all of those in the guise of debility and depression, but most, above all, it was defeat, and I would not see that.

I fought it; I sat and thought that it was relaxation. I behaved as if I was carefree. I wondered out loud that I had become so easy, that I was no longer provoked by grubbiness and disorder, and I made myself comfortable. I sat still and lay down, thoughtless, fearless; I sank and floated, drowned in sleep and sickness. I did not try to consider the future or question the present. I told myself that it was temporary, recoverable, that nothing was altered, that they were indistinguishable.

'I can't,' I said to Carmel Summers, when she began to ring again to suggest I went with her to the Wisden Centre or even that she came to visit me. 'I'm sorry.' I sounded genuinely regretful. 'You'll let me know when you've found someone?' I asked, and pretended that she would.

I did not do anything. I hid from my resolutions, I looked back on them as misguided inspirations, ideals of purpose I was too weak or too wise to pursue. I yearned for their strength and I could not bear it, I yearned for the self who had pursued, I was bereft and I was relieved. I was powerless and I did not try to alter that; I lay still and traitorous, emptied and vacant.

I did not stay thoughtless for long, though, and when it came back it was him I thought about.

When I was asleep I dreamt of him; when I was awake I sat with my eyes shut and was similarly transported. I was taken into another world, I became familiar with a different scheme of behaviour. I became unseparated from him, initiated into a world he inhabited.

It was an enclosed world, bounded, but it was not unpleasant. In fact it was full of toys. There were slides, chutes, roundabouts, and they were all for children like him. There was a huge wired playground full of them. Standing around it, staring from the boundaries were women like me, smiling, hating, full of adaptation. We stood, we commented, we laughed at all the tumbles and recoveries, we cheered, we applauded at nothing and pretended delight and relief. We turned blind eyes to one another, we could not distinguish our own children, let alone ourselves, and we were silent. We never spoke, we never allowed ourselves to whisper, 'He's getting better,' because that was not what we could hope for. It was not only unrealistic, it was wicked to hope for alteration. Our place was to participate, to endure, and to be private in it. Sometimes, when I had looked at that world for a long time I found I was crying or shouting to the women I saw going in and away from that place. I saw them encourage and praise.

I shouted, 'Don't, stop,' and when they did it was not to ask me, 'Why?' but, 'How?' Then I beat my fists against my bed or chair because I could not explain, I had not managed it. All I had managed was sitting in this chair crying, I could not teach anyone to apply comfort or control, I could not be responsible for anything like that. I looked round the kitchen or sitting room or bedroom and thought I would make something to drink and watch television or change my dress, that was all that was left; those were the only alterations I had discovered, then I could not talk any more to the woman who had watched the nursery and cried, and I did not let her talk to the woman who watched television and changed her dress. I kept them well apart from one another, strangers because they had quite different ideas.

I have no idea if the two of them would have ever talked to one another, I have no idea if they would have ever coincided; if Cathy's pram had not been knocked over I do not know what their separate futures would have been.

After that collision, though, there was no chance of unification; that collision did not just smash her pram, after that happened neither of those women existed, neither of those women could go on at all any longer.

When it did happen I would have preferred to have practised for the event. In the hospital it would have been better to have rehearsed that sort of reality, to have found some familiarity with desolation. If I had practised I would have been able to respond, I would not have been a dry vessel, empty of sensation.

'We've got hold of the father, he's with her now,' I had heard. I would have liked best to retaliate, but it would not have been a bad thing just to have answered, shouted back, because until then, until I heard what those words meant, I would have known what to do. I had believed all the words until that point. I had taken them into me and acted as I had thought fit. I had adapted events and I had allowed for my needs and I thought I had managed to show reality the part it was allowed to play, but I had miscalculated, it had got the better of me.

I had thought, ringing Carmel Summers, arguing, planning, pleading, that I could determine the resolution to our lives.

Even when I stopped pretending it had never occurred to me that there were different directions, that I was not experiencing events straightforwardly. I did not realise because when it happened, on the day Geraldine's neighbour panted and banged the door and gasped, 'Your sister's baby, your sister's baby,' and told me the name of the hospital, I had thought that I was recovered, that I was competent to deal with anything. While I drove to the hospital and found the room Laura was sitting in, I planned for it.

If Laura's baby were badly injured I would argue that I would not have time to look after both of them, that I had the right to choose where I devoted my attention.

'She'll want me,' was what I rehearsed, that was the interview I was practising. 'I won't have time for Cathy and him, you'll have to take him, I don't possibly have the time any more.' That was what I anticipated, that was what I still expected to come out of it.

When I arrived at the hospital I was welcomed, I was thought to be helpful while I sat with her in that little room. I was there to quieten and interpret, to translate accident into fact; I put out of my mind entirely that I had been a victim in a room like this. I was not paying back any of that, I was there because of a new injury, the past was discounted. And although Laura was shocking, beside herself, I found I had the right words. I could justify hysteria, I even felt for her in it, and I could put it aside, I could bend and talk to her, stroke and whisper and promise. I could make sense of her, I could come as close as I could to reassurance by love. It was better than anything we had grown out of, it was past history because it transcended it. While I was there beside her I was needed without measure, I was wanted beyond comparison.

'Laura,' I said, and I hugged her. All I desired was to absolve her from desperation, comfort and succour, to bring her back from a state I knew to be unbearable.

'Laura, listen to me,' I pleaded, as though it was truly within my power to provide consolation, as though as soon as she paid attention to me her daughter would be mended. 'It'll be all right. We'll hear soon. Don't worry, don't cry, it'll soon be over.'

Through all the time the nurses came and went and told us nothing, through all the time she howled and rejected I held onto her; it was only towards the very end that I doubted, it was only just before his arrival that I wondered if I was really helping.

Five minutes before I went back into the room where Graham was standing and the nurse announced, 'The father, we've located the father,' I thought it might be better to leave her beside herself, because that would make it easier to accept bad news. I stood up to go and search for a doctor or sister, someone who would know the best action to take.

'I can get her quiet,' I would tell them, 'but there isn't any point if it turns out badly. It's easier to bear grief if you aren't sane about it.' They would be able to nod at the truth of that and tell me to leave her moaning or continue to comfort.

As soon as that idea occurred to me I could not bear to remain, I had to find out as quickly as possible what to do.

'I won't be a minute,' I said to the nurse, and in that instant of speech, when I stood and made the moments in that room over and done with between us, I wanted to reach out and back into the ghost of that comforting, the ghosts of my reaching out to her, her turning to me; I wanted us back like that, enwrapped. I missed it so much, the pang of leaving was like a sickness. Outside I leant against the door. I was dizzy, I could have retched with regret, but I went on, I went down the corridor to a door where I had read *Mr Winch*, and knocked and explained my difficulty. All the time I talked his hand reached slyly sideways to keep the door open, and when I backed into the corridor to go to the room she was in, as I opened her door again I thought, I could have stayed in there all the time, I need not have separated us, I found out nothing; exactly on top of that knowledge I saw them and heard the nurse say, 'We've located him, we've found the father.'

'I would not have found this out either,' I thought. He would have seen me in the room with her, that is what would have happened; he would have ducked, avoided, confused and the moment would simply have passed. Nothing would have happened except confusion and now what was happening was a roaring inside me, a great din as everything splintered, I flew apart, I had nothing, not anywhere to grasp, no knowledge of what there was as reality.

'But nothing hurts,' I said. I must have said it to myself because no one moved and no one else spoke and then they all did, all at once. There was a great deal of activity, senseless, my senses made nothing of it: tangled words, guiding hands, noises and air as other people sat down and walked and came close to me. I watched their figures and did not want to remember why they should be behaving in this way, what cause and repercussions their activity had. I did not want to apply my mind to their presence. I did move then, I stopped, I remembered that word as I did it, I went to the window and looked out. I must have stood there for some time because after a while I understood they would not go, they were performing tasks for my benefit, making indications of care, sitting me down, talking again, giving me a cup of tea, even making a joke.

'Just like Audrey,' I heard Laura say, as though that link existed between us any more. I answered as though it still did, as if it was a statement that required sisterly reprimand, and I stopped because it was a betrayal; I should have bitten into my tongue; there was nothing. I stopped because I had no part now in what went on between other people, I had only myself to speak and answer to, there was no other connection.

There were other people there, though, because Mr Winch came in and I could not understand the words he was saying; the noises were disconnected, the baby, going, staying, discussion and decision. None of it had anything to do with me and nor did Laura weeping; nor did sitting and waiting and nor did Graham holding my coat and taking my arm or the nurse smiling at me or walking, or recognising the corridors I had run down to comfort her, or the hall and swing doors and asphalt I came to outside.

'Give me the keys,' I said, and that phrase connected with the white car in front of me. I knew how to put myself in the driving seat. Out of the corner of my eye I could see wheels and bumpers and clambering feet. It was cold, there was a freezing patch across my hands from the open window. Then features blurred close to me and I clenched myself against the nothing he had become.

'Go away,' I said because he was holding the door, he was trying to get in and I could not understand that, I did not see why, when everything was over and done with.

312

'Go, leave me alone, go right away, right away, right,' and I nodded to emphasise that, keeping my profile to him.

'I will, I will now,' he said and as though that guarantee was limited to the present and because that could not be what he meant, I wound up the glass between us, turned the key and pulled the choke, pressed, moved. I must have moved because when I looked again he was reflected, small, he was refracted back at me, receding too fast as other things around me grew to a different size.

When I got to Geraldine's house I was lucky because she was outside, fumbling for her purse. Anna and Melissa were holding onto the baby's carry-cot. I left the engine running and the car door open and called,

'Stop, don't take them inside.' She turned round. 'I've come to take them with me.'

'What's happened?' she asked, and as I started down the path she tried to take hold of my arm, but I shook her off. I walked past her so fast that she stepped off the path into the earth. I pulled the carry-cot away and took Anna's hand in mine.

'I've got to get there. I've got to go,' I said.

She nodded, she even pushed Melissa into the muddy border for the urgency of my exit.

'I'll speak to you,' she said as I swung the pram round, 'later.'

I hauled Anna beside it, lurched as if it was intoxicating, staggered onto the pavement, and then Geraldine was beside me again, unstrapping the carry-cot from the wheels, folding where my fingers were numb.

'Is Cathy all right?' she asked. 'Is it bad? Is she damaged?'

I said nothing and pushed the carry-cot and Anna into the back of the car and closed the doors.

'Ring me,' she called. I drove away.

'Where are we going?' Anna asked. 'What's happened to Cathy? Are we going to see her?'

I said nothing, I went as fast as I dared.

'Get out,' I said when we were outside our house. She did not protest that it was too difficult to unfasten her seatbelt, she was immediately obedient.

'What about Tim?' she asked when I did not start to unload the carry-cot.

'He can wait,' I said, 'he's quite safe in there. I've got to take him soon, anyway.'

I shut the door on him and she did not ask where, she followed me patiently up the path and waited while I looked at my key in my hand, in the lock, in my hand again. My mind would not move, it could not even recognise the automatic any longer.

'I want to go to the loo,' Anna said, and pulled my arm. 'I told Geraldine and she said I'd have to wait for her house.'

'This is our house,' I said. I leant against it; I could not keep upright otherwise.

'Let me in,' she said.

'All right,' I agreed, as though it was simple. She was gone a long time and when she came down I had got to the kitchen. I had leaned against the wall and bumped, shoulders, hips, one after the other, until I came to the door. Then it had been easier. I ached, I ached as if I had been drawn like canvas on a stretcher but I was becoming used to it, I was beginning to understand pain. After some time, because I had looked at the clock and out of the window and they had changed, and I could hear the television; I knew that it was time to go; that soon, anyway, he might be seen in the back of the car. I could not be bothered with that, bringing him in and out, back and forth, I could only manage that lifting once.

'Anna,' I said, 'listen.'

I warmed some milk and opened biscuits for her and it was not as difficult as before, it did not hurt quite so sharply in every part of me.

'I've just got to pop out' – it sounded easy, a trip to the corner shop, I had left her alone for that before – 'in the car.' She stopped eating, she stopped looking at the screen to stare at me. 'I'm just taking him,' I said. 'It won't take long. I won't stay, that's the point, I'll come straight back.'

'Where's he going,' she said.

'He's got to,' I answered. 'I always meant that. It's just taken a long time.'

'Where?' she asked. 'Will I go to?'

I could have smiled. His future was of no concern, it was the implications it bore for her own.

'You stay here with me,' I said. 'It's right that you stay. You're fine here. When you've eaten your biscuits,' I said, 'you can have an apple.' I focused on my watch. 'I'll be back before television's over.

It won't take any time at all, it's just a question of getting there and back.'

'Where?' she said but I did not answer. Now I saw the time I was worried; it had disappeared, gone in a flash that I could not account for. I did not know whether they locked the doors, even if they put barricades up, iron gates to shut away intruders. I had to make properly sure of security, I could not do it carelessly, that would make me irresponsible. I could invalidate my cause with a mistake like that.

'Just out,' I said. I remembered those words. 'My mother used to tell me that. And I was all right. I must have been, mustn't I, or I wouldn't be here now? I'll bring you something back,' I promised, because although every part of me was fixed on going, the back of my mind appreciated that she did not want cartoon images for comfort, she wanted my presence, and not the presence I gave her now, but a past one, previous past yearning for. I must not allow a second's memory of that to impinge or it would stop me, keep me still.

'I'll bring something nice,' I pleaded, 'a surprise. A wait-and-see.' I buttoned my coat. 'I'll be no time at all. Promise.' I walked as though there was no link between us which transferred her doubts to me, which hurt as her face tightened to uncertainty. 'Wave out of the window,' I called as I opened the front door.

I was so loud in my reassurance that it could be heard as far away as the roadside, and that was what I saw happen. I opened the door and he was by the car, he was crouching and peering into the back as though he did not recognise either the vehicle or its contents. Then he straightened up and looked across the pavement at me.

'Going out?' he said.

He shouted it rather, because there was some distance between us. 'Where are you off to?'

I did not reply. I stepped back in the porch and put the door on its chain.

'Where?'

He opened the gate and came up the path towards me and yet I experienced nothing more than annoyance.

'It can wait,' I said. I stood with the door and chain between us, that was all I imposed. 'There's no hurry. Another day will do as well. It might be too late, anyway. A lot's happened for one day.'

'I'll get him in, then?' He nodded back to the car. 'I'll bring Tim indoors. OK?'

'Why?' I said. He stared.

'Because he can't be left in the car, of course.'

'No?' I leaned against the door jamb as if these were normal conditions, as if we were having a rational discussion.

'No,' he repeated. 'He can't. I'll get him.'

I did not answer. Instead I called over my shoulder, 'It's all right, Anna, I'm not going after all.'

I watched him put the carry-cot and transporter together and push them up the path to stand in front of me. Then I pushed the door further shut.

'Look,' he said, and adjusted the brake. It was on a flat path between a closed gate and a solid house but he was not irresponsible enough to leave the cot unsecured. 'Open the door. He must need feeding. I can't leave him here.'

'Leave him where you like,' I answered and he came nearer then, he walked round the cot. We were very close. 'You got him out,' I said. 'It's nothing to do with me. Do what you like with him.'

He placed his hand on the hood.

'I see. It's nothing to do with him, but you'll make him suffer for it. Whatever you're going through, someone else has to bear the brunt as well. You've every right to be angry,' he said. 'In your book you've every right in the world. But even you ought to be able to direct it against those who deserve it.'

'So who does?' I asked.

He turned away.

'If you want me to go, I will. I'll clear off and then you can take him indoors. He's waited long enough. You ought to see to him. It must be time he was fed again.'

'You stay there,' I said immediately. 'You're not coming and telling me what to do, interfering and then running off—'

'Barbara,' and he was still reasonable. 'We'll talk if you want. I'll go if you want, it's your decision. All I'm asking is for you not to use him like this. It's not his fault. He isn't involved.'

'Not involved?' I asked. 'I don't quite see that. I don't think that's quite right. Imagine,' and I nodded at the logic, 'imagine if your father had given you a half-sister, you'd feel involved, wouldn't you? Of course, he doesn't realise that, you're right there, but if we look at it theoretically, he does have a right to involvement. You should remember that, you shouldn't ignore his rights because he's not able to voice them.'

'I'm going. It's better. I'll ring you later on.' He turned away.

316

'If you do,' I said immediately, 'I'll leave him out here all night. You can go, but don't forget what that means. You've made him stay outdoors. And if you tell anyone, if you get the police or a doctor, other people to come and see him, I'll tell them what you've done.'

'Let me in,' he said, not immediately, but after he had thought about it. 'Let me in, too, then. If that's what it's about. If revenge is what you're after you've got something to answer for as well. You're not entirely innocent. Are you?' he asked.

I heard a noise behind me.

'Where are you, what are you doing?' Anna called.

I slid the chain away and let the door swing open. I did not watch, I hung up my coat and went back into the kitchen without seeing him enter.

We did not look at one another then or any other day he stayed. For that time we pretended we knew who we were talking to sightless. If we had seen, if in abuse and torment and deceit we had recognised the other person, we would have been undone; we would have experienced such grief and love and waste that there would have been no revenge to make loss bearable.

He pretended there was no such thing as bereavement and I connived. Quite deliberately I kept it from myself that in every other moment we unwrote history, that every exchange was larded with betrayal. From the moment I let him in I should have known what he would do; from the first moment of observation I should have realised that I had no immunity to him. I should have known his strength and weaponry.

When I let him in we circled in preparation, we said nothing, hung up coats, boiled kettles, found chairs, exchanged tasks across the table like knives. All I saw around me was a bedroom; it was full of caressing. I could not take my eyes off his hands. I watched while he peeled an orange, minutely dissecting pith and fruit, succulence and waste. He fed the slices to Anna's lips and a nail grazed her chin, and it was not penetration that I visualised but their fingers and faces.

He sat at the table, he walked the room, he came nowhere near me and I wanted that adulterous touch, I shivered with wanting to wrench it to my possession, substitute my body for where hers had been. I wanted them dead in embracing, I wiped it out, I yearned for it, I was beyond control with its impossibility.

'Tell me why. Why?' I said. I steadied my hand to pour Anna's milk. 'Tell me,' I meant, 'tell me you and Laura hasn't happened.'

'Not now.' He sounded quite reasonable. 'I can't talk with them here. Leave it until they're in bed.'

'No,' I said. 'Now. You don't care about them. They aren't your first concern. They can listen too.'

He shook his head.

'Don't play games,' he said. 'Don't pretend. You provoke. That's what you were doing out there, that's what you're doing now. You provoke and then say I've no right to react.'

'Ah,' I said, 'was that what it was? Was that what Laura was about? You were provoked. Laura was a reaction. Fucking her, fucking your sister-in-law, is that what it's called, a reaction?' Yet the words did not make it real.

He turned his back and went and stood by the door.

'I told you to stop. I said, leave it until they've gone to bed.'

'I shouldn't be asking,' I said, 'is that what you mean? I should pretend it's unmentionable, act as if it's too painful to discuss.'

He shrugged.

'I don't care,' he answered. 'I don't care what you make of it. It doesn't bother me any more.'

I did not move, I kept hold of my desire to keep him in the room and I stayed still.

'Not now,' Anna said, she tried to imitate his voice, and then I stood and walked as if I would break, as if I was negotiating cracking ice. I went and sat down at the table a little way away from her. I looked at the butter and cups and my neat folded hands and then I leaned across and took her empty mug. She had hardly eaten anything. She had moved her fork around, her plate looked no different from when I had filled it.

'Finished?' I asked. When she nodded I said, 'Give it to Dad. He'll wash up. I'll get you ready for bed. Is that all right?'

Sideways, I could glimpse that although he did not answer he took off his jacket. As he rolled up his sleeves I wanted to stare, I wanted to pore over every inch of flesh he revealed.

'You help Daddy,' I said to Anna. 'You take everything over to the sink, that'll be a great help.'

In my mind's eye I saw her stand and lift the plate to hand to him at the sink, but I did not let that happen. Instead I reached out and took it from her. I balanced it on the palm of my hand. When he looked round that was what he saw.

'I've changed my mind,' I said. 'I want you to go, after all. I don't want you here. I don't need you to wash up. It's ridiculous. Go.'

'Stop it,' he said. 'Put that down.'

'No,' I said. 'Go. I don't want you, I won't have you.'

I stood up, I was still balancing the plate and, of course, I threw it, but that was a blind, that was a distraction to take his mind away from the weight of me, so that when I jumped he was knocked sideways, he stumbled and fell against the table, he righted himself on the sink, he had only one hand with which to fend me off and I had both to tear at him, to dig into his cheeks, find bone to drag out from under his flesh. I pulled, all the strength I had went into tugging, trying to drag his head level with my teeth, I could see his mouth moving as I did it, he was muttering, we were both silent, that was the only noise and then it was over. Upright, pushing, I stood no chance against him, he had my hands quite tight and he twisted. It did not look as if that was what he was doing. He turned me round with my back to him, it looked as if he was making me secure, but he pulled unnecessarily. He hurt to prove his point. I would have killed then, I would have mutilated for that sly supremacy.

'Don't cry,' I said instead, 'don't cry Anna. I got too angry but you mustn't cry, it's not to do with you. Let go,' I said to him.

'Is that it?' he asked. 'You'll stop now?' I could understand torture quite well, agony in return for humiliation. 'You'll stop,' he repeated.

He made me nod agreement, but probably he could not have held me longer, anyway, because I had begun to shake. It was involuntary, it was not a hidden bid for clemency; I would have avoided it if I could. Even when he let go the spasms did not go away.

'You'd better go upstairs,' he said, but I measured the distance between us and I crouched, I bent as low as a child and shifted from foot to foot, flexing my hands as if I would lunge. It was as if I was staked, that the pain I felt through every part of me was a solid body to lean on. For a moment I was full of strength and then I could not go on. There was nothing but pain and the impossibility of containing it and I began to cry. I could hear howling, which came nowhere near my feeling, but it came close for him. It came too close for him and he pushed me down, he tried to muffle me with force and solicitude. None of it did any good. He put his hands over my mouth, rocked me against his chest, and in the end held my shoulders with one arm and poured brandy into a glass with the other. He put it into my hand and then he put me aside.

'Drink that,' he said. 'Sit down and be quiet. I'll see to the children. Stay where you are. I'll put them to bed.'

After a time I followed him. I looked to make sure Anna was asleep and then I went into our room. He was sitting on the bed; he could have been waiting for me. I took the chair by the window. I put my glass safe on the floor and looked out into the garden.

'I'll go,' he said, 'if that's what you want. If you really want me to, I'll leave.' He chose his moment well; I could not make any choice. In that room all I had was yearning. 'But we'll get one thing straight first.' He nodded firmly. 'That scene mustn't happen again. Whatever's gone on. Anna and Tim don't deserve to be put through misery. They don't deserve pain for the mess we've made.'

'I could agree with that,' I said. It was nice to have the glass of brandy to pick up, it nestled and was friendly in my hand. 'But I didn't cause it. I don't deny that I had hysterics, but I had a reason. I had quite a good reason—'

I stopped, I did not state it again, I did not want to remember what he had done. Later, later on when anger had reconstituted me I would look at the cause, but at the moment I wanted to forget.

'No,' he said. 'It's not as simple as that. I think that you did it intentionally. You used Anna and Tim for your benefit. Whatever you were feeling, however I accept my part in what you were feeling, you had no right to make them witnesses. Can't you understand that?'

I sat back as though I was considering.

'I could explain to them,' I offered. 'I could tell them why I screamed. Not now, Anna's too young to understand, and he never will. But later, when it shows she's badly affected by it, when it's obvious that that one outburst wiped out five years of lovingness, then I could tell her why I did it. That might help. It seems odd,' I added, 'how it's become such a focus. How my behaviour matters so much more than anything you've done.'

'They're one and the same,' he said, and leaned across the room to me, as though he wanted to make things plain. 'That one outburst was the expression of a great deal more. Covering up all these

years has had its effect on all of us. It might not be such a bad thing
to bring it out in the open, it might do less harm to be open about it.
I think we should. We can't separate our responsibilities. We've
both contributed.'

I shook my head. I could not listen, I could not argue; it hurt my
throat, all over it hurt, but most in my throat to try and speak. I got
up and went to the bed, I wanted to fall on it. He stood up, he
almost leapt away and started to walk across the room. He did not
look round at me, he seemed quite content to pace up and down. He
was ruminative, not troubled. I lay down, that was all I could
manage.

'Did you do it in here? In this?' I asked. I hit the bedcover.

'What difference would it make?' he asked. 'No, if that's what
matters, not there. But I don't see that where and when affects
anything. It's why it happened and what happens next.'

'No,' I said, pulling the duvet to cover me. 'Not now. What
happens now is that you go. I want to sleep. I won't sleep with you
here.' I thought he took no notice. 'Go,' I said.

He looked past me at his pyjamas and as though I had not spoken,
as though it was an eccentric whim, he picked them up and took his
dressing gown off the door.

'I'll be in Anna's room,' he said.

When I woke in the night I hung onto sleep in terror, but in the
morning it lessened, and after that time was not hard to get through.
As soon as I woke I knew nothing existed except turmoil; there
would be no opportunity to succumb to grief. Time was to be taken
up with something quite different. It was a dangerous feeling, I had
to be on my guard. I had to be watchful for myself because the
company had changed, he had altered from the man I had spent
years of my life with to an adversary. I had difficulty in remembering the original cause, that was the trouble; whenever I tried to
pinpoint it I became confused. Laura, the baby, they escaped me, it
was only when I saw him that I remembered to be angry.

'Tea? Coffee?' I asked when he came downstairs, as though his
placement in Anna's room made him a visitor with unpredictable
tastes, or as though we had started a holiday where circumstances
dictated a change of habits. When he gulped water at the sink and
did not answer, when he sat and waited to be served, I did not ask
again. He was not my concern.

321

'Did Anna wake you?' I asked. 'She was up early. And he cried, did you hear that? We were all up early. You're late.'

'Do you hear me?' I meant, because he was mute as he raised his cup, and it was not my place to coax.

'We've finished breakfast,' I said, 'there's bread if you want it.'

He lifted his cup again and without looking put out an arm to draw Anna beside him.

'Get your shoes,' he said. 'Find your things, I'll take you to the nursery. We'll walk, there's lots of time, we won't be late.' She drained her milk and let him hug her. 'You'll be all right,' he told her, as though any doubt concerning that was nothing to do with him.

I leant across to put the butter and marmalade back into the cupboard and take his cup away.

'I hadn't finished,' he said. I shrugged.

'It's ten to. Go on, Anna, it's time.'

'It's a five-minute walk,' he said. I turned back to Anna.

'Get your coat, or your blue jacket, you can choose.' She stood between us.

He pushed his chair away from the empty table, keeping his back to me; he went and took his coat off the door. He wound his scarf about him with care, covering his mouth up as though it was foggy and he did not trust it out in the open. He took as long to do those things as Anna did to go up and downstairs.

'Here,' I said.

One by one she put her shoes forward to be tied, her coat to be buttoned, her bag to be fastened. He held out both his hands to her.

'I'll be back,' he said. 'I'm not working. I've decided to have time off. I'll be back after I've dropped her. I'll be ten minutes.'

When he came I sat down at the table with the baby on my lap.

'Did it last long?' I asked. Feeding, sitting with furniture between us, I could not be intending another attack. 'You and Laura? Or was it just a brief encounter?'

'It's not important,' he said from the door, 'it's not a relevant question. When and where and how long aren't what matter.'

'To her they do,' I said. 'Since she got pregnant they're not irrelevant at all to her. What you mean,' I said, 'is that it's private. The meetings, the wondering, anticipation, weighing it up, they just belong to you. Did you,' I asked, 'decide? Was there ever a moment's doubt? Or was it all a foregone conclusion? What made you? What did she do, what was it that happened between you?' I sounded no more than curious, idly intrigued by motivation. 'Or is it all too painful? Is that what you want me to think?'

He shook his head.

'We don't need to discuss Laura,' he said, 'it's what happened between us, that's what's important. You don't need to think about her.'

I held onto the table. It was more difficult to be calm, there were pictures I was receiving, smiles between them, hands, the first touching, all the manoeuvrings before flesh on flesh.

'I do,' I said. 'I don't completely grasp it yet. I've got to talk about it. I still need to believe you've done that.'

'You can believe what you like.' He came and stood nearer to me. 'I've got no control over that. All I'm saying is that you're mistaken. You don't listen. It's what's happened between us, that's what I told you. Try and see what happened there.'

'Him,' I said, and pointed to where he lay dribbling. 'That's what happened. That was where it began.'

'Not him,' he said. 'You. Not just how you've been with him but how you've been with everyone. Shut in. Closed off. You're private, your feelings are private, you're the only one you allow near. Laura was a consequence. We've got to examine the cause.'

'I don't believe you,' I said. 'Liar. I won't even listen to that, that's abuse. You did it, you and her and she's got that baby, hers, yours. It's nothing to do with how I am, it wasn't because of me. You,' I said, 'you and Laura fucking, Laura having a baby, there aren't excuses—'

He was close enough to stand over me and reach down.

'Give him to me,' he said. 'I asked you not to do this. I asked you not to make scenes in front of Anna and Tim.'

I stared.

'Tim? Look,' I lifted him off my lap and he did not move, he did not care which of us held him. 'He's calm,' I said. 'He hasn't got the least idea, he'll never have the least idea. Have him, here, he's all yours,' and Graham took him in his arms and cradled him. 'Tell me,' I said, trying to stand up, 'tell me where I've got it wrong. I'm finding it difficult. You sleep with her, she's had a baby; that's not important, that's not up for discussion. You can do that and say it's something else that matters, something between us I should be giving my attention to. It's this I'm asking about, you and her, what I'm supposed to make of this.'

'That's your choice,' he answered. 'I'll take him upstairs.' He bent his head so that their faces touched. 'I think that's best.'

They stayed there together, and I did not hear crying or walking; he must have sat for hours, nursing. All the rest of the morning it was silent.

When Geraldine brought Anna home he came downstairs and had to open tins and cook food because I would not. He touched Anna; every time he came by her chair he paused for a hug. I heard her small exclamations and smiled to myself. It amused me to think he believed that would achieve something, that I had wasted years in continuous nurturing when it was that easy. He brought the baby down, to play with, stimulate, he must have thought. I smiled at that, too, I particularly relished every moment of that disappointment. I wanted to ask if he thought the worst was over, if he imagined I was assessing the points at which I had failed. Every time he came near me I shook.

'You wait,' I wanted to mock as he offered Anna treats of affection, 'wait and see,' but I had nothing to threaten him with. He loomed above me, he followed, stood in front of me, he stepped in and out of my way with deliberation.

'Mind,' he said as I moved, interposing and disappearing, suiting himself when he spoke.

'Sit down,' he said when I was picking up the toys Anna had left on the floor. 'I want to talk.'

I locked the lorry and books more firmly under my arms.

'We're going out now. To the park,' I said.

He stroked Anna's cheek.

'Would you like to do that?' he asked, as though it was his place to offer an alternative. 'Suppose I took you? Suppose we went to the playground and I took you on the swings.' He turned to me. 'You could rest. You could have the afternoon off.'

'I'm not tired,' I answered.

He nodded as if that made for an amicable solution.

'We'll all go,' he said, and we did, a family outing. I pushed the pram and held Anna's hand.

324

'Go on,' I said to her when we had crossed the main road.

She ran ahead. Behind her we walked slowly, we could have been idly dawdling, heads bent in discussion over whether to get a baby-sitter, who to invite for supper.

'Tell me something,' I said.

'I have,' he answered, 'but you don't take any notice.'

'Why didn't you talk to me? If you're telling the truth and she didn't matter, why didn't you try?'

'I did,' he said. 'You didn't listen. I wanted you to realise, I wanted you to be able to alter. I was waiting.'

'You mean you waited too long? You deserve a reward for patience? Liar,' I said. 'You never tried.'

He pulled at my arm. 'Liar. You never let me.'

'Didn't she want you?' I asked. 'Is that why you've stayed for me to find out what happened? Is that why you're lying about it, so that you can stay here?'

'You don't understand,' he said. 'You still won't try.'

'Was it because you thought she'd be better?' I asked. I still could not quite recall what I referred to; when I came close to that image it eluded me. 'Better at sex. Was that it?' I was astonished, I could not believe that I could ask the worst so soon and so easily, but I did not wait for an answer. 'And better at everything? Talking, being together? Or was it just a one-night stand, neither of you meant anything by it? Was it exciting? Like we used to be, was that what you wanted?' He stopped dead in front of me. 'Was that what you got out of it? Is that going back far enough, was that why it started? Did you miss what we used to be like together?'

'Like we used to be?' he repeated. 'When? When we met? You don't know what you're talking about. When I first met you I thought you were icy cold, that's how we were together. I thought that you needed thawing, that I could persuade you to be open. But I couldn't,' and he looked down the road, at Anna. We were within sight of the playground; we could hear children shouting. 'Laura was nothing like that. With you I thought it was a question of confidence, that providing I gave enough reassurance I'd compensate for your insecurity. I told you, "I love you." I said that every day at Exeter, and when I left I sent letters. I visited every week and every time I had to start from scratch. It was as though we'd never met before. Every time I had to persuade you I wasn't set on perfection and you wouldn't ever see the contradiction. What it was,' he said, although I didn't ask, 'was that you wanted it both ways. I was supposed to say I didn't want perfection but that you embodied it. With her none of those things mattered.' I went on walking as though it was important to reach the park gates very soon. 'I listened,' he said. 'When I met you I listened to every word you said. I answered and none of it made any difference. When you talked about your parents I wanted you to see it wouldn't have hurt you to act differently, to try and see outside Audrey's regime, but you wouldn't try. At fourteen you gave up, as if you were maimed for life. You didn't have to be, you didn't have to follow in her footsteps. But you've never admitted that. You've pretended, you always have, and we've never got any further.' I watched Anna go through the gates towards the swings; she would find the one she wanted and wait for me to push her. 'It doesn't work,' he said. 'It didn't ever work, but I wouldn't admit it. It wasn't all bad, but it wasn't worth that effort. All those stories we told one another. Going to work abroad, going to live abroad, buying a van, roughing it. You never meant it. You knew in the long run you only had to say, "No, I want a house," and that'd be the end of it.'

'Don't lie,' I said, 'don't make it up. It was your money, you agreed.'

'I didn't have a choice,' he said, 'you always made that perfectly plain. Every decision had to have your approval or life would be unbearable. You only had to cast one doubt and I abandoned an idea. You put it differently; you made it seem as if you possessed a divine light of revelation as to how we should spend our lives, as if you alone knew the appropriate moment to buy a house, have children, renovate the kitchen, change a job. It was all up to you. I couldn't argue. I couldn't break into you.'

'You could,' I said. 'You could have tried. You could have made your stand.'

'Opposition to you,' he said, 'was the equivalent of annihilation. No one can deal with inflicting that.'

'You wanted me in the beginning,' I said. I slowed down because Anna had gone to the horse and she could rock herself on that. 'I wanted to get a job abroad and you said, "No, we'll get married." You made that choice. Don't lie, you remember that.'

'You'd have come back,' he said. 'I made a mistake. I thought you'd have gone and been so lonely, done so badly you'd have crept back and become even worse. More dependent, more frightened, more full of false bravado. I thought I could save you from yourself,

326

give you confidence, leave all that bragging, all the proving behind. I got it wrong. You've got what you want now, though,' he said.

I watched as Anna climbed onto the seat, held tight to the handle and began to kick as though the wooden animal was real.

'What's that?' I asked.

'Distance.' He followed my eyes but he did not see the same thing. 'Further away than your mother, even. You're barely human any more. Untouchable. Bear that in mind,' he said. 'Try and remember that when you're looking at Tim, think about that influence. It might not be all genetics, pre-natal; heredity can have an influence too.'

I walked away from him after that. I helped Anna on and off all the toys she wanted. I was as closed away as that child in the pram, smiling, nodding at nothing.

'Let's go home to tea,' I said. No one argued, but when I had spread butter on bread and boiled eggs, I could not eat. I would gag on every mouthful and he was the one who should choke.

'I'm not hungry,' I said. 'I'm cold, I'll have a rest now. Leave me. Don't come near.'

I was upstairs before he said anything; I was undressed and in bed before he called, and it was loud, he could have frightened Anna. But he did not care, he had to be heard.

'It's changed,' he said. 'We don't talk when you want, keep silence because you say so, that's over. I've finished with letting you be, I trusted you not to take advantage of that, but you've used, warped it for power. I'm telling you where I want the blame.'

His voice was lower and nearer, halfway along the landing I judged. I slid out of bed, took hold of the armchair, pulled it over to the door and wedged it against the handle.

'Why can't you listen?' he said. He was outside the door. He turned the handle and nothing happened; he must have felt the weight.

'You don't try,' he said. 'Nothing alters you. Please, I want you to see why it's happened. You can't spend the rest of your life shut away. Can you hear?' he said quietly, like a whisper, except it echoed.

'Not now,' I answered. It sounded as though I was asking indulgence for a temporary indisposition. 'Leave it for now. I need to sleep now, leave it. I'll talk to you tomorrow, I promise.'

Whether or not he believed me, after that he went away and I lay still and waited.

In the night I could have given up. I woke blanketed in dread because I could not see what would come out of it; I could not go through this without violence. Words had no connection with what we wanted to do to one another, they were no more than a device. We should have had our tongues tied, nailed up, I thought, and be made to battle with picks and swords; that would be more honest. Whenever I closed my eyes I saw us feinting with shields, locked and armoured on the kitchen floor. But I knew he would not fight, stabbing would not be as satisfactory a hurt as he wanted; he could inflict worse.

'I've been thinking how it's been,' he'd said. 'You're barely human any more. Remember that. Look at him and remember that.'

I realised that all evening I had not remembered him, I had left him unfed while I hid away. So I got out of bed, quietly so that I could not be heard anywhere else in the house, and without looking in his cot I took him out. I laid him on our bed and thought of obscenities and smiled at him. They were not so difficult, I could learn them too, words instead of stabbing.

'Sweetie,' I lied. 'Little pickle.'

I bent and picked him up and swung him to and fro in front of me, I let him rise and fall in my arms.

'Who's a good boy now? Who's the best his mummy ever had? Who's a pretty boy?'

I bent into him, questioning, searching for another hidden face, the fine lines that would show up under fleshiness, a narrowing, a swiftness that had been temporarily blurred.

'What does he want?' I asked him. 'Is he tired? Is he bored? Does he want walkies?'

I pushed him over my shoulder and went to his cupboard.

'Shall we go out, then? Make him warm for a little trip?'

I rummaged through the shelf carefully, looking hard until I found exactly what I wanted, a red and blue bonnet that had been Anna's. I fitted his head into it tightly; it squeezed him into a muscleless parody even of himself.

I found a jacket that I put on over his nightclothes, a navy cloth coat that looked strange over winceyette.

'He's a pretty pickle,' I whispered. 'He doesn't know if he's coming or going.' I picked up a blanket and wrapped it round him. 'Time to be off.'

As though he might cry out I put my hand over his mouth as I opened the bedroom door; as though he needed amusing into silence I made faces at him all the way down the stairs.

'Hush-a-bye,' I said as I opened and closed the front door behind us. 'Daddy's asleep, Daddy's in big sister's room. No noise,' I said as I unlocked the car door and fitted him into Anna's seat. 'Belt up, keep him safe, be a good quiet boy now.'

As I drove I sang, I turned on the radio but it was too late for any music and so I made some; I found tunes that had lodged away for years, croonings I would never have used on Anna. I looked back over my shoulder as I caught phrases of love and I laughed because he was not hearing them.

'We used to do this with your sister,' I told him as I pulled up at a red light, 'your daddy and me. "Good girl, Anna," we'd say, and when she was fast asleep we'd tiptoe back and put her back to bed. What a noisy girl she was.

'Whose's a quiet boy?' I asked him. I could have heard the noise of his dribbling if I had not accelerated, there was nothing else to hear.

'Nearly there,' I said several times. It seemed to take longer than it had at Christmas, although the roads were just as empty. I was still careful.

'Mind how we go,' I said, and when I turned the corner into her road I turned off the engine and let the car glide to an empty place outside her house.

'No fuss and bother now,' I said to him, and I reached into the back seat. I extracted him firmly and put my hand over his mouth again.

The road was quite clear, there were no stones anywhere. There were no lights anywhere from houses to see by; it would be useless going into gardens and rummaging about in the dark for pebbles or rocks, trespassing, waiting for arrest with him clutched to me.

'This'll do,' I said, and took off my shoe. 'This'll do the trick.'

I hopped along the pavement until I was outside her gate. I balanced him against my hip, and with the shoe in my other hand I took aim.

'Laura,' I shouted. I timed it exactly, I threw just as I called, and although it did not break the window it hit hard against the glass.

'Laura,' I yelled again. 'Come on.' I made my voice as loud as it would go. I thought she must still be at the hospital, I thought neighbours would appear and tell me to go away.

'Laura,' I tried again. That time it sounded more like a scream, and she looked out of the window.

'Come down,' I called. 'I've come to see you. We've got things to say to one another.'

'Don't,' she said when we were in her room. She wrapped her dressing gown tightly round her for protection, standing with her back to the wall. I wondered if she would stretch out her arms to protect all her innocent trappings, all the guiltless books and furniture I had come to attack. 'Whatever you've come for, don't. Please.' She turned to face me so that I could see the shadows and tears on her face. 'I can't take it, I can't take it or take it in. All I can think about is Cathy.'

'I haven't come to do anything,' I said, 'only to see you. To talk. Just words.' I looked to where I held him at arm's length. 'Where can he go?' I said. 'I can't hold him forever. Let me put him down. On here?' I pointed to her bed, and the scarlet spread that had covered them. 'Can I put him here, that'd do? Or there?' I pointed to Cathy's cot. 'That's the obvious place, isn't it?'

She flinched and shook her head.

'Don't look like that,' I said. 'He's not infectious. It's not a contagious disease. He can't pass it on.' I reached over the side of the cot and rearranged the pillows. 'He'll like it in there, won't you?' I nuzzled his mouth as though to quieten any denial. 'He'll have a lovely time in her bed.'

'No,' she said, 'don't. Take him out. Stay a minute if you like but then you'll have to go. I can't have you here—'

'Why not?' I asked. 'You haven't got anyone else. Cathy's in hospital, Graham's asleep, there's only you and me left to talk. Except for him, of course, but he'll keep quiet.'

'Take him out,' she said. 'Take him out of her cot. It's creepy.'

'Where then?' I asked. 'Your bed, is that better?' I dropped, almost threw him onto it, and sat down beside him and reached up for her arm. 'You, too,' I said. 'You sit here as well.'

She sank down, rubbed her eyes and hid her face.

'What is it? What do you want? Why are you here?'

'Why are you?' I asked back. 'I'm surprised to find you're not at the hospital. Why don't you stay with Cathy? Why don't you stay in

330

the ward, to make sure she's all right? Tell me,' I said, not unkindly, because I knew the answer.

'I'm frightened. Ever since Mercy I've been frightened of hospitals. This is the worst time of all. I feel awful but I can't stay.'

I covered my mouth to hide my smile.

'Poor thing. Don't be frightened,' I said. 'Just listen. Just talk to me. Just tell me. You,' and I pointed at her, 'what did you and Graham talk about? You tell me that and I'll tell you what I know. Fair's fair.'

She turned away. 'There's nothing I can tell you, it was nothing to do with you. It was just him and me.'

I moved nearer to her so we were very close on the bed.

'No,' I said. 'For you it was only to do with me. Whatever he said, whatever he did, he was nothing. It was you and me.

'I know,' I said. 'He's said you were nothing. I mean it, I wouldn't come otherwise; I'd be frightened of what I'd hear. I wouldn't come and ask you if I might not like it. If I might hear about love. You must have said something.' I shook her. 'What did you think up that would interest him? What did you try?

'All right,' I said, when she was silent. 'I'll tell you. He lay there and he pretended. He told you stories, and he tried to forget. He used you to pretend it hadn't happened. He used you to put that' – and I nodded at the baby – 'out of his mind. He put a baby inside you to stop thinking about this one. What did you tell him? That it didn't matter? That it was love? Lying here,' and I squeezed harder to make her take notice, 'did you think he was thinking about you? Stroking and fucking, did you believe that? "Come away with me," did he say? "I don't talk to Barbara," did he say? But, "I fuck her," did he tell you that? "Laura, Laura."' Although I did not do it well, it could be taken as an imitation of his voice. 'Did he say your name, did he say, "Love, I can't leave you?" Did he walk round this room as if he would never go?'

I looked, I fixed on each corner and each object in the room as if I could nail him to them, fix him for ever. She tried to move but I held on, I would be pulled flat across the bed before she got out of my grasp.

'You,' I said. 'I can see you, I can see both of you. This room isn't yours, it's wide open for me too. I can see you here and everything of what it was like, but that's not all I want to see, what I want to watch. What I'd most like is seeing you like you watched Mercy. I want to see you in real fear.'

She pulled then, she wanted to escape.

'I can,' I said, and I let her go so fast she almost toppled backwards, 'I can tell you what I came for. You wait until you hear that.'

She sat up.

'Hear what? That Graham didn't want Cathy? That's not news. Cathy's mine, she's nothing to do with him. You can have Graham—'

I started to smile.

'Cathy,' I said, 'that's the pity of it. Poor little thing. Just like my poor baby. Poor Laura, too.'

Then she grabbed me, she was off the bed and hauling at my shoulders, she was screaming, 'Stop it, liar.' I let myself be pulled, I thought we could tumble together on the floor.

'There's nothing wrong with Cathy, there's nothing wrong, you're making it up.'

I smiled, I nodded.

'Is that what they told you? It's probably for the best, then.'

She shouted in my face, 'You're mad, you're lying, there's nothing wrong.'

I looked hard at her.

'They send you away at nights,' I said. 'The doctor doesn't talk to you. I saw him. He was alone and he talked to me, he said, "Unbalanced," and I thought he meant you. But I was wrong, it was her he was talking about. Haven't they told you yet? Haven't they said what might happen? She's different,' I said, 'altered. You must have noticed. She won't ever be the same again. You'll have to watch, all the time you'll have to keep looking at her and wondering when it will show. "Unbalanced," he said, and he meant it. "She'll have to be watched," he told me. "We can't say that to her mother yet, but she'll have to face it sooner or later." I'm just telling you,' I said and she stood up.

'Take him,' and she pointed at the baby, 'take him and get out of it. I don't believe a word you're saying. I've seen her X-rays, I've talked to the consultant every day. He'd have told me, I don't have to listen to anything you're saying. Go on, pick him up, get in your car and go, we've got nothing to say to one another.'

'Nothing that you want to listen to.' I slid myself across the bed. 'Graham knows. I came to tell you. If you don't believe me, ask him.'

She stood in front of me, she put herself in my way.

'Go on,' I said. 'Get him to tell you. Make him admit it, twice, two children gone wrong, see what he says.' I picked up the baby.

'But he doesn't complain, he calls this one his best boy. But he should tell you the truth, you ought to know.'

'Get out,' she said, wrapping her arms round herself. 'I don't want you here.'

'We're on our way,' and I tightened the bonnet on his head, as though he might have wriggled it loose. 'Look.' I pushed him at her as she stood there, rigid, and because the strings of the hat were very tight he looked distorted to someone else's eyes too, I could see that in the way she turned away. 'Who does he remind you of? Who will Cathy look like?'

I picked up one creased fist and let it flop backwards and forwards. I waved it at her until she would not look any more, until I was out of her door.

'We won't tell anyone,' I said to him as he slept in the car and I drove back. 'That was our little jaunt. Yours and mine.' When we went in the house was still quiet. I had hardly been gone from it; there was nothing to show what I had done.

In the morning I asked Anna, 'Did you hear anything in the night?'

'No,' she said. 'Daddy slept in my bunk again. Will he always now?'

I half-nodded and she dipped and lifted her spoon, considered her cornflakes.

'Laura did, too,' she said and she frowned. 'Once. A long time ago when you were at the hospital.'

I put my hands round the teapot as if warmth would help because the words clung, they rang in my ears as I heard Graham coming downstairs.

'Did she?' I asked. 'Are you sure? Why don't you ask Daddy? Make quite sure.'

He came in, buttoning his cuffs, rubbing his eyes and she did. She phrased it carefully, it was unambiguous and he looked from her to me, he did not answer.

'Don't you remember?' I asked. 'Have you forgotten already? Was it that insignificant? What do you remember?' I asked as he walked past me and sat beside Anna. 'Come on.' I jogged his shoulder, it could have been accidental except for the care we took not to touch one another. 'Tell us what you do remember. There must be something. Out of all those weeks, months, all the years beforehand, something must have inspired you.'

333

He nodded and folded his arms.

'You're right. When we first lived in London. When you were teaching and we used to meet her in a pub, I looked forward to that more than almost anything. That prospect would keep me going all day at school, the idea of getting on a train to Tottenham Court Road and knowing she'd be at the other end. Her enthusiasm. It was like a breath of fresh air, she'd try anything. She didn't always consider what she had to lose. She didn't work everything out before she did it, she was spontaneous. She wasn't looking for retribution. She laughed a lot,' he said, loudly, as though I had tried to interrupt. 'I could spend evening after evening trying to work out how to bring you back from despair, how to convince you that perfection in all things wasn't a necessary condition of happiness, and she'd stuff her face with crisps and giggle at failing her driving test again.'

'She didn't notice you,' I said. 'You could have been anyone. Any man did for her then. Did she tell you how many, did she let you count up? You should have said you fancied her.' I moved Anna's bowl and passed her toast. 'She wouldn't have minded me being first, not if she was desperate. She's never been fussy. But she wasn't that desperate in those days, she might have said no, you were too dull, she might not have fancied you. But that wasn't what happened, was it?'

I looked over the table, I tried to lift the teapot but it spilt, it shook heavily because I remembered. I saw her room again, I saw them floundering together, I heard the whispers, I watched her face.

'Are you glad?' I asked. 'Was it worth it? Go on, you've said everything else. It was good and you miss it, and you want her back. I was lying and looking at that boy, watching him in a cot next to me, dribbling, foolish, and you escaped. You and she, you and her—' I was leaning so far across the table he grasped my arm.

'Stop,' he said. 'Stop this. You promised . . .' He turned his head towards Anna. 'They don't have anything to do with this.'

'She does.' I pointed at Anna. 'She told me. What is it she shouldn't know about? And him, don't say he doesn't come into it. Don't say that without him it would still have happened. Where did Anna come into it that night? What did you stop her ears with, what did you tell her? Where did you put her? What about the morning, down here, what went on then?'

'Shut up,' he said. 'You're making it up. You don't know what

334

you're talking about. Why don't you look at what matters, what's really happened? Look at all this, here, us; look at what you've made of this. Tim. Tim,' he repeated, 'that's what I'm talking about. Look at what you've done there. What's supposed to happen to him when you've made him into a monster? You've gone mad with him' – I nodded because he put it so plainly – 'and you've made it impossible for anyone else to be sane. You've shut him even further away than you. You've made him a judgement on you and you won't let anyone else have any say in it. You've captured him, you've taken advantage. You want him worse than you are. You appal me,' he said. 'What you've done is disgusting. You've maimed; nothing I've done is as bad as that. You'd rather he was dead. Because he doesn't live up to your standards you wish you'd killed him, don't you?'

He waited in vain for me to deny it.

'Get out,' he said, 'go away. You're unfit, you're not fit to be with anyone. Go on, get out. Stop it.'

All I had done was stand.

'I shouldn't have said that. I should have waited. I should have remembered.' He leaned across the table. 'Come on, Anna. We'd better get going. You don't want to be late.'

She slid away and went upstairs and he stood, too, he went to look out of the window at the day outside.

'I'll wait,' I said, 'and you wait. We'll talk about fitness. What you consider to be right and what you've done. We'll talk about that.'

He looked at his watch as though he wanted to arrange an appropriate time.

'All right,' he said. 'When I come back from taking Anna. Is Geraldine collecting her?'

I did not answer, I did not see why he needed to know that.

'Will she bring Anna back here?' he turned round. 'Or do you want me to do that?'

'You?' I asked. 'You do what you want. You go. You go and think, all the time you walk along the road, all the way there, all the way back you can think about explaining, about telling Anna what's happened. You can practise saying, "Cathy's more of a sister to you, Anna," because that's what's going to happen. When you come back, you can look damage in the face, too.'

He went and got his coat from the hall.

'Just a minute,' he said and ran upstairs. I heard his footsteps in our room, he was crossing to the corner where the cot was; yet he hardly paused, time for a glance, that was all. 'Anna, we're going now, come on, it's time,' he shouted. 'Goodbye,' he called, and neither of them came into the kitchen to say it to me.

'Goodbye,' I answered back.

As soon as they were gone I waited for him to come back. I bathed the baby and brought him down and fed him; this time I did not put him back in his cot, I walked about holding him. I went to and fro across the window because then I would see the first moment he turned into the street. I stood and sat and strode about, I had no idea how long, I could not let myself believe it was more than minutes. When my arms began to ache I still did not look at the clock, I put the baby down in his cot. I tucked him in with great care and then bent over each side in turn, stared from different angles. I took a chair and sat on it beside him, levelling my face to his to discover what images swam to him from where he lay. He half-moved, he attempted to flounder across the sheet to me. I stood up; I did not have to pick him up, there was something else I had to attend to.

'You,' I said, and before I made up the rest of the words I caught the sound of his dialling before the phone even rang. It did not surprise me at all to hear his voice. I was quite calm, only curious as to what delay had occurred, what excuse he would give for his late return.

'I'm at Laura's,' he said. 'You know that, don't you? You knew that was what I'd do? You knew there wasn't any other choice. Cathy's fine, they'll let her out of hospital. I'll let you know—' He stopped, it must have occurred to him that it was not of interest to me how she progressed. 'I took Anna,' he said, 'and I saw Geraldine. I checked, and she'll be bringing her back, there's no problem about that.'

'Why are you phoning?' I asked. 'What's happened? What are you doing, where are you going?'

'I'm staying here,' he said. 'I can't stay with you while we do that to one another. You don't give me any option. I'm trying to be constructive, we can't keep behaving in that way. At this stage, this is all I can think of. There isn't any alternative. I've tried, you know that, but it's in a vacuum, it doesn't have any effect. I've tried and

336

it's no good, and that's not the point any more. It's what happens next.'

'Surely not,' I said. 'After all you said? Is that talk all over and done with? Is that all there was to it?'

'We have to find what to do next,' he began, but I interrupted.

'Next?' I was not sure if I had grasped the point. 'You've gone,' I said, 'isn't that it? You're already there and I'm here. I'm in this place with Anna and him.'

'We'll talk about that,' he said quickly. 'Of course we'll have to discuss them, but we can't stay in the same place and do it, we've got to get away from one another.'

'You have,' I said, 'and that's why you've left. You've got away from me and you've got a different baby crying and a different little girl to look at. So that we can talk later on.'

He did not answer.

'It's a change,' I said.

'I wanted to tell you what I said to Anna,' he said. 'I decided that as far as she's concerned I'd be staying with a friend. I wanted to let you know what she thought was going on. I expect she'll ask who, why, how long, but at this stage I'd rather just leave it at that.'

'She'll recognise her,' I said, 'when you all meet. Unless she wears a mask, she'll see straight away who Laura is.'

'Barbara,' he said, 'I don't have a choice. I haven't worked it out yet. It's not possible to be anywhere else. That's not just my choice. Let's leave it at that, I'm ringing to let you know. I'll talk to Anna, I'll speak to her this afternoon or evening. I'll do that every day. There's nothing else either of us can do now, is there?'

'Is Laura there?' I asked. 'There too? In the room? Listening? Or have you shut her out, made her go downstairs to the lavatory? Is she pretending she can't hear, or is she sitting next to you? Is she laughing, is that what that noise is?'

'I'll go now,' he said. 'Tell Anna I'll speak to her later.'

'No,' I answered. 'I won't tell her anything. I won't let you anywhere near her, you're not having a chance to maim her, you're a monster, you're distorted, you've gone there, into that room with her again because of nothing except her, it's not what you say about us, it's her, that's what it is—'

'No,' he said. 'I've left you. That's what it is.'

I heard him put the phone down but I still shouted into it, because whether he listened or not I could see them standing together, I could be in that room with them.

337

'You,' she would have said with such wonder when he arrived, and put her hands either side of his face. 'What did you tell her? What did you say you were going to do?'

He would have closed her words back in her mouth, they would have stumbled, clinging, across the floor.

'It's nothing to do with her,' he would answer. 'It's us,' and she would rock him very gently, cradle his head against her. 'Tell me,' he would ask, 'tell me what's happened to you, what have you done, what have you thought about?'

'Don't,' she would say, and put him a little away from her.

'You're hurting, you're making my breasts hurt.'

He would touch, one finger would be distracted from torment to feel her nipple.

'All I feel, all I want to talk about is you. Nothing else is bearable,' he would say. 'What will you do to me?'

'Here,' she would say and he would look at her, their eyes matching as they undressed.

'What did you think about?' he would whisper; no thought would be further from him. 'All I feel is you, all that I want to talk about is you, nothing else is bearable.'

He would do it gently to pretend it only served as a function of comfort.

'Better?' she would ask and he would nod without hesitation, because anything was better than nothing. He would cross his legs on her bed, I could feel his weight beside me. 'What are you thinking?'

He would shake his head in answer.

'That you're the only one I can talk to.'

But then there would be no words, there would be none needed for that staring, that mesmerising into love.

'You.'

He would find every feature, every muscle, every nerve, he would stroke each single part until there was no division, and no end to sensation; she would want to weep with it, there would be nothing else.

'What will you do to me? What will happen?' she would ask.

I wanted to answer that.

I held the phone to try and tell her and it was only because of him, the sounds that were coming from his cot, that I put the receiver down. I went over to see, and then I remembered that this did not have to continue. I looked at him, flat and marooned and considered

the prospect of righting him, feeds and smiles. I realised I did not
have to stay watching; he did not have to remain in this house. I
could make it quite plain what my reasons were, I need leave no
doubt or guilt over that. I could put him away with those he
belonged to, I could go back to the point I had been trying to reach
from the very beginning, from months before, I could forget all of
his future. I could go back two days to him ready in the car outside,
I could write the note to Carmel Summers and in half an hour
deliver him to her. I too could deliver abandonment. It was not
exclusive to Graham, there was no reason why I should not find my
own dry satisfaction in his couplings. It was not even a difficult note
to write when I sat down; it was not as hard as the lines to Audrey
and Leslie had been, it was composed already, waiting for the right
moment.

Dear Carmel,
    Tim Browne is yours to be adopted. He has no place here,
he is not possible to live with, I am not able to look after him.
It should have happened when I first asked, that would have
avoided a lot of knowledge, but this is not too late. No one
needs to be consulted, and only I am here. Graham is with his
other child, my sister's. There is no reason for this baby to go
on staying with me.

I signed my name, sealed it in an envelope and then dressed him. I
dressed him like a parcel, protective layers against cold or bumping.
I was clumsy, it took a long time, and I tried not to look at him. I
would not change my mind but I wanted no contact with him; there
was no reason for anything but separation, there never had been any
other state.

When he was zipped and buttoned I fitted him in the carry-cot
and locked him tight under the cover. He touched every perimeter
of it now. It was heavy, a cumbersome package. When I lifted it into
the hall I had to rest the weight before I took it to the car. I leaned
between the two doors and looked back into the kitchen where it
had stood all that time, but the lack was hardly noticeable; it did not
look empty, it was how I used to remember it, it had been restored.

I drove carefully, slowing before I came to traffic lights and crossroads because the car had lulled him to sleep. I could hear snores

from his flat nose, I had to be cautious not to wake him. All the way there Friday crowds were gathering, especially by the market and shopping centre. I had to drive at a walking pace; passers-by could have looked through the windows. When I got to the Town Hall I was grateful, though; it would take longer for the pram to be noticed among so many people. It would allow me the time I needed to leave him and shut myself safely back indoors.

I parked dangerously, on a double-yellow line, but when I stood on tiptoe and scanned the street there were no wardens or police to be seen. I hauled the carry-cot and wheels onto the pavement, and fixed them together and locked the car doors. As I wheeled him I did not look down at all. I looked in the passing shops, a jeweller's, a toy shop, a butcher's, I blinked across them and gold and plastic and cutlets dazzled me. When I came to the civic steps I pulled the pram up, concentrating on the grey steep slope to the grey brick building. I hauled and lurched and then we were outside the main door, and I put on the brake and stood to look at the opening times. I walked towards the side door, inching further and further away. I kept quite still for a minute until I could see no danger. No one ran down from the offices, no one ran up to ask what I was doing; I could leave, I could walk away and let him go. Then I could hardly move, I had great difficulty letting go of the handle of the pram. I thought if I had nothing to balance, to hold onto, I might fall, but I did it, I took steps until it was not possible to keep hold any longer and then I had let him go.

I walked back slowly, past the same windows; there was still no one to be seen by the car, no uniforms, no ticket. I got in and drove and was back at the house without consciousness. I was inside it effortlessly, except I could not stand properly. I sat quite still, as silent and deserted as the rooms, and waited until Anna was brought home. I waited until that happened before I began what had to be done next, before I set about making us secure.

'Have a good morning?' I asked and cooked her lunch. She told me about the quarrel over the sandpit. While she ate and chattered I weighed furniture in my mind, displaced heavy pieces to the doors and the hall, calculated what I could lift and what would have to be emptied and pushed.

'Where's Tim?' she asked. 'What about his feed? Where's he got to?'

'He's asleep,' I said. 'He had his lunch early, he fell asleep over it. He's gone, I took him upstairs in his carry-cot. He's tired, he needs a long rest today.'

'Where's Daddy?' she asked. 'Will he be back after work? Has he gone there today?'

'You'll see him,' I said. 'Later, you will. Not yet, though. Now, this afternoon, you and I have got a lot else to do. We've got a moving job on, that's what we're going to be busy with. Rearranging. All the furniture's got to be found a new place. We'd better get a move on with it.'

She laughed, she understood the pun.

'Put your plate in the sink,' I said, 'and then go and stand by the door. Keep it held open for me. I'll do the heavy stuff, you can help in a minute. I need you to guide me first, tell me when I can't see.' She stood there, solemn and obedient, while I took the trolley out, the clothes airer, her stool; all the small things that would make a warning noise if they fell.

'Is it a game?' she asked when I had done that. I started to pull the table over to her, stumbled, and told her to get out of the way. I shoved and levered it all the way down the hall to the front door until it was wedged against the lock.

'It's for us,' I said, 'that's all. That's all I'm doing it for.'

I went back to the kitchen and started to carry the chairs out one by one, putting them upright on top.

'Is it for hide and seek?' she asked.

'In a way,' I answered.

'Can I hide, then?' she asked and started to run upstairs.

I shouted, 'No, keep still, stay where you are, keep where I can see you.'

She sighed, because if I did not want to let her out of my sight that made it quite the reverse.

'What will happen when we play it?' she asked, and waited as I took Graham's Windsor chair and found a place on the table top.

'We won't let them in,' I said. Then, 'Sit still,' because I could hear her moving, every time I turned she did not keep where I told her. She sat on the stairs, but whenever I looked away she crept up, further and further from me. 'Come down,' I encouraged, 'help. We'll do the dresser next, we'll move that. I'll really need a hand with that. We'll empty the drawers and see what we can find there. Photos, there was some hair ribbon last time I looked. Maybe even some Smarties.'

'Why?' she asked.

I frowned, I thought she understood.

'I told you,' I said. 'We're staying indoors and we don't want anyone else to come. We've got to stay here. If anyone tries we've got to show them they can't get in.'

'Why?' she asked again.

I pushed past her on the stairs.

'Move,' I said.

The dresser would be too heavy, instead I needed to get the chairs from Graham's room. She shrank into the banisters while I bumped them past her.

'Keep to one side,' I said and pushed them down.

It didn't matter if they cracked or splintered. What I wanted was to stand in his doorway and hurl them, but I measured the distance, I let them go slowly so all they did was roll down the stairs. When I picked them up at the bottom they were undamaged. I did throw them then, hard onto the pile against the door; they became attached, leather limpets at the foot of the table.

'That'll do,' I said. 'We'll do the rest upstairs now. The sitting room.'

I ran and started to pull the bookcase and then the armchair out. I was panting a little but I did not think of stopping. When I got them both into the hall I slammed that door shut and stood on the chair to do it, rocking in the small unsteady space like a victor in a child's game. I jumped off and rammed them both tight under the door handle.

'Look out,' I said; she was standing too close to me.

I went back into Graham's room and stood in the corner. I could have launched myself into the centre but I held back. I teetered and then grabbed his small table, if I had wanted I could have waved it like a flag.

'Mind out of the way.'

I crashed it against the door and the wood did split then, but I left it hanging. I was taking too long. I looked from one door to the other and nodded to Anna.

'I've got to get all the doors shut tight. Then, if anyone tried to get in through a window, they wouldn't be able to get out of the room into the hall. They're very firm, you couldn't move them from inside, you feel.'

She shook her head and stayed where she was.

'What about him?' She turned to my bedroom door. 'Why can't

you get him here, why can't he play, too?' She whined because she knew quite well it was not a plausible request, her contact with him was never more than passing.

'Because he's asleep,' I said. I was quiet now, I said it reasonably. 'He doesn't want to. He doesn't understand, you know that.' Then I shouted, 'Come out,' because she had made to dart past me into our bedroom, 'there's nothing to see in there.'

I tried to grab her but she clung to the door handle, twisted it with a disobedient smile.

'I'm just listening,' she said. 'I want to hear when he wakes up. Then he can come downstairs with us. You'll have to get him when he cries,' she said, 'when it's teatime. Why can't you wake him up now? He could have his cot here. He could be in the hall, too.'

I took no notice, I went from door to door, making sure they were caught tight.

'Go down now,' I said to her and followed close to make sure she did. 'In here.' I pushed her into the kitchen. 'This door,' I said, 'the one to the garden.'

I took hold of the fridge to put in front of it and shoved it all the way across the tiles. It rattled, all the stoppered containers of his day's feeds bumped about inside; I could hear them falling like ninepins onto the cushion of butter on the shelf below.

I put the armchair and spin dryer against the fridge. Anna would not move, she stood in front of the stove. I could not shift that further than the length of its cable so I left her there, holding the oven door, scuffing her shoes while I fitted all the remaining chairs into a block.

'Where's he gone?' Anna asked. 'He'd want to play, really. Why can't he come down? He could watch us. It's not fair.' She trailed across the unaccustomed space. The whole floor was empty except for a pile of his clothes that had been folded on the edge of the table and had fallen as I moved it. She picked up a blue jumper and rubbed it against her face. 'I want to put it on,' she said and thrust her hands into the sleeves, holding it across her chest so that its narrowness pulled her arms together. 'It makes me walk funny. I can't balance.' She wobbled from side to side towards me. 'Look,' and she lolled, she was a rocking clown in the centre of the displaced room.

I did not go to catch her. I watched her imitation and wondered how she knew that was what he would have been like. I stood still as she staggered in the huge space around her, giggling with excitement. It was no joke at all, she might have known that, but she did not know how to put a stop to it.

'Let's do your bedroom,' I said, because it echoed now in the kitchen.

When I stood in the door, waiting for her, and looked into the hall I was shocked; I had put that barricade there and I wanted to get away from it.

'Do what?' she asked, skidding to a halt. She put her hands on her hips. 'What are you up to now?'

'I'll show you,' I said. 'Come on.'

But she did not follow. 'I don't want to,' she said. 'I want to leave my room how it is.'

I swallowed because I had to be persuasive, I could not run up and downstairs between all the places where there could be a break-in; I had to make a secure place for us to wait in.

'If we change where you sleep,' I said, 'it'll be nicer. It'll be cosier if we're down here together. It'll be like camping. We'll make camp beds for both of us, we don't want to have to bother about all the rest of this place. There's no reason for us to keep going up and downstairs. We'll make it like a giant tent, we'll just live in here. We'll have our food stores and our stove and our water supplies. Except for the loo we don't ever need to go outside. You could watch television in bed. And have your supper there,' I said. I did not mean to bribe her, only to stop her looking unhappy.

'I want to leave my room. I like it how it is,' she said again, but with less conviction. She could see I did not mean to be difficult or selfish, I quite seriously believed it to be necessary.

'It won't take long,' I said. 'Come and help.'

'Why can't he camp too?' she asked when I had pulled her mattress halfway out of the bedroom door. It had been cumbersome and my hands hurt with bending. I stopped to roll the duvet and pillow into a bundle and kicked them ahead of me. I thrust them hard across the landing so that they fell, spreadeagled and tangled, half-way down the stairs.

'Move those,' I said. 'I've got to get this down, you can pull those out of the way. Pull them,' I repeated, because she did not move. 'Drag them behind you. All you have to do is walk to the kitchen and pull them behind. It's not difficult.'

'What about his bed?' she said and started, very slowly, downstairs. 'Why don't we take his, too?'

The mattress jammed as I heaved it, wedged between the walls, and I could not get any purchase. I pushed and it stayed still; I kicked and pulled and it bent but did not shift.

'Shut up about him,' I said. 'You could help, you can see what I'm doing, you could try and do something too.'

'Let's leave it,' she said. 'Let's go for a walk.'

'Listen,' I said. I punctuated my words by pushing my shoulders against the obstinate softness. 'I've told you what we've got to do. We've got to stay indoors, just you and me. When we've taken your bed down, then it'll be better, you see.'

When I finally wrenched the mattress free she walked downstairs in front of me, proceeded so slowly that I shouted, 'Move, move.' I could see her crushed by my weight on top of her. Even when I had pulled it into the kitchen, gone back for the bedclothes, when I had everything unpiled and made into a bed on the floor, with a pillow propped in a corner and the television balanced at the foot, she would not look.

'You can watch your programmes,' I said. 'I'll come in a minute. I've still got things to do. You can see, it's time for the cartoons. You'll be all right, just stay still.'

I had left it until last to move the armchair out of our bedroom to bar that door and I did not want her following me, looking into the empty cot, questioning and discovering.

'I'll only be a minute. I'll only be upstairs.'

She did not look up but sat on the edge of the mattress, gingerly, hardly turned enough to see the screen. She looked at the inches, the feet, the whole expanse of blank tiles surrounding her, the lack of wooden legs, the bareness of the new room she inhabited.

When I opened the bedroom door I did not expect it to be different, because there had been plenty of occasions before when he had been out of it, but as I went in I knew it was changed. It was nothing like the room it had been when he was out in his pram, down in the kitchen or the garden; it showed he was gone, it was not waiting for him to re-enter. I had not misjudged what had to be done, or the effect of it; it was better – I had not made a mistake – but it was shocking. It would never revert to before he was born, it would never lose this loss; it was over and that was final.

I stared into the corner where his cot had stood. It had become alien, deserted by function. His presence did not haunt it, he was a ghost; it was worse than that, the reverse, he was missing. I looked all round, waiting, as though it would alter back and then I started to shiver. It had become cold. There was no question of moving any furniture to another place. I shut the door, pulled it tight behind me and ran downstairs.

'Is he asleep still?' Anna said. 'I heard you go in there.'

'Probably,' I said. 'I don't know.'

It was no longer important whether I told her, whether she knew from me or Carmel Summers or Graham. As soon as I was back in that kitchen, the disarray, the inappropriateness of the bedding and guarding made it necessary to be plain, to let her see all of it, everything I had let us in for. I was frightened as I came downstairs. I had run to get back to her, I was not horrified but I was taken aback; I needed reassurance for how far I had taken it.

'He's not there,' I said.

She looked up and then back to the television.

'I've taken him away,' I said. 'I thought it would be better. I thought it would be easier,' but that was not true, rightness, ableness, ease never came into my mind. 'I can't have him any more,' I said. 'I've been telling her, that woman who came here, I've said it for months but she took no notice. I've shown her now, I've shown her what can't be done. He'll be all right, there's nothing the matter; I just explained what had to happen. It's got nothing to do with you,' I said. 'You can't see him now, I don't mean that, but it's got nothing to do with what happens to you. I'm not taking you anywhere, you can see that, can't you?'

She did not look up then either, she stared ahead at the dog and talking cat on the screen and although they shouted and jumped and squawked she did not laugh.

'It's just him,' I said. After a minute I went over to where she sat and crouched beside her. 'Look. You've seen what I've done, you've helped me do it.' She turned away. 'Stand up, come and look again.'

'No,' she said. 'I want to stay where I am.'

I sat down beside her and we watched together. At intervals I went back to look at the hall. Against the front door it was formidable, the table and chairs were nearly as high as the fanlight. Behind me, upstairs, all of the landing was blocked and the entrance from almost every room was impassable; it was all heavy, everywhere balanced with wood.

'Please come and see,' I said to Anna. 'Come on, come and look at what we've done. No one could get in through that lot, we're fine, nothing can stop us staying here.'

But she refused to move; she hardly spoke at all. Even when I sat

346

next to her she did not lean against me, take my hand or talk about what was on the screen. Before the usual time I started to cook supper.

'We'll sit on the floor,' I said and propped her with a cushion. 'This is a very comfortable camp. And this is luxury food for campers. Pancakes. Beans and sausages is usually the best they get.'

When I had thrown away her half-eaten food I asked, 'What story would you like before you go to bed?' but she shook her head.

'Then shall we watch television?' I offered. She was right, neither food nor fiction was sufficient distraction. 'I'll sit with you. Let's have a drink,' I suggested. That was all I could think of, comforting, liquid. 'We'll both have one,' I said. It seemed appropriate, hot milk, sweet tea, brandy, I could offer us all of them, we would be better equipped then.

We sat there a long time, warm, half-lit, and I began to believe that it would not happen, that I had made us secure enough for it not to come to an end. I could not foresee days. I could not see the next morning clearly, but neither could I imagine it finishing, it seemed to be so much of what I had striven for that it could not be terminated.

'It's all right. It's worked. It's lucky, too, it's all gone smoothly.' I said, stroking her head. 'Poor Anna. It'll be better now, though. Remember the mattress?' I reminisced. 'We should have left it on the stairs for a while and then you could have had slides on it. And when everything fell over in the fridge. And all the things in the dresser drawers, we never did find out those, did we? We could save that for tomorrow, it's too late to start anything else now. Isn't it nice like this?' I asked. In the blue light of the television the room looked softer and she moved closer and closer to me. 'Go to sleep soon. When you wake up it'll be another adventure. Tomorrow will be different, too. We'll do some rearranging then. We'll see one another as soon as we wake up, that'll be nice.'

'Yes,' she said. She did not ask where he was or why this was happening, she was not frightened or unhappy any more. I had made things quite peaceful.

I was half-asleep when the telephone rang but I picked it up and walked to the other side of the room so that Anna would not be disturbed.

'I'm still here,' I said. 'You saw, didn't you?' Twice in the afternoon I had heard a car stop outside and watched Carmel Summers get out, try to see in through the letterbox and then go away. The first time I had been frightened; I expected her to return with other people who would try to force a way in. But the second time I knew that she was worried by what she had to deal with.

'I got your note,' she said, 'and I did as you suggested. I'm with them now, your husband and sister. Would you like to talk to them?'

'No,' I said. 'You know that. You didn't have to see them, that wasn't what the note said. You didn't have to go there, you only had to tell them. They don't want him, you've got to be the one to deal with that. "Tim Browne," I quoted, "is to be adopted." That was what I said, that's what you've got to do. Tell Graham, by all means, but it's nothing else to do with him.'

'He'd like to talk to you,' she said. 'He wondered about your daughter.'

'She's here,' I answered, 'we're both here,' and his voice cut in, like a film effect, too fast for me to hear properly.

'Where is she, what is this, what's happened?'

I answered patiently, as though he did not know, 'Anna's here, I told Carmel Summers; I wrote a note to tell her what it was about. I'm not having him any more, I told her months ago. She was supposed to be doing something about it. She didn't have to come to you, I didn't tell her to do that.'

'We came to the house,' he said, 'but no one answered the door. Where were you?'

'Here,' I said.

'And Anna? Her, too? Let me speak to her,' he said. 'Let me talk to Anna.'

'Why?' I asked. 'It's late. She's asleep.'

'Just a moment,' he pleaded. 'It's easier, it'll stop Carmel coming round again.'

'Why should she?' I asked. 'It's got nothing to do with Anna. He's the only one she's got to see to.'

'I'm not sure.' He hesitated. 'She seemed to need to check on Anna before she could go ahead with him. Barbara,' he lowered his voice, 'I'm not arguing, I'm just saying how it seems.'

'All right,' I said, not because I believed him but because Anna had woken up and was listening.

'I want to talk,' she was saying, 'it's my turn, you said I could see

348

Daddy, I heard you say his name.' Her voice became raised. 'I want to talk to him.'

I carried the phone back and put it beside her.

'Go ahead,' I said.

She listened a moment. He must have asked how she was and what we were doing, because she answered, 'Watching television. And I went to sleep. All right.' And then she said, 'I can't. From inside. Mummy blocked up the doors. Chairs.' She looked at me. 'You tell him,' she said, pushing the receiver back at me.

'There's nothing to tell,' I said. I was quite pleased to give him an explanation. 'It's just a safety measure.' And, because I thought it would help him to believe we trusted one another, I said, 'It's like what you told me about Carmel Summers having to check on Anna. This is the same, but different.'

'I'd like to see,' he said. 'Especially I'd like to come and see Anna, that goes without saying, but as well I'd like the chance—'

'No,' I interrupted. 'No one needs to see us here, we're not going anywhere. It doesn't require anyone to make that effort. If you do,' I said, 'if you do try and come near Anna or me, you'll have to stay outside. Anna and I are staying here, just us, and when he's taken care of we'll come out. There's nothing to worry about, it's just a way of making sure. I'm keeping her and I've got rid of him. He's nothing to do with me, Carmel Summers can see to him. She didn't need to tell you, even, she could have just done it.'

'Don't be—' he began, but he did not call me stupid; he did not want to antagonise me into foolishness. 'Suppose I came and talked,' he said. 'I'll try and arrange something about Tim and come and tell you what it is. How would that be?'

'I don't want to hear,' I said, 'it's nothing to do with me any more.'

'There may be papers to sign,' he said.

I laughed. 'Papers? Now? After all this time? On a Friday night?'

I could see them sitting round Laura's phone. Laura and Carmel Summers would be whispering to one another, whispering back to him, 'Tell her this, say we'll do that'; or writing notes so I did not hear their hushed voices.

'I'd like to see Anna,' he said. 'You've said yourself, it's Friday night, what can anyone do now? You're prejudicing your chances. Be reasonable. If you go on it won't be easy to talk your way out of behaviour like this.'

'I'm not having him back,' I said. 'I don't have to talk my way out of anything. I've said it all.'

'Let me talk to Anna, then,' he repeated.

'No,' I answered. 'She's fine, she's told you that. When Carmel Summers says she's arranged—'

He said, 'Hang on.'

'Listen,' he would be saying to Carmel Summers and Laura, 'what can we do? She dumps him on the Town Hall steps, locks Anna away. I've got to stop her. What is it she's going to try next?'

'No,' I said, and then I shouted it. 'No, I don't care, I won't see anyone, it's nothing to do with me, it's up to you, you and her, leave me alone. When it's all settled, when he's gone we can talk, when that happens you can see Anna. It's an exchange, it's my exchange and I'm not stopping until after that.'

I slammed the phone down, I threw the whole box to one side of the room. I would have smashed it, pulled the wires out from the wall if Anna had not begun to cry.

'Take it all down,' she said. 'Let's go out, let's stop staying here. I don't want to any more.'

I put my arms round her. I tried to tell her that this was reasonable, that if we stayed like this we could come to no harm.

'What's going to happen?' she said.

'We'll wait,' I answered, 'that's all we've got to do. We're fine, we've just got to wait for it to be over. Sit on my lap,' I said.

I made her comfortable against me, stroked her face, tried to lull her out of worry.

'Listen,' I said, 'I'll tell you what.' I told myself I had nothing to be ashamed of. 'When Daddy rings again say to him, "I don't want to come out." Just for a tease, just to pretend, and we'll see if that'll make him hurry things up. Say,' and I considered the exact words that would sound both authentic and urgent, '"Mummy's told me what's got to happen and you've got to do it quickly. We won't come out until afterwards, you know that."'

Eventually, she said, 'Yes'; she did not ask what it meant.

I sat and rocked her. It was completely dark outside. I turned down the sound on the television because I thought I heard, I was waiting for any tap at the door, the slightest bang, the noise of a car, a ladder against an upstairs window. I knew Graham would not leave me alone. I knew also he would not come by himself, he would bring others with him. I was not ready for that, I had no more answers ready. I did not have another bargain to make; I did not know what I would have to do to keep us like this.

Then Anna said, 'Listen. What's that? Is that Daddy?'

I had heard it a moment before, the dying engine, the garden gate. I got up very quietly and ran to look out of the window. There was only one car and only Graham and Carmel Summers got out of it, they must have left him with Laura. At least they were not trying to bring him to give back to me. I heard the key turn in the lock. I took hold of Anna's arms.

'Be quiet,' I said. 'I mean it. I'll tell you if you can talk to him.'

'Barbara,' he called.

'Stay still. Stay here. I'm going to see,' I said to Anna. I pushed her to sit on the edge of the mattress. 'I'm going into the hall.' I crossed the room and put the light on in the hall. 'You can see now,' I said, 'and you can hear me. I'm not going far.' I walked up to the furniture in front of the door. 'Stay there,' I said through it. 'Stay out. Don't try. I've said what I want, you tell her to do it.'

'Barbara,' he said, 'I'm not playing. I'm telling you what I want. Let Anna out and we'll see what can be done, but that's got to happen first.'

'No,' I said.

'Where is she? Let me talk to her. I'm telling you, that's what's going to happen. Bring her here or I'll knock this down, all I've got to do is push, there's nothing there, I could be in in seconds.'

'Don't,' I said. 'Don't do that.'

I leaned against the wall and looked from Anna crying to the front door. I looked at what had happened in the house.

'Go away,' I said. 'I don't believe you. I know what you've done, you won't give anything, you'll take her, that's all. You'll have him back in here and pull her out. She's here to make people see,' and I kicked the table and all the chairs on it banged against the door. 'She's all right, it's you who's the trouble.'

'I want to hear her,' he said. Then he shouted, 'Anna, what's happened?'

She got up and ran, she was starting to cry, and before she could answer I grabbed her. I held her tight and whispered, 'Stop it, you were all right before he came. Go back and wait.'

But she shook her head, pulled away from me and clung to the table leg. When I tried to take hold of her she strained away from me. She put her hand over her mouth to stop the noise of her tears and when I reached out to wipe them she stood rigid. We waited, we had nothing to say.

'Just be quiet,' I said. She nodded. I did not like it, I wanted us back when we had been enclosed with one another and he had not encroached.

'Barbara,' he said. It was so low and calm I jumped. 'I've got a suggestion. Listen, don't shout, it's what you want, just listen. I'll do what you say, Carmel will do what you say, but there's got to be something in return. Otherwise it's not fair. Barbara,' he said, 'do you understand that? If you want co-operation, if that isn't what you're prepared for, we'll have to take other steps. This way you'll get what you want, there's no risk of that not happening, but if you don't co-operate it'll be a lot more difficult.'

'You mean Anna,' I said. 'That's not co-operation, that's not fairness. I started this and I say she's got to get rid of him but Anna stays. She's here with me, she's here to show you.'

'Say Carmel does,' he said softly after a while. I wondered if they had just agreed that, conspirators in the porch. 'What happens then? When you've got what you want, what do you do after that? Monday, say. Next week, not now, but when it's fixed, what'll happen to you?'

I had thought that far ahead, I had always known that I would have to dismantle things, it was never meant to be a permanent state.

'I'll have shown you,' I said. 'I'll have got what I wanted.'

'You've got that now,' he said, 'you've shown us.' Then suddenly he called, 'Anna, are you all right, Anna?'

It sounded like a scream.

I shouted back, 'Stop it, go away, leave it, Anna's all right, you don't have to do anything except go again, leave us alone. You've done it once today, you've gone to her and your other baby, it's not hard, you're not unpractised, go and do that again, go where you want to belong, you've gone and you can't come back, you've got nothing to do with here any more.'

I turned to Anna. 'Tell him,' I yelled, 'go on, you tell him,' but she shook her head. I took hold of her arms and shook her. 'Tell him, what do you want him for?'

'I don't believe you,' she said through the door, and she cried, 'Don't.'

Then I began to scream, I screamed nothing at all, only sounds, a noise echoing down the hall and through all the house, it made no sense at all, it was nothing I remembered saying before, I could not understand what I was asking, it took a time to turn it into words that I could use on him, a phrase that he could understand.

'Get Audrey,' I was shouting. 'She'll tell you, get Audrey, you'll have to believe it then.'

When I thought he had gone away I took Anna's hand, led her back to the kitchen and wrapped her duvet round both of us.

'Don't cry,' I said. 'You couldn't help it. When I was little I sat like this. I sat and watched my mother and all the furniture in her house. When I went to bed and Laura went with me, we both lay all night and watched cupboards and chairs. We'll wait, that's what we'll do now, we'll wait for Grandma to come. That's what I told Daddy I wanted, that's what he's got to do, get her. She'll tell them.' I smiled to myself with certainty. 'She'll make them do what I want.'

'She won't be long,' I said at intervals, because however long it took it was inconceivable that she would need to be persuaded. The delay was because of the lateness, bad traffic conditions, she had to be told of all the passing of information and negotiations.

'She'll be here any minute,' I said. I promised that all the time. Anna ground herself into me. Every time I tried to quieten her she stiffened.

'Don't hold me so tight,' she said.

'I'm not letting you go,' I answered.

'I won't go anywhere,' she argued. 'Let me go and see.'

I held her rigid in my arms.

'Wait for Grandma,' I said, and she cried. Every few seconds she tried to break away. It was an age, it took an hour before it stopped and there was a knock at the door. No one called, there was no banging.

I said, 'Stay here,' to Anna.

I crept, I bent and shook so much I had to descend to all fours. I went like that, again, across the kitchen floor into the hall.

'Who is it?' I said and straight away she answered. 'Is anyone with you?' I asked.

'Open that door,' she told me. 'I'm not shouting through this.'

'Is anyone else there?' I repeated, but I did not care if there was. I

353

had recognised the sound in her voice and I felt hollow all through, a sadness I had forgotten all about. All at once I knew I should not have done this, that nothing would happen, nothing would alter. She would come and it would be like every day I had returned home from school and sat with her in the kitchen or eaten a meal or gone for a walk; there would be nothing between us except disappointment.

'All right,' I said.

One by one, slowly, because I had forgotten how heavy they were, I took the chairs away from the table and put them on the floor behind me. I did not even start to move them back to the kitchen. Then I took hold of the table and hauled and it was like a dream where objects are beyond any shifting and then weightless. I could not manage it. I fell as I pulled and then it was effortless.

'Get this chain off,' she said. I realised Graham must have given her his key. 'Get out of the way.'

She pushed the door hard and it opened and she came in. She did not look at me or the furniture in the hall or at what was stacked all up the stairs, she went straight into the kitchen.

'Stand up,' she said to Anna. 'Are you all right?'

'Yes,' Anna said. She did not shrink or cry; she stood up as if she was in a classroom.

'Let me look.' Audrey turned her in a little circle, 'Sure?' When Anna nodded she pulled her towards her, it was a hug. 'That's good,' she said. 'Had your tea?' Anna nodded. 'Well, then—' and she hesitated. 'You got something to read?' she asked. 'You find your book for five minutes and then we'll get this sorted out. We won't be long, soon have you in bed.'

Then she turned to me.

'Do you know what time it is for her to be up?' As if that was the only issue she had come about. 'What do you think you're doing with her?' she asked. Because I could say nothing she answered herself. 'Using her. I thought better of you.' She pointed to the hall. 'Out there,' she said. 'I'll be five minutes,' she said to Anna, 'and that's the lot of it. We'll be sorted out after that.'

She followed me out of the room and we stood with everything around us. We were boxed in, it was inescapable.

'You,' she said. 'You and that whore. You and him, her and him, that's what it's about, isn't it?'

'No,' I said. 'It's that baby.'

'You're stupid,' she said, 'you're cracked. All this,' and she stopped then to look at it and it was mountainous; beside it she only looked angry. 'I'm not putting up with the place like this to suit your ideas. We've had enough of your funny ideas. Get it done.'

I stood still, I could not believe that was what she meant. She came up close to me, her face white and her neck blotched; she held her coat belted tight round her, the leather end of it in one hand and her bag in the other.

'You make me sick,' she said, turning away and making a retching noise. 'She's got to go to bed, that's what's got to happen here. She's got to be seen to, you're not leaving her with all this to wake up to, you're putting things right. That stuff out there, you got it in this state, you straighten it up. Put the whole lot back as it was, get it right. Tell her to help.' Her voice softened. 'She can give a hand.' She started to pull open her coat. 'Go on, get a move on.'

She almost ran back into the kitchen, tripping over the step in her haste.

'Come on,' she said to Anna, 'you, too.' She pulled the duvet off the mattress and bundled it at her. 'Get that outside, and these,' and she dived on the pillows, she pulled all the soft cushionings I had given us into a heap by the door. She was bent and bowed with the effort. 'Get these back,' she said. 'Get that stuff off the landing, we can put this back where it belongs.'

I went into the hall and began to carry the chairs back to the kitchen. I did not want to, there was no longer a need to be protected by them, but I did not see any point in restoration. I did not want her hauling the spin dryer, dragging the fridge. 'Stop,' I wanted to say, but no one ever did to her.

'If you came to do this,' I said, 'what did they tell you? What did Graham and Carmel Summers say when they came to get you?'

'Say?' She pushed in front of me, grabbed a stool from under my fingers. 'They said what'd happened.'

'What?' I asked. 'What did they call it.'

'You can tell me.' She pushed me. 'You tell me what to call it, you save it and think up what you'd describe it as. They said what you'd done, that was what they told me, what else were they supposed to do? You', she said, and banged the wooden legs on the floor, 'you know what they talked about, you can't start pretending now. This,' she said and let the stool rock between us while she shook her fists, 'get this done, get upstairs, start there. I want it shifted, I want all that lot put straight, get it cleared up so I can do what I said I'd come for. Get it right so I can put Anna to bed.'

355

'Was that why you came?' I asked. 'Was that what they said, was that what they said I wanted you for?'

'That's what I said,' she answered. 'What've they to do with it?'

I did as she told me, I opened doors and sorted and tidied and stacked. I could hear her voice downstairs, instructing, encouraging, and Anna answering as if it was an ordinary visit. I put objects away and I wanted to keep my eyes closed; I did not want to be part of this ending.

'What do you think?' I wanted to call out. 'What do you think happened here? Guess, what do you think I did this for?' I wanted her to face me and talk about the truth.

She shouted up at me, 'Nearly done? You finished yet? I want to have this mattress up, I told you. I want to see about getting Anna in bed.'

I went down the clear stairs and took my share of the weight she was holding. She could have been on a bus platform asking for the fare I had to pay, she did not look at me.

'Move it,' she said. 'Push it up, it can't stay down here. Look where you're going, look at what you're doing.' I pulled helplessly. 'You got it here, you see to it,' she said.

I waited for her to leave me stranded and helpless with it, but she did not, she clung and shoved and sweated with the effort.

'You,' she hissed, 'doing this. You're cracked, you don't know what you're up to.'

'I didn't start it,' I answered back.

She did let go then, she tore her hands away and lunged at me across the mattress.

'Don't give me that. What's that supposed to mean, what's that supposed to alter?' She flung herself back against the banisters. 'Is that supposed to put all this right? Is this supposed to make you put up with it?'

I remembered the stairs rattling when I was a child, the force of attack she would mount against them when we had walked in snow or mud.

'Nothing'll make me put up with it,' I said.

She was ready to spit; she gathered it in her mouth ready, she rolled it between her teeth and looked at me.

'You,' she said, but she faltered; it came out as a dribble, it was nothing more than an offensive little stream down the side of her chin. Then she clenched her teeth. 'Get on. Get this shifted. That's what matters. Get it on the bunk,' she said when we hauled it to the door of Anna's room.

I took the corners and helped her lift it.

'They did it here,' I said. I hardly had the breath left but I was not letting that struggle go for nothing. 'Anna told me. This was where it happened. That,' I said, 'that's what happened. I had him and they had this. That's what you could think about.'

She turned her back on me, she ran downstairs and back up again with the bedclothes.

'Make it,' she said. 'She's ready enough, if you can't see that I can. If you won't see to her, take proper care, I will.'

She swung to face me and it was like staring at a broken reflection of the face that looked up from his cot.

'I can do that, whatever I can't do, I can do that.'

'That's what I came for,' she said, and she pushed past me to the door. 'Anna,' she called down the stairs. 'Come on, up here, I'm waiting. I'm waiting to see to you now. Get undressed,' she said.

Anna took off her clothes; together they folded them and made a pile on the chair.

'Jump in, come on, it's late, lie down now,' she said and flattened the pillows and tucked the duvet round her. She made it tight as swaddling. 'See you in the morning,' she said and pointed to me. 'Kiss Mummy goodnight. Say "See you in the morning" to her.'

Anna lay still under the stretched covers and looked at Audrey instead.

'Where are you going?' she asked. She had not spoken to me since Audrey arrived.

'To see to her,' she said, and nodded at me. Then she bent over the bunk. 'Go to sleep, be a good girl,' she said. Anna put her hands under her hair. 'Come on,' she told me, 'downstairs.'

'Look at it,' she said in the door to the kitchen. She switched the light on. 'It looks broken into. Vandalised.' She stepped back so her shoulder was against me; she leaned as if she would tip me head first into the room. 'You,' she said, and took hold of my shoulder and shook it. 'Look at what you've done to everything.'

I did not understand what she meant me to do next.

'Stop it,' I said. I pulled away and faced her. 'Listen, stop taking

357

notice of what it looks like, listen to what I'm saying. I told you up there, I wanted you, I said it then. I wanted you to tell them, I'm not having him back. That was what this was for, that's why I did it, I was showing them.'

She walked away from me into the room.

'Listen.' I wanted to shout. 'What would you have done? How would you show them? What's your answer?'

She looked at me and she did raise her voice.

'You know,' she said. 'Don't give me that, you know what I'm talking about.'

'No,' I insisted. 'What? I wanted you and you came to clear up and see to Anna. You've done that, so what next? Who's out there, what have you promised them you'll do? I asked you to tell me, I asked you to find out what else I could do to show them.'

'Show them?' she repeated. Her voice was even higher. 'You don't fool me like that. You know what you're on about, you can show them any time you like, but it's not them you want to see. That's why you brought me; it wasn't them at all, it was me who had to look at it.' She clenched herself; I recognised every muscle in her body. 'You don't need telling,' she said, 'you'd got it all worked out. I knew that the minute I saw her.' She pointed to the door. 'That one who brought me, you'd never pick someone like that, who'd make a mess of everything. She doesn't dare do anything, she told me that, she can't do a thing for anyone: you, that baby, no one. Don't tell me you believed her.' She snorted in my face. 'You chose her deliberately, you got her so you could do what you wanted.'

'Carmel Summers?' I said. 'I didn't choose her, I don't know what you're talking about. I've tried to get her to help. I trusted her.'

She almost spat again.

'Liar, you knew, you knew what you were doing. She's useless, she's nothing, she said so, she told me in the car on the way here. She hasn't done a thing about that baby, she's not bothered with you. You're a joke to her. That's why you let her carry on, so you had the chance to do this.'

'No,' I said.

She wiped her hands up and down together, clenched them into a fist.

'You never used to be a liar. "I never took Barbara seriously," that's what she told me. "Barbara managed so well." She doesn't care, anyone could see that. You knew.' She took a step, it was all

358

there was between us. 'Except that wasn't enough. Finding a way of getting away with it, you had to make me watch. I had to be brought along to see it. This,' she said, 'you wanted this fuss and commotion, you wanted me to see what it was like, you wanted—'

'No.' I tried to grab her. 'I didn't want you to see Laura and Graham, what would you care about them for? They don't matter, they're nothing beside what matters, the only thing that matters to me is not to have him, to get him out of this place, that was what I wanted you to make sure of—'

'You knew.' She pulled her arm back. 'What am I supposed to show you? You knew there was nothing I could do. I didn't do it, did I? I tried, but it didn't work. I had a go at making my house safe. I put her upstairs, and look what happened. Laura brought her down. Laura dragged her round the place, shoved her up against me all the time. I've nothing to show no one. You watched,' she said, 'you were there the whole time, keeping your eyes open, head down over your homework, but you saw, you knew everything about it, I don't need it shoved down my throat. You leave him, you do it, but I don't need showing you can manage what I couldn't.'

I did grab her then; I took hold of her shoulders and held the tops of her arms tight to her sides. I kept her still enough to look, I made sure she had no escape from understanding me.

'I thought you'd managed,' I said. 'I thought you'd be the best person. I wanted you because of that. That was what I meant, that was what I thought.'

She closed her eyes, she screwed them up tight so that she did not have to see how much I meant it.

'You're out of your mind,' she said.

'It's still true,' I answered.

She turned her head away.

'Let go,' she said.

I did, there was nothing to hold onto her for.

I walked to the stove and rubbed at the scratch marks I must have made when I dragged the fridge past it. I pulled the armchair a little way from the door, I opened the fridge; there was enough food to last another day, after that I would find it difficult.

'What am I going to do, then?' I said. I swung on the door as if I was deciding what supper to cook.

She moved too, not in my direction; she went and looked out of the window and then she went over to the sink and studied her hands, turned them over.

'Filthy,' she said, and leaned over to the tap, but slowly, as though it was too much effort even to make herself clean. 'You'll be all right.'

She started to run the water; she ran it hard and it was difficult to hear her voice above it. Very slowly I went nearer to her so that she did not have to shout and I did not have to ask, so that I could concentrate on what she was saying.

'I thought you'd done it,' she said. 'That was what I thought you wanted me to see. She's done it, I thought, she's got her, she's got Laura to take him. She's got Laura and Graham looking after that baby, she's fixed it up, turned the tables, no trouble, no outsiders involved, she's managed to hand him over, I thought, given him to just the people who deserved him. That was what I thought you'd done. I didn't think you needed telling.'

'I did.' I raised my voice so that she could hear. 'I didn't see it like that.'

She turned off the water.

'Why not?' she said. 'What's wrong with that? Isn't it obvious? What's wrong with doing that? You think about it.' She turned her back to the sink. 'Go on,' she said. 'Go on. Think. I would,' she said. 'I would have.' Then she looked right away from me; she shook herself as if she'd come in from the cold and looked round the room.

'This was a nice place,' she said.

I stared at it again, there was the table I had scrubbed, the chair where Anne Berrington had sat, the place that was Anna's, where all of us had fitted; the corner his cot had been, the cupboard Laura leaned against. Instead she was there, facing me, wiping her hands, patting between her fingers, and she had her head turned; I saw she thought she was smiling.

'I'll tell you,' she said. 'You wait till the morning. You go out then and tell them, that's what you can do. You take Anna to show them there's nothing wrong with her and you tell them. "He's yours," you say. Go on, let them get out of it, let them find out what it feels like. You go to bed now,' she said, 'and that's what you do in the morning. That's all there is to it.'

I didn't answer.

'Come on,' she said. 'I haven't got all night.'

I didn't move.

'All right,' she said. 'I'll go. I'll sleep in Anna's room. I'll sleep in that bunk, then you can think of me being there in future; you can think that was the place I slept in when I came here. That's what it'll be. Now, you go to bed,' she said.

I did not want to move. I did not want to go past this stage ever. I wanted to go on as if it was possible, as if it was reasonable for there to be a solution I could find bearable. I sat still. For as long as it took her to hang up the towel and come and stand over me I looked at the pictures she had made. I was as quiet as if they could be the end, as if I could see, or she make me believe them, I practised as though she or I had any chance with reality.

All Futura Books are available at your bookshop or
newsagent, or can be ordered from the following address:
Futura Books, Cash Sales Department,
P.O. Box 11, Falmouth, Cornwall TR10 9EN.

Please send cheque or postal order (no currency), and
allow 60p for postage and packing for the first book
plus 25p for the second book and 15p for each additional
book ordered up to a maximum charge of £1.90 in U.K.

B.F.P.O. customers please allow 60p for
the first book, 25p for the second book plus 15p per
copy for the next 7 books, thereafter 9p per book

Overseas customers, including Eire, please allow £1.25
for postage and packing for the first book, 75p for the
second book and 28p for each subsequent title ordered.